THE CAPTAIN'S BRIDE

A ravishing beauty with an irresistible air of innocence, Lady Violet Rochelle has no end of worthy suitors—not one of whom interests her in the slightest. For though seemingly demure, she harbors a secret yearning for adventure . . . and for a lover who is anything but proper. . . .

Captain Trevor Dane, lately of the king's Navy, is a man known for his daring exploits and his victories in battle. But when, on a furtive mission of his own, he breaks into Violet's bedchamber and impudently avails himself of her kisses, he unleashes a passion that will soon seal both of their fates. . . .

Shadowed by intrigue and unrelenting danger, the last thing Dane needs is to be saddled with a wife. Yet when Violet vows to marry him not to save her own reputation, but to save his, Dane finds himself up against a most formidable—and disarming—opponent: a raven-haired temptress who will not be denied! And now, as rumors swirl amid the *ton* that Dane is the elusive agent *Le Corbeau,* Violet sets out to show the world they have the wrong man . . . making her a target of his implacable enemies, and leaving Dane desperately searching for a way to keep his lady wife safe . . . and safely in his arms. . . .

Books by Sara Blayne

PASSION'S LADY

DUEL OF THE HEART

A NOBLEMAN'S BRIDE

AN ELUSIVE GUARDIAN

AN EASTER COURTSHIP

THEODORA

ENTICED

A NOBLE DECEPTION

A NOBLE PURSUIT

A NOBLE RESOLVE

A NOBLE HEART

HIS SCANDALOUS DUCHESS

AN IMPROPER BRIDE

THE CAPTAIN'S BRIDE

Published by Zebra Books

THE CAPTAIN'S BRIDE

Sara Blayne

ZEBRA BOOKS
KENSINGTON PUBLISHING CORP.

http://www.kensingtonbooks.com

Chapter 1

Captain Trevor Dane pulled his steaming mount to a halt at the edge of the barren spinney and slid stiffly from the saddle to the ground. From his vantage point on the crest of a low rise, he had an unimpeded view of the stately Tudor house lit from within by glittering chandeliers and from without by a full moon, set like a pale, gleaming eye in a clear, luminous sky. The muscle leaped along the hard line of his jaw as the strains of a country dance wafted gaily to him on the chill breeze.

"The devil," he cursed, presented with indisputable evidence that a gala was in full progress. He would be a bloody fool to brace Granville now before a house full of guests, never mind that he had traveled by coach nearly the breadth of England in only three days for the express purpose of demanding an audience with the man. Reason cautioned him to bridle his impatience and return to Exeter and his rooms at the White Hart Inn until a more propitious time. Sir Henry, after all, would hardly be amenable to leaving his guests in order to speak with a man whose name he had sullied and whose integrity he had called into doubt. But then, Sir

Henry had thus far made it a point to deny Dane *any* opportunity to face his accuser.

His eyes hardened to cold, steely points. In the three months Dane had lain near death's door, Sir Henry had done his work well. In spite of the sixty-two gun *Antiope*'s single-handed victory over a French seventy-four, Captain Trevor Dane had been overlooked for promotion. Far more importantly, for the first time in his nineteen years at sea, he had been denied a ship.

What the devil had Granville hoped to gain by seeing Dane cast on the beach, his career finished, his reputation in ruins? Granville *could not* have known of the meeting with Philippe Lambert. The devil, he had taken every precaution to make certain no one knew.

Unfortunately, it would seem the same could not be said for that other, far more dangerous visit to St. John's Cathedral. Someone had been waiting for him to emerge from the church. The attack, coming on the steps leading from the cathedral, had been swift and silent.

Only by the merest chance had he not ended up with a knife in his back. Still, if there was some sort of evidence Dane had failed in his duty, why had he not been brought before a court-martial?

That was perhaps the most unnerving part of all, Dane decided, drawing his cloak more firmly about him against the brisk chill of the mid-February night. The bloody damned silence!

Not even Admiral Sir Marcus Llewellyn, who had been captain of the first ship upon which Dane had served as a midshipman and who over the succeeding years had fostered Dane's rapid rise to post rank, had been willing or able to help him this time. His door, along with the others at the Admiralty, had remained closed to Dane.

The message had been clear. Captain Trevor Dane was not to be given command of *any* ship ever again. No doubt he was fortunate he was to remain on half pay for the time being, he thought cynically. *Colette,* the French seventy-four, had foundered and sunk almost within sight of Gibraltar. The prize money she would have brought him, it seemed, was to have been his last. Hellfire! His career in the king's Navy was finished. It had been better had he perished from the back-shooter's cursed bullet!

Briefly, he wondered what his uncle would say when he learned of his nephew's fall from grace. Not that it would matter. No doubt Blackthorn had long since forgotten all about the young scapegrace he had sent off to sea in the hopes the king's Navy could do what he himself could not—tame the wild streak that had landed the boy at loggerheads with his uncle more often than not.

It had been a bitter parting. In nineteen years, there had not been so much as the exchange of a single letter between Dane and the earl, who by now must surely have sired himself an heir to replace his younger brother's orphaned brat. As for Dane himself, he would rather be reduced to penury than petition his uncle for assistance of any sort.

But then, he was far from being either helpless or penniless yet, he reminded himself. Nor was he disposed to accept tamely his present turn of fortunes. He would not rest until he bloody well knew who had condemned him and why. And Sir Henry Granville would seem to be the man who had all the answers.

Turning back to his mount, he vaulted to the saddle and rode at a brisk canter along the track that led to the rear of the house.

He did not doubt how he would be received were he to call in the manner of a gentleman—at the front door. Bloody hell! It had been four months since he left his sickbed. Four months of writing letters petitioning an audience with their bloody lordships. Four months of cooling his heels in a waiting room crowded with unem-

ployed officers as eager as himself for a ship. He had
been put off long enough.

Still, he was in no mood to be turned away amid the
curious stares of Sir Henry's fashionable houseguests.
He would await Granville in his study, he decided with
grim appreciation of the irony of his position. No doubt
at least there, he reflected acerbically, he would have
access to a grog tray and a brandy to warm his insides
before Sir Henry had him shown to the door.

Moments later, finding a measure of shelter for his
mount in the lee of an outbuilding, Dane stripped off
his cloak and slung it over the horse's back. The mount,
whose use had been arranged for him ahead of time by
William Parker-Stanhope, Dane's former second lieutenant, should fare well enough for the time being,
Dane decided with a mirthless twist of the lips. No doubt
young Parker-Stanhope would be more than a little chagrined if he had to report to his father, the admiral,
that the prime bit of blood had succumbed to an in-
flammation of the lungs thanks to the carelessness of
the lieutenant's disgraced former captain.

A hard glint came to Dane's eyes at thought of Parker-
Stanhope's unshakable loyalty. What did men like Sir
Henry Granville know of those who fought and died at
sea? Amid the smoke and the fury of a broadside, sailors
fought for the ship and for their shipmates. The sea
and the horror of battle forged iron bonds between
men who knew little of the reasons for why they were
in the fires of hell, but only that they must fight in hopes
of surviving to another day. In the heat of battle, they
looked to the captain to see them through. The captain
had no one to look to but himself.

There was a purity of truth in that which not even
the spite and secret ambitions of the powerful could
sully, Dane thought grimly, as he made his way across
the mews to the back of the house and let himself in
through French doors that overlooked a rose garden,
stark in its winter fastness.

The withdrawing room in which he found himself was happily deserted, the fire in the white marble Adams fireplace reduced to little more than glowing embers. Dane crossed the room and noiselessly opened the door a crack to peer out into a deserted corridor, dimly lit by a hall lamp. From somewhere above came the distant strains of music, denoting the ballroom located in the west wing. No doubt the rooms adjoining the ballroom would be taken up with card players, which must surely mean Granville's study would be somewhere here in the east wing, far from the sounds of gaiety.

Slipping out into the corridor, Dane made short work of locating the servants' stairs. A few moments later found him traversing the second-story hallway.

It had been nineteen years since he had been in anything resembling the tasteful elegance of his present surrounds. The thick carpet that muted his footsteps was a far cry from the canting deck of a ship of war. His quarters aboard the two-decker *Antiope* had been luxurious in comparison to his cramped stern cabin on *Mercury*, the fleet eighteen-gun sloop-of-war, which nearly eight years before had been pounded into oblivion off the coast of France.

Nevertheless, even aboard the *Antiope* his quarters had been spartan at best, the accommodations of a man who had spent his life at sea and known nothing but war for far too long. And yet, given the choice, he would gladly have taken the many discomforts of even the meanest, most weather-worn, barnacle-encrusted ship of war over the finest house in England if it had meant he would be returned to the life for which he had been born.

He was a sailor and the son of a sailor. Not only had he no taste for the opulence around him, but he felt out of place on land, like a bloody damned fish out of water.

Perhaps it might have been different, he reflected, conscious of a sharp twist of hollowness in the pit of his stomach, if there had been someone to give him a reason to start over in a new life on land. The devil. The last thing he should have expected upon coming home to the house he kept in the unfashionable part of London was to discover the single slender thread that was his only bond to the land was severed. Lynette, that sad, lonely girl who had loved him, was dead.

Could the fault for that, too, be laid at his door? he wondered bitterly. He had owed Lynette Lambert his life. He had given her precious little in return. When she needed him the most, he had been away at sea, as he had ever been.

What the devil had possessed her to set out on her own for Blackthorn Manor in the north of Devon? Had it been purely by chance a masked rider had tried to rob the post chaise, only to be frightened off by the guard's blunderbuss? Was it truly only a tragic coincidence that the single shot from the assailant's pistol had found Lynette?

She had died alone. She had deserved far better than that. The devil! She had deserved far better from *him*.

Angrily, he shoved all thoughts of Lynette from his mind. There would be time enough for recriminations later, he reminded himself, peering into an empty sitting room and moving on to the next door. For now, there were questions to which he would have answers.

Only briefly did it come to him to consider the possibility that Sir Henry, occupied with a house full of guests, would not come to his study before turning in for the night. In the few days Granville had been aboard the *Antiope*, Dane had become unavoidably familiar with the habits of the man who had displaced him from his quarters. He was, if nothing else, methodical.

Every night, with a precision that had not gone unremarked among the officers whom he engaged in whist before turning in, Sir Henry spent an hour at work on his journal. It was not unlike a captain and his ship's log, Granville had remarked one evening to Dane, who had entered the chartroom to find Sir Henry bent over the map table and jotting down notations in his brown leather-bound book.

"Been at it since I was a boy," Sir Henry had added, closing his journal and rising in preparation of retiring for the night. "Helps clear the mind to put the day's events in order, what?"

It came suddenly to Dane to wonder if that was all Sir Henry had been doing in the chartroom, which, due to the civilian's presence on board, was being made to double as Dane's living quarters. He had not failed to note at the time that the ship's log lay open among the ordered debris of navigational charts and various personal papers, among them the last letter he would ever receive from Lynette.

He had tried then to recall whether he had failed in his usual practice of locking the log away in his sea chest when he had done with it and could not. They had been beset by a swift and sudden storm so violent that he had been on deck without respite for the better part of eighteen hours. Hardly had Sir Henry vanished into his cabin than Dane had flung himself, fully clothed, upon his cot and sunk into the sleep of utter exhaustion.

He had not thought of the incident again until after the battle with *Colette,* when he had swum up out of the depths of a coma, fretting with fever and pain over the nagging questions of who had shot him in the back from the deck of his own ship and why.

If Sir Henry had fired the shot that had felled Dane, no one had witnessed it—or at least no one would attest to it. Even Murdoch, Dane's burly coxswain, had failed to come up with so much as a single seaman who would admit to having seen anything. But then, all but a handful of men had been occupied with following Dane in his mad scramble over the gangway to take the French ship. Perhaps it was true no one had seen anything.

Dane cursed under his breath. No matter how hard he tried, he could not shake the conviction there was a conspiracy of silence surrounding everything that had happened to him. Someone had wanted him out of the way. Someone did still. And no one was talking—at least not yet.

Someone would be made to talk, Dane vowed grimly. The silence would be broken this very night by Sir Henry Granville.

Hardly had that thought crossed his mind than Dane came to an abrupt halt, his every nerve taut with awareness. Before him, only a few steps away, a door off the main staircase landing stood slightly ajar.

From somewhere within had come the faint but unmistakable sound of movement. He was sure of it, and all of his fighting instincts warned it was not Sir Henry Granville beyond that door. It was an hour till midnight—hardly the time for a host to take leave of his houseguests.

Furthermore, it would hardly seem reasonable to suppose Sir Henry, or anyone else who had a legitimate reason for being in that room, would be relying on a single taper for light when there must have been lamps conveniently at hand.

There! He heard it again, the distinct shuffle of papers.

Noiselessly, Dane stepped to the door. Peering through the narrow opening, he could make out little beyond the eerie shadows cast by the flicker of candle-light—little, that was, save for a book-lined shelf along the far wall, indisputable evidence he had located Sir Henry's study.

Bitterly he cursed his lack of foresight in coming unarmed. But then, he had not planned to *shoot* Sir Henry, much as he might liked to have done in some of his darkest moments. Dane did not doubt, however, that whoever was in that room had not come similarly unprepared. He had not spent more than half his life in the king's Navy without having developed a keen sense for danger.

Cynically, it came to him to wonder why he should stick his bloody neck out to intrude on a probable burglar at work in the home of the man who had quite possibly attempted to put a period to Dane's existence and who had most certainly, for all intents and purposes, ruined him. Hellfire! Far from thanking him for it, Sir Henry was more than likely to have Dane thrown in gaol for entering his house uninvited. Indeed, Dane could not think of a single good reason why he should interfere in something that was in reality none of his affair.

Hardly had that thought crossed his mind than he was assailed by the distinct sound of a groan issuing forth from the confines of the study.

"Coming around, are we, Sir Henry?" murmured a low voice, remarkable for its chilling lack of compassion. "A pity. You leave me little choice but to silence you again. I do hope for your sake it will not be permanently this time."

The devil! Dane cursed, silently, to himself.

The next instant he had flung the door wide.

He was met with the chilling scene of Sir Henry seated in a chair, his head and upper body slumped over a desk littered with papers. Standing over him, a pistol ominously raised for striking, was a masked man draped in a black cloak, the hood pulled low over his forehead. Through the holes in the mask, glittering eyes leaped up to meet Dane's.

"Captain Dane! By all the saints, this is fortuitous," exclaimed the masked man, his white teeth flashing in a grin of unholy amusement. "You are just in time to die, Captain, for the villainous attack on Sir Henry."

The pistol lowered and fired. Dane, hurling himself to one side, felt the breath of the pistol ball whip past within inches of his cheek. He landed hard on his side and, rolling, bounded to his feet—in time to see his assailant vanish through the doorway. On the point of following in pursuit, he went suddenly still as Sir Henry, uttering a groan, stirred.

Bitterly Dane cursed. In an instant it came to him, the peril of his present circumstances. The vanished assailant had spelled it out for him. He would have the devil's own time trying to convince anyone he had not bludgeoned Sir Henry. The real assailant, after all, was nowhere in sight.

At least he was sure Sir Henry was alive. Equally certain, his only hope of avoiding being accused of the crime was to find the masked intruder before he himself was discovered. Dane sprang for the door.

"Bloody hell, who—you there—stop, I say!" Granville rasped after him as he bounded into the hallway and came to a sudden halt.

The corridor stretched before him—deserted. Reasoning the blackguard must have fled up or down the curving staircase within easy access, Dane made to descend the stairs, only to go suddenly still at the sound of voices in the foyer below.

"It was a pistol shot. Could hardly be mistaken in that."

"I daresay it came from the floor above, Sir Oliver."

"The study!" exclaimed a woman's voice in tones of rising alarm. "Faith—Sir *Henry!* He said he was going to fetch a sample of his favorite blend of snuff for Lieutenant Cordell."

"Lady Granville is in the—the right of it, sir. Sir Henry and—and I were discussing the merits of a new blend of Turkish r-rappee he had recently acquired."

"There would seem little point in standing around indulging in speculation," observed Sir Oliver, with pompous self-assurance. "I suggest someone ought to go up and investigate."

Dane, about to be caught on the staircase, did not wait to hear more. Turning, he bounded up the stairs two at a time and fled along the upper-story hallway, only to turn back as a door opened at the far end of the corridor and three gaily appareled females emerged, laughing and chattering among themselves.

Dane opened the door nearest him and stepped inside—and found himself staring directly into the startled eyes of a singularly spellbinding blue-violet hue.

Given the instant impression of a stunningly beautiful countenance framed in luxurious curls the blue-black of ravens' wings, Dane was momentarily deprived of the power either to move or to speak. Indeed, he had the most peculiar sensation that time itself had been suspended for the space of perhaps four or five heartbeats as he stared into what could only be described as the face of a veritable paragon of loveliness. Then, inexplicably, a becoming tinge of color rose to her silken-smooth cheeks.

"This is all very flattering, I am sure. Nevertheless, I'm afraid, sir, I must protest," declared the paragon of feminine loveliness, seemingly torn between wry amusement and a rising indignation. "As it happens, I have had quite enough adulation for one night. Therefore, if you don't mind, perhaps you would be so good as to—"

She was not allowed to finish what her uninvited caller might be so good as to do. Dane, hastily pushing the door to with the heel of his boot, caught her to his chest and covered her mouth with his.

Telling himself his sole intention in availing himself of the young beauty's lips was to silence her before she attracted the notice of the three passing gaily by outside in the hall, Dane yet could not but note when the slender form clasped in his arms changed from rigid bestartlement to something on quite a different order.

Egad, the paragon of beauty, it would seem, was a female of uncommon passion. Indeed, he could not be mistaken in thinking she had melted against him or that she was returning his kiss with a sweet, untutored fervor as unaffected as it was innocent.

With no little sense of bemusement, he released her

lips and lifted his head to behold the young beauty's eyes closed, her lovely face wearing a singularly dreamy aspect that brought a wry twist to Dane's lips. Then the beauty's luxurious black eyelashes fluttered against her cheeks and drifted open.

Dane's smile froze and slowly faded as he stared into the unguarded depths of the eyes that gazed wonderingly back at him. She remained unmoving, her eyes fixed on his, for so long that Dane suffered the birth of misapprehension. She was clearly past the first blush of youth, not so young as he had first supposed. Still, she could not have been above two or three and twenty. More than that, she was obviously a female of quality unused to being kissed by strange men who came bursting uninvited into her bedchamber. He was a brute to have used her in such a manner.

A long, tremulous sigh broke from her lips. "Finally," she breathed. "It has all been made clear to me. I believe I must thank you, Captain. You cannot begin to know how long I have waited for this moment. Still, I cannot but wonder. Why did you do it?"

Her first words did little to assuage Dane's uneasy feeling of guilt. Indeed, it was immediately to come to him that the shock of his ungentlemanly transgression must have unhinged her mind. Or perhaps she was deliberately mocking him, he thought suddenly, struck by her use of his naval rank in addressing him.

She was here, at the home of the man who had ruined him. Perhaps it was not so farfetched to think she might know perfectly well who he was or even entertained some absurd girlish fantasy about dallying with the infamous Captain Trevor Dane. No doubt she was not so innocent as he had supposed, but one of those spoiled young beauties who delighted in playing men for fools.

A dangerous glint came to his eyes. Perhaps she should be taken down a peg.

"How not, my girl," he replied, flicking her under the chin with a careless forefinger, "when you are pos-

sessed of lips as luscious as ripe, red berries—and just
as bittersweet?"

"Bittersweet?" echoed the intriguing young woman,
a flicker of interest dispelling somewhat her dreamy
expression. "Thank heavens! I was afraid for a moment
you were going to ruin everything by concocting some
extravagant simile in praise of my beauty. I believe,
Captain, I never should have forgiven you for such a
lapse."

Dane, given to behold a bewitching gleam of humor
light up the paragon's magnificent orbs in accompani-
ment to that final, unexpected announcement, was
made to reassess his earlier, hastily drawn conclusions.
Beautiful, yes, but not spoiled. She was far too unassuming in her manner to be one of those heartless jades
who collected unsuspecting men and then discarded
them as soon as they had lost their charm of unattain-
ability.

Nor did he judge her to be of the highest ranks of
society. Although her gown of lavender sarcenet
appeared of the first stare of fashion, she was far too
lacking in the haughty airs of one used to command
the deference of her inferiors. No doubt she was the
daughter of a younger son of aristocracy who had
embarked on a career at law or in the Church. Or
perhaps she ranked no higher than the offspring of a
country squire. Whatever the case, she was undeniably
enchanting.

In spite of the fact his finely honed instincts for self-
preservation were warning him against tarrying in the
house of his enemy for so much as a moment longer
than was necessary, Dane found himself leaning over
the girl. "From which am I to presume you do forgive
the liberty I took in kissing you?" he queried, noting
that, despite his own generous inches, she had only to
tip her head back to look into his eyes. "I warn you, I
am sorely tempted to do it again at the smallest provocation."

"No, are you?" she had the temerity to answer him. "Perhaps I should tell you, then, that my grandpapa says I am provoking in the extreme."

The little devil! thought Dane, keenly appreciative of the fact that she *had* tipped back her head not to look him in the eyes, it would seem, but to give him unimpeded access to her lips! Furthermore, her arms had slipped up around his neck, causing her lissome form to press against his lean, masculine length.

Egad! Her grandpapa, Dane did not doubt, was deserving of sympathy.

"Well, Captain?" demanded the paragon of beauty, her eyes questioning on his. "You did say, did you not, at the smallest provocation?"

"Impertinent little baggage," declared Dane with a wry twist of his lips. "If you are not careful, you are like to discover what happens to young ladies who deliberately provoke strange men."

If he had thought by that to bring her to a sense of her own peril, he was to be immediately disappointed.

"I believe, sir," she had the temerity to reply, "that was precisely my intention. My name, by the way, is Violet, and I do not find you in the least strange—save that you would seem inordinately pale for a naval officer." A frown darkened her lovely eyes as they gazed searchingly into his. "I fear you have been ill, Captain."

"If I have, it is nothing to concern you," Dane answered, perhaps more coldly than he had intended.

To his chagrin, the girl's demmed enticing lips curved quizzically upward. "Dear, have I offended you? That was never my intention, I assure you. It is not my usual practice to pry, but I did wonder. You are young, sir, to wear the twin epaulets of a post captain. I believe you must be one of England's many unsung heroes. You have the look of one who has known little of peace in his life and a deal too much of war."

"Have I?" Dane queried harshly. "What the devil could you possibly know of me—or of war, for that matter? You are a beautiful young woman. Why the deuce are you hiding out in your bedchamber when by all rights you should be in the ballroom surrounded by a host of fawning admirers?"

"Precisely *because* I was besieged by a plethora of doting swains," retorted the singular young beauty, making it clear he had slipped a cog in her estimation by his insistence she should behave in the manner of an Incomparable. "I did tell you, did I not, that I had had enough of adulation for one night? I came to my chamber to escape all that sort of nonsense before it was discovered that, far from being either a goddess or an enchantress, I am simply a woman, and a rather prosaic one at that. I fear you would find I am neither exciting nor dangerous, but hopelessly commonsensical, were you to come to know me at all well, Captain." To his discomfiture, she favored him with the full force of her compelling eyes. "Certainly it would seem I have failed utterly to be provocative in *your* view. How very lowering it is, too. Must I remind you, Captain? You have yet to kiss me again."

Hellfire! fumed Dane, who, for no little time, had had to exercise his considerable willpower *not* to give in to the urge to do far more than kiss the wholly desirable creature residing in his arms. This exquisite child had not the smallest notion what she was doing to him.

It had been two years since he had taken a woman to his bed. Two years since he had been near enough to *any* female, let alone one on the order of this one, to inhale the sweet, clean scent of her. The aroma of lavender mingled with rosemary assailed his nostrils like intoxicating wine. Worse, the warmth of her firm, young body pressed against his was eliciting a decidedly masculine response that, left unfulfilled, promised to afford him no little future discomfort.

"You, my girl, are in danger of provoking a deal more than you bargained for," growled Dane. Judiciously, he pulled her arms down from around his neck and held her wrists captive at his chest. "Are you not in the least curious as to why I should have burst unannounced into your bedchamber? I might be a desperate man, a burglar perhaps, intent on knocking you alongside the head and absconding with your jewels."

"If you are, Captain, you are going to be exceedingly disappointed. Other than my mother's locket," she said, touching an exquisite gold relic of another age that hung on a chain about her slender neck, "I'm afraid I haven't any jewelry of any value."

She frowned, gazing up at him. "It did occur to me at first that you had followed me in here," confessed the surprising young beauty, seemingly not in the least disturbed at such an eventuality. "Not to rob me, but to woo me. On the other hand, it is true I did not see you in the ballroom, in which case I daresay you had some other reason for breaking into my room. Not that it matters. You are here, are you not? I daresay it was an inevitable result of a chain of circumstances which will in turn instigate any number of further chain reactions, one of which I yet dare to hope will lead to that second kiss you promised me."

"Little baggage," uttered Dane, startled into giving vent to a deep-throated laugh. "I never promised you anything."

"On the contrary, Captain, you stated plainly that you would kiss me at the smallest provocation. I, in turn, have given you every provocation. Next I daresay I shall be reduced to pleading, which would be the shabbiest thing. You cannot know how long I have waited for a man like you to do what none other has ever dared before. I was beginning to think I should never know what it was to be—"

Whatever she had thought never to know, she was not to be allowed to say.

"Hush!" whispered Dane, touching the tip of his index finger to her lips before she could finish. In the ensuing silence, the unmistakable clatter of footsteps up the stairs to the landing sounded clearly. "Much as I should like to continue our discussion," he murmured, his face grim, "I fear I have already lingered too long. Needless to say, no one must find me here."

"Are you indeed a burglar, then?" queried his companion, reaching without hesitation behind him to turn the key in the lock. Then, taking his hand, she led him to the window and threw open the sash. "Never mind. I am perfectly aware you are no such thing. I do hope you are not afraid of heights."

"No sailor who has ever trimmed a sail in the midst of a storm long entertains a fear of heights," declared Dane, thrusting a leg through the opening. He paused, clasping the girl's hand as she glanced over her shoulder at the peremptory assault on her door. "I am not a burglar, but I am a man with implacable enemies. Promise me you will do nothing to bring harm to yourself. If they guess I was here with you, tell them I gave you no choice but to help me."

"Never mind about me, Captain. I am well able to fend for myself. There is a ledge. Make your way along it to the corner of the house. I believe the drainpipe is firmly enough lodged to bear you safely to the ground." She looked at him, her eyes expressive of regret mingled with urgency. "I shall keep them occupied as long as is necessary for you to make your escape. Pray take your time, Captain. I should be greatly displeased if you were to fall to your death."

"No less than should I," said Dane feelingly. Pulling her without warning to him, he kissed her soundly on the lips. "Thank you, sweet, lovely Violet. I shall not soon forget you—or what you have done to me this night."

"Done to you—?" she gasped, a hand pressing unconsciously to the tumultuous rise and fall of a firm, well-rounded breast.

His teeth flashed in a rueful smile. "I daresay you will haunt my dreams at night for a long time to come."

The next instant, he was on the ledge groping his way in the dark, while behind him came the sounds of shouts and finally the window sliding shut.

He was conscious of an unwonted pang of regret when, some moments later, he dropped from the drain-pipe to the earth and stole through the grounds to where he had left his mount. No doubt it was fortunate he would never know who his sweet, incomparable Violet really was, he told himself wryly, or that he in all likelihood would never lay eyes on her again. Those few, fleeting moments in her presence had wrought havoc on his usual cool composure, and in the weeks to come he would need all of his wits about him if he were to have any hopes of untangling the dangerous web of intrigue that seemed to be closing in around him. Reminding himself that the last thing he needed was to be distracted by a paragon of beauty with eyes the mesmerizing hue of violets, he sent his mount at a swift canter away from the great Tudor house set in the swale.

Tomorrow he would have need to consider his future course of action. If he dared not now approach Sir Henry, he had at least been face to face with his enemy—a masked man who had known Captain Trevor Dane on sight and had not hesitated to try to put a period to his existence. A man, moreover, who had managed to disappear seemingly into thin air.

Dane did not believe for a moment the man's vanishing act could be attributed to anything of an extraordinary nature. Patently, Sir Henry's assailant had been one of the invited guests. It would have been a simple matter, after all, for the masked intruder to divest himself of his disguise and rejoin the rest of the company in the ballroom without undue comment. It was even possible he had been among those who had assembled at the bottom of the stairs.

Dane's lip curled in sardonic appreciation of that overheard conversation. 'Sir Oliver' could have been none other than Vice Admiral Sir Oliver Landford. Naturally, where Landford was, one could expect to find Lieutenant Alastair Cordell, the admiral's aide, in attendance.

It would seem it was a small world after all, thought Dane with ironic appreciation. Landford had ordered Dane to transport Sir Henry to Gibraltar, a duty better suited to the sloop *Bluefin* or one of the frigates, not a lumbering two-decker. Dane had thought it strange then. How much more suspicious had it loomed in the wake of subsequent events!

Unfortunately, the attack on Sir Henry would seem to make little sense in light of the incidents aboard *Antiope* that had nearly put a period to Dane's existence. If Sir Henry had fired the shot from *Antiope*'s deck, then who had assaulted Sir Henry in his study? Presumably, the assailant had been in search of something among Sir Henry's papers when he had been surprised by Sir Henry's unexpected arrival. Dane would have given a great deal to know what that something was. It would seem it was not Sir Henry himself the intruder had been after, else Sir Henry would undoubtedly be dead.

Clearly, there was a deal more involved than the attempted murder and subsequent discrediting of a lowly naval captain. The question was, what had the one to do with the other? The answer obviously revolved around the events in Malta—his secret meeting with Philippe Lambert and the assignation to which he had been drawn in St. John's Cathedral. He had been a bloody fool to listen to Lambert. Hellfire! He was a naval captain. The last thing he could have wished was to play the part of a bloody spy.

Grimly, it came to him he was at a distinct disadvantage in the sort of game in which he had inadvertently become engaged. He was a naval captain, lacking in both fortune and influence. On the deck of a ship in the line of battle, he was a force with which to be reckoned. In the salons and closed rooms in which the

powerful waged their wars of intrigue, he would have
been out of his element even if he were not barred from
those inner sanctums. The devil, he thought, relinquishing his mount to a stable lad at the White Hart
Inn in Exeter. It was a twisted coil in which he found
himself, and he had only suspicions and a multitude of
unanswered questions from which to start.

Curiously enough, however, Dane's last thoughts
before he fell into the sleep of utter exhaustion some
twenty minutes later concerned neither Sir Henry nor
his masked assailant, but a slender girl with eyes the
deep, mesmerizing blue of violets.

Chapter 2

Lady Violet Clarice Rochelle, smiling and nodding from one to another of the roomful of suitors who surrounded her, all of them jockeying for her undivided attention, could not imagine what had possessed her to attend Lady Granville's house party little more than a fortnight ago. Even before she had arrived to discover Vice Admiral Sir Oliver Landford, the brother of the man who had ruined her father, was in attendance, she had known she would be made to regret it.

Of course, Violet could not deny it would have been frightfully rude to refuse the invitation of the woman who had been her mama's bosom bow. Lydia, Lady Granville, had ever chosen to treat Violet with consummate kindness. Violet abhorred the merest thought of doing anything to hurt her godmother's feelings—or anyone else's, for that matter.

Still, she should have cried off, pleading a case of the chicken pox, measles, or the plague, if need be—*anything* to have avoided the ridiculous predicament in which she presently found herself as a result of her one error in judgment.

But then, it had not really been *left* to her discretion as to whether she would attend Lady Granville's house party or not, she wryly reminded herself, judiciously averting her gaze from the sight of Mr. Franklin Mayberry, a middle-aged nabob in search of an aristocratic wife to elevate his social standing, as he strove to balance a Longton Hall blue and white octagonal tea bowl and saucer on one bony knee. The truth of the matter was she had gone solely because Albermarle had suddenly taken it into his head to order her to do so.

Really, it was too bad of her grandfather, the duke, to have interfered when she might least have wished for him to do, she thought, stoically ignoring Geoffrey Whitlow making grotesque faces at Johnathan Whitlow, his twin, over Mr. Jacob Little's bald pate. She could have told Albermarle what was like to come of it. As a matter of fact, she *had* told him, and in no uncertain terms.

Little good it had done. There was no reasoning with the duke when he took one of his queer notions to meddle in the lives of those who depended upon his largesse for their very existence. And Violet, in the infelicitous position of having been orphaned nearly seven years earlier and having further been left, like her older brother Gideon, the Marquis of Vere, with neither a fortune nor the merest competence to sustain her, was most definitely dependent upon Albermarle.

In the norm, she was able to forget she lacked the independence which, deep down, she craved as an essential part of her nature. After all, involved, for the most part, in any number of obscure projects, like demonstrating that redheads in Devon tended to occur in families who had redheaded ancestors even if neither the mother nor the father were redheaded themselves or that wind currents were apparently affected by seasonal temperature changes as was evidenced by kite flying from the castle parapets from January to August, Albermarle was like to overlook Violet's existence for weeks, even months on end. Left to her own devices, she had learned to be content with the illusion of independence afforded in long walks along the beach, in dreamy contemplation on the cliffs overlooking the river gorge, or in reading.

Only on one of those rare occasions when Albermarle came down out of his airy fastness to observe he was not the only family member residing in the castle was she made to wish she had accepted the invitation to live with her elder sister Elfrida and her husband, Guy Herrick, the Earl of Shields. That she had not was due to her own stubborn sense of pride, which would not allow her to be a pensioner on her brother-in-law, never mind that he was as rich as Croesus and would gladly have welcomed her into his household—to that and to the realization that the impetuous Elfrida never would have ceased to try and launch her into society.

It had taken Violet nearly two years of exile at Albermarle to rid herself of the last scourge of suitors that had resulted from her single Season in London, a Season she most adamantly had not desired but which Elfrida, determined on one of her irresistible schemes, had made it impossible for Violet to refuse.

Despite the fact Violet had not exerted herself to take part in the whirl of social events, she *had* succumbed to the temptation to attend the theatre and the opera and, really, she could not have forgiven herself had she not gone at least once to Vauxhall Gardens.

And then her Aunt Roanna, who despite her indolent nature was ostensibly sponsoring Violet's come-out, had suddenly and inexplicably roused herself to insist her charge really must accept the vouchers to Almack's Assembly Rooms which Lady Sally Jersey had been so kind as to send to her.

Faith, it had been the height of folly to so much as show her face at the assembly rooms, let alone actually consent to dance with any of the host of gentlemen who had thronged eagerly to her! She had had in the end to depart London under cover of darkness in order to avoid the painful necessity of rejecting any number of marriage proposals that had clearly been in the offing. She had even gone so far as to deliberately promulgate the fiction she had become a total recluse in order to discourage any further inquiries in Devon.

Violet hated above anything to have people make a fuss over her, especially impressionable males who, professing to having been instantly smitten by her beauty, insisted on comparing various parts of her anatomy to any number of ridiculous things. Johnathan Whitlow had claimed her skin was as soft as the underbelly of his half-grown hound, Rupert, when Violet was only ten and Johnathan nine. Since that momentous event, she had had her raven locks likened to "the velvet fall of night inviolate," her eyes to "unplumbed amethystine pools," her complexion to everything from "the pristine purity of virgin snow" to "the milky bloom of maiden bower"—egad! Tonight Sir Jeremy Biddle had declared his intent to paint her in the guise of Venus rising from the sea foam!

Good heavens, thought Violet, hiding behind her vellum fan the impish grin that lurked beneath the surface of her carefully maintained outward façade of demure self-composure. She could not but wonder if Sir Jeremy contemplated a Venus in the natural state. Ever practical, Violet could not conceive of Venus emerging from the sea foam fully formed *and* fully dressed. But then, neither could she conceive of herself in the guise of the goddess of beauty.

It was all a parcel of nonsense, and while she had in the past derived no little amusement from the absurd protestations of her ardent admirers, she would far rather be left alone to lose herself in the pages of a delectably lurid novel of Gothic romance by the Earl of Oxford or Ann Radcliff.

Indeed, she would rather be doing *anything* other than what she was doing—attempting to come to a decision as to which one among those vying for her favor would receive the promise of her hand in marriage. Really, thanks to Albermarle's interference, things had gone far beyond mere absurdity!

Violet could not but be keenly aware of the irony of her position. She had, for as long as she could remember, attracted members of the opposite sex much the way sugar water attracted bees. She had only to enter a room to entice a swarm of adoring gentlemen to her. For Violet, who heartily disliked being at the center of attention at anytime and who further could never bring herself to do or say anything that might wound the sensibilities of anyone, her peculiar gift for drawing gentlemen admirers was more of a curse by far than an asset. She could neither repulse their attentions nor derive any real enjoyment from them.

Worse, her reputation for being demure and retiring, defensive measures she had long since adopted to preserve her from the more importunate of her would-be swains, had made her the object of intended matrimony of only the very young or the most respectable sort of gentlemen, all of whom she privately must categorize as crushing bores.

Not that she would ever have revealed to anyone her abhorrence of suitors of obvious virtue. She was far too sensitive of the feelings of others ever to say or do anything that might be construed as censorious. In truth, only those who knew her most intimately had ever been allowed to glimpse the frivolous side of her nature, which was given to a strong inclination to levity. Privately, she entertained what she greatly suspected was a lamentable appreciation for the absurd, not at all in keeping with what should be expected of a lady, and a secret yearning for a lover who had not the smallest leaning either to prudence or moral rectitude.

No doubt she could attribute that particular desire for a mate who not only possessed all the unredeeming qualities of a rogue, but the sort of questionable virtues

of a dyed-in-the-wool black sheep—a man, in short, who
would not bore her as soon as they had got past the
pleasantries to a more intimate knowledge of one
another—to a perversity in her character, or perhaps
to the fact she had been born under the sun sign of
Pisces, personified by two fish swimming in opposite
directions. Certainly her older sister, Elfrida, who entertained an unshakable belief in the extraordinary powers
of the mind as well as in the merits of astrological prog-
nostication, would have said the fact Violet's beau ideal
fit more the criteria of the romantic villain than the
virtuous hero of fiction was due to the influence of her
upstream fish personality seeking to strike out against
the current.

Perhaps Elfrida was in the right of it, Violet sighed
to herself, even as she pretended to be fascinated by
the efficacy of paregoric draughts and mustard baths
in the treatment of the grippe, a subject which Wilfred,
Lord Cranston, was espousing with glowing enthusiasm
at the moment to Mr. Jacob Little, a widowed country
doctor in search of a wife to share his life of ministering
to the sick.

Certainly, Violet knew what it was to be perpetually
pulled in opposing directions. Her natural instinct to
avoid the smallest sort of disturbance to her dreamy
existence was in sharp contrast to a rebellious urge to
fling caution to the wind and embrace all life had to
offer. The first, overpowering inclination had dictated
she remain at Albermarle Castle under the aegis of her
grandfather. The second had compelled her to devour
every sort of novel depicting Gothic horror, intrigue,
and romance upon which she could lay her hands.

The truth was Violet had, for as long as she could
remember, yearned for a life of adventure far removed
from the reality of her uneventful existence tucked away
in the protected environs of Albermarle Castle in the
south of Devon.

Violet, however, had very little hope of ever realizing

her secret ambition. Unfortunately, no one but herself and those who knew her most intimately had the smallest inkling she was anything but a wholly proper female of the sort to make a conformable wife for any one of the paragons of virtue presently ensconced with her in the emerald withdrawing room at Albermarle Castle. Therein lay the crux of her present untenable predicament.

Since having made the error of attending Lady Granville's house party, Violet had found herself the object of a determined pursuit by not one or even two but half a dozen of just the sort of praiseworthy gentlemen who least fitted her ideal of a husband. Worse, having followed her en masse to Albermarle Castle, they had proceeded to lay siege to it with a pertinacious zeal that had served finally and irrevocably to attract even the notice of the duke.

His Grace, eschewing his usual practice of dining in solitary splendor in his private quarters while perusing a variety of weighty tomes concerning any number of esoteric subjects ranging from Erasmus Darwin's *Zoonomia, or the Laws of Organic Life* to Hufeland's *Macrobiotics, or the Art to Prolong One's Life*, not to mention Watson's *An Apology for the Bible* and Hegel and Schelling's *Critical Journal of Philosophy*, had descended upon Violet and her swains one evening in the midst of what had become a tiresome rivalry for the privilege of leading the object of their divine inspiration into the dining room.

Wilfred, Lord Cranston, claiming that right by virtue of his holding the highest hereditary rank, was in a standoff with Mr. Franklin Mayberry, who did not hesitate to point out that, while he might not yet lay claim to a title, he was, thanks to a fortune acquired in textiles, possessed of more than ample means of getting himself one.

Mr. Jacob Little, a widower who, having become convinced that beneath the demure exterior of one possessed of an angelic beauty must reside a self-sacrificing soul suited to be the wife of a country doctor, was not to be outdone. Stolidly he observed that the logical, as well as fair, solution to the problem was to draw straws for the favor of the lady's arm, a proposition subsequently and wholeheartedly endorsed by Sir Jeremy, the aspiring portraitist, who rang immediately for the butler to fetch a straw broom—upon which Johnathan Whitlow, exchanging a wink with his inseparable, not to mention identical, twin brother Geoffrey, moved in concert with Geoffrey to claim the prize.

It happened, in consequence, that Violet, braced on either side by identical Whitlows, glanced up to find herself face-to-face with her ducal grandparent.

"Your Grace!" she gasped, assaying, despite the impediment on either arm, to drop into a curtsy. "How kind in you to join us."

"Yes, I daresay," observed the duke, surveying the motley gathering of gentlemen with a singularly dispassionate blue eye, grotesquely enlarged by means of a quizzing glass held up to that ducal orb. "I confess, miss, to some little confusion," he added, allowing the glass, suspended on a ribbon about his neck, to drop. "I was unaware we were engaged in entertaining guests, an oversight which can no doubt be attributed to my lamentable memory."

"Your memory, lamentable or otherwise, is not to blame, Your Grace," murmured Violet, having toyed for only the briefest of moments with the notion of giving in to temptation.

Albermarle, whether due to the fact that he was an Aquarius with his Moon sign in Leo, as Elfrida was wont to claim, or because he was simply too wrapped up in his various esoteric pursuits to take notice of the more mundane matters transpiring around him, was noted for his lapses in memory—lapses, however, which had a disconcerting habit of ceasing to exist without a moment's warning.

"I'm afraid I have been derelict in my duty. As it

happens, I neglected to inform you these gentlemen had been so kind as to drop in for a visit."

"A visit, is it?" queried the duke, appearing to appraise in turn each of the gentlemen caught in various attitudes of sudden, acute awareness. His penetrating gaze, recording recognition of the identical countenances of his godsons, Johnathan and Geoffrey Whitlow, came to rest on Sir Jeremy Biddle's pleasant, if rather vague, expression. "Am I not mistaken, I encountered at least one of these gentlemen wandering about Gideon's Tower. He was inquiring, as I recall, how to find his way out of 'the Scythian maze,' by which I must presume he thought himself cast among barbarians. How fortunate it would appear he was successful in making his way out. Our chance meeting occurred better than four days ago." Albermarle looked directly at Violet. "Precisely how long have we been honored with the presence of guests?"

"A little more than a se'nnight, Your Grace," Violet answered simply. Really, there would seem little point in hedging the truth. "I did mean to tell you, Your Grace. When the gentlemen made their appearance, however, you were occupied with reading aloud to your hothouse variety of *Peristeria elata* and had left explicit instructions you were not to be disturbed. Then immediately thereafter Lady Rutherford arrived, and under her auspices you began your planned meditational retreat to cleanse mind and body of contaminating external influences. It was my understanding you had not planned to emerge from seclusion for another two days, Your Grace, or you may be certain I should have prepared you to expect company for dinner tonight."

At that observation, offered with unimpeachable gravity, Albermarle's eyes narrowed sharply on Violet. "Yes, well," he said, clearing his throat, "Lady Rutherford and I unfortunately reached something of an impasse in our quest for sublime understanding. In consequence, we agreed to curtail our endeavors for the time being."

Violet, who had little difficulty in surmising from that grudging admission that her grandpapa and his mistress of several years' standing had come somehow to loggerheads, which had led to Lady Rutherford's departure in a huff, could not but wish the duke and his lady friend had managed in this instance to avoid one of their all-too-frequent contretemps. Clearly, Albermarle was in one of his perverse moods, which Violet knew from extensive past experience tended to make His Grace even more unpredictable than was normal for an Aquarius with his moon sign in Leo.

"Which does not entirely explain your failure to keep me apprised of the fact that we have visitors," appended the duke.

"If I may be so bold, Your Grace," Lord Cranston manfully stepped forward. "I daresay the fault, if fault there is, does not lie with Lady Violet, who is Beauty and Virtue personified, but with these, her humble supplicants come to worship at the shrine of feminine perfection."

"Feminine perfection, is it?" commented the duke, his gaze coming pointedly to rest on the object of Lord Cranston's divine inspiration.

Violet, meeting that look, had been hard put not to give vent to a groan. There had been no mistaking the speculative gleam in Albermarle's eyes. Indeed, in retrospect, she did not doubt that was the moment His Grace had conceived his Grand Notion.

Certainly, Albermarle received the news he had been host for a little more than a se'nnight to several uninvited gentlemen houseguests with a sangfroid she had immediately distrusted. Had Elfrida been present, Violet was certain her sister would not have needed recourse to her crystal ball to divine that their grandfather was up to Something that boded ill for Someone. Violet herself had been visited with an instant sinking sensation in the pit of her stomach, which had hardly been alleviated by the discovery that Albermarle intended to sit down with his guests for dinner.

It had, at the very least, been a meal to be remembered, Violet reflected wryly. It was made immediately evident she had failed in all her efforts to persuade Henri, her grandpapa's French chef, that the duke's insistence on engaging a Chinese cook versed in the philosophy of yin and yang in food preparation was merely an aberration in His Grace's behavior that must soon be set to rights again. Upon lifting the covers to find not *poisson véronique* but a soup concocted from four-inch cuttings of seaweed combined with thinly sliced onion and a variety of grain resembling the mash fed to the livestock, she had little doubt Henri must have fled the castle in horror.

Still, Violet could not but grasp at the hope, as the soup was followed by a dish of steamed dandelion, mustard, and collard greens, that her admirers, faced with almost certain starvation in the days to come, must surely pack up their trunks forthwith and depart.

That hope waxed brighter yet over the main course of a mixture of various sorts of boiled brown rice and rye as Albermarle fixed the nabob with his unnervingly direct stare and pointedly observed their present fare was a panacea of youth for a man like Mayberry who, despite having one foot in the grave, so to speak, yet had unlikely ambitions of virility suited to the taking of a wife less than half his age.

"Would you not agree, Mr—er—Little, is it?" queried the duke, turning his attention without warning from the nabob, red-faced, his mouth working, but no sound issuing forth, to the doctor, who was gingerly sipping at his twig tea with the air of a man who suspects he is about to be poisoned.

"I beg—beg your pardon, Your—Your Grace?" stammered Little, waxing a sickly white from the top of his bald pate to his Adam's apple bobbing spasmodically above the knot of his neck cloth, tied, it would seem, in the Inelegant.

"You are familiar, of course, with Hufeland's learned treatise *Macrobiotics, or the Art to Prolong One's Life,*" Albermarle declared in tones of dire certainty. "For a physician, Hufeland must naturally be de rigueur. You have only to look at myself to see the efficacy of adhering to the Oriental principles of complementary opposites in planning one's regimen. Having attained the ripe age of eight and seventy, I find I am being rejuvenated daily by the consumption of foods reflecting the proper balance of yin and yang life energies."

"I daresay Mr. Little is more versed in Galen and Parcelsus than in Hufeland's espousal of Oriental philosophy in prolonging life, Grandpapa," suggested Violet, taking pity on Mr. Little, who, indeed, could not have denied His Grace was a remarkably well-preserved specimen of the male gender, his raven locks untouched by so much as a single strand of gray and his slender, well-knit frame as erect as ever in his youth and demonstrating a suppleness of strength surprising for one of his advanced maturity.

"Then I suggest Mr. Little, along with an inordinate number of his colleagues, is woefully ignorant of an important alternative to leeching and the preponderant reliance on purging to treat everything from dyspepsia to lunacy," the duke declared flatly. "I daresay the king himself would not find disfavor with the notion of a more enlightened approach from his numerous and thus far ineffectual physicians."

"The king is hardly competent to judge, Your Grace," Lord Cranston had had the temerity to interject, thus drawing notice to himself. "His Majesty, as everyone knows, is quite mad."

"And who, Lord Crankston, is to blame for that unfortunate turn of events?" the duke shot back at him. "The charlatans, Lord Crackenberry. The practitioners of quackery who, like Mr. Little here, have not bothered to familiarize themselves with Hufeland's learned book. That is who is to blame, Lord Crockstone."

"Lord *Cranston*, Your Grace," Violet gently corrected. "His lordship is the Earl of Cranston."

"I shouldn't wonder if he is," agreed the duke with what would seem a dark significance. "And what of you, sir?" he asked of Sir Jeremy Biddle, who was in the process of examining a roasted pumpkin seed, a dish of which had been set on the table in lieu of sweetmeats.

"I, Your Grace?" Sir Jeremy replied. "I am not the earl of anything, I assure you. And as for Mr. Hufeland's no doubt scintillating writings, I fear I haven't any opinion. I say, what do you call these curious tidbits? I daresay I have never encountered anything quite like them before."

"They are pumpkin seeds, Sir Jeremy," supplied Violet, suppressing a smile.

"Are they indeed?" said Sir Jeremy. "And what does one do with them?"

"One presumably eats them," speculated Johnathan Whitlow. "Though I should think they were better suited to a pigeon's palate," he confided to Geoffrey across the table from him.

"I daresay a pigeon were better suited to *my* palate at the moment," muttered Geoffrey Whitlow beneath his breath to Violet, who, seated at the foot of the long table opposite the duke at its head, had a Whitlow at either elbow. "Say you will marry me, dearest Violet, and I swear you will never be required to eat birdseed again."

"It would serve you right if I did say I should marry you, Geoffrey Whitlow," retorted Violet, who was heartily wishing her entire retinue of admirers at Jericho. "You know you haven't the least wish to be wed to me. You are here only because Johnathan has taken the absurd notion that he is in love with me, when we both know he is only enamored with the idea of being in love. I daresay you would both turn tail and run if you thought for one moment I should ever be so foolish as to take either one of you seriously."

"Damme, Violet," complained Johnathan, his youthful face assuming a chagrined expression. "You know very well Geoffrey and I have been head over ears in love with you practically since we were in short coats. It has always been only a question as to which of us you will finally have."

"Faith, what fustian!" Violet uttered with a comical grimace. "We have been friends for far too long to pretend there could ever be anything of a more serious nature between us. Even if I could ever bring myself to choose one of you, I should feel as if I were marrying my little brother. And pray do not say there is hardly more than a year between us. I feel ages older than the two of you."

"At least if you settled on one of us, you would not be in danger of wedding a man old enough to be your father," Geoffrey grumbled, "as would be the case with either the doctor or the nabob."

"And as for the remaining pair, you could not actually *prefer* Biddle or Cranston over Geoffrey or me," Johnathan did not hesitate to interject with a moue of disgust. "Egad, the one fancies himself an *artiste*, and the other, besides being oppressively fond of mustard baths, resides yet with his doting mama. What you need, dearest Violet," asserted Johnathan, swelling his chest, "is a man."

"Hear, hear," agreed Geoffrey, warming to the subject. "Someone dashing enough to woo you away from your demmed beloved solitude in the country."

"And then man enough to keep you bloody well interested," Johnathan concluded with an air of sapience.

"A naval captain, I should think," Violet dreamily asserted, instantly deflating any fantasies the two may have entertained that the object of their aspirations would see one or both of them in the role they had depicted. "Indeed, a brave captain in the king's Navy

I daresay would be just the thing. Does either of you know where I might find one?''

Naturally, they had not had any suggestion to make regarding a naval captain to supplant them in her affections. But then, they could not know she had not been making an idle remark. In view of the coil in which she presently found herself, her chance encounter with just such a paragon as they had described was made to seem all the more poignant to Violet, who had spent the past several days thinking of little else.

A pity her mysterious captain had neglected to tell her his name or give her some clue as to where he might be found when he was not about the business of breaking into people's houses, not to mention ladies' bedchambers, unannounced, she mused. Having excused herself from her doting swains for the ostensible purpose of resting before dinner, she made a precipitate retreat from the emerald withdrawing room and wended her way along the winding stairways and corridors to her chambers overlooking the sandy beach at the foot of sheer cliffs. She did not believe for a moment he was the desperate character Sir Henry had painted him—a clever and exceedingly dangerous French agent, as it happened, whom someone whimsically had given the name *Le Corbeau*, of all things.

The Raven indeed, she thought with a sardonic quirk of her lovely lips. He was in truth quick enough of wit, she recalled, to be thought more than clever, and she did not doubt for a moment he was dangerous—eminently so, and especially to her peace of mind. He was, however, no more a French agent than was she herself!

Even now, she had only to close her eyes to conjure up a mental image of his lean, handsome countenance—the high, wide, intelligent brow and long, straight nose, the slash of stern, sensitive lips above a firm, stubborn jaw. The intriguing mark of a razor-thin scar along his left cheekbone had only added to the aura of controlled recklessness about her mysterious captain.

Possessed of hair the same midnight hue as her own and black, demon eyes that had had the peculiar effect of setting her emotions all in a turmoil, he was undoubtedly the most fascinating man she had ever encountered, not to mention the most provoking. Faith, she had never known anything like the thrill that had coursed through her upon finding herself imprisoned without warning against the hard, masculine length of him. Certainly it seemed he had awakened feelings she had never previously suspected lurked deep within her.

Without knowing anything about him, let alone his name or his purpose in breaking into Sir Henry's house, she had not hesitated to help him escape capture! And all because of a kiss that had shaken her to her core and left her warm and tingling with the newfound knowledge of what it was to be treated like a real flesh-and-blood woman by a strong, virile man.

The devil! Fierce, passionate, and proud, he was everything she had ever dreamed of in a man, and he was gone, vanished like the merest will-o'-the-wisp. Really, it was too bad of him!

Who was he, really? she wondered, as she had done repeatedly since that single fateful meeting at Lady Granville's house party. Sir Henry, his head wrapped in a bandage, could hardly be considered objective in his assessment of the intruder, whom he had not hesitated to describe as a villainous devil with the heart of a viper.

Still, she could not deny Sir Henry had indeed been bludgeoned unconscious. She simply could not convince herself her mysterious captain and Sir Henry's assailant were one and the same man. No, she decided, shaking her dusky curls with utter certainty, it was quite impossible. It simply defied all logic, not to mention every one of her highly developed feminine instincts.

Violet had ever prided herself on being an excellent judge of character. Further, she had always been accounted a female of uncommon good sense. Surely no man could have so thoroughly pierced her formidable defenses if he were the sort to cowardly strike Sir Henry from behind with the intent of purloining secrets of the realm from his defenseless victim's desk. Her mysterious captain was not capable of betraying anyone, let alone king and country. Violet would have staked her life on it. She, after all, had looked into his eyes.

Really, she wished she had not. She had not been at all prepared for what she had been given to glimpse—a strong man in the grips of unaccustomed doubt, a brave man who, though not himself violent by nature, had seen too much of violence and suffering.

There had been more, things that, being Violet, she had known instinctively. Her dearest captain, she did not doubt, was a lonely man. More than that, he was a man in bitter torment.

Why? she wondered, not for the first time, as she sat, her knees folded to her chest, in the window seat in her bedchamber and gazed down on the sandpipers wading in the shallow wash of waves along the curve of the beach. She had known almost instantly he had been recently ill. It was not only the finely etched lines of suffering about the eyes or the unmistakable pallor of his face. It had been evident, as well, in the loose fit of his uniform coat, in the powerful frame devoid of excess flesh.

He had not been quite himself yet, and Violet had been swept with an almost overpowering desire to have him to herself for an extended length of time. She did not doubt that, given the chance, she would have returned him to his normally robust health. More than that, however, she had wished for the opportunity to chase the shadows from his marvelous eyes.

It had been that which had haunted her, disturbing the normal tranquillity of her dreamy existence at Albermarle Castle—the unshakable conviction her mysterious captain had needed someone. If only she knew his

name, she thought. At the very least she might have
inquired after him.

Not that it mattered anymore what or who he was,
she sighed. All that had been rendered singularly aca-
demic by her grandfather and his Grand Notion, which
he had related to her only a few short hours ago in his
study.

She supposed it was true *something* had had to be done
about her suitors, who thus far had demonstrated a
tenacity of purpose not even a three-day regimen of
macrobiotics could discourage. Certainly, the duke had
made it clear that he was not prepared to allow his
home to be overrun for an indefinite period by a pack
of hangers-on.

On the other hand, it would seem really too bad of
Albermarle to give her the ultimatum of choosing one
of the six to be her husband when he might just as easily
have rid himself of his unwanted guests by the simple
expedient of ordering the lot of them to immediately
vacate the premises. It was not as if he were not perfectly
capable of doing whatever he pleased, mused Violet.
He was the duke, after all. Unfortunately, it pleased him
at the moment to have Violet husbanded and out of
the castle once and for all, whether she herself willed
it or not.

Nor was he disposed to put up with her propensity
to indefinitely defer matters she found not to her liking
in the hopes they might simply go away. She would
bloody well choose one of her suitors to be her husband,
or Albermarle would do the choosing for her! He was
demmed if he would have his granddaughter waste her
life away mooning about the castle when she might have
her pick of any number of eligible partis. That much
he had made abundantly clear—the old devil!

And there it was, she reflected ruefully. Albermarle's
Grand Notion. How kind in him to give her until her
twenty-fourth birthday on the seventeenth of March,

little more than two weeks away, to decide who was to be her husband.

As if she *could* make up her mind, when she was being constantly bombarded with protestations of undying affection by the gentlemen in question! Really, it was too much to ask of her. Not only was she unable to make up her mind, she was exceedingly reluctant to hurt the feelings of those whose offers she would reject, especially as each had sworn he could not contemplate a life without her.

In truth, she would gladly have consigned them all to the devil if she could. Unfortunately, that was not a viable option. Indeed, she would seem to be in a devil of a coil.

In the norm, Violet might have looked to her sister Elfrida for an ally to aid her in her dilemma. Unfortunately, Elfrida and Shields were at Claverling, Shields' principal estate, in Cheshire. Certainly, she could not look to her brother Gideon, the Marquis of Vere, for help. Having quarreled with his grandfather—*again*— Vere had taken off for parts unknown.

How very *like* Vere not to leave word where he might be reached! thought Violet, who did not doubt her brother, as head of their immediate family, would not have hesitated to send her suitors packing. With the possible exception of Johnathan and Geoffrey, Vere would hardly have approved of a single one of the lot to be his future brother-in-law.

How much less could *she* conceive of such an eventuality! Never mind that she was a firm believer in the tenet that whatever was meant to happen would happen, she could not but feel a trifle uneasy at the realization her grandfather was not to be swayed from his determination to see her settled with a husband.

Really, it would all seem quite utterly hopeless. She simply could not make up her mind on such short notice—or ever, if one went right to the heart of the matter.

Certainly, she could never choose between Johnathan and Geoffrey. Indeed, they were out of the question. Even more impossible, however, loomed the thought of marrying Lord Cranston, who came with a plethora of real or imagined ailments and an exceedingly virtuous, not to mention overindulgent, mama. Or Mr. Mayberry, for that matter, who, despite his much vaunted fortune, demonstrated a disturbing propensity for penny-pinching. As for Mr. Little, she did not doubt he would have been an indulgent husband if only he did not entertain impossible hopes of a sizable dowry and a wife who would be willing to devote herself to drudgery. And then there was Sir Jeremy Biddle, a penniless baronet who was decidedly out of touch with reality.

How she wished she might put some distance between herself and her importunate swains! Perhaps then she could achieve some sort of objectivity by which to judge who she might be most able to tolerate as a husband.

Hardly had that thought presented itself than it came to her—the one place to which she might escape to contemplate her course of action in solitude. The house which had belonged to Violet's mama and which, upon the death of the marchioness, had gone to Elfrida, offered just the sort of haven Violet needed. Bath, after all, was less than forty miles from Honiton, a mere day's journey by coach.

Suddenly she was on her feet, her thoughts racing. She had more than sufficient funds saved up from several past quarterly allowances to buy passage on the mail coach and to provide for her comfortably for as long as she might wish to stay at her sister's house. Fortunately, perhaps, tucked away in Albermarle Castle, she had had little opportunity to indulge what she considered her feminine weakness for shopping for pretty things. Money, or the lack of it, need not be a deterrent to the plans taking shape in her fertile brain.

Albermarle, on the other hand, loomed as a formidable obstacle. Naturally, she could not expect the duke to give his blessing to a plan that would remove her from a castle overrun with suitors for her hand. Indeed, she did not doubt the very notion would be enough to send His Grace into the boughs. And therein lay the greatest stumbling block for Violet, who could not like the notion of causing her grandpapa distress.

Obviously, there was but one course before her. She must simply take the bull by the horns and go without asking leave. No doubt when faced with *un fait accompli*, Albermarle, being Albermarle, would conveniently suffer one of his memory lapses and relegate the entire matter of her unwanted husband to where it belonged—oblivion.

With Violet gone, her devoted swains must inevitably follow suit and abandon their siege of the castle. And then, when her birthday was safely past, she would return to find everything as it had been before she made the error of attending Lady Granville's house party.

It was all so simple, she thought, setting about making preparations for her departure. Indeed, she could not imagine *why* she had not thought of it before!

Violet was not altered in her conviction that she had arrived at the ideal solution to her dilemma when, half an hour before sunrise the next morning, she slipped out of the castle and made her way along the lane to Honiton carrying naught but a small grip, a bandbox, and her reticule. Since the arrival of her suitors at the castle, she had abandoned her usual practice of rising early in favor of putting off for as long as possible the necessity of entertaining her houseguests. Consequently, they had become accustomed to amusing themselves until she made her appearance just before breakfast was removed from the sideboard at ten.

With any luck she would not be missed until well after midmorning, and by then she should be on the mail coach out of Honiton and well on her way to Bath. Anyone who came to her rooms in search of her would find a note addressed to the duke in which she informed

His Grace that, in need of solitude in which to contemplate the decision he had given her to make, she had
deemed it prudent to go into retreat for a time. Assuring
him of her obedience and her undying affection, she
promised to send word when she was safely arrived at
her destination.

And in truth, it seemed all was going marvelously
according to plan. She was fortunate to find, upon
reaching the posting inn at Honiton shortly after the
sun had come up, a mail coach even then was preparing
to make its departure. In moments, Violet's bandbox
and grip were stowed away in the boot and Violet herself
was happily settled in a seat next to a window.

The other passengers—two tradesmen who manifested symptoms of having overindulged the night
before in strong spirits, a draper and his dour-faced
wife, who, no doubt noting her fellow passenger's lack
of a traveling companion, eyed Violet with chilly disap-
proval—appeared content either to doze or sit in stony
silence. Violet, who, with the exceptions of a previous
brief stay with her sister in Bath and her single Season
in London, had done very little traveling in her life, was
more than happy to be left alone to gaze out the window
at the passing scenery.

It had been a mild winter, and the first signs of
approaching spring made for a pleasant journey along
the narrow, high-banked lanes resplendent with azaleas
and magnolias already bursting forth with flowers. It
seemed hardly any time had elapsed before the coach
arrived at a posting inn on the outskirts of Yeovil and
stopped to change horses.

Violet, glad for the opportunity to stretch her legs,
stepped down into the cobblestoned courtyard. She had
forgotten since her previous journey to Bath how lovely
was the countryside surrounding the town of Yeovil,
which boasted nine springs, all of which flowed into a
sylvan lake somewhere close by.

Not loath to be quit of her traveling companions for

a spell, she allowed herself to be drawn down a wooded path along the banks of a purling beck. The keen scents of gorse and sorrel sweetly assailed her nostrils, even as the gurgle of the chuckling stream lulled her into a fanciful daydream in which a certain dashing naval captain played a significant role. She came abruptly back to the present, a blush on her cheek and a rueful smile on her lips and yet strangely at peace with herself.

Faith, she had not realized how greatly she missed her long walks along the beach or the hours spent in solitary dreaming on the cliff tops overlooking the river gorge!

Reminded at last that she dared not linger overlong, she reluctantly turned her steps back the way she had come. Too late. Hardly had she stepped free of the woods than she was greeted with the blare of a horn and the clatter of wheels over cobblestones, followed shortly thereafter by the sight of the mail coach wheeling out of the courtyard onto the road to Bath!

Really, it was simply too absurd, she thought, hardly knowing whether to laugh or cry at the new coil in which she found herself. Certainly there would seem to be little point in standing in the courtyard with her mouth agape. After all, things could be worse. She could be at home surrounded by her adoring suitors.

No doubt a day and night spent in the lovely environs of Yeovil would prove a not unpleasant interlude, she told herself as she made for the entrance of the inn with the intent of engaging a room for the night.

She was soon to discover things *could* be worse—that, indeed, they were prone to deteriorate with alarming rapidity.

"Naturally, you will be wanting a cot, miss," asserted Mr. Ambrose Tankersley, the innkeeper, in response to her inquiry concerning a room. Speculatively, he eyed her over the rimless tops of the eyeglasses perched halfway down his rather bulbous nose.

"I beg your pardon?" said Violet, who had more in

mind the comforts of a four-poster complete with a warming pan. "A cot?"

"For your maidservant," expanded the landlord with frosty significance, "who, I daresay, is waiting outside with your trunks."

"Oh, I see," declared Violet, who did, indeed, begin to grasp the significance of the innkeeper's apparent reluctance to welcome into his establishment a female lacking both baggage and a traveling companion to lend her countenance. Plainly, he suspected she was a wholly improper sort of female intent on practicing her feminine wiles on his male guests! "As a matter of fact, I am traveling without a maidservant. I was, however, in possession of a bandbox and valise until a few moments ago. They, as fate would have it, are at present on their way to Bath in the boot of the mail coach, which was so disobliging as to leave without me."

"So you say, miss," said the landlord, clearly unsympathetic to her delicate situation. "On the other hand, it might be Frank Jessop had good reason not to wait for a passenger who was so heedless as to wander off just when he was preparing to set out. Mayhap you had ought to be told this is a respectable house that doesn't take to females of questionable plumage."

"*Plumage?*" choked Violet, torn between sardonic amusement at being taken for a woman of ill repute and consternation at the prospect of finding herself without a roof over her head for the night. She drew breath to inform the innkeeper that, far from being a Cyprian, she was the daughter of the late Marquis of Vere and the granddaughter of the Duke of Albermarle and, further, it was hardly her fault she should find herself stranded when she had paid good brass for passage on a mail coach that could not bother to announce it was preparing to leave without its passengers.

Before she could give utterance to her protest, however, a soft, compellingly masculine voice did it for her.

"I find it passing strange the landlord of a respectable

house should employ language that is rude at best and boorish by any standard. I am moved to inquire what the trouble is."

Violet turned, her heart inexplicably behaving in a wholly unseemly manner. She had little difficulty recognizing in the tall, uniformed newcomer her devilishly handsome captain from Lady Granville's house party. Indeed, it would have been difficult to mistake the black, glittering eyes beneath the firm set of his tricorn, never mind the man's tall, powerful physique, made to seem somehow even more formidable draped in a blue single-caped cloak that enveloped the entire impressive length of him from his indecently broad shoulders to his booted feet.

The innkeeper, presented with the looming presence of an obvious force to be reckoned with, swallowed dryly. "Begging your pardon, Captain, but you would seem to be laboring under a misunderstanding. There's nothing amiss. Certainly nothing that need concern you."

"On the contrary," Violet objected, "there is a very great difficulty here. Mr. Tankersley was just on the point of sending me away without a room."

"No, was he?" queried the captain, turning the hard glitter of his eyes on the hapless landlord, who was suddenly moved to wring his hands in the soiled fabric of his apron.

"It seems he is not in the habit of letting rooms to unattached females who have neither baggage nor a feminine traveling companion to lend them countenance. I am afraid he thinks I should be something of a bad influence on his masculine guests."

"Do you indeed, Mr. Tankersley?" murmured the captain in chilling accents. "Obviously you are incapable of recognizing a lady when you see one, an error for which you will directly apologize. You have, Mr. Tankersley, the honor of addressing my *wife*."

Chapter 3

It was difficult to say who was more startled at the captain's unexpected announcement—the innkeeper or Violet. Certainly it was clear who was the more unnerved by it.

"Your—wife?" echoed Mr. Tankersley in fading accents, his expression reminiscent of one who had just been made the recipient of a dire premonition.

"My *wife*," the captain affirmed with chilly certainty.

"B-beggin' your pardon, C-captain," stammered the landlord, spreading wide his hands, "b-but how was I to know? It looked queer, it did, her not having so much as a bandbox. And being left behind by the coach— well, it's not the usual thing, is it?"

"Is it not?" murmured the captain with a daunting lack of sympathy. "No doubt you would know better than anyone. But then, my wife is not of the usual sort. You have only to look at her to apprehend she is hardly accustomed to traveling by means of a public conveyance."

Violet, suddenly finding herself the cynosure of two pairs of masculine eyes, resisted the absurd compulsion to reach up and check if her white felt hat with the upturned brim and blue-violet ostrich plume curling smartly over one ear sat straight on her head. Indeed, it was all she could do not to give vent to a vapid grin.

"Bless me, I do see what you mean, Captain," said the landlord, swallowing hard as he took in her tall, graceful figure, appareled in a Spanish pelisse of blue velvet lined with ermine and trimmed in ivory Mechlin lace. "I was wrong to think what I thought about you, madam. In spite of the—er—questionable circumstances, I should've seen right off you aren't what I suspicioned you to be."

"You should, indeed," agreed the stern-faced officer in accents that made the innkeeper wince. "However," tempered the captain, who, having forcefully made his point, was apparently disposed to relent somewhat, "perhaps you may be excused in part for what might in those aforementioned circumstances be considered a not unnatural error. As it happens, my wife and I were likewise victims of an unfortunate misunderstanding— one that led to her unannounced departure from home early this morning."

At the discovery that not only was she married but a runaway wife as well, Violet choked on an astonished burble of laughter. "You may be sure I was driven to it," she uttered in a strangled voice, which the captain pointedly ignored.

"Which is why," he continued as if he had not been so rudely interrupted, "she was traveling by mail coach without benefit of her abigail. Very likely it also serves to explain why she should have been so remiss as to be off somewhere woolgathering when the coach was brought to leave without her."

"I daresay I was contemplating mariticide," Violet sweetly postulated. "As in Latin *maritus,* for husband, and *cidium* from *caedere,* to slay."

"*Fortunately,*" persisted the captain quellingly, "it

allowed me to happen upon her before she could proceed further on what was a wholly unnecessary journey.''

At last he looked straight at Violet, who despite the
sudden and distinct flutter in the pit of her stomach
could not but be struck by what would appear a feverish
glitter in the magnificent coal-black depths of his eyes.
A soft thrill shot through her as his strong fingers
grasped her right hand in his.

"Did you think I should not come to you, my sweet
Violet?" he queried, his compelling look seeming to
cause her heart most peculiarly to skip a beat. "Would
it surprise you to learn you have been constantly on my
mind since our last parting? I wish only that you might
trust me in this. In spite of anything you might have
been told to the contrary, you may believe I should
never intentionally do anything to harm you."

"I pray you will not be absurd," declared Violet, who
realized suddenly he was speaking naught but the simple
truth. Inexplicably, she experienced a melting pang at
the knowledge of what he was willing to dare for her,
no doubt out of the mistaken belief he was somehow
indebted to her. He was, as he himself had confessed
to her, a man with implacable enemies, perhaps even
a hunted man. He hardly needed the complications he
was inviting in taking up for her with an innkeeper who
would soon, in any event, have been made to see the
error of his ways.

Indeed, it really was not in the least necessary. She,
after all, was Lady Violet Rochelle. She might pretend
to be demure and retiring because it suited her purposes, but she had the blood of dukes in her veins.
She did not doubt she could bring Mr. Tankersley to a
proper understanding of whom he had all but accused
of being a ladybird. Certainly she could not allow her
gallant captain to place himself in jeopardy for her sake.

"You must know perfectly well I never believed any
of the absurd things that were said of you. Nevertheless,

I cannot forget the circumstances of our—our last moments together. Really, for your sake, I—I—"

It was on Violet's lips to bring an end to the ridiculous charade by denying that she was anyone's wife when it came to her that her self-proclaimed husband not only was most unnaturally pale, but a distinct sheen of perspiration on his handsome brow should not have been there. Furthermore, on closer inspection, she was made uneasily aware he was holding his left arm peculiarly stiffly at his side. It was, in fact, all she could do to stifle a gasp as she beheld a sudden trickle of blood down the back of his left hand, which held hers!

"—shall endeavor to be a more conformable wife!" she blurted, appearing in a sudden gush of emotion to fling herself against his broad chest. "Forgive me, my darling. I never should have taken off the way I did. You are quite right. It was all a stupid misunderstanding." Even as she felt him stiffen in surprise, Violet surreptitiously pressed the corner of her muff to the blood before it could drop to the floor to leave a telltale stain.

A shadow of sudden suspicion flickered briefly across the captain's stern, handsome features. "I daresay there is nothing to forgive, my dove," he said measuringly. "You were understandably upset."

"Thank you, my darling. You are all that is generous," returned Violet with only the barest hint of irony. "I, on the other hand, shall not soon forgive *you* for undertaking to come to me. When I heard you had been wounded, did you truly think I should be content to wait at home for you until you were well enough to quit your sickbed?"

Violet, made the object of the startled leap of the captain's black, piercing orbs, could feel only a measure of perverse satisfaction at having at last pierced his cool reserve.

"I confess I never know quite what to expect from you, my sweet," replied the captain with a wary quirk of an eyebrow. "It has been my experience you never cease to surprise me."

"Has it, my darling?" murmured Violet. Searchingly, she gazed up into his face. "I promise you can trust me to understand what you are going through, my dearest, if only in future you will not keep me in the dark. I daresay I never should have let us part without making it clear that I should always wish to help you in any way possible if you would but let me."

She was rewarded for those words of assurance with a grim narrowing of the captain's gaze on her. "You are everything a man could wish for in a wife. Nevertheless, I have told you, my precious, there are some things of which you are better off remaining in ignorance. No doubt I shall endeavor, however, to be rather more forthcoming in future."

"Really, heart of my heart, that is all I shall ever ask," Violet said, only to sustain a sudden constriction of her throat as she beheld the captain sway on his feet. "My darling!" she exclaimed sharply, quick to slip a sustaining arm about his waist. "You are ill! Faith, why did you rise so soon from your bed?"

Ignoring the captain's sharply quelling look, Violet turned her glance pointedly on the landlord. "I feel sure Mr. Tankersley is to be forgiven his error in judgment, dearest," she said in the cool, commanding tones of a true granddaughter of the duke. "You were about to show us to your finest chamber, were you not, Mr. Tankersley? One which includes a private sitting room?"

Mr. Tankersley, only too happy to be acquitted of any offense against the gimlet-eyed officer and his unpredictable wife, was quick to comply with Violet's request. "Indeed, ma'am. You may be sure I have just the thing. If you would both be so good as to follow me, we'll soon have you comfortably settled in."

In his eagerness to atone for his prior mistakes, the innkeeper himself bent to take up the captain's leather pouch as he ushered them toward the stairs.

Violet, keenly aware of the captain's weight against her, found herself hoping they had not far to go. Indeed, glancing up into the grim cast of his face, she suffered a queasy sensation in the pit of her stomach. She knew very little about injuries and wounds and the like. Still, she had the most dreadful feeling her gallant captain had the look of a man who had lost a deal more blood than was strictly good for him.

She could only be exceedingly relieved when presently the landlord ushered them into a cozy sitting room pleasantly furnished with braided rugs and dimity curtains, two tapestry-covered wing chairs, a settee, a tea table, and a lowboy. Adjoining was a low-beamed bedchamber, which to Violet appeared to be dominated by its massive oaken bedstead.

"This will do splendidly, Mr. Tankersley," Violet remarked, casually dropping her muff on the settee as the innkeeper knelt to light the fire already laid in the inglenook fireplace. "And now if you would be so good as to send up a tea tray and hot water and towels for washing, we should be ever so grateful. Oh, and I daresay my husband," she added, marveling that her tongue did not stumble over the blatant falsehood, "would not be averse to something rather more stimulating than tea."

"Brandy, if you have it," interjected the captain, who, moving away from Violet, came to stand in the open doorway to the bedchamber, his shoulder propped against the frame. "Or port, if you have not."

"As it happens, we have a peach brandy that is made hereabouts. I believe you will find it to your liking, sir," the landlord offered, bowing as he happily took his leave of them.

Hardly had the door closed behind him than Violet rushed to the captain's side in time to prevent his legs from giving way beneath him. "Quick, we must get you to the bed," she breathed, one hand going about his waist, while the other drew his uninjured arm over her shoulders.

"The devil," he cursed between clenched teeth. "Never meant to involve you in this. What the deuce possessed you to miss your coach?"

"I'm afraid I was doing just as you said, Captain," replied Violet, helping him across the room to the bed. "Woolgathering. It hardly matters now, does it? How badly are you hurt?"

"I have suffered worse . . . and lived . . . to tell of it. Flesh wound." His strength spent, the captain sank heavily onto the bed. "Couldn't stop. Bloody hounds on my trail. Mostly, I am in need of a rest." As Violet reached to undo the straps at the neck of his cloak, the captain's hand closed hard about her wrist. "No matter what happens, you will leave on the coach tomorrow, my sweet Violet. Promise me. I will not have your life put at risk because of me."

"Hush, Captain," Violet admonished, surprised her voice should sound firm and steady when she felt all quavery inside with dread anticipation of what she might find beneath the heavy fabric of the cloak. "You must not spend your strength foolishly. While I am perfectly capable of looking after myself, I shall require your help in removing your clothing."

Ignoring the darkling look Dane bent upon her at that pointed evasion of the promise he had demanded of her, she pulled the heavy cloak open to reveal his coat sleeve saturated with blood. "The devil, Captain!" she exclaimed, steeling herself against the faintness that threatened. "This is no mere flesh wound. You have need of a doctor."

"No!" the captain ground out between his teeth. "No doctor." A chill coursed through his lean, strong body. Shuddering, he gasped, "The ball . . . passed through . . . cleanly. No bones broken. Cleanse and bind it. It will be enough. It will bloody well have to be."

Violet bit her lip to still the numerous objections that

leaped to mind at those less than reassuring words from the captain, not the least of which was that he was clearly on the point of going into shock and was quite likely to develop a fever before the day was out, never mind the ever-present danger of putrefaction. A single look at the hard set of his strong, masculine jaw was enough to convince her that remonstrations would prove useless.

"Very well, Captain," she said, resolutely removing her hat and her pelisse, "though I cannot but think you are being foolish in the extreme. I suppose," she added, reaching with grim determination to undo the buttons down the front of his coat, "you do not intend to tell me *how* you came to be wounded. No, of course you do not," she continued bitterly, talking in order to keep a tight rein on the emotions rising like bile to her throat. "At the very least you might tell me your name. I daresay I shall soon use up my store of affectionate appellations by which to address you in front of Mr. Tankersley."

Violet, easing the bloodstained coat off her patient, caught her bottom lip between her teeth at the captain's sharply indrawn breath. After a single glance at his face, ashen and taut with pain, she could not bear to look again. She was hurting him, and somehow she must go on hurting him until the thing was done—she, Violet Rochelle, who could not abide so much as the thought of hurting anyone!

"Of course, I suppose I might resort to terms of a less endearing nature," she said feelingly, willing her fingers not to tremble as she fumbled with the buttons of his waistcoat. "Indeed, I can think of any number of names I might call you at this moment." Freeing him of the waistcoat, she tossed it impatiently aside. At last, unwilling to submit him to the pain of removing his shirt, she grasped the linen fabric of his blood-soaked sleeve and ripped it open from the cuff to the shoulder to reveal congruous holes oozing blood high up at the front and back of his arm. "Faith, Captain," she uttered, dismay lending an edge to her voice. "It is a wonder you have any blood left in you."

"It looks worse than it is," grunted the captain with a wry grimace. "It is fortunate you are not the sort to swoon at the sight of blood."

"I am not the sort to swoon at the sight of anything," declared Violet, acutely aware of his eyes on her. Grimly, she fought down the sense of hysteria welling up inside her as she tried to remember everything she had ever heard or read about the treatment of wounds. Most important at the moment was to stop the bleeding. Of that she was instinctively certain.

"No, I daresay you are not," agreed the captain with a sardonic twist of the lips. "I knew from the first you were a most remarkable female."

"I am nothing of the kind," denied Violet, feeling unreasonably cross with him for being in the state he was in. How dared he come so near to tossing his life away! "I told you before, I am dreadfully prosaic."

"And wholly commonsensical," he recalled with a whimsical gleam of a smile. "Which is why you managed, no doubt, to be left stranded without your maid or your trunks."

"No, how can you say so?" Grasping his other sleeve with fingers made fierce by necessity, Violet ripped the fabric from his arm and bound it about the wound. "The one has nothing to do with the other. Really, it is the shabbiest thing that you should bring up that particular when it is all your fault that I was left behind."

"*My* fault!" The captain winced as Violet, in her agitation, fairly yanked at the ends of the knot.

"Yes, *your* fault."

Where the deuce were the hot water and brandy? she fretted, silently, to herself. The wound must surely be cleansed before it could be permanently bandaged. Hardly had that thought crossed her mind than a scratching at the outer door announced their timely arrival.

"I was thinking about *you*," she said, "when I should have been attending to the coach. Keep the bandage snug until I return," she added, ineffectually trying to wipe the blood from her hands on the tattered remnants of his shirt. At last, realizing the futility of her actions, she impatiently tugged on her blue kid gloves. "I shan't be long, Captain."

"Dane," said the captain, grasping his injured arm. Then, at her look of puzzlement, "My name, sweet Violet—Trevor Dane."

"Yes, of course it is," agreed Violet, with a flashing smile that momentarily banished the strain from her eyes and must surely have taken his breath away. "Pray do not stir while I am gone, Captain Dane. I shan't forgive you if you use your strength needlessly."

Hastily, she made her escape then, slipping out of the bedchamber and closing the door behind her.

For the briefest moment, she stood with her back to the oaken barrier as she schooled her features to reveal nothing of the turmoil within her breast. Captain Trevor Dane, the hero of countless naval battles, a man of whom even her uncle, Commodore Richard Rochelle, had written in glowing terms, waited in the bedchamber for her return. A great deal had suddenly been made clear to her, not the least of which was why her gallant captain had looked as if he had only recently left a sickbed when first she had met him. She had read it in the *Gazette;* indeed, everyone had: Dane had been grievously wounded in his valiant defeat of a French seventy-four in the Mediterranean, an event that had occurred only a few months before his unexpected appearance in her guest bedchamber at Sir Henry Granville's.

Faith, there had been mention of something else. Violet remembered quite clearly her Aunt Roanna writing that Captain Trevor Dane, being well known among his naval contemporaries for his daring exploits and his victories in battle, had taken a French ship single-

handedly, a feat which, instead of earning him the lau-
rels he richly deserved, had led to his having been
skipped over for promotion and denied a new ship to
command. Roanna's dearest Richard very much feared
Dane had incurred the enmity of someone powerful
enough to quash the captain's career.

Who? Violet speculated. And why? Indeed, who in
England could possibly wish the captain dead? she wondered with a chill along her spine. And why had Dane
felt it necessary to break into Sir Henry's house?

There was a mystery here she did not understand—
not yet, at any rate. What was patently clear to her was
that, in his present state of vulnerability, she and she
alone stood between Captain Trevor Dane and those
who wished him ill.

She would not fail him, she vowed, crossing to admit
two chambermaids in the company of no less a person-
age than the landlord's wife, a rotund, middle-aged
matron who, bustling into the room, gave the impression of boundless, good-natured energy.

It was immediately evident Mrs. Tankersley had been
made privy to the events that had transpired earlier
and, further, she was possessed of a strong motherly
disposition, which Violet suspected bordered on being
meddlesome, though kind in its intention. She had not
only commissioned the maids to bring a tea tray, hot
water, and clean towels, but had taken it upon herself
to fetch numerous other items as well for the use of the
captain's lady. These had included a cotton nightdress,
a cap, a wrapper, all of which Violet was duly informed
belonged to Mrs. Tankersley's daughter-in-law, and a
brush and a comb.

"I hope you'll not think me forward, missus, for bringing you these few things to tide you over," appended
the landlady, carefully laying the articles of clothing
over the back of one of the chairs.

"No, how should I?" exclaimed Violet, smiling,
though she could not but soon be wishing the lot of

them at Jericho. "I must naturally be grateful for your kind generosity, Mrs. Tankersley."

"There's no need to be," replied the landlady, directing one of the serving girls to set the tray on the tea table and the other to put the towels and the ewer of water on the lowboy. "It's little enough to make up for Mr. Tankersley's unfortunate error in judgment. I hope you'll not think too badly of him, missus. He's a good man for all he's a mite hasty to jump to conclusions."

"I have no doubt he is, Mrs. Tankersley," Violet answered, her thoughts anxiously on the wounded man waiting for her in the other room. "You may be sure I am not one to hold grudges. And now, if you will excuse me, I really must be getting back to the captain."

Violet, noting the woman's glance go to the closed bedchamber door, had the sinking feeling Mrs. Tankersley was a deal more discerning than her husband. Certainly Violet was acutely aware, as she reached into her reticule for a coin for each of the serving girls, that she herself had become the object of the woman's keen-eyed scrutiny. She was left little doubt that the landlady had suspicions of something amiss when, after that single, penetrating look, Mrs. Tankersley shooed the chambermaids from the sitting room.

"Now, missus," she said, closing the door behind the exited servants with the air of one who will not easily be put off, "you may say it's none of my never you mind, but Mr. Tankersley mentioned the captain looked a mite peaked. He's a sight worse than better, isn't he, missus? You needn't tell me if you don't want to. There's a stain on your gown that says it all for you."

Violet, robbed of speech, stared in disbelief at the blotch of crimson on the front of her skirt. Really, this could not be happening, she told herself—not now, when she needed above everything to be free to return to the captain.

"You poor dear!" exclaimed Mrs. Tankersley. "Why

don't you let me help you? I may be a meddlesome old woman, but I know how to hold my tongue."

Did she, indeed? wondered Violet, aware she might very well be adding to the captain's peril if she trusted the landlady with his secret. Still, the woman had already guessed most of it, and Violet did not doubt Mrs. Tankersley would be of invaluable aid should the captain take a turn for the worse, which seemed all too likely for Violet's peace of mind. Would it not be better to take the landlady into her confidence and trust her to be ruled by her motherly instincts than to send her away and leave her to brood over her suspicions, perhaps even to nurse a growing resentment against her unconfiding guests? It seemed to Violet she had very little choice but to enlist the landlady's help.

Drawing a steadying breath, Violet looked straight into the older woman's eyes. "He is Captain Trevor Dane of the *Antiope*, and he was wounded as he tried to make his way home to me," she stated baldly. "I am in grave fear for his life, but he will not give me leave to send for a doctor. Nor, I suspect, would it be in his best interests were it to become known outside of this room that he is in a vulnerable case. He has enemies in England who wish him dire harm, though he will tell me nothing of them." At last her voice cracked with the strain under which she had been laboring. "He has served king and country with courage and honor, Mrs. Tankersley. He does not deserve to die like this."

"Then we must do our best to see he doesn't," declared Mrs. Tankersley, a martial light in her eyes. "I lost a son in the Battle of the Nile. I expect England has given enough of her sons to war without losing another to road agents. And so I'll tell Mr. Tankersley if he should ask me."

"*Thank* you, Mrs. Tankersley," breathed Violet, clasping the other woman's hands in both her own. "I shall never forget you or your kindness. And now I think we must hurry. He has lost a deal more blood than is good for him."

Violet was to wonder ever afterward what she would have done had Mrs. Tankersley failed to take it upon herself to make it impossible for Violet to refuse her offer of aid. Upon entering the bedchamber, they had been met with the daunting scene of the captain crumpled unconscious on the floor. Whether he had been trying to reach Violet or in a fit of delirium had risen from the bed only to lose consciousness was not clear. She could not have been away longer than a few minutes, though in her state of anxiety it had seemed more like an eternity. Still, she tormented herself with her failure to have been with him when he needed her.

At least she could be in a measure relieved to discover her hastily applied bandage had served to stem the flow of blood. Her gallant captain had not lost any more of that valuable commodity in her absence. Nevertheless, it was of little comfort to find his brow was cold and clammy to the touch or that he appeared wholly oblivious to the sound of her voice entreating him to awaken. Faith, how still and limp he lay!

Mrs. Tankersley had proven a veritable tower of strength. Somehow, with one on either side of him, the two women had managed to lift Dane to the bed, there to turn to the work of relieving him of his clothing.

How strange she had felt neither embarrassed nor self-conscious as, having removed his boots and stockings, she struggled with Mrs. Tankersley to strip the white breeches from Dane's inert form. At the time, she had been too occupied with the tasks at hand to dwell on the reality of his nakedness. Not until much later was Violet, who had never before been given to see a grown man in his natural state, to feel the blood rise hot to her cheeks at the memory of her gallant captain, lying helpless and unaware, beneath her gaze.

And truly, he was in all respects a magnificent specimen of his gender. It had not, however, been the stark
masculinity of him that had drawn a gasp from Violet's
lips, but the record of his years at sea in service of king
and country written in scars on his body.

Indeed, only when they cut the ruined shirt from him
had Violet's courage nearly failed her at sight of that
older, graver wound and the tale it told of how near he
had come to death's door. God's mercy! He had been
shot in the back!

Violet, seated wearily in a chair by the bed in which
Dane, cleansed and bandaged, for the moment thankfully slept, shuddered at the thought of how near she
had come to losing him before ever she had met him.
Clearly, he had been fortunate that the ball, entering
below the right shoulder blade to exit beneath the arm,
had apparently missed both the ribs and any vital organs,
else it was doubtful he would have lived to tell of it.

It had, nevertheless, been a harrowing wound. She
had read as much in the *Gazette,* not to mention her
Uncle Richard's account of it in the letter from her
Aunt Roanna. The jagged relic of a sword slash across
the ribs on his left side told yet another story of the
captain's reckless valor, as did the thin, white line along
his cheekbone. And now here he lay wounded yet again.

Really, thought Violet, her lovely brow puckering in
a frown as she gazed down at the still face against the
pillows, it would seem to her Captain Trevor Dane had
given enough for king and country to last a lifetime.
How, she wondered, could he persist in flinging himself
into danger's way? Certainly the odds had all been
against his continued survival the longer he remained
at sea. On the other hand, they would not seem to have
improved greatly since his return to land. Faith, she
thought, had he no one to care what happened to him—
a father, a mother, a sister? Or—a sweetheart perhaps?

Violet, made ruefully aware of a sudden hot pang
through her midsection at the merest thought that the

captain might have a lover waiting for him somewhere, sternly made herself consider that distinct possibility. He was a sailor who was away at sea for months, even years at a time. A wife might be expected to wait patiently for those few, fleeting moments when she could be together with her seafaring husband, but the same could hardly be said of a spinster, who, when one went right to the heart of the matter, could not afford indefinitely to put off marriage and the hopes of a family. And he had kissed her, Violet, not once, but twice. Surely he could not have done so had his heart been engaged by another.

A bemused smile touched the corners of her lips at the memory of those two stolen kisses. How different from the chaste salute of her knuckles by all those gentlemen of unquestionable virtue who had declared she was their divine inspiration!

Faith, Dane's lips on hers had sparked a fire within her that had had little to do with divine inspiration. In his embrace, she was a woman in the arms of a man.

Violet, who had been plagued with male admirers ever since she had left the schoolroom behind her, could not but think it strange to contemplate that she had never before been given to experience anything remotely approaching the tumult of emotions Dane seemed capable of inspiring in her. Even sitting at his bedside as he slept had the effect of infusing her with a curious warmth quite unlike anything she had ever felt before.

Analyzing it, she could not but note that it little resembled the searing heat that had pervaded her limbs at the touch of his lips to hers. Indeed, this was something of quite a different order—quieter, subtler, and far more difficult to understand.

It came to her that she owed its source to a feeling that somehow it was right for her to be at Dane's side during this, his hour of need. Whatever else might come of the curious sequence of events that had brought them there together, at least she should have had one adventure of quite an extraordinary nature in an existence that had hitherto been characterized by a dreamy uneventfulness.

More than that, she was acutely aware that, having embraced a course of action that must inevitably land her in a bumblebroth from which there was little promise she would emerge unscathed, she was remarkably free of any sense of trepidation. If anything, she felt serene in what loomed as her fall from grace. Certainly, she had never felt *that* before with anyone! But then, she could not deny she had never before met anyone quite like Captain Trevor Dane.

Wryly amused at herself, Violet resisted the tender impulse to brush a stray lock of hair from Dane's brow lest she awaken him. How *young* he looked, she thought. In sleep, the stern lines were banished from the corners of his mouth. The grave air of command he wore when he was awake too was in abeyance, set aside for the moment like his uniform and the sword that seemed so much a part of him.

Still, even in sleep there was little of softness about him, certainly not in the lean, hard jaw limned with the shadow of a beard or the masculine chest bristling with its black mat of hair. He was all muscled firmness, a man to whom it would never occur to spare himself in battle or the execution of his duty. And yet she knew full well that beneath the hard veneer was a man of sensitivity not even the years of war had served to eradicate.

It was that man she had been given to glimpse upon their first encounter, a man haunted by some secret anguish. Who was he, really, wondered Violet, so far forgetting herself as to lean over to trail the tip of her index finger lightly along the line of the scar on his cheek. Who had hurt him and how?

A low gasp burst from her lips as, unexpectedly, she

found herself staring directly into Dane's black, feverish eyes. A frown of bafflement creased his brow.

"Lynette? *C'est toi?*" A merciless hand closed hard on Violet's wrist. "*C'est toi?*"

"Captain, no," breathed Violet, alarmed at his sudden violence. "You mustn't—"

A blur of pain darkened his gaze.

"*Non, c'est impossible. Lynette est morte.*" Releasing her, he closed his eyes and turned his head away, his uninjured arm flung over his face. "Bloody illusion. Lynette is gone, and now Philippe has no one but me." A low sigh breathed through his lips, and his arm dropped to his side on top of the counterpane. "Shouldn't have been alone," he muttered fretfully. "Why the devil was she going to Blackthorn?"

Violet sat very still as she willed her heart to cease its pounding. Dane lay quiet now, his breathing slow and regular in sleep. She did not doubt he had not been truly awake, but caught up in a dream into which she had inadvertently intruded. He was dreaming now, she thought, seeing his eyes moving beneath his eyelids, dreaming of his lost Lynette. Faith, how greatly he must have cared for her!

An involuntary stab of something very like jealousy as quickly gave way to a silent ache for the captain. It had all been there in his voice—grief, bewilderment, despair, and something more. Guilt, she thought with a pang. He blamed himself for her death.

But then, who did not upon the loss of someone dear? she reflected, vibrating to a painful chord of memory. One blamed oneself and then one blamed the one who had died. One blamed the fates or God. And, finally, when the pain had been dulled by time, there came some sort of acceptance. There had to, or one simply could not go on.

She had gone on, allowing herself to be carried on the current of daily living, never fighting it, drifting through the days and months and years while she waited until it might be safe to feel again. It had been like being lost in a dream, one which might have continued indefinitely had not her grandpapa, the duke, disturbed her tranquillity. Well, she was awake now, she mused with a wry twist of her lips. Awake and poised at the brink of something that promised to forever alter the serene flow of her existence.

She did not fool herself into believing she could escape the consequences of her latest actions. She would leave the posting inn at Yeovil either as a ruined woman or a married one. Gazing down at Dane, she rather thought she would prefer the latter.

And how not? she mused, when he was precisely the man she would have chosen to be her husband, if only he had been among her determined suitors. Far from desiring her or her hand in marriage, however, he would undoubtedly wish her at Jericho when he was himself again. He, after all, was a man of duty. As such, he must inevitably be exceedingly reluctant to take on the burden of a wife now, when he was embroiled in something quite obviously fraught with danger.

His concern would be to protect her from his enemies; that much he had already made patently clear. Indeed, she did not doubt when he awoke to find her still at his side, he would be exceedingly put out with her. Rather than pledge himself to do the honorable thing and wed her, he would be far more apt to nobly take infamy upon himself and send her away, both their reputations in shreds, but her physical safety assured. It would be just like her gallant captain.

Really, it was too bad of him, she thought, shivering in the growing chill of the room. Drawing her knees to her chest, she tried to tuck her bare feet into the folds of her borrowed wrapper, to little avail. Obviously, Mrs. Tankersley's daughter-in-law was more generously endowed in certain areas than in others. While the nightdress and wrapper hung on Violet's slender frame with fabric to spare, the hems reached well above Violet's ankles.

Still, even the ill-fitting night clothes were better suited to her present circumstances than her thin chemise and drawers must have been, she told herself, as she tried to ignore a growing ache in her back, which she did not hesitate to attribute to the straight-backed chair upon which she sat.

The afternoon spent watching over Dane had taxed both her strength and her inner reserves. Indeed, it had been fraught with frequent restive spells in which Dane had lapsed into rambling incoherence, sometimes, curiously enough, in French, but more often in language that must have made her ears burn had she not been intent upon striving to keep him from thrashing about in the bed. Though she had made little sense of his utterances, she could not mistake the nature of those wild ravings. They owed their substance to the scenes of battle he had lived and was reliving yet again in his dreams with the anguish of a brave man who had seen and given much.

And he would go on giving, she knew instinctively, driven to seek out and engage the enemy in battle. He was, after all, a captain in the king's Navy. Ordered away to sea for months, sometimes years, at a time, he was expected to endure hardship and danger. More than that, he was expected to achieve victory in battle. It was, after all, the tradition of the British navy to win in the face of overwhelming odds. To do less was not to be thought of. Certainly, the tales of the captain's daring exploits demonstrated he had adhered to that tradition of glory—but at what cost to himself?

It was something beyond Violet's understanding— war and a warrior's lust for battle.

Or was it? pondered Violet, acutely aware that, having lived a sheltered life of rank and privilege that demanded very little of her, she had hardly had occasion

to test her mettle. Was there somewhere deep inside
her an instinct for danger?

There had been a Rochelle in the company of William
the Conqueror when he swept across the Channel to
take by force the throne he claimed had been promised
him. A Rochelle had distinguished himself in the campaign to lay waste to the Vale of York, conducting himself with a savage ferocity that had won him the title of
baron with lands in Devon. His successor had reaped
further rewards in William II's three campaigns into
Wales, earning for himself the office of viscount and
the landed estates that went with it.

The Earl of Rotham, the Marquis of Vere, the first
Duke of Albermarle, all of them Rochelles, had been
soldiers and statesmen well-known for their ruthlessness
and skill in the art of war. If redheads could be born
to parents who were not redheaded themselves, as Albermarle had postulated from his extensive investigation
into the subject, then perhaps it was not inconceivable
Lady Violet Rochelle might possess the innate capacity
for a combative spirit.

Certainly her brother, Gideon, the Marquis of Vere,
having by the time of his twenty-second year fought
three duels from which he had emerged unscathed and
victorious, was a Rochelle in the truest sense, Violet
mused with a sardonic grimace. And Elfrida, born under
the warrior sign of Aries, had ever demonstrated a
quickness to leap to the defense of her loved ones—or
anyone else, for that matter, who she perceived to be
in need of a savior. She, too, had carried on the Rochelle
tradition of boldness in the face of adversity.

Violet had always considered herself the black sheep
of the family in that respect. Indeed, she had often
wondered if she were not in truth a changeling left in
the Rochelle nursery by mischievous faeries, she so little
resembled her siblings in temperament. Rather than
involve herself in a squabble, Violet's first, overpowering
instinct had ever been to retreat into solitude. It was,

after all, the far more sensible course when one took into account that seldom was anything of a positive nature ever really accomplished in participating in a direct confrontation.

She had long since observed that not only did arguments rarely serve to change the points of view of those who engaged in them, they far more often than not lent themselves to a greater alienation of the participants. How much more must that be true of wars, which must inevitably lead to a greater misunderstanding between disparate peoples? Really, there would appear to be little sense in any of it.

And yet it seemed that wars, like disputes between individuals, were an inevitable facet of the human condition. As such, to fight them, there must be warriors into whom were bred the precepts of patriotism and duty and the instinct to preserve those things to which one owed one's identity. She had no doubt Captain Trevor Dane was just such a one. And if it should ever occur that a retreat into solitude was no longer a viable solution to aggression, might not she, Violet Rochelle, be similarly moved to take up the cudgel in defense of that which she held dear?

She did not know the answer to that question at the moment, or to any of the other multitude of questions whirling about in her brain. She knew only that she was cold and exceedingly weary and that, further, she would like nothing better at the moment than to slip into the bed beside her sleeping patient if only for an hour or two of restful repose.

And why should she not? Violet suddenly asked herself, sitting up in the chair. Her reputation need not be a prohibiting factor. *That* had been damaged beyond repair the moment she entered the bedchamber with Dane.

As for Dane himself, he was sleeping peacefully at last, a circumstance for which she could only be grateful, since it would seem to indicate the captain's fever had

already begun to subside. There would appear to be
every reason to hope the wound would not become
inflamed.

Perhaps he had been aided in that respect by the free
flow of blood, she theorized, yawning. Doctors often
bled a patient to lower a fever, after all. Or perhaps the
cleansing application of brandy to the wound had served
its purpose.

Whatever the case, she could not think it would be
to the detriment of her patient if she stretched out
beside him in the bed for a short while. There was every
chance he would never even know she was there.

Stiffly, Violet unfolded herself from the chair and,
slipping out of her borrowed wrapper, ever so carefully
lifted the counterpane. Easing down on the bed, she
slid her feet beneath the bedclothes and, pulling the
covers to her chin, settled on her side with her back to
the captain. Enveloped in a delectable cocoon of
warmth, she breathed a long sigh of relief and let her
body go wonderfully lax. Slowly, inevitably, her eyelids
drifted down over her eyes.

From a dreamy distance a tiny voice whispered in her
ear that she was not behaving at all in the manner of a
wholly commonsensical female—that, indeed, she must
see that she very likely was courting a deal of trouble,
if only she were not too tired to think in the least coher-
ently. She was asleep before she could give the matter
any proper consideration.

Chapter 4

Dane, drifting just beneath the surface of wakefulness, lay still, his eyes closed and his mind toying with the intriguing puzzle of why there should be a weight draped across his chest. There was something else, too—the sensation of something soft and warm snuggled against his right arm and shoulder and, yes, the scent of lavender teasing his nostrils. Deciding these peculiarities were not altogether unpleasant, he felt himself giving in to the temptation to simply drift away again.

And then it came to him what it was, precisely, that was nestled cozily at his side!

Dane's eyes flew open. *Good God*, he thought, turning his head to find himself staring into the lovely face that had haunted his dreams at night and left him with a memory both poignant and sweet somehow.

For the length of several erratic heartbeats, he told himself he must be dreaming, a supposition put immediately to rout by the soft swell of the unmistakably flesh-and-blood bosom pressed against him. There was the indisputable evidence, too, of the girl's arm flung across his bare chest, not to mention the light caress of her breath against his neck.

All of which served to bring him to a startling new revelation—not only was he lying in bed with the paragon of loveliness who had helped him escape certain discovery in Sir Henry Granville's country manor, but he was doing so without a stitch of clothing on. Egad!

Clenching his eyes shut, he tried to recall how he came to be in his present circumstances. It immediately returned to him—the scene upon which he had happened upon entering the inn.

The devil. When it had become clear to him he could go no farther without stopping to tend the cursed hole in his arm, the last thing he had anticipated was encountering the young beauty on the point of being turned away by the innkeeper. Obviously, the landlord was a man lacking in the most rudimentary understanding, Dane grimly reflected. Only a fool or a blind man would ever have mistaken the sweet, lovely Violet for a Paphian.

A faint, whimsical smile played about the captain's lips as he conjured up a mental image of the exquisite creature clad in the first stare of fashion, her dusky curls caught up beneath a wholly fetching concoction of white felt with blue velvet trim and a feather dyed to match her pelisse. She had radiated grace and beauty and something more—that indefinable quality that marked her as a lady born.

Opening his eyes again, he turned his head to gaze with no little bemusement at the girl's delicately wrought features composed in sleep. Good Lord, she was even more beautiful than memory had served him! More than that, she was both generous and pluck to the backbone, as was evidenced by the clean bandage about his arm as well as the indisputable fact she had stayed to care for him when he was unable to care for himself.

He suffered a pang of shame mingled with dismay. A man's sickroom was no bloody place for a woman, especially one of her obvious breeding. But then she was hardly in the usual style of female, he mused, noting his pistol, primed and loaded, set out on the bedside table.

His lips twisted in a smile that was distinctly sardonic at the memory of how readily she had leaped to his aid. He might have known then she would never be content to leave him once she had seen to his wound. Indeed, he could not but find it ironic in the extreme he had thought to come to *her* rescue only to end up once more in her debt—not to mention in her bed.

Who the devil was she, and what had she been doing traveling on a mail coach without benefit of a companion, female or otherwise? he wondered grimly. In spite of the elegance of her attire, which must have cost a pretty penny, it would seem the mysterious Violet was in straitened circumstances. That would, after all, be the most plausible explanation for her presence on a mail coach. If that were the case, she must have spent nearly the entirety of her slender means on the gown, pelisse, and other accoutrements, he speculated—in order to go where and do what?

And then it came to him, insidiously, like a mawworm gnawing away at his pat assumptions. Perhaps the innkeeper had not been so far from the truth of the matter when he had questioned the propriety of her peculiar circumstances. A gently born female with little or no fortune of her own, after all, would have few options open to her to provide for her existence. She could marry, or she could hire herself out as a paid companion or a governess—or she could accept the protection of a gentleman of means without the formality of matrimony.

Dane suffered an unexpected wrench as it came to him—an exceedingly plausible explanation for why his sweet Violet, dressed to the nines in the first stare of fashion, should have taken passage alone and without baggage on a mail coach and, further, why she should have neglected to tell him more than her name. Good God, she could not be a wealthy gentleman's discarded mistress! Not *this* girl. Not again!

He was not to be given time to ponder the answer to that disturbing question. At that instant, Violet, breathing a long, contented sigh, opened her eyes to his.

For a long moment, neither occupant of the bed moved as eyes of spellbinding blue-violet stared uncomprehendingly into orbs of coal-black glittery intensity.

Dane, waiting for the young beauty to arrive at a proper understanding of the singularity of their present circumstances, was not sure what reaction he had expected from her. Certainly, it was not to behold Violet's lovely face suddenly light up with a warm, vibrant glow that seemed peculiarly designed to bring on an instantaneous resurgence of his fever.

"Captain Dane," declared Violet, who was noting with no little gladness the return of rationality to her patient's otherwise grim aspect.

"Sweet Violet," Dane acknowledged with only the barest hint of irony.

"You are awake," Violet helpfully pointed out.

"As you see," agreed the captain without the flicker of an eyelash.

"And, am I not mistaken, feeling much more the thing."

"I daresay you are *not* mistaken," Dane confirmed, wondering when she would see fit to arrive at the crucial point of their thus far unproductive dialogue.

"I could not be more pleased, Captain," Violet earnestly confessed, "for, if you must know, you gave me quite a scare."

"No, did I?" queried Dane, grimly noting what would seem the young beauty's complete lack of discomposure at lying in bed with a man who, besides being quite utterly as nature had intended was for all practical purposes a total stranger to her. "No doubt I beg your pardon for any inconvenience I may have caused you."

"Pray do not be absurd, Captain," demurred Violet, thinking he had certainly awakened in a rare taking. Plainly, he was not disposed to be in the least helpful in what could only be described as a delicate situation, the devil. "It could hardly have been otherwise. You were, after all, quite out of your head with fever."

"A circumstance that undoubtedly explains why *I* should be in my present peculiar circumstances, but hardly what the devil *you* are doing here. I distinctly recall before losing consciousness ordering you to be on the next coach."

If he had thought by that to impress upon her the enormity of her failure to abide by his wishes, he was soon to be disappointed. Violet, arching a quizzical eyebrow at him, appeared anything but daunted.

"I am reasonably certain I heard the coach arrive and depart no little time ago. You did not actually expect me to go, did you?" she said, making it clear he had dropped a peg in her estimation. "You were hardly in any case to be left to your own devices, you know. I daresay you are not ready yet to leave your bed, no matter how anxious you may be to dash bravely off once more into danger."

Dane could not but be ruefully aware she had hardly misstated his case. Even without the fiery ache of his wound, he suspected he had not the strength to travel beyond the confines of the room. Wordlessly, he glared at her as she leaned over his chest to examine his bandaged arm with an insouciance that would seem to be wholly impervious to ill-tempered naval captains.

"You have a sad notion of my character," she continued, apparently satisfied the bandage did not require her immediate attention, "if you think I should ever be brought to abandon a friend in need." Settling her chin on the back of her hand on his chest, she gazed speculatively into his glowering visage. "No doubt I am sorry if I seem to have placed you in an untenable position, Captain. Naturally I had meant to be out of your bed before you awakened."

"But not, it would seem," he observed dryly, "out of the inn and safely embarked once more on your journey."

"No, not that," Violet smilingly agreed. "It never occurred to me to leave you. However, I should wish to have spared you this present added awkwardness. Upon being awakened by the coach's arrival, I fear I was far too content where I was and, having foolishly talked myself into a few more minutes of self-indulgence, I fell asleep again. Oh, you needn't glower at me, Captain. I am perfectly aware I have been remiss. The truth is, however, I cannot regret what simply cannot be helped. To do so, you would agree, would only be an exercise in futility."

"Viewed in such a light, futility would seem to take on a whole new dimension," observed Dane in tones heavily laced with irony. "What is done is done and the devil with the consequences."

"I knew you would understand," applauded Violet, positively beaming her approval, though privately she thought Dane's particular choice of phrasing rather harsher than was needed. "And that is why, having come to the conclusion that, since my reputation was past being a consideration, there would seem little point in stoically suffering the chill in the room, I finally succumbed to the temptation to climb into bed with you. I'm afraid I have never thought much of people who insist on playing the martyr for no good reason. I wonder," she reflected, thinking it was a shame her gallant captain seemed prone to frown far too much of the time, "do you think I could be prey to moral turpitude without my being aware of it?"

Dane regarded her out of eyes that seemed capable of burning holes through her. Moral turpitude—egad! She had all but admitted she was a fallen woman with little left to lose by climbing into bed with a man she hardly knew.

No doubt that would explain why she had not been discomposed upon being forcibly kissed by a stranger who had broken into her room on one exceedingly memorable occasion. Far from displaying the offended sensibilities he had expected of her, she had all but seduced him into kissing her again! Nor had she been overly concerned at the distinct possibility Sir Henry and his houseguests would come to realize she had been locked in a bedchamber with the intruder who was undoubtedly alleged to have bludgeoned Sir Henry.

If she were someone's acknowledged mistress, she would hardly have been worried about any damage to her already tarnished reputation. Egad, it was hardly beyond reason to suppose she had indeed been accused of that very thing, and, further, that her protector had seen fit, because of it, to withdraw from her the mantle of his protection.

Dane was prey to a sudden slow, burning rage at thought of the blackguard who could callously thrust Violet out into the world without so much as a trunk of clothing to her name. Kept woman or not, she had not deserved that from anyone. How much less did she deserve to be made an unwitting target of assassins because she had helped a stranger in need, he mused darkly.

"What I think," he said grimly, "is that you are utterly lacking in a proper sense of self-preservation. The devil," he growled, "you haven't the smallest notion who I am or in what you are involving yourself. You should remove yourself from this bed and this inn— now, before you discover to your regret that I am far from being your friend."

"Naturally you would say that," Violet rejoined without hesitation. "You are, after all, exceedingly worried at the moment about the compromising state of circumstances in which we find ourselves." Snuggling down once more into the warmth at his side, she left little doubt that she was quite pleased to remain where she was. "Obviously, you are trying to frighten me away."

Frighten her away? thought Dane. He had faced a fleet of enemy ships in the line of battle with greater assurance than he had now against a slender girl with spellbinding eyes and alluring lips that, despite his infirmity, were having a telling effect on his anatomy.

He was ruefully aware of a distinct stirring in the region of his groin, a circumstance that could not be allowed to come to full fruition under present conditions—in bed with a female who had succored and saved him.

Hellfire! Whatever the state of her virtue, he was demmed if he would take advantage of her generosity! It was time she was made to realize the danger she was courting.

Ignoring the hot stab of pain in his arm, Dane heaved himself on to his uninjured side. "You, however, are not easily frightened, is that it?" he demanded, as, lifting himself to lean over her, he ruthlessly pinned her to the bed with a hand braced on the pillow beside her head and a muscular thigh thrust over her legs.

Violet stifled a gasp of bestartlement at suddenly finding herself in what could only be described as a wholly intriguing position—flat on her back with a superb specimen of masculine virility all but astraddle her! Aware of a most peculiar, not to mention unfamiliar, tingling sensation rippling through her from her head to her toes, she stared speculatively up into black, demon orbs.

Dane, staring back at her, could not but be struck by his enigmatic Violet's unnerving composure.

"On the contrary, sir," she returned, apparently not in the least discomfited at this sudden turn of events. "I am noted for being timorous and prone to take flight at the merest threat of any disruption to my tranquillity, which is why, as it happens, I found myself stranded in Yeovil in the first place."

"Are you saying you were running away from something?" queried Dane with no little skepticism. In his few brief encounters with her, she had thus far demonstrated a coolness of nerve that would have done credit to a veteran sailor under fire. "No doubt you will pardon me if I find that difficult to believe."

"It is true, nonetheless," insisted Violet, giving in to the urge to trail her fingers experimentally through the bristling mat of hair on Dane's hard, muscled chest, which seemed conveniently placed at the moment for that very purpose. "I was, as it happens, fleeing the necessity of having to choose from among a plethora of suitors, none of whom I had the heart to refuse and not one of whom I was pleased to accept."

"Suitors!" declared the captain, staring hard at her. He had brought himself with no little reluctance to accept that she was very likely a man's discarded mistress. Vaguely, he had assumed there had been only the single lover. Now it would seem she was pursued by a bloody *host* of gentlemen eager to take her under the mantle of their protection!

Clearly she had need neither of his pity nor of his concern for her material welfare. Somehow that realization afforded him exceedingly little gratification. In fact, he was made sudden prey to an unfamiliar, rending pang somewhere in the vicinity of his stomach.

"Indeed, suitors," Violet confirmed with a comical grimace. "Absurd, is it not? The thing is, I am an orphan, you see, dependent in the absence of any fortune of my own upon my grandfather. And he, as it happens, has decided it is past time I was wed and out of his hair."

"Wed!" Dane rasped, ruefully aware of feeling a cumbersome weight had been launched from his breast. What a fool he had been to doubt in his sweet Violet's virtue! He should have known she was talking about suitors for her hand, not her favors.

Unfortunately, the news, while causing him to experience an unexpected, not to mention inexplicable, stab

of relief, had also the perverse effect of placing him
in a most damnable position—naked and astraddle a
virtuous maiden in search of a husband! "The devil he
does!" he uttered harshly.

"I'm afraid he was quite adamant on the subject,"
admitted Violet, moved to trace with her fingertips the
magnificent cord of muscle down the side of the captain's neck to the broad set of his shoulder.

Faith, she had never realized before how beautifully
sculpted a man's physique could be! Indeed, there
would seem to be something exceedingly stimulating
about smooth, firm skin with bands of muscle rippling
beneath it in all the most intriguing places!

But then, she had never been given before to observe
a representation of male perfection au naturel and certainly never before at a proximity that could only be
described as exceedingly intimate. The experience was
having a most peculiar effect on her emotions, not to
mention any number of her vital functions, not the least
of which was the sensation of a mounting heat in her
veins accompanied by the rapid acceleration of her
pulse rate.

Really, she thought, observing the rigid set of Dane's
handsome countenance as she explored the muscled
firmness of his chest with her hands. It was the shabbiest
thing that while *she* would seem inordinately susceptible
to Dane's compellingly masculine presence, *he* would
appear odiously impervious to any reciprocal attraction
to her!

"Grandpapa even went so far as to declare that if I
did not choose a husband for myself, he would choose
one *for* me. Which is why I decided it was prudent to
make myself scarce for a time in the hopes he would
come to forget all about this sudden start of his to marry
me off whether I should wish it or not."

"But of course you did," Dane uttered on something
between a gasp and a groan.

She had not the smallest notion what the devil she

was doing to him! Hampered by the fact that his weight was propped on his right elbow while his left arm was not only prone to a throbbing jolt of pain at the slightest movement, but was occupied with holding down the subject of his intended object lesson as well, he could do little but suffer the exquisite torture to which Violet's exploratory manipulations were subjecting him.

"For a sensible female, you seem to be remarkably prone to reckless endangerment. Not only have you run away from home, but you managed to be left behind by your coach, not once, but twice. And now see what has come of it. Have you the least notion how close I am to treating you as you so richly deserve?"

"That depends," replied Violet, running the pad of her fingertip over a masculine nipple that, intriguingly, had grown perceptibly hard before her very eyes, "on what you believe I deserve for taking care of you when you could not take care of yourself."

"For that, you undoubtedly have my gratitude," Dane ground out between clenched teeth. "For ignoring my order to embark on the first bloody coach away from here, you are perilously close to experiencing just what happens when a man awakens to discover a beautiful, desirable woman in his bed."

"No, am I?" queried Violet, gazing up at him with wide, interested eyes. "My poor captain, I'm afraid you could not have determined on a worse argument for chasing me from your bed. Doubtless you would be doing me a favor if you ravished me. At least I should not be compelled to marry where I have no wish to do, for, if you must know, I am pursued by gentlemen of great moral rectitude who would not be pleased at all to be saddled with ruined goods. I daresay I should, in fact, not be required to marry at all in such an event, which would suit me very well if I cannot have a man to whom I would willingly give my heart." Violet, marveling at her own brazenness, lifted her arms around the captain's neck. "Do you, sir," she asked, "intend to ravish me?"

Dane, finding himself gazing into quizzical blue-violet eyes of a spellbinding loveliness, was sorely tempted to do just that. The young beauty, far from demonstrating the least trepidation at such a prospect, presented a wholly alluring aspect of innocence combined with the dreamy air of one not quite of this world.

Who the devil *was* she? he wondered, keenly aware she still had not told him any more than that she was a penniless orphan dependent upon her grandfather and that her given name was Violet. Good God! She was as lovely as the flower for which she was named and just as enchantingly unpretentious.

Every instinct of self-preservation warned him that this dreamy-eyed enchantress was the sort of beauty who captivated men without even being aware of her singular power to do so. And the very last thing he could have wished at the present time was to become entangled with a female of quality who had not the least idea with what she was flirting. But then, who was he trying to fool? He had inextricably committed himself to a course of action the moment he declared her to be his wife.

A man, if he was a man, must be honor bound to make the lie a truth. Unfortunately, the price of honor would be to place the young beauty in immediate peril of her life. Hellfire! He could not think how the devil he had allowed himself to be caught in such a damnable coil!

Having come upon the scene in the inn that left little doubt as to the young beauty's dilemma, he had hardly intended to put himself forward as her protector. Far from it. He had only two hours earlier been struck by a sniper's bullet. The *last* thing he had contemplated was saddling himself with a maiden in distress, especially one of obvious gentility, not to mention innocence.

With a feeling of having lost command of his senses, he had found himself declaring the female was his wife!

No doubt he could attribute his irrational act to the circumstance that he had lost a deal of blood and was feeling more than a trifle light-headed at the time, he told himself wryly, and not to the fact that he had not, since his folly in stealing a kiss from her upon the occasion of his illicit entry into Sir Henry Granville's manor, been able to eradicate her from his mind.

Upon entering the inn, he had not only recognized her immediately, but had done so with an instantaneous, unwonted leap of his senses that took him wholly by surprise. That she had subsequently ministered to his needs with a quiet, composed determination one would hardly have expected in a gently bred female had done more than place him under her obligation. It had served to impress on him the fact that she was as sweet, caring, and generous as she was breathtakingly beautiful.

She was also most damnably desirable, not to mention elusive of understanding, he acknowledged wryly to himself. Little wonder her grandfather wanted her wed and off his hands. Dane strongly suspected that beneath her dreamy façade of otherworldliness, there lurked a stubborn will and an unassailable streak of independence that promised fair to wreak havoc on his own peace of mind. Nevertheless, his impulsive act in interceding on her behalf had sealed both their fates.

Not marry? he thought with a dawning sense of his own foolheadedness. There was never any choice but that she should marry him. That much should have been made unavoidably clear the instant he opened his eyes to find her in his bed. How much more painfully obvious was it now that he knew her to be penniless and an orphan! He might be Captain Trevor Dane, a man who had been cast ashore, his reputation in doubt and his career at an end, but he was not the sort to ruin an innocent female and then abandon her to an existence of penury and shame.

And yet how could he forget that he had failed just such another girl who had risked everything for his sake? She, too, had been a woman of breeding, used to a finer kind of existence than he had been able to provide for her, and she might very well have paid the ultimate price of her life for his failure to protect her.

Hell and the devil confound it! How could he risk bringing the beautiful Violet to a similar fate?

The answer was that he could not. He was a bloody fool to think he might keep her safe. He could not even be sure from one moment to the next if he were about to be targeted by a sharpshooter's bullet, just as he had been on the decks of the French ship *Colette* and then again only yesterday on the road a few miles outside of Exeter. Violet might this very moment be in deadly peril, and all because of him.

"Captain? Captain Dane."

Violet's low murmur brought Dane to the awareness that he had been staring at her for some little time while he wrestled with his conscience. Silently, he cursed as he felt himself drawn into the liquid blue-violet depths of her eyes. The bloody truth was that, no matter what might come of it, he wanted her—wanted her with a hard, burning need that had nothing to do with honor or duty.

Her sweetness and innocence, so far removed from everything he had known since he had left his boyhood behind at the age of twelve, aroused in him longings he had thought long since dead and forgotten. The fresh woman's scent of her, mingled with lavender and rosemary, awakened memories of his extreme youth spent growing up in the cottage on the outskirts of Combe Martin with his two older sisters and the gentle woman with warm, laughing eyes who had been his mother.

How long had it been since he had last heard from his older sister Anne? And from Kate, the sister who had been betrothed to a young cleric? Seventeen years—or longer? Anne had married the son of a local squire upon the death of Meredith Dane less than a year following the loss of Captain Morgan Dane at sea, and Kate must surely be wed to her curate and have a family of her own by now.

He, on the other hand, had gone to sea without a backward glance, glad to escape his hateful existence at Blackthorn Manor and the uncle who had never overlooked an opportunity to punish and humiliate him. Dane had never understood why Blackthorn had so obviously despised the only son of his younger brother.

But then, long before the earl had taken him in to live with him, Dane had known, vaguely, in the way a child knows, that there had been some dark thing between his uncle and his father, some secret that, in the earl, had festered over time. It was something that Dane's parents never discussed, but it had been there, nonetheless, waiting until his father's son, placed at the mercy of the earl, should be made to feel the brunt of it.

Angry and rebellious, he had severed every tie to the land without a single regret—until a slip of a girl with dreamy eyes and a sweetness that brought back forgotten memories of a happier, more innocent time had dropped unannounced into his life. The devil! She was a magical creature who wielded an uncanny power over him, a power he had not the desire to resist. And yet if he were to be left with a shred of decency, he *must!*

The gentle touch of Violet's palm to the side of his face jarred Dane out of his dark reverie. "My dearest captain," she murmured, unable any longer to watch the bleak play of emotions across his hard countenance. "Pray do not take it so to heart. Whatever forces have brought us to this point in time and wherever they might in future lead us, you need not torment yourself. We have been given this moment. It is that simple. I have every faith all will be precisely as it was meant to be."

Dane stared at her, his mind reeling against the impossible naivete of her logic. Egad! He had never heard anything quite so absurd. A man forged his own destiny by the choices he made. His life, in consequence, was the sum of his decisions—good or bad.

And yet for no little time he had been aware that, deep inside him, there was a hollow place, an emptiness that war and his adherence to duty had held in abeyance and that he had surrounded with impregnable barriers. Not even Lynette had known how to breach the walls he had built up over the years of solitude and single-minded dedication to his naval career. Lynette had believed he was driven by a lust for glory, and he had never tried to make her see it for what it truly was.

But with Violet, he sensed it was different. He had the unnerving suspicion this slender woman with her air of otherworldliness could see straight through to his very soul. More than that, he had the strangest sense when he was with Violet that he need never feel alone again.

Hellfire! Whatever or whoever she was, she was here and she was willing, and he was filled with an aching weariness that might be assuaged for a few blessed hours in the arms of a woman—*this* woman, who from their first encounter had cast her spell over him. Perhaps she was even right that the future was beyond requiring his concern. Certain it was that in the eyes of the world it would make little difference whether he bedded her this day or not. It was enough that she had spent the night in this room and in this inn with him.

Then so be it, he thought, and lowered his head to press his lips to her brow, her eye, her cheek. Then, suddenly struck by a chord of memory, he paused, his lips poised over hers.

"Tell me one thing," he said, gazing quizzically down into her beautiful eyes, like blue gems casting mysterious lights. "That other time—what was it that you had thought never to know?"

He watched, fascinated, the smile of memory, her face growing still as she returned his look, searchingly.

"You kissed me," she said simply. "That was something none of my numerous suitors had ever done. Believe me, being a divine inspiration leaves a great deal to be desired. In all truth, I had begun to think I should never know what it was to be treated like a real, live woman of flesh and blood.'' Her eyes darkened with some new thought. "Captain, I—"

"Hush," he whispered, marveling that any man could be so blind as not to see Violet for what she was—a vibrant, vital creature with the face and form to incite a man to successive acts of utter madness. Uttering a groan of submission, he covered her mouth with his.

Violet, to whom it had come somewhat belatedly to think perhaps it was a trifle unfair not to give Dane *some* inkling as to the possible minor complications she envisioned before them if they continued on their present course, had parted her lips to insist she be allowed to finish what she had been about to say. After all, in spite of the indisputable logic that her reputation, for all practical purposes, could not be more ruined than it already was, it occurred to her that he had ought to know that there were pertinent others who might not view it in such a light.

She was summarily silenced by Dane's kiss, accompanied as it was by the wholly unexpected thrust of his tongue between her teeth, a circumstance that had the startling effect of sending a shock wave pulsating through the entire length of her body. Really, it would seem too much to expect she should have the presence of mind to do anything but return his kiss—fervently, with the same melting passion that was coursing just then through her veins.

Certainly, she did so unreservedly, a circumstance that could hardly go unremarked by Dane. Good God, she was all sweet passion and innocence, was the dreamy-eyed enchantress. Worse, she aroused him as no other woman ever had before her. Not even Lynette's practiced lovemaking, he thought with a merciless stab of guilt, had served to make him forget who and what he was. But then, he had never wanted anyone the way he wanted Violet, had wanted her from the very first moment he looked into her cursed lovely eyes.

"Violet," he uttered huskily, releasing her to press his lips into the curve of her neck. "Beautiful Violet. I never meant for this to happen. This is madness."

"Pray do not be absurd, Captain," said Violet, who, sustaining a shudder of pleasure occasioned by his having found the most exquisitely tender spot just below her right earlobe, was having a deal of difficulty focusing her thoughts. "No one *meant* for this to happen. However, now that it has, you must see it is only the natural culmination of events leading up to this moment. I wish you will not concern yourself."

Not concern himself? Dane uttered something between a laugh and a groan. Good God, she could not be so green as not to realize it was the possible natural culmination of events leading *from* this moment that should bloody well concern them. He was keenly aware, if she was not, what came from pursuing courses of this sort to their unmitigated conclusions.

Offspring resulted from it. The prospect of fathering a child under these or any circumstances was hardly one he found devoutly to be desired. Not at this particular point in time, with unknown assailants stalking him with the intent of cutting his stick for him and a cloud of uncertainty hovering over his horizon.

On the other hand, he owed his sweet Violet for having come to his rescue, not once, but twice, without thought for her own safety or well-being. Moreover, she had done so without asking for anything in return. Egad, she had been *grateful* to him for taking advantage of her!

Very well, he thought grimly. If nothing else, he would show her precisely what it was to be a real flesh-and-blood woman in the arms of a man who, far from being one of her admirers of moral rectitude, wanted nothing more than to savor every delectable inch of her.

Savagely, he flung the counterpane aside.

Violet had never, before Dane, known what it was to be so much as kissed by a man. Certainly she had never before known what it was to have a man untie the bows at the front of her bed gown deliberately, one after the other, and then, holding her spellbound with the black glitter of his eyes, bare the white swell of her breasts to his smoldering gaze.

She could hardly have been prepared for the tumult of sensations aroused by suddenly finding a strong, masculine hand mold itself to one of her breasts. How much less could she have anticipated the dizzying swell of emotions occasioned by having him lower his head to circle an already peaking nipple with the tip of his tongue?

No doubt it was perfectly understandable that other, more immediate concerns should take precedence for the moment over such a trifle as the probable reaction of a certain powerful duke, not to mention a marquis noted for his propensity for dueling, to events going forth in the bed. Violet was more than a little distracted by the sudden awareness that Dane was steadily working the hem of her night dress up over her legs.

Nor was that all or the least to occupy her. Dane, having reached the vicinity of hitherto forbidden places, paused to slip his hand between her thighs. A low gasp fairly burst from her lips, as, delving into the moist warmth of her secretmost regions, he unerringly found the tiny bud nestled between the swollen petals of her body.

"*Cap*tain!" keened Violet, moved suddenly to writhe beneath him with a strange, mounting sense of urgency. "Captain, before you—before *I*—be-before—! *Faith*, Captain, I really had ought to tell you—"

"You need say nothing, sweet Violet," rumbled Dane, marveling that he should find her already flowing with the heady nectar of arousal. Egad, she responded to his lovemaking with a readiness he had hardly expected of his dreamy-eyed enchantress. More than that, she was an angel of seduction who threatened to push him beyond the edge of his self-control!

"This is only the first in a sequence of events," he uttered thickly, trailing kisses down the slender column of her neck to the throb of her pulse at the base of her throat, "whose natural culmination"—he lowered his head further yet to mold his lips to a delightfully taut nipple—"promises to be"—running his hand downward over her firm, flat belly, he found once more the moist cradle of her desire—"all you might have wished for. You are about to discover what it is to be a flesh-and-blood woman," he said, and slipped a finger inside her.

Violet, who had never before known the power of her own body to transport her to rapturous heights, frantically sank her fingernails into Dane's shoulders and arched herself against him.

Faith, nothing she had ever imagined before in her most fanciful daydreams, indeed, nothing she had ever read before, not even the most lurid of her Gothic romance novels, had prepared her for what it was to be a real flesh-and-blood woman in the arms of a strong, virile man—and most particularly this man.

He, from the very first, had breached her defenses as no other man ever had—indeed, ever could. Perhaps it was only that she had sensed from her first glimpse into his eyes that they were kindred spirits, both of them solitary creatures to whom loneliness had become a way of life.

With Dane she had known almost at once she could dispense with the mask of the demure, self-effacing Violet. With him, she could gloriously be herself.

More than that, she had seen behind the hard glitter of his eyes to a soul in bitter torment, and, being Violet, she had suddenly wanted nothing more than to woo him out of the dark place in which he seemed to have found himself. At the very least, she had wished she might bring him to smile, something she had instinctively known did not come easily to him. How much more had she been given to see as she lay a captive witness to the battle going on inside him!

For the first time in her life, Violet, far from feeling the urge to retreat to someplace of peace and solitude, wanted nothing more than to remain precisely where she was. Dane needed her, whether he realized it or not. He needed someone to draw him out of himself. And if he did not love her, at least she would have the satisfaction of knowing what it was to be in the arms of a man she was quite certain *she* would have come to love had she been given the chance.

Indeed, she had the most peculiar feeling, based, no doubt, on her extensive past experience with a plethora of adoring suitors, that she would never find another to whom she would willingly give herself. In which case, it would obviously be better to have loved once than never to have loved at all, she told herself, as, breathing a low, tumultuous sigh, she clung to Dane, her entire being focused on the glorious torment of his manipulations.

Her resolve to apprise him of her formidable kinsmen and the certainty of their displeasure receded in a swirling heat of sensations building toward some magnificent culmination just beyond her comprehension. Fleetingly, it came to her that, whatever Albermarle and Vere might think of her recent, unprecedented show of rebelliousness, at last she had found something that was worth risking the forfeiture of her safe, tranquil harbor at Albermarle Castle. *Dane and all he made her feel were worth it!*

That was Violet's last coherent thought as she was swept up in a rising swell of unbearable torment. With all of her strength, she strove for the thing that eluded her.

Dane, feeling her reach for it, pressed the palm of his hand against her swollen bud.

Faith, it was too much for her! She erupted in a rapturous explosion of release the likes of which she had never imagined in her wildest fantasies.

At last, feeling trembly and weak and yet marvelously sated in the aftermath of her first experience in the power of her woman's body to transport her to glorious heights, she went wondrously limp in the bed even as Dane collapsed facedown on the pillow beside her. It came to her on a wave of tenderness that her gallant captain had awakened her to a whole new world fraught with endless possibilities for discovery of just the sort to appeal to her as yet untapped spirit for adventure. And yet, in spite of the magnitude of what she could only describe as a moment of sublime inspiration, she could not but be aware that all was not quite as it should be.

Dane had taken her to the rapturous heights, but *he* had remained conspicuously behind!

"Really, it is too bad of you, Captain," she said, turning her head to look at Dane.

He, far from displaying the delicious languor that made Violet feel as if her bones had been turned to pudding, was lying in prone rigidity.

"Though perhaps I should not blame you," she added, wishing to be fair in her judgment. "I fear I have become far too used to being the object of male adulation. No doubt I ought to be relieved to have met one man who, far from thinking to make me his divine inspiration, does not even like me very much. And who can blame you? I fear I have been a sad trial to you, Captain. I daresay it will prove good for my soul, if not for my vanity, that you are apparently impervious to my much vaunted beauty."

Dane, who was in the painful throes of self-abnegation, uttered something between a laugh and a groan. *Impervious to her beauty?* Egad, she was like to drive him mad with wanting her. She would never know how close he had come to casting away his last shreds of honor.

He doubted there was a man alive who could have

been in Violet's sphere of influence for any length of time without coming to entertain aspirations of bedding her! She was the sort of woman every man dreamed of possessing but never really believed the opportunity would present itself. No doubt it was the height of irony that it had presented itself to him now, when he was at the bottom of his fortunes and faced with seemingly insurmountable odds against his own survival.

"Captain," Violet persisted, her initial pique at Dane's failure to respond giving way to the sudden birth of concern at the realization every muscle in his magnificent body appeared tensed and that he was covered in sweat.

Faith, how *could* she have been thinking only of herself? She should have known it was far too soon for Dane to be exerting himself. Very likely he had thrown himself into a relapse and all because of her.

"Dane," she said, tentatively touching a hand to his shoulder, "pray *say* something. I shall never forgive myself if I have led you to further harm."

Dane, occupied with willing his respiration and heart rate, not to mention the turgid state of a most particular part of his anatomy, to return to a semblance of normalcy, mutely shook his head. The response did little to assuage Violet's mounting sense of alarm.

"Dear, this is all *my* fault," she uttered in no little distraction. "I never should have allowed you to exert yourself on my behalf. The devil, Captain, look at me. I should not like to summon Mr. Tankersley to help me with you, but I shall if I must. I will not allow you to perish because of me."

In spite of the absurdity of her fears, based on innocence, Dane could not but feel a measure of perverse satisfaction in having at last pierced the dreamy-eyed enchantress's demmed unruffability. "Softly, my girl. I may be in irons at the moment, but I'm a far cry from slipping my anchor."

Stifling a groan, he heaved himself over on his back.

He had dishonored and ruined his sweet Violet, but at least he would not leave her unprotected and with child. Whatever the natural culmination of this day's events, he would not have that ignominy on his conscience to add to all the rest.

Somehow, in his present extremity, that thought was cold consolation.

To Violet, who was given to view for the very first time in her life a man in a full state of arousal, the moment was one of supreme illumination. "Faith, Captain," she breathed, "I believe I begin to understand. Indeed," she added, her eyes, wide with wonder, lifting to his, "I believe a great many things have been made suddenly clear." Carefully, she drew the counterpane up to cover his nakedness. "It would appear your gallantry knows no end, which really is the shabbiest thing."

Returning her nightdress to a semblance of decency, Violet removed herself from the bed with as much dignity as she could summon in her tousled state. "I am sorry, Captain, to have been such a sad trial to you," she said, gathering up her clothing, including her gown, which Mrs. Tankersley had been so kind as to clean and press for her the night before. "Though I did try and tell you, you needn't have worried."

Her clothing clasped to her breast, at last she looked at him. "I'm afraid your noble gesture has changed nothing. No doubt I should be sorry for that, too, but in all truth I cannot bring myself to regret what simply could not be helped. It would, after all, be—"

"An exercise in futility," Dane finished for her with only the barest hint of irony. "You have already told me." He paused, a frown darkening his eyes. He had the strangest feeling his life had taken a sudden, sharp turn from which there would be no coming back again and that, furthermore, this slender girl with eyes like moonlit gems knew it.

The devil. It was time she was made to understand there could be no place for her in the future he envisioned before him. Tomorrow or the next day, when he had strength enough, he would depart alone from the inn and never look back again. It was the only way he knew to keep her safe.

"Violet," he began, searching for the words to make her see it as it must be, "I—"

He was interrupted by a furious assault on the sitting room door that sent him reaching for his pistol on the table.

"Yes? Who is there?" called Violet, her gaze quizzical on Dane.

"Open up, I command you, in the name of His Britannic Majesty!"

It was hardly the answer she had expected.

Chapter 5

Dane uttered a curse and started from the bed, the pistol clasped in his hand.

"A moment, please," Violet called out to the soldiers in the hall as she reached to press Dane back against the pillows. "I am not presentable."

"Stand away, girl," growled the captain. Roughly, he thrust Violet's hands aside. "If you wish to help, fetch me my clothes."

"I shall do no such thing, Captain," retorted Violet, refusing to yield before the fierce leap of his eyes. "Pray stop this foolishness instantly."

"*You, in there,*" issued from the hallway. "*Open up at once by order of the king.*"

"Yes, yes. I am coming," Violet flung sharply over her shoulder before turning once more to Dane. "You will ruin everything, Captain," she whispered. "Stay where you are and trust me to see to these gentlemen."

Then, without waiting for an answer, she left him and, crossing quickly to the bedchamber door, called out before closing it, "Perhaps you would be so good as to come in and wait in the sitting room, gentlemen. I shall join you as soon as I am dressed."

The protest that rose to Dane's lips was summarily quelled by the sight of Violet, hurriedly shrugging out of the sleeves of her nightdress to allow the gown to slide down her slender form into a pile about her bare feet. Good God, he groaned silently to himself upon being presented with the unimpeded view of the paragon of beauty in all of her magnificent womanly perfection. If the king's men did not cut his stick for him, his unsatiated desire for his gloriously unpredictable enchantress was like to do it for them.

Violet, in the process of pulling on her stockings, first one and then the other, followed swiftly by her drawers and her shoes, was unaware of the devastating effect she was having on the captain.

Really, she wished Dane could bring himself to trust her. If the king's men were in pursuit of her gallant captain, then he was in a perilous toil, indeed. Obviously, his enemies were not only implacable, but in a position of no little power.

She, on the other hand, in spite of the lamentable fact that she was an orphan without a fortune of her own, was not without influence. It was time Dane's enemies discovered he had an ally capable of bringing considerable force to bear on his behalf.

Of course it would mean Dane would have to marry her, she reflected, pulling her chemise over her head and slipping her arms through the armholes. That, however, was surely a rather inconsequential stumbling stone when set against the benefits to be gained from it. She, after all, required a husband to make her grandfather happy, and Dane was in need of the mantle of protection that she could provide him.

It would seem to be a perfect solution to both their problems. Violet smiled, reaching for her gown. A pity there was not time enough to bring Dane to see it in a similar light before the final die was cast. But then, she did not doubt matters would proceed according to their natural course.

The only thing with which she need concern herself at present was the matter of the king's men waiting on the other side of the closed door and the story she was already formulating. Then Violet, having slipped into her dress, was hastily running a comb through the luxurious mass of curls that were the envy of many of her feminine contemporaries—those who had to resort to curling papers or hours spent with a curling iron to achieve a similar effect.

Dane, watching her, could not but be painfully sensible of his vulnerable state, unclothed and far from in his customary strength, not to mention in an agony of unrequited desire. He chafed at the necessity of entrusting his fate to a courageous slip of a girl who had already done more for him than he had any right to ask. Nor did it help to know she offered the only practicable means of avoiding the sort of confrontation that must inevitably lead to disaster.

He would not allow himself to be taken, not before he had finished what he had started, and he would not fire on king's men, not even to save his own skin. He had not so far sold his soul to the devil as to take the life of a British soldier in the pursuit of his duty. Egad, had he sunk so low on the other hand that he could allow a woman to fight his battles for him? And at what risk to herself?

"There," said Violet, taking a last rueful glance at her reflection in the looking glass. "I suppose that will just have to do. I cannot think our brave soldiers will wish to wait for anything more elaborate." She turned from the glass with a swirl of silk skirts to favor Dane with a conspiratorial grin. "Remain in bed, I pray you, Captain. And I suggest you put this on," she added, flinging him his nightshirt, which had been laid out at the foot of the bed. "I daresay this will not take too long."

"Violet—" Abruptly Dane stopped, hardly knowing what he wished to say to the vision of beauty preparing to issue forth in his defense. Indeed, the sparkle in her eyes was enough to rob him of the power of speech. It came to him with a horrifying flash of insight that his irrepressible Violet was *enjoying* the prospect before her! "The devil," he growled, prey to the thought she had not the smallest notion of the risk she was incurring, "this is not some bloody parlor game. It is entirely possible those men are here to place me under arrest."

"No, truly?" queried Violet, a decided gleam of interest in the look she bent upon him. "No doubt you will tell me why—after I have sent them on their way."

Turning to the door, she paused only long enough to don the mask of serene composure with which she customarily faced the world. Then, reaching for the door handle, she left Dane to stare after her in a thunderous silence.

She was met with the sight of three seasoned soldiers armed with muskets, their crimson regimentals bearing distinct signs of travel, and a fair-haired young lieutenant who fairly snapped to attention at Violet's entrance.

"Pray be at ease, gentlemen," said Violet, smiling as, softly closing the door behind her, she came to stand before the lieutenant, who was regarding her with the fixed stare of a man who had been suddenly struck with a divine inspiration. "I beg your pardon for keeping you waiting, Lieutenant. I had not anticipated morning callers. I fear I have yet even to break my fast. Indeed, I was on the point of ordering a tray sent up. Perhaps you and your men would care to join me?" She paused, gazing doubtfully at the young man's stricken countenance before gently adding, "Lieutenant?"

"*Ahem!*" declared the officer, clearing his throat.

"Indeed, sir," observed Violet with a gravity belied by the twinkle in her eyes.

With an effort, the lieutenant appeared to recall himself to the unpleasant duty before him. "It is kind of you to ask, ma'am," he replied, no doubt acutely aware of his men, who were standing at rigid attention and staring exceedingly stone-faced at a point somewhere beyond their superior's shoulders, "but regretfully we must refuse. I am afraid our visit is of an official nature."

"But of course it is, Lieutenant," said Violet with only the barest hint of amusement. "You made that quite clear, did you not? Still, I fail to see why we cannot converse in comfort. At least allow me to offer your men a pint at my expense. They appear to have traveled a great distance and would no doubt do better with some refreshment."

Reaching for her reticule on the sideboard where she had left it the night before, she gazed appealingly at the young officer. "Come now, Lieutenant, where is the harm? I fear the brave men who risk their lives to keep our country safe are too often in the pursuit of duty denied the simplest of pleasures. Will you not allow me to make it up to them in some small measure?"

It was, in spite of her peculiar circumstances, the simple truth, spoken from her heart. Dane, listening from the other side of the door, smiled grimly as he shrugged gingerly into the nightshirt. There were officers who might have resisted the beautiful Violet's sweet appeal. Clearly, the lieutenant was not among them.

"Well, since you put it that way, ma'am," came gruffly from the officer, "I suppose there is little harm in it. Corporal Blanchett, you and the men will retire to the common room, where you will limit yourselves to victuals and one pint per man. Keep your eyes and ears open for anyone who appears suspicious. I shall join you there as soon as I have concluded my business here."

"Yes, *sir*," replied the corporal, clicking his heels smartly together. "And thank you, ma'am. It's been a long ride, and that's no lie. The lads could do with a wet."

"And so, I fancy, could you, Corporal," observed Violet, placing the coins in the man's callused palm. "Enjoy your wet, Corporal. I am certain you deserve it."

"I'll do me best, ma'am," promised the corporal, a

twinkle of understanding in the look he bent upon her. 'Twas clear his young lieutenant was in way over his head. On the other hand, it was equally plain to John Blanchett that whatever the game the lady was playing, she meant no harm to the lad—unlike them what had sent the lieutenant on what looked to be a bootless errand. Whoever the blighter was that had give them the slip, he wasn't no lily-livered sniper what had been shot trying to ambush an admiral. John Blanchett would eat his hat if he was.

The fellow they were chasing had been shot at, right enough, but he was the one what had been ambushed. There wasn't no mistaking the bloody signs. Anywise, they wouldn't have sent a green lieutenant after a Frog spy, not if he was the real thing. It was all a bloody lot of nonsense, and John Blanchett needed a wet to wash the sour taste out'n his mouth.

"You heard the lieutenant," he barked at the soldiers. "We've our orders. Smartly, now. A-b-ou-t *face. March!*"

"And now," Violet said when the men had departed in quickstep, no doubt to take full advantage of their unlooked-for furlough, "how may I be of service to you, Lieutenant—Lieutenant . . . ?"

Without waiting for an answer, Violet sank gracefully onto one of the wing chairs, then gestured for the lieutenant to sit across from her.

"Freeman, ma'am," replied the officer, awkwardly attempting to settle in the chair, but hampered greatly by his sword, which ended thrust rigidly straight out before him like some unwieldy appendage. "Lieutenant Nathan Freeman of the Coldstream Guards."

"But of course you are," agreed Violet, dazzling him with her smile. "I am pleased to make your acquaintance."

The lieutenant shifted uncomfortably. "I'm afraid you may change your mind, ma'am," he said, clearly in a quandary as to how he came to be conversing with an Incomparable whose beauty was apparently surpassed only by her kind disposition. Obviously, he had expected something quite different.

"No, why should I?" queried Violet, gently quizzing.

"Because, ma'am," he answered manfully, "I am, as it happens, under orders to track down and apprehend a dangerous French agent known only to us by the alias of *Le Corbeau.*"

"And so you have come to me?" demanded Violet, her lovely eyes wide with astonishment. "Surely you do not believe *I* am this mysterious *Le Corbeau*? I have seldom been beyond the borders of Devon, I assure you. You may ask my grandfather, the Duke of Albermarle, or my brother, the Marquis of Vere, or perhaps my brother-in-law, the Earl of Shields. They will be sure to tell you I haven't the smallest interest in politics."

Dane, who had been listening to the exchange going forth in the next room with a wry appreciation of the lieutenant's exquisite dilemma, at those revelations fell heavily back against the pillows.

Good God, he thought, any amusement he had been feeling at the expense of the lieutenant gone suddenly and quite utterly into eclipse. The dreamy-eyed enchantress had done a deal more than bedazzle a callow youth in an officer's uniform. She had utterly pulled the wool over the eyes of Captain Trevor Dane, who bloody well should have known better—with the result that he had not only compromised an innocent, but one who could claim kinship to a house second only to royalty.

Egad, if he managed to escape arrest for treason by the Crown and to succeed in avoiding having his stick cut for him by his enemies, he might very well be looking forward to the pleasure of facing a marquis at twenty paces!

With a sense of unreality, Dane heard the young lieutenant stammering an answer.

"No, m-milady, of—of course you have not. I never thought, I mean it never entered my head that—that you . . ." Abruptly the lieutenant stopped and straightened his shoulders. "*Le Corbeau* is a man, milady," he blurted. "A—a black-hearted villain who would stop at nothing to achieve his nefarious ends. Only a fortnight ago, he broke into the home of Sir Henry Granville for the purpose of stealing government papers. One could never mistake you for such a one."

"You cannot know how relieved I am to hear it, Lieutenant Freeman," said Violet, taking pity on the officer, who, having leaped to his feet, presented every manifestation of one who wished the floor might open instantly up and swallow him. "But if I am not under suspicion, then what has brought you here to me in your quest for the Frenchman?"

"Not a Frenchman, milady," emended the lieutenant, suddenly seeming to find himself. "*Le Corbeau* is believed to be an English subject and therefore a traitor to king and country."

"How perfectly dreadful," breathed Violet, a hand going to her throat. "And you must think he is somewhere in the vicinity, else you would not be here interrogating me."

"I beg your pardon, milady." Red-faced, the lieutenant extended a hand in contrition. "I never meant it to seem as if I were submitting you to a Spanish Inquisition. The truth is it was never you I thought to find here."

"Not I?" Violet queried, displaying a pretty bewilderment. "But then who, Lieutenant Freeman? Indeed, why are you here at all?"

"I am here, milady, because the man we seek was reportedly in Exeter no later than yesterday morning when an attempt was made on the life of Vice Admiral Sir Oliver Landford. Thankfully, Sir Oliver's aide was on hand to thwart the attempt. It is reasonably certain he wounded the assailant, who escaped capture and managed subsequently to elude his pursuers."

"He sounds a remarkably clever villain," observed Violet, who, despite having gone from hot to cold during the course of the officer's narrative, refused to believe for one moment the man she had succored and saved was a would-be assassin. On the contrary, she did not doubt that, had Dane wished the vice admiral dead, Sir Oliver would no longer have been among the living. "You really must not blame yourself for losing him, Lieutenant. Very likely he has gone to earth to lick his wounds and will not be heard from again for some little time."

"I believe you are quite in the right of it, milady," replied the lieutenant, appearing more than a little troubled. "As it happens, we traced his movements to within a league of Yeovil before he managed to give us the slip. We have since been making inquiries about the town."

"Oh, I *see*," said Violet, her lovely features expressive of sudden enlightenment. "You were told the gentleman who took these rooms for the night was gravely indisposed!" Violet came eloquently to her feet to favor the lieutenant with the full force of her eyes. "You think I am harboring your spy! Faith, I believe I should be greatly offended, Lieutenant, if it were not all so patently absurd."

"If I am mistaken, milady, I shall naturally offer my sincerest apology," replied the lieutenant, straightening to attention. "However, duty requires that I examine the man in the next room."

"And so you shall, Lieutenant," replied Violet with a fine disdain that might have impressed even her brother Gideon, who was well known for his ability to quash the loftiest of pretensions with naught but his chilling stare. "There is a wounded naval officer in that bedchamber, a man who has served his country with courage and honor. I daresay you may have read of his victories at sea. He is Captain Trevor Dane, most recently of the *Antiope*, which single-handedly defeated a French seventy-four in the Mediterranean."

"Captain Dane. By the saints, I have heard of him!"

exclaimed the lieutenant. "And in truth the sinking of *Colette* was bravely done, milady."

"Indeed it was, and you may be sure he has done nothing to merit anyone's censure, save perhaps to fall in love with the granddaughter of a duke and then marry her in secrecy. But then, you will see for yourself how little he is deserving of your suspicion. Come, Lieutenant Freeman," she said, crossing to the door with a cool dignity that belied the fierce beating of her heart.

With her whole being, she willed Dane to be in his bed, ready to play the part she had set for him. "I ask only that you do nothing to excite him," she added, her hand on the door handle. "He is far from fully recovered from wounds suffered in defense of king and country."

It was exceedingly doubtful that the lieutenant, entering solemnly in Violet's wake, had the least notion of the unutterable relief she felt upon beholding the captain lying convincingly in bed, the counterpane pulled up to his chest and his eyes closed in apparent sleep. Indeed, she could not but offer up a small prayer at noting the gun was nowhere in sight.

"Wait here, Lieutenant." Violet stepped carefully to the bedside. "Dearest?" she murmured, touching a hand gently to Dane's shoulder. When he failed to move so much as a muscle, she leaned over him to say softly in his ear, "Dearest, there is someone here to see you."

Violet, acutely aware that Dane must have heard every word she had said to the lieutenant, was not sure what to expect from her gallant captain. She was hardly prepared to have Dane suddenly turn his head and brush his lips to hers. "My sweet Lady Violet," he said with only the barest hint of irony, "you have come back to me."

Violet, who could not but note the darkling gleam in his eyes, only just managed to stifle a gasp. Patently, he was bent on punishing her for her failure to be wholly confiding in him, the devil! It was not as if she had not *tried* to tell him about Vere and Albermarle, after all. Her back to the lieutenant, she favored Dane with a comical moue. "But of course I have, my darling. Surely, you did not think I should not?"

"I'm afraid I was dreaming, my dearest," said Dane, looking Violet straightly in the eyes. "I was away at sea again, and you were at home in Devon surrounded by a bevy of admirers—as well you should be. The grand-daughter of a duke is clearly above my touch, I told myself. She belongs in a castle with luxury surrounding her, not in the modest house of a lowly naval captain. She should forget me and return to her grandfather directly, before it is too late."

"But it is too late, my dearest," crooned Violet, heartily wishing Lieutenant Freeman at Jericho. "I should even go so far as to suggest we burned our bridges behind us the moment I was pronounced your wife. You may be sure I have no intention of leaving you now, when we have just almost managed to have our honeymoon."

Dane, presented with an image of Violet at her sublimely sweetest, which was tellingly belied by a dancing imp in her eye, was able to suppress the urge to shake her until she begged for mercy only because of Lieutenant Freeman's uneasy presence and his own debilitating wound. The little devil! She knew perfectly well she was sinking herself further into disrepute and himself into a toil from which his only avenue of escape was to wed her. The question that baffled him was why?

The only answer that came to him at the moment was that she was an impossibly headstrong, meddlesome female with an overgenerous heart. Worse, he was damnably aware that, if circumstances had been different, he would not have found the thought of falling into his sweet Violet's snare in the least undesirable. Egad, he did not doubt there was a man alive who would not envy him such a wife!

But she was *not* his wife and never could be. Hell's

teeth, it had been better had he died at sea than to drag Violet down with him! It was time she was made to realize he was nothing like the respectable suitors she was fleeing. As soon as he had dealt with the lieutenant, he would send Lady Violet Rochelle promptly on her way. No doubt her ducal grandparent would have the wherewithal as well as the credit to wrap the unfortunate incident in clean linen. Certainly, the last thing His Grace could wish was to have his granddaughter wed to a penniless naval captain with a tarnished reputation.

"There is not a bridge that cannot be rebuilt, my dearest Violet," Dane said gravely, brushing a stray lock of hair from her cheek. "And now I suggest we have kept our visitor waiting long enough."

"Yes, I suppose we have," Violet agreed slowly. She gave Dane a long, thoughtful look before turning away. "Lieutenant Freeman, I should like you to meet . . ."

Lieutenant Freeman, however, was nowhere in sight. Indeed, the only evidence he had ever been in the room was the bedchamber door closing softly behind him.

It had occurred to Violet often in the past several hours that the mischievous fates must have dropped Captain Trevor Dane into her life for the sole purpose of teaching her a lesson in humility. Indeed, she could not but think it was ironic in the extreme that the only man she had ever met who was determined to hold her at arm's length was the one man to whom she was irresistibly attracted.

Attracted? she thought, as she strolled dreamily back along the wooded path from the sylvan lake. It was far more than that. She very much feared that she had fallen head over ears in love with Dane!

There, she had admitted it. But then, she did not doubt she had lost her heart to Dane from the first moment he had snatched her into his arms and kissed her.

Of course, it was not *just* because he had kissed her, she told herself, trailing her fingers through the leaves of a clematis vine. She could not be such a gaby as that. And it was not because he was devilishly handsome or exuded a delectable aura of mystery and danger, though she could not deny those particular attributes did him no harm in her eyes. Neither did the fact that he so far topped her own generous inches that she might easily have worn shoes with high French heels in his company and still been made to feel uncommonly small and feminine next to his splendid height.

Certainly she could not dismiss the influence on her of his magnificently broad shoulders, which seemed expressly designed to show off to advantage the snug-fitting blue coat bearing the twin gold epaulets of a post captain. She did not doubt all of these attributes had had a telling effect on her emotions and that they further had played a part in her willing fall from grace.

But she had known tall, strong, handsome men before, and never once had she felt the smallest urge to abandon her every instinct for self-preservation and embrace ruin and disgrace, not to mention all the unavoidable disruptions to her previously tranquil existence, for one of them. Certainly she never could have conceived of doing so for the sake of a man she had met only once before and under exceedingly questionable circumstances. Really, it would seem to defy understanding.

No one, least of all herself, could possibly fancy her doing anything remotely similar for Jeremy Biddle or Lord Cranston or any of the other suitors who had for all intents and purposes driven her from her quiet refuge straight into the arms of a stranger. But then, she had never before met a man like Captain Trevor Dane, who exuded the same sort of quiet strength tempered with compassion that so poignantly reminded her of her dearest papa.

Added to that were a sense of strong purpose coupled

with a firm resolve, which markedly separated Dane from the fribbles and polished town beaus of her acquaintance. Then, too, there was a reckless, unruly streak beneath the well-honed disciplined will, which she could not but find dangerously attractive. Faith, it was little wonder that he had razed her defenses with but a single kiss and then gone on to capture her unprotected heart!

She had never stood a chance against her gallant captain, never mind that he tried to hide his sensitive nature from the rest of the world with a sternness through which she had seen at once. If nothing else, his tormented dreams had revealed that beneath the hard exterior was a man who cared, perhaps too much. He was, after all, a warrior and a commander of men. Carried on the lust for battle, he would fight with a ferocity of purpose that would leave little time for contemplation of the horrors around him, thought Violet, who had been sickened with dismay upon overhearing her Uncle Richard once describe an embattled ship's scuppers running crimson with blood. And when the battle was over and the bill in life and limb taken, what then? A warrior, a captain of men, must somehow bury the dead and look to making his ship ready to fight again.

The navy was a stern taskmaster. She did not doubt Dane had learned to bury his emotions along with his dead. Nor would he hesitate to do what he considered his duty—in this case, to save her from himself.

Really, it was too bad of him, she reflected with a wry quirk of her lips. Since he had awakened to find her in his bed, he had done all in his power to be rid of her, even going so far in the wake of Lieutenant Freeman's departure as to attempt to dress himself with the intention of summoning his mount and riding away without her.

It was cold comfort to her that he had yet been too weak to do more than struggle into his breeches before

he collapsed once more on the edge of the bed or
that he had lacked the strength to resist when she had
pressed him down against the pillows and covered him
with the counterpane. He had made it abundantly clear
he would leave her just as soon as ever he was able. And
all because his pride would not allow him to marry a
duke's granddaughter to her detriment and his advantage!

Good heavens, as if advantageous matches were not
the motivating principle for marriage among those of
her kind! she thought with a wry appreciation of the
irony of her position. Not one of her determined suitors
had entertained any qualms about marrying above his
station. She did not doubt her noble lineage was what
made her loom in their eyes as a prize so devoutly to
be desired. But then, Dane had been in the right of it
on two cogent points. She quite possibly would not have
liked him had he not been intriguingly different from
all of her previous suitors, and she very likely would not
have formed a fascination for him had he not loomed
as irresistibly unattainable.

It was too bad of him to fling her own feminine frail-
ties in her face. On the other hand, he had failed utterly
to take into account that love was wholly unpredictable,
not to mention beyond the bounds of reason. The truth
of the matter was he was precisely what she had always
looked for in a husband, which naturally meant he was
different from all her previous admirers, else she would
have married one of *them.*

Furthermore, it would seem fatuously pointless to
argue what might have been, when it was clear their
situation was unavoidably meant to be. Not that she
could ever convince him of that, she reflected with a
rueful grimace. He was a ship's captain. It was unlikely
he relied on intuitive reason to conduct his affairs.

Dane would do what he thought was best for her,
which must naturally presume he considered her incapable of determining that much for herself, the devil!

That realization had led her that morning to facilitate the natural course of events, something she was by nature exceedingly reluctant to do at anytime. In truth, he had left her little other choice. She, after all, was convinced the best thing for them both was for Dane to make her his wife.

Faith, who would ever have thought that she, Violet Rochelle, who had always been the sort to flee at the smallest threat to her independence, would take it upon herself to get leg shackled to a man who made it plain he did not even like her very much?

With her characteristic practicality, she made herself consider the possibility he might never come to feel the least fondness for her. She could not dismiss out of hand, after all, the mysterious Lynette, who had met an early, lamented end. Violet suffered a hollow pang at the memory of the anguish in Dane's voice when he had cried out in the throes of delirium to his lost Lynette. She did not need to have Dane tell her Lynette had been his lover. In her woman's heart, Violet knew it. The question was, had he loved her with the all-consuming passion of a Leander for his Hero or a Romeo for his Juliet—or, for that matter, an Edmond, Duke of Albermarle, for Genevieve, his duchess?

A tender smile played about Violet's lips at the thought of her grandfather's devotion to the memory of his dearly departed wife. The old bugbear had never found another like his fiery-haired Genevieve, who had stolen the Albermarle betrothal ring and forever won his heart. Perhaps Dane, too, was the sort who could love only once.

Even if that were the case, however, Violet was keenly aware it changed nothing. *She* loved *him*, and she would let nothing deter her from her resolve to do all in her power to help protect him from his enemies, especially if Vice Admiral Sir Oliver Landford happened to be among them.

An icy chill coursed down her spine at the mere possibility that Landford was in league with Dane's enemies. Landford, after all, must ever be inseparable in her mind from his brother, the Earl of Blaidsdale, and from the pain of all that had been forever lost to her—her dearest mama and papa and the carefree innocence of extreme youth.

She was sixteen when her father's yacht had gone down, carried, it was said, in a raging storm onto the rocks and then, foundering, swept out to sea. It had never made any sense to her, not even after the sharp edge of grief had given way to an aching, hollow emptiness, leaving her with little else to do but contemplate the vagaries of fate.

Numerous images of her tall father at the helm of his beloved *Swallow* were forever etched into her mind from her earliest childhood. To her, he had always seemed invincible. More than that, the Marquis of Vere had been a sailor of no little remove, and that fateful day he had had on board his marchioness.

It was inconceivable to Violet that he could ever have been so remiss as to allow his vessel to be caught on rocky shoals, even along an unfamiliar coast. In her heart she knew somehow he had been betrayed. How much more certain had she been when she learned the *Swallow* was carrying a fortune in gold smuggled out of France!

Then, as if to give the final proof of the pudding, Lord Blaidsdale had presented a marker against Vere's estate. *Poor Gideon,* she thought, recalling the hard veneer of her brother's pride as he had sold out of the Funds to honor what he had never doubted was a fabricated debt against the meager remains of his inheritance.

The Marquis of Vere had never been an inveterate gambler, but when he had played at the tables, he had won far more often than not. More significantly, his sense of what he owed his name and his family would never have allowed him to risk the greater part of his fortune at a single game of faro, even though it was a game at which he excelled. Certainly, Gideon had never believed for one moment that Lord Blaidsdale had ever seen the day that he could beat his old rival at faro— or any other game of chance, for that matter.

Violet, having absently pulled a magnolia blossom from a low-hanging branch to inhale its sweetness, without thinking crushed the flower in her fist. No one had ever been able to prove Blaidsdale had cold-bloodedly plotted to destroy her father. There had not even been evidence to point to piracy and murder in the demise of her parents.

Still, there was not a Rochelle who did not believe the earl had engineered the tragic misfortunes that had befallen them.

There had ever been a dark rancor between the two houses. And now it would appear Captain Trevor Dane had somehow fallen under a similar shadow of menace.

Vice Admiral Sir Oliver Landford would most certainly seem a part of it, and if he were, then Dane was in perilous waters, indeed. Landford was as maliciously devious as Blaidsdale was ruthless, she thought, feeling the painful reopening of old wounds. Together, they had destroyed the Marquis of Vere, who should have been beyond their malevolent touch.

Faith, what chance had Dane alone against men like these? The answer, she very much feared, was that he had no chance at all. Together, however, Dane and the granddaughter of the Duke of Albermarle would present a formidable alliance to make even Sir Oliver think twice about making Dane the object of his rancor. A pity she could not depend on being able to persuade Dane of that. But then, Dane would surely come to it in the normal course of events.

Still, he was a proud man who would not take well to the notion that a woman had manipulated him seemingly to her own ends. She had every intention of keeping that little tidbit of knowledge from him out of the firm belief that what he did not know would not hurt him. Besides, it was not really manipulation, after all, she told herself. She had only facilitated what was bound to occur anyway, which was perfectly acceptable, since the end result was to provide Dane with the means of defending himself from his enemies.

It had come to her with startling clarity as Lieutenant Freeman quietly left them to themselves. It was all perfectly logical to her and must surely have been to Dane as well, if only he could be made to see beyond his unshakable male code of honor. Her gallant captain was adamantly resolved to separate her from him in order to keep her from harm's way, when it was patent that the only way to neutralize his enemies was to align himself with a force that was at least the equal of theirs. And certainly the Duke of Albermarle, for all of his eccentricities, was a power with which to be reckoned.

With Violet as his wife, Dane would have entrée into doors that would otherwise have been barred to him. More than that, he would find few would willingly incur the Marquis of Vere's displeasure. Indeed, Violet could not but view her brother, Gideon, as Dane's ace in the hole—if, she reflected ruefully, he did not first put a period to Dane's existence for having compromised his little sister. Vere was as dangerous as he was unpredictable.

Still, Violet did not doubt she could bring Vere to stand as Dane's ally once the captain was her husband. Vere was, for all of his cold-bloodedness, fiercely protective of his sisters, especially Violet, who had been nominally left in his keeping upon the death of their parents. Once convinced that Dane was indispensable to her happiness, Vere would be implacable in his defense of the captain, all of which made Gideon a double-edged sword in her present circumstances.

While Vere would fight to the death, if need be, to insure his sister's happiness, he would undoubtedly cut Dane's stick for him if the captain persisted in his resolve not to marry her. But then, the latter would never arise, Violet assured herself, as she dropped the crushed magnolia blossom into the bourne and watched it carried swiftly away with the current. She, after all, had taken steps to make certain it would not.

Violet might have been less sure of herself had she been aware that Dane, dressed in his breeches and a clean shirt, was even then with the help of a stable lad in the process of pulling on his boots.

He was sweating profusely by the time the task was completed. Cursing his weakness, he shoved himself to his feet and tossed a coin to the boy, who was eyeing him doubtfully from beneath a thatch of unkempt hair.

"You don't look so good, gov'nor," said the boy, shoving the coin deep in the pocket of his shabby coat. "Belike it's a mite soon for you to be out'n your bed."

"The devil it is," rasped Dane, willing the room to stop its cursed spinning. "Rather than giving advice to your elders, I suggest you tend to your own business." Immediately, he caught himself. Hellfire, he had no call to vent his anger on the boy. The child, after all, was in the right of it. He was far from recovered enough to have left his bed. On the other hand, he was cursedly aware that if Violet would not leave him, he must remove himself forthwith from her. If the king's men could find him, so, too, could others.

Drawing a deep, steadying breath, he said quietly, "What is your name, boy?"

The child, who could not have been above nine or ten, answered guardedly, "Tommy Ellers, gov'nor."

"Well, Tommy, I should not have spoken to you in such a manner. You have been a great help to me. And now I should like my horse saddled and brought around to the yard. I shall be leaving directly. Can you see to it for me?"

"No, I fear he cannot," pronounced a feminine voice from the doorway.

His teeth clenched, Dane steadied himself. "Tommy,"

he said without turning to look at Violet. He did not have to have done. He could feel her cursed lovely eyes on him. "You will do as I say."

"You will do no such thing, Tommy," Violet said quietly. "The captain is far from being fit to ride. Instead, I should be obliged if you will inform Mrs. Tankersley that the captain is ready to take his broth."

At that, Dane did turn to look at her, his demon eyes glittery in the candlelight.

Tommy, glancing from the grim-faced captain to the lady, wasted little time coming to the decision he was where he had no business to be.

"Beggin' your pardon, gov'nor, ma'am, but I think I hear old Jemmie Coggins, the head groom, callin' me name." Giving a tug at his forelock, he edged past Violet and bolted from the room.

"Do not think," said Dane in the sudden silence, "that this changes anything. You have only put off the inevitable for a short time longer."

Violet favored him with a whimsical smile. "Strangely enough, I might say the same to you, Captain. As it happens, however, I am in no mood to argue with you. I have had the most splendid walk and find I am in complete accord with the world. Can you not cease for a little while to regard me in the light of a gaoler and instead join me for tea in the sitting room?"

"The devil, Violet," pronounced the captain, torn between frustration at the weakness that kept him a prisoner to the allure of his sweet enchantress and a disgust of his own boorishness toward her. "You have a sad notion of my character do you think I regard you in the light of a gaoler. Do you think I am not aware that everything you are doing is motivated out of a desire to help me?"

Seeing him sway on his feet, Violet crossed calmly to his side.

"No," she said, slipping an arm about his waist and guiding him into the sitting room, "I feel quite certain that you have ascribed the highest possible motives to my actions. No doubt you are exceedingly grateful, too, when really that is the last thing I should wish from you."

"The last thing." Dane went suddenly still, his dark eyes probing hers. "Then, if not my gratitude, what is it, precisely, that you *do* want from me?"

"At the moment, I want you to sit down while I send for a tray to be brought up," replied Violet, striving for a lightness of tone at sharp variance with the sudden flutter of her heart. "I daresay you will do better with some nourishment inside you, and I, as it happens, am quite famished."

"The devil you are," said Dane, who was neither blind nor a fool. He knew perfectly well the maddeningly elusive Violet was deliberately evading his question. "Damn it, Violet, it is not tea and biscuits you want from me."

"No," she agreed with a rueful smile, "though I should have liked to fortify myself before having this discussion. I cannot think at all well on an empty stomach."

"But then, it is not necessary for you to think," said Dane with velvet-edged softness. "You have only to tell me what new scheme you have hatched for my benefit."

"Scheme?" queried Violet, appearing genuinely puzzled. "I am not in the habit of hatching schemes, Captain. Something has come up, however, on the order of an unavoidable circumstance resulting from a recent chain of events."

"But of course there has," conceded Dane in exceedingly dry tones. "What circumstance, I wonder, and from which chain of events?"

"The circumstance of my having compromised you, of course," declared Violet, as if stating the obvious. "Dear, you needn't glower at me, Captain. I am perfectly aware I am the one at fault. Further, I am fully prepared to put everything right."

"No doubt," returned Dane, eyeing her warily. Egad, he thought, what the devil was this? If he had learned anything about Lady Violet Rochelle in the past several hours, it was that behind her dreamy air of otherworldliness throve a maddeningly independent female who was capable of doing anything she thought was to his benefit. "And how, I cannot but wonder, do you propose to do that?"

"It is very simple," replied Violet with an impossible calm. "I propose to marry you, Captain, as soon as possible by special license."

Dane, who did not know what exactly he had expected to hear from his dreamy-eyed enchantress, was hardly prepared for that particular announcement.

"You are proposing to *marry* me—to make an honest man of me? Good God, Violet, you are not lacking in originality."

"I wish you will not be absurd," demurred Violet, who was hardly surprised at Dane's lack of credulity. It was, after all, only what she had expected from him. "It has nothing to do with making an honest man of you. I daresay you are that already. At any rate, it is not *your* reputation that has been compromised."

"No, it is *your* reputation, and still I will not marry you," Dane said harshly. "I will not make that mistake again. You will return to your grandfather, who will no doubt prevail upon one of your numerous suitors of virtue to do what I would not. You will wed and you will learn to be happy, and if you fail in that, at least you will be alive and well."

"You, however, are certain to be dead, thanks to me," Violet stated flatly.

"Now you are being foolish beyond permission. Even if I should so far fail in my endeavors as to end up in an early grave, it could hardly be laid at your door. You are not planning to shoot me while I sleep, are you?"

"Not while you sleep, Captain," observed a dry masculine voice at Dane's back. "And most assuredly not Violet. I, however, might be persuaded to oblige you."

Coming about, Dane beheld a tall, slender figure, elegantly clad in a black, double-breasted cutaway coat with mother-of-pearl buttons, dove-gray pantaloons, and black leather Hessians polished to an uncanny sheen, unfold itself from the high-backed wing chair facing the fireplace. Singularly keen blue eyes surveyed Dane from beneath drooping eyelids.

"Your Grace," declared Violet, dropping into a curtsy.

"As you see," replied Albermarle.

Chapter 6

Dane, finding himself facing the Duke of Albermarle across the expanse of a great mahogany desk situated in the library at Albermarle Castle, could not but reflect that this new twist of fate had caught him cursedly unprepared. Egad, the last thing he had been contemplating when he awakened that morning in the inn at Yeovil was that evening having a téte-à-téte at Albermarle Castle with Violet's ducal grandparent on the subject of marriage settlements, though obviously he should have been prepared all along for just such an eventuality.

He had not, since the startling discovery of Violet's identity, tried to fool himself into believing a man of Albermarle's stature would not demand satisfaction of any man who compromised his granddaughter. Nor had he thought indefinitely to evade responsibility for his actions. He had been prepared to answer for his transgressions, if and when the time came he was no longer on the run from his unknown enemies.

His one thought had been Violet's safety. Egad, he most assuredly had not anticipated that, far from separating himself from her, he should be persuaded to depart with Violet and her grandfather to the duke's ancestral pile. No doubt he could attribute his several lapses in judgment to the powerful distraction of a dreamy-eyed enchantress who had the uncanny knack for bringing him to indulge in fanciful dreams of the sort that should have had no place in the life of a sailor and most especially one with his singularly uncertain prospects. But then, all that had changed in a matter of seconds, along with the charted course of his life.

Hellfire, he was not dreaming now, he thought with a wry twist of his lips, though it bloody well felt as if he were. He was awake and caught up in a bizarre unreality.

In retrospect, he supposed there was little he could have done to avert this particular outcome. How did one, after all, convince a duke the best thing for his granddaughter was to overlook the circumstance that she had spent two days and a night in an inn in Dane's company, even to behave as if it had never happened? If he were in Albermarle's shoes, he would bloody well horsewhip to within an inch of his life any man who had used Violet in the manner he had done. Cynically, he mused that it would only be what he deserved for having been a demmed fool from start to finish.

At least, Dane told himself, he should feel a measure of relief that the duke had seen fit to exclude Violet from the present proceedings. He might not agree with the duke that the business before them must naturally be considered a private matter between gentlemen, but he could not deny he had rather face the duke alone, without the beautiful Violet to distract him.

Far from being relieved, however, he was prey to a demmed uneasy premonition. And how not, he thought grimly. Violet had accepted her grandfather's pronouncement with a pretty meekness at sharp variance with the serene intractability of the determined angel of mercy Dane had come to know. Not even one who espoused the philosophy that events determined by a never ending chain of cause and effect must proceed according to their natural course could so blithely submit to her grandfather's assumption of authority over her fate unless she were demmed certain what the outcome was going to be.

It came to him with grim conviction that Violet knew something he did not. But then, his unpredictable enchantress had thus far proven full of surprises, Dane reflected wryly. Egad, who but Violet, having freely embraced ruin for the sole purpose of tending to the needs of a wounded stranger, would subsequently arrive at the conclusion she was honor bound to marry him because she had compromised his hopes for survival?

A mirthless smile played about Dane's lips at the memorable event of Lady Violet Rochelle's proposal of marriage to the disgraced Captain Trevor Dane. Perhaps the most surprising part of all was that she had been so obviously sincere in her conviction she was become the instrument of his destruction. And in truth, she had painted a chilling enough picture of the peril she envisioned before him.

Even if he should manage to prevail over his enemies—which, alone and without help, she considered exceedingly doubtful—he would never survive the Marquis of Vere.

"I love my brother dearly, Captain," Violet had declared, her lovely eyes beseeching, "but I should be the first to admit he is a cold-blooded devil. He would most certainly cut your stick for you without batting an eyelash."

It had been cold comfort to Dane to realize she was undoubtedly in the right of it. Even if he was Vere's equal in a fight, he could hardly fire on a man who was defending his sister's honor. He had not sunk so low as that. But then, neither had he so lost all sense of his own manhood as to marry Violet for the reasons she had put forth.

Angry with himself and the impossible dilemma he had created for himself, he had responded ungraciously, heedless of the duke observing them with keen interest from the comfort of an overstuffed wing chair. "If your brother is half as formidable as you have made him out to be, then I must be glad for your sake you have a protector of his remove. You bloody well need *someone* to take you in hand, Miss Rochelle."

"Then marry me, Captain," the little minx had not hesitated to come back at him. "You may be sure Vere will thank you for relieving him of his obligations to me, and with you to instruct me, I daresay I should prove a most conformable wife."

"You, my impossible girl, would prove nothing of the sort," Dane had retorted with utter certainty. "Nor should I wish you to do. The last thing I should desire is a conformable wife."

"And the last thing I should wish is to be made to conform to something I am not." Smiling in complete accord with him, she said, "It would seem we are perfectly suited, Captain."

"The devil we are!" exploded Dane, who was as close as he had ever been to losing his patience with the irrepressible Violet. "You are the granddaughter of a duke, and I am a man without prospects. In my present circumstances, I not only could not support you in the manner to which you are accustomed, I should be hard-pressed to keep a roof over your head. We are not *suited*, my lady. We are as far removed from one another in station as day is from night. Are we not, Your Grace?"

"Perhaps," had replied the duke, absently tapping his quizzing glass against his ducal chin. "On the other hand, there is a philosophical implication. Can day truly be said to be removed from night? Are they not in fact inseparable parts of the whole and therefore indistinguishable one from the other? When the sun is shining on Devon, has it not set in Manchuria?"

"I daresay it has, Your Grace," Violet had agreed, smiling. "I should even go so far as to speculate that in the cosmic order of things, all of existence is one and

the same and therefore inseparable. However, for our
purposes here and now, would it be amiss to address
the more specific question?''

Then the turning point had come, and with it the
bizarre chain of events that had culminated in Dane's
present circumstances—sitting across from the Duke of
Albermarle presumably to discuss the seemingly
unavoidable arrangements for his nuptials.

"I suppose if you insist, my dear. It is, nevertheless,
an intriguing conundrum, is it not?'' queried the duke.
"Or shall you protest it is all only a matter of semantics?
Whatever the case, I daresay my granddaughter may
count herself fortunate at the prospect of wedding an
earl. As for having a roof over her head, I should think
Blackthorn Manor will do splendidly. Should I object,
in short, to a marriage between our two houses? Hardly.
If nothing else, removing the source of so much divine
inspiration would, at the very least, serve to rid Albermarle Castle once and for all of its cursed plague of
suitors.''

Reeling from the peculiar sensation that the duke
had just slipped one in under his guard to land him a
hard-fisted blow to the belly, Dane struggled to sift
through the plethora of observations to the one significant implication in Albermarle's unexpected pronouncement: Blackthorn was dead.

No doubt Dane should have felt something—regret,
relief, a perverse satisfaction—something. Strangely, all
of the old resentment was little more than a vague memory that seemed to belong to someone else. He could
not even recall his uncle's face with any clarity.

The truth was he felt nothing beyond a vague sense
of surprise that Blackthorn had died without issue. If
anything, he should have expected the earl to make
certain the young scapegrace he had sent to sea would
never inherit the title or Blackthorn Manor.

Certainly Dane had neither coveted nor expected
anything of his uncle's. It was consequently with the

greatest sense of disbelief that Dane explored the dawning realization he was become the new Earl of Blackthorn.

Something of his emotions must have shown on his face. Dane was drawn from his thoughts by Violet's exclamation of wonder and chagrin. "You did not know! Dane, I *am* sorry you should have to learn about the loss of your uncle in this manner."

"There is no need to be," shrugged Dane. "There was little love lost between us." A wry smile twisted his lips at the look in Violet's eyes. "Do not imagine I rejoice at Blackthorn's passing. I do not. But neither can I find it in myself to grieve. The truth is, I have heard nothing of my uncle in the past nineteen years. I was twelve when he sent me to sea at my request. By mutual agreement, we never saw or communicated with one another again."

"Mutual or not, it is queer nonetheless," declared His Grace. "By all rights, your uncle's solicitor should have notified you of the earl's demise. When a title is involved, not to mention entailed properties, it would seem damnably irregular to allow seven months to elapse without informing the heir."

Irregular, perhaps, had thought Dane, but not really surprising. He had been away at sea for two years and in a sickbed in Gibraltar for three months. Upon his return to England, he had found it expedient to remove from the house in London and take less costly quarters. The boy, after all, was settled in with his nurse in a cottage she shared with her widowed sister in Kent. He was safe for the time being. And Dane was left to move freely about in his own search for answers to the questions that plagued him. Any emissary sent to find him would have had the devil's own time of it.

He went suddenly still as icy fingers explored his vitals.

Of course an emissary had been sent. He had not found Dane, who was lying in a sickbed in Gibraltar. He had found Lynette.

Then suddenly it was clear to him why Blackthorn Manor had been Lynette's chosen destination. With the heir summoned to the earl's deathbed, she had taken the offered coach and gone in Dane's stead. The question was why she should have done it. The earl would little have welcomed one he would see in the light of a usurper to all he was about to leave behind. All of which brought Dane to the proposition that something had compelled Lynette to go—and that someone had been waiting for her on that road.

Try as he might, Dane could not dismiss the nagging suspicion that it was not by chance Lynette's coach had been waylaid. The more he dwelt on the events leading up to and surrounding that fateful night, the greater was his feeling a robbery had never been intended.

Someone had deliberately set out to put a period to Lynette's existence, just as he himself had been targeted by a back-shooter's bullet.

True, he had not thought it curious at first that she had sent Philippe with his nurse to the cottage in Kent. On a long journey, a child would have been an inconvenience she would rather do without. Nor had it seemed entirely unreasonable that she should have left instructions that, in the event that something untoward should occur to prevent Philippe's mother from returning for him, the nanny was to send word directly to the captain. There was always an element of uncertainty in travel. Lynette would have wished to provide for every contingency before setting out.

Or so he had told himself. Increasingly, however, he had become less sure there had not been something far more sinister at work. Indeed, it had come to him, like a mawworm gnawing away at his insides, that she had been taking the precaution of removing Philippe to a place of safety before she herself set off knowingly into danger.

Why? What possible threat could she have perceived to cause her to leave Philippe in an obscure house in the country and then depart on a journey to Blackthorn Manor, a journey not only patently unnecessary but singularly futile—unless she had gone to draw danger away from Philippe. What the danger might have been or from what source it might have come was somehow tangled up in the web of intrigue into which Dane himself had been drawn. It had to be. Dane did not believe in coincidences any more than he believed Philippe Lambert had sent him to St. John's Cathedral on a whim.

If Lynette were alive, Dane strongly suspected she might have explained a deal more than why she had tried to flee London. If both events were related somehow to her brother, Philippe Lambert, then they must surely be linked as well to something from Lynette's past, a subject about which she had been singularly reticent.

The devil! It had been seven years since he and Lynette had fled France together. In all that time, he had come to know precious little about her. She was the daughter of the former *Comte de* Delacourt, who had, along with his *comtesse*, fallen victim to the rampage of the mobs; and she was the sister of *Capitaine* Philippe Lambert of Bonaparte's imperial navy. That was all she had revealed of herself or anything concerning her life before the twist of fate that had landed an escaped British prisoner on the doorstep of her country house in the north of France.

She had survived the death of her parents by doing what was necessary, she had confided with a vague little shrug that had conveyed a great deal more than she intended. There had been a man. That much had been unavoidably certain—a man whom she had been willing to flee France to escape. What else had she kept from Dane? How much more might pose an unseen threat to himself, to young Philippe, and to anyone else who happened in the way?

It had come to him then that Violet had to be told

about Philippe—about the boy and about Lynette, his mother.

"It would seem by some queer twist of fate that I am after all an eligible candidate for marriage, even for the granddaughter of a duke," he had said, acutely aware of the irony of the sudden change in his circumstances. "You should know, however, that I have a son. Until seven months ago, I had a wife, as well."

A low sigh breathed through Violet's lips. "Lynette," she said, her eyes shimmering with understanding. "She is dead. I know. You called out to her in your delirium. And Philippe. You said that you were all he had now. Forgive me, I have wanted to ask. How did he lose his mother?"

"She was killed by a highwayman on the road to—"

"Blackthorn." Violet pressed a hand to her breast. "You kept wondering why she had been on her way to Blackthorn. She was going to the earl because—"

"My uncle had summoned his heir to him as he lay on his deathbed. Only I was away at sea." As he had always been, Dane thought bleakly. In seven years of marriage, they had had only four months together. He had given her his name and demmed little else.

But then, she had never asked more of him. She had never even asked that he love her. The devil, *he* should have been the one on that bloody coach to Devon! Now there was only one thing left he *could* give her.

"If it is marriage you want, Miss Rochelle, then no doubt I should be honored to ask you to be my wife," said Dane, looking Violet straight in the eye. "I suggest you take time to think, however, before you give me your answer—now that you know I have a son."

"A son who has lost his mother and who is in need of a home and a family. Oh, yes, Dane," breathed Violet, her lovely face alight. "I know I could never replace her. But I should hope I might in time win Philippe's affection. At the very least, he should have his father. I daresay it is past time he came to know you."

"Very commendable of you, to be sure," observed Albermarle in exceedingly dry tones. "I believe, however, you are missing the key point, my dear. If there should be a male issue from your marriage, your son would not be the first in line to inherit."

"No," replied Violet without hesitation. "But then, if he is *our* son, I daresay he will wish to follow in the footsteps of his father in any case. He will be a sailor, like his father and my father. The sea is in our blood, too, you know, Grandpapa. *Are* you asking me to be your wife, my lord?" she said then, turning compelling blue-violet eyes on Dane. "It was never my intent to entrap an earl, though doubtless that will be what the world will say I have done. As it happens, I *did* ask you first—*before* I knew you had ascended to your lofty station. No doubt I shall in future salve my conscience with that knowledge."

"Are you not getting ahead of yourself, miss?" interjected the duke quellingly. "I believe it is customary for a suitor to ask permission first of the male head of the household. And since my grandson and heir is conspicuous by his absence, it would seem to devolve upon me to act in this matter. It is my decision that we shall remove at once from this miserable excuse for an inn to Albermarle, where we may discuss in more congenial surrounds what is to be done."

The devil, thought Dane, easing his arm to a more comfortable position inside its sling as he watched Albermarle, standing with his back to Dane, pour two glasses of brandy. The morning's events, far from clarifying matters, had served instead to cast a darker shroud of mystery over them. Worse, he had now not only to consider the risk to Violet's safety should he do the unthinkable and marry her, but he had to contemplate as well the very real possibility Philippe's life was in danger, too.

Hell and the devil confound it, he mused with a faint, baffled smile. He might have known Violet would see the added complication of a motherless child not as a deterrent to their marriage but as a reason to proceed with the ceremony as soon as possible!

He suffered a sudden, swift pang of guilt as quickly quelled. There would never be a child between them, he told himself. If they married, it would be a marriage of convenience only. And then, when the business of *Le Corbeau* was finished, he would leave it to Violet to decide for herself how best to end it.

"You are pensive, Lord Blackthorn," Albermarle observed. Handing Dane a glass, he took a seat in the leather-upholstered chair behind the great desk. "As well you might be. You had never any intention of marrying my granddaughter. That much was made abundantly clear to me. And now here we are in the peculiar circumstance of coming together to discuss what is to be done to salvage the situation. I wonder if I should not do better simply to shoot you where you sit."

At those words, Dane glanced up—and found himself staring down the muzzle of a pistol which not only gave every evidence of being primed and loaded but also was trained unswervingly on his chest. Dane went perfectly still, his gaze lifting to the duke's, regarding him with chilly dispassion over the barrel of the gun.

"What say you, Blackthorn?" Albermarle queried, as if they were discussing nothing more momentous than the prospect of a change in the weather. "Shall I bring the whole untidy affair to a close?"

Silently, Dane cursed. He was not in love with life, nor was he afraid to die. The devil knew he had faced that bitter prospect often enough in the past. Nevertheless, he had a strong dislike of the notion of being shot down where he sat. Death in battle was one thing. Being slaughtered like a fatted calf for the duke's perverse pleasure was something else altogether. Still, he would bloody well rather die than beg for his life.

"You will no doubt do as you please, Your Grace," said Dane steadily. "Nor could I blame you. As it happens, you have every reason to mistrust my intentions toward your granddaughter—in all save one. You may believe I should never willingly do anything to hurt Lady Violet and, further, I should always do all in my power to keep her from harm. Beyond that, I can promise nothing. In all truth, I believe she would do better without me."

"Do you?" The pistol held steady on Dane. "Perhaps I agree with you. The scent of trouble clings to you, Captain. On the other hand, I am constrained from shooting you." The duke laid the pistol aside and leaned back in his chair to regard Dane with his cursedly unfathomable eyes. "No doubt you will pardon this little exercise. There are few things as effective in revealing a man's true nature as the belief he is staring death in the face. I had to be sure you are what you seem to be. For whatever reason, my granddaughter has set her sights on you. I, naturally, must feel obligated to uphold her in her decision. It was I, after all, who ordered her to choose a husband."

"You could hardly have had me in mind," Dane observed dryly. Ever so slowly he felt the muscles in his shoulders relax as it became apparent he was not to meet an immediate demise at the hands of the duke.

"I daresay you could not possibly know what I had in mind, sir," Albermarle did not hesitate to point out. "You will know this, however. I should be exceedingly displeased to discover Violet's happiness had been sacrificed for any reason, no matter how noble sounding. She has known enough grief in her young life. Thus far, you would seem to demonstrate a remarkable understanding of my granddaughter. But then, that is hardly surprising, since you are obviously in love with her. Pray do not bother to deny it. It is the only possible explanation for the irrationality of your behavior these past few days."

"No doubt I am relieved, Your Grace," said Dane,

who found little to amuse in the sudden turn of conversation. "At least you do not think I am by nature a fool."

"I shall thank you not to take snuff with me, my lord," snapped the duke. "All men are fools in love. It is the nature of the malady. It is also the wise man who knows enough not to squander the experience in inconsequentialities, which is what I strongly suspect you are in danger of doing, more's the pity. But that is neither here nor there. Violet has made up her mind to have you, and have you she shall, or I will know the reason why. It is all that needs to be said on that particular subject. As for the practical matters, she will come to you with a not insubstantial dowry."

Dane stiffened in the chair. "Then it will remain her own. The dowry is of no consequence to me. If I am going to marry Lady Violet, it will not be for any fortune she might bring to me."

"You, sir," pronounced the duke coldly, "would not be marrying Lady Violet at all if you were allowed to have your way—or I mine. In which case I suggest you do not fling my generosity in my face."

Dane, cursing himself for a bloody fool, sharply curbed his temper. Hell and the devil confound it! He had lived more than half his life under the navy's harsh discipline. He had not reached post captain on the promotional chain of command by behaving in the manner of an undisciplined recruit—or by losing his self-command in the face of the enemy.

"You are right, of course," Dane said with only the barest hint of irony. "I spoke out of turn. Naturally, it was never your intent to bribe me. Respectfully, however, I submit you are mistaken about one thing. As it happens, I have every intention of marrying your granddaughter."

"You astonish me," submitted the duke, touching his fingertips together to form a pyramid of his hands at his chest. "You will no doubt pardon my curiosity. What brought you to change your mind?"

"Only that it has occurred to me that, in light of today's events, marrying her may prove the only way to keep her safe. If I have learned anything about your granddaughter, it is that once she has set her mind on a thing, there is no dissuading her from her chosen course."

"No, have you?" murmured the duke, who could not recall Violet had ever determined on any course other than avoiding committing herself to anything that might require her to do something she had no wish to have done. But then no doubt his lapse could be attributed, he told himself, to his notoriously lamentable memory. "And to what particular course do you perceive she has committed herself?"

"To driving me mad, I doubt not," Dane replied grimly. "From our very first encounter, she has not hesitated to put herself at risk for my sake, and she has not stopped since. You heard her at the inn. She proposed a united front against my enemies. She is even willing to marry me in order to prevent Vere from challenging me to a duel. Next she will undoubtedly suggest that, as his brother-in-law, I should enlist Vere's aid in rooting out my enemies."

"I should not be at all surprised," agreed the duke, who knew his granddaughter too well to suppose otherwise. Violet had always looked to her older brother as a hero and protector, while Gideon, the young scoundrel, would stir up a hornets' nest purely for his own amusement. "You, however, prefer to involve no one in your endeavors, is that it?"

"I prefer not to have the death of another woman on my conscience," Dane answered, setting the brandy aside, untouched. "I daresay she will find little opportunity to fling herself in harm's way if she is occupied with her duties as chatelaine of Blackthorn Manor. No doubt she will be well enough amused learning to be a mother to Philippe. As for me, I think it is time the Earl of Blackthorn acquired a measure of town bronze."

A dark, inquisitive eyebrow arched toward the ducal hairline. "You intend to leave your wife in Devon while you pursue your pleasures in town? Now why, I wonder, did I not think of that?"

"I doubt not you did think of it, Your Grace," rejoined Dane, who had long since come to the conclusion that Albermarle, far from being the absentminded eccentric he presented to the world, was every bit as astute as he was dangerous to cross. "I should go so far as to say you are perfectly aware it is not my pleasure I shall be seeking in London."

"No, of course it is not. You may have been elevated to the rank of earl, but you think like a naval captain. I had wondered when it would occur to you that the Earl of Blackthorn is a far different proposition from Captain Dane of the British Navy. Having ascended to the peerage may not render you unassailable, but it does confer certain advantages previously denied you. A gentleman would use his position to broaden his awareness of the subtleties around him. Your vision— unfortunately, it would seem—is limited to military objectives."

Dane's lip curled in cynical appreciation of the duke's assessment of his shortcomings. "The devil," he said. "It would seem I am a hopeless case."

"It is early days yet," replied Albermarle, rising dismissively from his chair. "As it happens, I have every expectation my granddaughter will be a beneficial influence on you, whether you wish it or not. And now I suggest we join Violet, who, along with Bishop Long, is awaiting our arrival in the chapel."

In the chapel! Good God, thought Dane. Albermarle had wasted no time in making sure of him. He had summoned no less than a bishop to do the leg shackling. But then, it would take a bishop to dispense with the usual formalities.

It was soon made evident to Dane that Violet had indeed entertained few doubts as to the outcome of the meeting between Albermarle and himself. Stepping through the arched doorway into the quaint stone chapel, Dane was met with a vision of femininity arrayed in flowing white embroidered in pale yellow rosebuds. Over her raven curls, she wore an embroidered veil wreathed in a garland of yellow silk roses, while in her gloved hands, she carried a bouquet of yellow tulips interspersed with purple violets no doubt garnished from her grandfather's hothouse. Never had she appeared more beautiful. Inexplicably, he felt a small ache awaken somewhere in the region of his breastbone.

"It was my mother's wedding gown," said Violet, her lovely eyes searching on his. "I hope you do not mind. It has always been my fondest wish to be married in it."

"Then you shall have that much at least," Dane said more harshly than he had intended. Immediately, he caught himself at the hurt in Violet's eyes. "Forgive me," he murmured, cursing himself for a heartless brute. "This can hardly be the sort of wedding in which you envisioned yourself wearing it. I regret I have robbed you of that, sweet Violet—and of so much more that should rightfully have been yours."

Violet, peering up at him, smilingly shook her head. "I wish you will not be absurd, Dane." Placing her hand on his arm, she turned toward the bishop. "As it happens, this is precisely the wedding of which I have always dreamed."

It was not the answer he had expected, though no doubt he should have done. Naturally, Violet would never admit to disappointment. She was far too practical to cavil over what could not be helped.

Still, she was a woman, and he could not dismiss the conviction all women entertained fantasies of weddings with all the folderol that normally accompanied them. At the very least, she should have wished her family and friends to be present. But then, no doubt it was better this way, he mused darkly. When all was said and done, it would be easier for her to end it.

Somehow that thought struck a hollow note as his glance fell upon the profile of Violet's face through the gossamer veil. How different she was from Lynette, that sad and lonely girl whose heart had been wounded and left forever scarred! For all her passion in bed, she had remained distant, unreachable, like a flower encased in crystal.

And now there was Violet, all sweet, untouched innocence in the full bloom of young womanhood. His blood stirred at the mere recollection of her untutored, fiery response to his lovemaking. It came to him with bitter regret that she deserved much better than him. Then, in a haze, he heard a voice request the ring.

In the sudden wash of confusion, he became aware the duke had stepped forward.

"I have the ring." Albermarle's eyes sought Violet's. "It was the happiest day of my life when Genevieve, Lady Albermarle, condescended to wear my ring. I daresay she would have been pleased to know one day it would grace the hand of her granddaughter." His gaze held hers for a moment longer; then, as unfathomable as ever, swung to the captain, who had not missed the shimmer of tears rise to Violet's eyes. "The ring, my lord."

"The ring, indeed," murmured Dane, accepting the exquisitely carved band of gold with a queasy sense he had just been made an unwitting party to something rare and fine between Violet and her grandfather. The moment, fraught with emotion, was a far cry from the hasty ceremony performed by the captain of the East Indiaman that had picked two refugees up out of a stolen fishing boat at sea. As Dane slipped the ring that had graced the hand of the former duchess on Violet's finger, he was hardly prepared to discover he was far from immune to the spell cast by the hushed atmosphere of the centuries-old chapel, the solemn presence of the bishop, but, most of all, the radiant beauty of the bride—*his* bride, good God.

It came to him on an unexpectedly fierce swell of tenderness that he had been lying to himself all along. Never had he wanted anything so much as he wanted this slender, dreamy-eyed girl. Whether God or chance had placed her in his way, he knew he had never any intention of giving her up.

Then Lady Violet Rochelle, the granddaughter of a duke who from the first moment he had laid eyes on her had woven her enchantment over him, was pronounced his wife, to love, honor, and cherish for as long as they both should live. Dane, lifting the veil to gaze into spellbinding eyes the color of violets, knew he would do all in his power to keep her, and the devil with the consequences.

Chapter 7

The three melancholy chimes of the hall clock struck and died away. Violet, shivering in the chill of her bedroom, tucked her bare feet beneath the hem of her nightdress and hugged her knees to her chest.

Dane was not coming to her tonight. It was long past time she accepted the infelicitous evidence of her own solitary state and left her perch in the window seat for the warmth of her bed.

She was being foolish. She knew it, and she did not care. She was a bride on her wedding night, she told herself, staring petulantly at the plash of raindrops against the window glass. A bride did not go to her marriage bed alone. That was not the way it was done; she was quite sure of it. And especially not when the bride was wearing her Grandmama Genevieve's wedding ring!

A lump swelled in her throat. Albermarle's generosity had taken her utterly by surprise. And how not? It never would have occurred to her he would be without the ring.

It had always been there, on his gold fob chain along

with the watch inside which he carried a miniature of her—Genevieve, his dearly beloved duchess, who had stolen the Albermarle betrothal ring and forever captured his heart. She had been the only love of his life, the ring his most precious relic of her. And he had given it to her, Violet, to wear in token of her own marriage, just beginning.

Faith, if only she were worthy of it, she thought, recalling how, as a little girl, she had used to wheedle her grandpapa into taking her in his lap to let her see and touch the shiny band of gold. In her childish imagination it had been a thing of fascination, like the story of Genevieve Hayden, the fiery-haired adventuress who had risked everything for love.

In spite of his lamentable memory, he had not forgotten, the dear. Nor had he given the gift lightly. It had been a rare demonstration of the affection in which he held her.

In truth, she did not know how she was to face him on the morrow—or anyone else, for that matter. No doubt everyone in the castle would know Lady Violet had spent the night alone!

How *like* Dane, she thought ruefully, to do the wholly unexpected. Or perhaps foregoing the pleasure of his new wife's company was precisely what she should have anticipated from him.

The wedding, after all, had not exactly been his idea. Very likely it had been a trifle overwhelming to discover a bishop already on the premises.

He could not have known that the Right Reverend Long was the duke's brother-in-law. Nor could he be aware that the bishop had made it a practice each year for the past forty to spend a few days at Albermarle before the onset of Lent in order to indulge his lifelong affinity for angling. It had been purely happenstance that Easter had fallen in the latter part of April that year and the bishop had arrived only that morning to start his retreat from the demands of his office.

Violet, on the other hand, *had* known it. Indeed, she had been counting on it when she sent the note to Albermarle to inform the duke of her compromising circumstances at the inn.

Once that particular chain of events had been set in motion, there really had never been any question as to its culmination. The duke, naturally, would never accept anything less than Dane's firm commitment to marry her. Unfortunately, Violet had not taken into account the possibility of this particular twist in the outcome—that Dane, once having seen the inevitability of making an honest woman of her, should choose not to consummate the marriage. Really, it was too bad of him, she thought, plopping her chin down on the tops of her bent knees.

In retrospect, she supposed she could hardly blame him for having taken exception to being maneuvered into a marriage he had made it plain he did not want. No doubt it had been a mistake to indulge her fondest wish to be married in her mama's wedding dress. Very likely it had given her part in the affair away.

And now, having formed a disgust of her, her dearest captain was determined to have nothing more to do with her. And, indeed, why should he? He was the Earl of Blackthorn now, with the fortune and privilege that went with it.

More than that, he had come into the title with the succession already secured with a son from his previous marriage. It was perhaps the height of irony that he had warned her beforehand how it must be, and she, thinking only of Dane and his motherless child in need of comforting, had missed the true significance of his words.

Faith, what a fool she had been to think that she should try to influence events! This was what came of striking out against the current. If she had only let things well enough alone, perhaps in the natural course of events Dane might have come on his own to the decision to wed her. Perhaps he might even have come in time to love her, if only a little. Now there would seem very little hope he would ever forgive her—and just when she had begun to think perhaps he had formed an attraction for her, no matter how rudimentary.

And in truth, for a single, breathless moment, as Dane had lifted her wedding veil and looked into her eyes, she had been almost positive he was not so indifferent to her as he wished her to believe. In truth, her heart had seemed suddenly to still as his gaze, piercing and black, had infused her with a glowing warmth.

Faith, she could not be mistaken in thinking his lips had touched hers with an aching tenderness or that they had lingered as if reluctant to part from her. And when, a seeming eternity later, he had released her, surely she could not have been so misled as to imagine he had cradled the side of her face with the palm of his hand as though she were infinitely precious to him.

No, he *had* held her with his touch and with that fierce, compelling light in his eyes which seemed now irrevocably etched in her memory.

Then why had he not come to her, she fretted, her gaze drawn to the table set for two, the covers laid but as yet untouched, the bottle of champagne sent up by her grandpapa in the way of a wedding present waiting to be uncorked.

Really, this was not at all the way she had thought things would turn out when she had conceived the notion of marrying Dane in order to save him from her brother's wrath, not to mention provide him with allies against his powerful enemies. She supposed that now, as the Earl of Blackthorn, he did not require the grand-daughter of a duke to give him access to doors that must have been closed to a mere captain in the navy.

Indeed, she did not doubt that an earl who was in addition a real live hero of countless naval battles would prove quite irresistible to the *ton.* No dinner party or

soiree, no gala would be accounted a success unless the
new Earl of Blackthorn deigned to attend.

Inevitably, she was prey to a sudden queasy sensation
at the realization he would be particularly attractive to
the feminine contingent. She did not doubt he would
have his choice of any number of barques of frailty who
would like nothing better than to be invited under the
mantle of his protection. And while he was pursuing
his pleasures in the arms of his mistresses in town, his
wife would be at home alone. Worse, she would be a
wife who was yet a virgin!

That was the shabbiest thing of all, Violet decided.
Indeed, she could not think of anything more appalling
than living the rest of her life as a wife who had never
lain with her husband. Faith, it simply was not to be
thought of to be doomed either to live a life of denial
or to seek solace in the arms of illicit lovers. Her every
instinct, not to mention her highly developed sense of
the romantic, rebelled against such a bleak scenario.

She was a young, healthy female who, thanks to Dane,
had been given to experience the power of her woman's
body to transport her to a state of ecstasy. It would seem
just the least bit unfair there was only one man with whom
she would wish to share the bliss of an all-consuming
love—indeed, who had the power to unleash her primal
feminine passions. It was the devil's own irony he
refused to consummate the marriage.

She might as well be confined to a convent, she
thought dejectedly. Indeed, she might as well not be
married at all.

But then, that was it, she thought suddenly, her heart
skipping a beat. If the marriage were never consum-
mated, Violet would have grounds to demand an annulment. It was Dane's way of giving Violet her freedom
without compromising her reputation, of insuring her
safety by keeping her at a distance.

Really, it was too bad of him! And yet, how like her
gallant captain to go to such lengths to prevent her

from becoming prey to the danger that might already have taken one dear to him and had come so close to putting a period to his own existence.

The devil take him! It should have been Violet's decision to make. But then, she thought, going quite still, it was her decision yet.

Suddenly she sat up, her heart thumping beneath her breast.

If he would not come to her, it would serve him right if she went to him! It was, after all, what her Grandmama Genevieve would have done.

And, truly, why should she, Violet, not do as her heart bade her? She was his wife, whether he liked it or not. If she had no wish to be treated like a hothouse flower in need of being carefully nurtured and protected, then surely she must cease to behave like one. She must make him see she was not to be dismissed lightly.

The next instant, she had left the window seat and was sliding her feet into her slippers. Pausing only long enough to take up a lighted taper, she let herself out the door into the corridor.

Dane sat sprawled in a tapestry-covered wing chair, his legs thrust out before him and his injured arm, freed from its sling, allowed to drape along the arm of the chair. He had earlier discarded his coat and waistcoat, along with his neck cloth, and then, yanking the neck of his shirt open down the front, had sloshed another brandy in a glass before dropping into the chair.

He did not know how long he had been staring, unseeing, into the glowing embers of the fireplace, his thoughts on the girl who must long since have given up on him. She would never know how close he had come to losing the battle against overwhelming temptation. Egad, he was nearly driven mad at the thought that he had every right to claim the sweet, passionate Violet as his own.

Every right but one, he amended darkly and, emptying his glass, reached for the decanter on the occasional table beside him.

Bitterly, Dane cursed. When he risked a meeting with his brother-in-law at Valletta as Malta had fallen at last to Nelson, he could not have known the price he'd pay would include the dreamy-eyed Violet Rochelle. It had been the devil's own luck he had spotted Lambert among the French officers taken prisoner.

Philippe Lambert, the former *Comte de* Delacourt, had survived the purges because he was among the few French naval officers with experience in battle. It seemed doubtful he would endure beyond the loss of Malta. Dane had owed it to Lynette to see Philippe though there had been little he could offer in the way of comfort. Nevertheless, Philippe had been right when he cursed Dane for a fool for coming.

"You would do better to forget you ever knew me. All the world will forget Philippe Lambert. The emperor does not look kindly on defeat, *Capitaine.*"

Still, Philippe had owed Dane a debt beyond repaying, and the Frenchman was as good as dead already.

"Beware, my brother," Philippe had said softly as his hand closed hard about Dane's wrist. "In battle you are a fearless warrior, but in the shadows where men deal in secret, you are little better than a pawn. You gave my sister sanctuary when I was powerless to protect her. *Maintenant,* I beg you will go to St. John's Cathedral. Tonight at midnight. Light a candle for me, *mon ami.* A warrior cannot fight what he cannot see."

The devil, thought Dane, the brandy sour on his tongue. Philippe's words had been cryptic at best, but his look had been fraught with meaning. In retrospect, he supposed he really had little choice but to go. Lambert might be an enemy to England, but he was a man of honor. He had been trying to convey a warning to the man who had married his sister. In that, he could be trusted to have Dane's best interests at heart. Dane had gone, knowing his actions might be misconstrued by others.

He had told no one of his purpose or his destination, not even the disapproving Murdoch. A grim smile played about Dane's lips at thought of his loyal coxswain. Murdoch would be chafing now at being left behind to watch over young Philippe, just as he had been left behind that fateful night in Valletta. His place had ever been at his captain's back, and Dane had keenly felt the burly coxswain's absence as he approached the austere exterior of St. John's Cathedral.

Erected by the Knights of Malta, the magnificent cathedral with its vaulted ceilings and its pavement of marble tombstones had seemed a brooding place steeped in the history of its founders. His experience with devotional houses had hitherto been limited to the modest church in Combe Martin to which his mother had taken him as a boy.

This massive structure, with its soaring roof bearing Preti's masterpieces, its rich tapestries recording the deeds of the knights, and its exquisite paintings depicting the life of John the Baptist was a foreign world to a sailor more used to the limitless expanse of sky and water. In the hush of approaching midnight, the polished suits of armor standing silent watch among the carved statues had seemed to mark his measured progress with vacant eyes.

The secluded apse with its hundreds of candles, in contrast, had seemed to offer a haven. Dropping a coin in the box, he had taken a candle and, lighting it, set it in its niche. Then, assuming an aspect of meditation, he had waited.

No doubt it was instinct that prompted him at the approach of footsteps to withdraw into the shadow of a statue and to remain in concealment at the arrival of a man, soon joined by another just out of Dane's range of vision. Dane, able to see only the grotesque cast of shadows of the two men against the far wall, had little difficulty discerning it was not an amicable meeting. The terse exchange of words, the sharp hand gestures gave evidence of a heated argument, and occasionally he had heard enough to garner that one of the men was not averse to employing coercion to achieve his object. In the end, a packet had been passed from him to the other.

Hell and the devil confound it! He would have given a great deal to know the contents of that packet. What a bloody fool he had been to allow them to depart without issuing them a challenge!

Worse, while they had remained shadow figures on a wall, it was to become painfully obvious that his presence had not gone undetected by them. The attack on the steps leading from the church had been swift and deadly in its intent. Something, the soft scrape of shoe leather perhaps, had brought him spinning around to glimpse a cloaked figure bearing down on him. At the flash of a knife, he flung himself sideways, his hand reaching for the sword at his belt. His assailant, having lost the advantage of surprise, had fled to a waiting carriage before Dane could regain his balance.

The day following the events at the cathedral had seen Dane ordered back to sea with Sir Henry Granville on board as his passenger. Why? Had someone meant to ensure Dane never saw Lambert again?

Vice Admiral Sir Oliver Landford had given Dane his sailing orders. It would seem damnably odd that Landford had been present the night Sir Henry was assaulted by a masked intruder. It was odder still that Landford had apparently been the intended victim of a would-be assassin approximately at the same time Dane was being targeted by a sharpshooter's bullet on the road north out of Exeter. The latter event had seemed suddenly to bring everything into grim perspective.

The devil, thought Dane, his hand clenching on the glass. It would seem his enemies, whoever they were,

were not content with having destroyed his career and consigned him to obscurity. They wanted him dead— shot down or hanged as the traitor *Le Corbeau!*

It was the only explanation that would seem to make any bloody sense. Lieutenant Freeman and his men had not come to bring in Captain Trevor Dane to face a court-martial for having consorted with the enemy. They had come in search of the French agent who was believed to have assaulted Sir Henry in his study and Vice Admiral Sir Oliver Landford in his quarters in Exeter. Someone had made sure they came straight to Dane.

That realization struck Dane most forcefully when he had had time to contemplate the events at the inn. Alone at last in his bedchamber at Albermarle and with his head completely clear for the first time since he had awakened at the inn to discover Violet in bed with him, he had seen the impossibility of his position. He could not in all conscience ask Violet to share the life of a man who was under a cloud of suspicion.

He had married her, but before he could claim her as his wife, he had first to clear his name of any hint of calumny. Bloody hell, he had to discover the real traitor's identity and expose him to the Admiralty.

To do that, he had to stay alive. More than that, he needed to find a safe haven for little Philippe. And now Violet, too, was become a part of the equation. But then, he mused cynically, there could hardly have been a more secure stronghold for her than Albermarle Castle.

A bleak smile came to Dane's lips. He would set out alone at first light. With his departure, his dreamy-eyed enchantress would be safe enough under her grandfather's protection. Tossing back his head, he downed the fiery liquid in his glass at a single swallow and felt it explore his empty belly.

Hell's teeth! She would forget him in time. Certainly she would never know what it had cost him to leave her.

For the first time since his nearly forgotten childhood,

he had been given to glimpse what it might mean to let someone near who could breach the walls of his defenses. With Violet, he need never have felt alone. He might even have come in time to know the meaning of domestic happiness. At the very least, he did not doubt she would haunt his dreams for as long as he lived, even as she now haunted his every waking moment.

"Christ," he groaned, as, glancing up at the brush of a sudden draught, he was even then visited with a vision of loveliness garbed in flowing white and bathed in pale candlelight. Hellfire, he thought, rubbing a hand over his eyes. It was not enough that he had only to think of the beautiful Violet to conjure up an image of her. Now she must appear to him as he had imagined her, waiting for him to come to her on this, their wedding night. No doubt that image would tease and torture him in the days and nights to come. Blindly, he reached for the decanter of brandy, only to discover it was empty.

"My poor captain. I'm afraid you will have to ring for another. On the other hand, it would be a shame to wake up Mr. Cousins at this time of night. You may be sure the old dear has long since gone to his bed."

At this series of observations, gravely voiced, Dane opened his eyes.

"Violet. Good God. It is really you."

"It is indubitably," agreed Violet, who rather thought her dearest captain must be more than a trifle bright in the eye. Just for a moment, he had looked at her as if he were seeing a ghost. "I daresay I should have come sooner," she said, hastily depositing the burning taper on the mantel and crossing to him. "Faith, Captain, you look perfectly dreadful."

"The devil I do," growled Dane. Setting aside the empty decanter and glass, he came to his feet to stand glaring down at her. "You should not have come at all."

"Naturally, you would say that," replied Violet with perfect equanimity. She, far from feeling daunted by his towering presence, could not but think her dearest captain had never looked more appealing than he did at that very moment with his hair tousled as though he had been running his fingers repeatedly through it.

Indeed, she could not but be thrillingly aware that his shirt was open to the waist, revealing the bristling mat of hair on his masculine chest. "You are, after all, up to your old tricks again of deciding what is best for me, when really it has never been your decision to make."

Afraid she might lose her nerve at any moment, she stepped up to him and clasped her arms about his magnificently lean, powerful waist. "I am, in case you had failed to notice, a grown woman."

Failed to notice? Egad, thought Dane, who was keenly aware at the moment that Violet's firm, well-rounded bosom was pressed against him in a manner certain to arouse his manly ardor. He had been driven to distraction by his enchantress's womanly attributes from the first moment he had had the misfortune to lay eyes on her! Bloody hell, she must know perfectly well she was a paragon of feminine perfection no man could long hope to resist. At their first encounter, she had been in retreat to her rooms to escape the adulation of a plethora of masculine admirers. Upon their second, she had been fleeing a siege of importunate, aspiring suitors!

"The devil, Violet," growled Dane, reaching to disengage her arms from about his waist. "I am neither a boy nor one of your virtuous suitors with whom you can play your bloody parlor games."

"No, my dearest Captain," Violet instantly rejoined, "you are a man who is determined to ruin everything with your obstinate adherence to the notion I am some sort of wilting violet." Marveling at her own audacity, she reached up to cradle his face between the palms of her hands. "Look at me. Do you truly believe I am incapable of determining for myself what is best for me?"

Dane, compelled in spite of himself to gaze into the

unguarded depths of Violet's eyes, stifled a groan. Egad, she had not the least notion what she was doing to him. She was all sweet earnestness and fire, was his glorious enchantress. The devil! She clouded his reason and melted away his resistance.

Clasping strong fingers about her wrists, he drew her hands down and held them captive at his chest. "What I believe, my sweet, impossible Violet," he said, a hint of bafflement in the look he bent up on her, "is that I was a fool ever to allow you to involve yourself with me. When I saw you in that cursed inn, I should have turned tail and run."

"But you didn't," Violet pointed out practicably. "I fear you would not, in any case, have gone very far. You know very well you were far better to entrust yourself to my care. I really cannot see it matters now."

"What is done is done?" murmured Dane with only the barest tinge of irony, as he was made tinglingly aware of the delectable woman's scent of her mingled with the suggestion of lavender.

"Now you are roasting me," accused Violet, wrinkling her nose at him. How dared he fling her words back at her! Her poor gallant captain, she noted, nevertheless had the look of a man who had been in the cruel grips of a dilemma. She was torn between pity and a perverse and purely feminine wish that he had been suffering from an acute case of unrequited desire. "Even so, you will agree it cannot be changed now. Dane, in all truth, I should not wish it to be."

A smile, exceedingly wry, flickered briefly about the corners of Dane's mouth. "No, I daresay you are pleased to be married to a man who had every intention of leaving you at first light."

"Yes, though I think it would have been the shabbiest thing to be left a maiden," reflected Violet, noting with a small thrill through her midsection his use of the past tense in his declaration. "Little good it would have done you. You did not really think I should be moved to have our marriage annulled, did you? I am not such a poor creature, I promise you. If you leave without me, my dearest, most provoking captain, you may be sure I shall only come after you."

It was true, thought Dane, marveling he had ever thought it could be otherwise. Releasing her, he turned away to stand with his arm propped on the mantelpiece, his gaze brooding on the glowing embers of the fire. She was his sweet, incomparable Violet. Naturally, she would have come after him. He might have known as well that she would work everything out on her own, even to realizing he had intended to give her up for her own good.

Obviously, there would be no annulment and certainly no keeping his bride at Albermarle Castle—or Blackthorn Manor, for that matter—while he pursued his own course in town. He did not doubt that as soon as his back was turned she would set off on her own after him. Indeed, there was no telling what the unpredictable enchantress might be capable of doing if left to her own inventive devices.

Inexplicably, the realization he would seem to have no choice but to take Violet with him when he left was not so disturbing as Dane might have anticipated. In truth, he experienced something that curiously resembled the lifting of a heavy weight from his shoulders, coupled with an unmistakable and familiar stirring in his loins.

With a distinct air of deliberation, he turned to look at her. "You, my girl," he said, his eyes suddenly glittery and black in the firelight, "would seem to have everything resolved to your satisfaction."

Violet, who could not but be struck by a sudden change in her dearest captain's demeanor, met his look searchingly. "Perhaps not everything," she ventured, aware her pulse had inexplicably begun to race. "There is still the matter of a bridal supper, which is as yet untouched. And a bottle of His Grace's best champagne waiting in my room to be sampled. It would seem a pity to let it all go to waste, would it not?"

"A cursed shame," agreed Dane, who could not have cared less at the moment about the most lavish of bridal suppers, not even accompanied by what he did not doubt was a champagne of the first order. "One which I fear is unavoidable. Tell me one thing. I find I am filled with curiosity; indeed, I think I really must have an answer, my sweet, irrepressible Violet. Why would you have come after me?"

It was not a question Violet was expecting. Indeed, she was hardly prepared to answer it. "It would seem obvious, would it not?" she evaded, lowering her eyes as though she found something suddenly quite fascinating in the vicinity of the captain's left shoulder. "I am your wife. How would it look if you left me the day after we were married? I should never have been able to show my face again."

"It would have looked as if I had left you to see to my affairs before I undertook to remove you from your home," offered Dane, who could not but be intrigued by his normally forthright Violet's uncharacteristic failure to look him in the eyes. "Or something to that effect. I doubt not you would have come up with a suitable story to satisfy people's curiosity. But then"—placing the side of his index finger beneath her chin, he gently forced her head up—"heretofore you have demonstrated a marked disregard for what people might think. No doubt you will pardon me if I find it difficult to believe you have developed a sudden concern for public opinion. Violet"—lowering his head to hers with infinite slowness, he brushed her lips with his—"why did you come tonight?"

A whimsical smile twitched at his lips as he raised his head to observe Violet with her face tilted up, her eyes closed, and her lovely features wearing a rapt expression. Egad, she was magnificent, was his sweet, generous Violet. She responded to his caresses as no other woman ever had before her. His breath caught as her eyelashes fluttered against her cheeks, then lifted to reveal the blue-violet depths of her eyes lit from within with a soft, wondering light.

"You kissed me," she said accusingly, "just when I most in particularly might have wished to keep my wits about me."

"Yes, and you may be sure I shall kiss you again," asserted Dane, thinking his new bride promised fair to cut up his peace of mind. "Often and repeatedly, until you answer my question. Tell me, Violet," he said, pressing his lips to her brow, her cheek, and, finally, the corner of her mouth. "Tell me why you would have come after me."

Violet, who was suffering from the peculiar sensation that her bones were being turned into melted wax, lifted her arms about Dane's neck and clung to him to keep her knees from buckling beneath her. Really, it was not in the least fair that Dane should submit her to a Spanish Inquisition when her head was spinning in a most ridiculous manner and she could not think at all clearly. Nor did it help in the least that his hands trailed over and down her back, until, finding and molding themselves to her firm, rounded posterior, they drew her to him.

A low gasp of surprise burst from her lips as she felt the hard bulge of his manhood against a particularly sensitive part of her anatomy.

"Why, Violet?" Dane whispered, nibbling most inconsiderately at her right earlobe.

"Faith, why do you think?" gasped Violet, letting her head loll to one side in order to give him greater access to the delectably tender flesh along the slender column of her neck. "I am a Rochelle, and I love you. I'm afraid I really could not help myself."

Dane went suddenly still. Violet had declared she loved him! Egad, he had not thought to hear those words from her. When she had persisted so sweetly in her determined pursuit of him, even going so far as to assert she would have followed after him and tracked him down had he left her, he had attributed her behavior to feminine pique. And how not, when he had done everything in his power to disabuse her of the notion he was made a victim to her sweet allure from the first moment he laid eyes on her? He had not dared to imagine Lady Violet Rochelle, who might have had any man of her choosing, would give up her heart to him! He was both humbled and elated by her confession.

The pain of his injury forgotten in a hot surge of desire to possess her, Dane bent down and lifted her high into his arms.

"Dane!" Violet gasped, instinctively clasping an arm about his neck. "Pray put me down. Faith, you will hurt yourself!"

Ignoring her protests, Dane carried her to his bed. Sweet, beautiful Violet was his wife, and she had said she loved him. He could let nothing now stand in the way of his claiming her as his own. His lips found hers, and he kissed her with a fierce, aching tenderness borne of all the years of his solitary existence. At last, holding her against his chest, he slowly let her feet slip to the floor so she stood leaning against him, her head tilted back, her lips blindly seeking his.

Meeting her kiss for kiss, he slipped the gown off her shoulders and over her arms to let it slide down her slender frame to the floor at her feet.

"Violet," he uttered huskily, his breath harsh in his throat as he beheld her, revealed in all her womanly perfection. Her eyes luminous in the pale oval of her face, she stood tall before him—unafraid and unashamed. A low groan sounded deep in his throat. She was Violet, his incomparable Lady Blackthorn. Flinging back the bedcovers, he lifted her to the bed.

Violet's breath caught as Dane leaned over her, a hand propped on the bed on either side of her. His eyes moved over her face, slowly, lingeringly, his look a silent caress that brought the blood hot to her cheeks and awakened a fiery heat in her veins.

She could not but sense this was not like that other time, when he had deliberately taken her to the rapturous heights while he, conspicuously, had remained behind. She had not understood at first the sort of man he was. Not until she had beheld the wonder of his magnificently erect male member had it been made poignantly clear to her. Her dearest captain was a man of rare integrity who, convinced he must walk away from her, had spared her the loss of her innocence and, yes, the risk of her conceiving a child out of wedlock. She had seen it all then in the rigid cast of his face.

How different now was his look. And his touch, she thought, moving her face into the caress of his hand against her cheek. Her heart swelled beneath her breast as it came to her that his was the look and touch of a man in the dawning realization of possession. She was his, and, fiercely tender, he would take her.

The knowledge awakened an aching in her heart. His name breathed through her lips, and he stilled, his gaze, searching, on hers.

Holding his eyes with hers, she carried his hand to her lips and, pressing a kiss into the palm, guided it next to the soft swell of her breast.

It was all there for him to read in her eyes. He was her dearest, most loved captain, and he was her husband. There was no other man to whom she would willingly give of herself.

The realization Violet had pledged herself to him and to him alone inflamed him. With a groan, Dane covered her mouth with his, his tongue thrusting between her teeth to taste her exquisite sweetness. A sigh breathed from her depths, and she reached to him, her hands moving feverishly over his chest. She was all fire and generosity, was his surprising Violet. Her sweet, untutored ardor ignited a burning desire like none other he had ever known before.

Hungrily, he molded his lips to the nipples of her breasts, first one and then the other. Shuddering with pleasure, Violet sank her fingers into his shoulders and arched against him. Then, lower still, he teased and tantalized her, until, spreading wide her thighs, he parted the swollen petals of her body. Marveling to find her already flowing with the heady nectar of arousal, he lowered his head to her.

"The devil!" Violet gasped, startled at Dane's liquid caress of the bud within its petals. Faith, what the deuce did he think he was doing? She was like to explode with molten fire, and he was not with her!

"Softly, my girl," Dane said hoarsely, lifting his head. "There is nothing to fear in what I am doing."

"The devil there is not," groaned Violet, clutching her hands in the pillows. "I fear I shall burst if you do not stop, and that I could not bear. I will not do this without you, Dane; I swear it. Not this time. Not again."

"No, not this time," uttered Dane with a harsh laugh that was more in the nature of a groan. He was painfully aware of the hard bulge against the front of his breeches. Egad, he doubted he could endure the agony of denying himself a second time his need to sink his shaft into her. Leaving her, he stripped off his shirt, followed swiftly by his boots and his stockings. At last, freed of his breeches, he turned back to her, only to halt at the sight of Violet.

She was breathtakingly lovely, all silken smoothness and feminine curves and valleys. Her breasts were full and high and magnificently rounded. Her waist was hardly larger than the span of his hands, her belly firm and flat. Her legs, long and slender, tapered to delicate ankles and shapely feet. In the pale glow of the shaded lamp, her eyes shone huge in her face like starlit pools of mystery drawing him into their depths.

Easing himself on to the bed beside her, he leaned over her, his eyes searching hers.

"Sweet, beautiful Violet," he whispered, touching his

lips to her hair. "I have been driven nearly mad with wanting you. Tell me you want me, too."

Violet, who had just been given to see her dearest captain in all his masculine glory, could not but think that a somewhat frivolous question. Dane in a coma had presented a magnificent specimen of manhood, sculpted to a muscular hardness by physical hardship and what she did not doubt was a spartan existence. Dane awake and fully aroused could not but serve as a glorious vision of male virility. Had Sir Jeremy Biddle been privileged to see him thus, she was quite convinced he would have been inspired to paint Dane in the guise of Prometheus unbound.

"I want you, Dane," said Violet, pulling him down to her. "So much so I think I should have perished from desire had you left me."

"Jade," unequivocally pronounced Dane, who had not failed to glimpse the gleam of laughter in her eyes.

Immediately she sobered. "How could you think I should not want you, my dearest, most provoking captain?" she said, taking his breath away with the warmth of her gaze. "From the moment you kissed me, I have been wanton and shameless in my pursuit of you. Should we live to be a hundred, I daresay I shall never cease to do all in my power to lure you to my bed."

It was a prospect to boggle the mind, thought Dane, who was singularly aware Violet would have to do little more than glance at him across a crowded room to inspire thoughts of bedding her. Egad, he was inspired now almost beyond bearing to plunge himself into her.

Leaning down to her, he aroused her swiftly with his hands and his lips until she writhed beneath him, her head moving aimlessly against the pillows, her fingers clutching at his shoulders.

"Hurry, Dane, I pray you," she cried out to him, as she felt herself deliriously carried on a rising tide of blissful torment. *"I am like to die of needing you!"*

"Soon . . . sweet . . . Violet," Dane hoarsely assured

her. Sensing her reach for the thing just beyond her comprehension, he hurriedly parted her thighs and inserted himself between them. Fitting the head of his swollen manhood against the lips of her body, he held himself over her. "I fear you may be in for something of a surprise," he cautioned, feeling the sweat pour over his body. "Trust me, Violet, to carry us both through perilous waters."

"You must know very well that I trust you, Dane," gasped Violet, wondering what the devil he was waiting for. Faith, she was deliriously near the point of exploding from sheer anticipation.

Then, theorizing her dearest captain might be entertaining some lingering doubts concerning plunging past the point of no return, Violet wrapped her legs around him. "I promise I am ready for anything," she offered in the way of encouragement. "I pray you will not be afraid to open the budget."

Grimly, Dane stared at her. She had not the slightest notion what lay before her. But then, there would seem little point in delaying the moment of enlightenment. Having reached the natural culmination of previous events, he saw but one course before him. Slowly but inexorably, he buried his shaft in her.

Violet, prey to a searing burst of pain, cried out.

Instantly, Dane went still, his every muscle tensed and straining with the effort to contain his torment of need. "My poor darling," he said, touching his lips to her forehead. "You are sadly disillusioned at the moment, but the pain is behind you, I promise." Carefully, he began to move inside her, making slow, shallow forays. "Trust me, Violet. I would never lie to you. We are merely at the threshold of a magnificent chain of events."

It was true. Violet had indeed felt her expectations dashed, but not her trust in Dane. *That* remained inviolate. Unclenching her misapprehension, she surrendered herself to her dearest captain's tender manipulations.

His slow, rhythmic thrusts reawakened a whole new range of pleasurable sensations quite unlike anything she had ever imagined before. It came to her in a delirium of exquisite torment that there was nothing quite so glorious as an all-consuming passion with this man to whom she had given her heart and soul. She was a Rochelle, and she knew she would never love another as she loved Dane, perhaps as he had loved Lynette.

She was aware of a swift stab of pain in the vicinity of her breastbone. Then even that was swept away in a frenzied sense of urgency. Reaching for something she did not understand, she clutched at Dane with frantic hands.

"Dane, *do* something, I beg you," she gasped, feeling she must surely explode if he did not help her. "Faith, I cannot bear it! I feel as if I shall die of it."

Dane, borne on a fierce swell of triumph, drove himself savagely into her, carrying them both swiftly to the heights. Then at last, feeling her explode in a shuddering wave of release, he plunged deeply, spilling his seed gloriously inside her.

Together they collapsed in a tangle of arms and legs, their hearts pounding and their breathing coming in ragged gasps.

It was to come some moments later to Violet that she had never before felt so wondrously sated or so gloriously languid as she did at that moment with Dane lying beside her, one arm flung over her waist and his face pressed into the curve of her neck.

For the first time in her life, she had let someone past the walls of her defenses into the secretmost recesses of her heart, and he had taken her to the heights of passion. Surely, this was the most sublime sort of communication possible between husband and wife.

A whimsical smile played about her lips as it occurred to her that in the months and years to come there must certainly be times of discord and misunderstanding; but so long as they could still retreat into the blissful realm of shared passion, they would never truly lose one another. This must surely be love's greatest gift.

Then Dane, stirring next to her, served perversely to remind her that she very likely was doing no more than building castles in the sky. Dane did not love her. He was drawn, like all the others, to her beauty, but his heart remained his own. Really, it was too bad of him, she thought.

Chapter 8

Violet, critically observing the small, erect figure dressed in a skeleton suit with its tight blue jacket buttoned above the waist to tapered nankeen trousers ending at the ankles, could not but think that motherhood was a far more complicated proposition than she had ever previously imagined it would be.

Of course, she could not but acknowledge that her experience with children had heretofore been limited to her cousins, Alexandra, Valentine, and Chloe, who were thirteen, eleven, and nine years of age respectively. That experience, encompassing two and a half years of living in Albermarle Castle in the company of Roanna and her three burgeoning hopefuls, should have been sufficient to quell any sentimental fantasies Violet might have entertained concerning the joys of motherhood. That it had not was perhaps due to Violet's penchant for slipping away to more serene environs whenever something threatened to disrupt her peace and tranquillity.

Nevertheless, the day Violet's Aunt Roanna had finally made up her mind to stand up to her father-in-law, the

duke, whom she had long held in dread for what she
did not doubt was his aversion to her, had led to the
not unhappy outcome of removing her and her young
family permanently to London.

How like His Grace to do the wholly unexpected,
thought Violet fondly. Certainly Roanna, when she had
been brought to an awareness that, far from confining
her and her children to the dungeons for her impertinence, the duke had undertaken to establish her in a
house, fully staffed and furnished, in the genteel environs of Stratton Street, had been overcome with surprise.

But then, Violet did not doubt that Roanna, until that
moment of enlightenment, had never understood that
Albermarle had only to be shaken out of his habitual
abstraction to see to the heart of a matter. What he had
perceived was a woman who was languishing for want
of her own domicile in a milieu calculated to stimulate
her domestic and social instincts. The remote fastness
of the castle had sapped her vitality. London had seen
her flourish, just as Albermarle had no doubt perceived
that it would.

Whimsically, Violet wondered what her grandpapa
would have seen had he been present today at Blackthorn House in London to witness Violet's first decisive
acts in the realm of the nursery. This was, after all, the
momentous occasion of the breeching of Lord Fennington.

Thus far, judging from his lordship's dour expression,
not to mention the unmistakable signs of recent tears
on his cheeks, she was not sure whether it was going to
prove an altogether satisfactory endeavor. But then, the
transformation from the outward appearance of frilly
femininity to one of unadulterated masculinity had
been profound, to say the least.

Somehow, when she had first laid eyes on the child,
she had known that somewhere beneath the voluminous

petticoats and mass of blond curls allowed to grow to unseemly lengths must be a dyed-in-the-wool boy.

She had not been mistaken, thought Violet, viewing with approval the boyish face beneath the short-cropped hair combed forward over the brow. The boy was slender but well made and promised fair to be judged more than handsome when he grew to manhood. In the meantime, he presented an aspect of injured boyish pride.

Violet could not but think it a pity it had been left so long to cast off the boy's petticoats. The child was nearing his seventh birthday. But she supposed it could hardly have been helped. The boy's mama, after all, had unfortunately perished just as Philippe reached the customary age of breeching, a circumstance that must naturally add to the gravity of Philippe's forced passage from infancy to boyhood. In his childish grasp of events, his petticoats and curls must naturally be associated with his memories of his mama and the only home he had known until he had unhappily been uprooted from everything dear and familiar.

And now he found himself once more transplanted, this time with strangers. Even his father, she thought with pity, recalling to mind the story Dane had related to her as they lay, sated in the wake of passion on their wedding night—the story of Lynette and the young British naval officer who had been taken prisoner after his sloop-of-war was sunk off the coast of France.

A surge of tenderness swept over and through her at the memory of Dane's voice, falling quietly in the silence. Afraid to disturb his train of thought, she had remained perfectly still, prey by turns to feelings of enthrallment, horror, and pity. Even now her heart thrilled at thought of the cold nerve of the man who had sailed his sloop in brood daylight through a narrow inlet into the very midst of the enemies' ships at anchor.

She marveled that she had sensed no rancor in Dane's dispassionate account of the intercepted French communiqué that had been the cause of the ill-fated mission. It had seemed rather too convenient that a fishing boat loaded with spare masts and spars should venture out into the teeth of the British blockade. That it had carried a shot-weighted pouch containing dispatches to Admiral Roche from Napoleon himself was too farfetched by half. The Frenchman's first instinct upon realizing he was about to be boarded must surely have been to toss the incriminating pouch into the sea, and yet, markedly, no such attempt had been made.

It had little availed Dane, a junior officer, to voice his misgivings to his commodore, who, eager for promotion, had dismissed them as preposterous. When Dane had persisted in suggesting a boat assault under cover of night and supported by marines on the shore, the commodore had even gone so far as to question Dane's loyalty and courage.

Violet had not hesitated to silently condemn the man's shortsightedness. He had ordered the fragile *Mercury* to lead the way into the baited trap, and Dane had gone, knowing what might come of it.

What had come of it was the loss of his ship and more than half his men to the waiting shore batteries. That he had still managed to disable a French two-decker and numerous small vessels before turning his own command into a fireship and ramming it into an anchored eighty-gun ship of the line had seemed to Violet nothing short of miraculous.

To Dane, the death toll added to the loss of his beloved *Mercury* had outweighed all the rest. The commodore had paid the ultimate price for his arrogance. Struck down in the first barrage by a splinter, he had not seen his command turn back in the face of impossible odds. His own flagship had limped to open sea under cover of the smoke billowing from the *Mercury* clasped in a death embrace with the French man-of-war.

For his impudence in having wreaked havoc on the

enemy, Dane was taken prisoner, along with the tattered remnants of his crew who had managed to swim ashore. Six months in a French prison had brought him to the reluctant realization that a prisoner exchange was not to be forthcoming.

Naturally he could not have known then that his capture had gone unreported or that, consequently, he was presumed to be dead. The one thing he had had to his advantage, however, was Murdoch, who had been allowed to remain to serve as his captain's personal servant.

One night, seven months into his imprisonment, he had hardly expected to be awakened in the middle of the night by his grinning coxswain. Having been employed by the captain of the guards to help carry a newly arrived load of wine casks to the cellars, Murdoch had taken it upon himself to disable his guard and relieve him of the keys to the cells.

Without access to so much as a rowboat, there had been no escape possible by sea. They had fled inland. Chance—or, Dane had added whimsically, the inevitable culmination of a particular chain of events, perhaps—had brought them to the isolated country house and Lynette Lambert.

Violet, for once, had been more inclined to the opinion that divine providence had had a hand in it. After all, Dane could have found no better an ally than a beautiful former aristocrat who, despite Napoleon's declaration of amnesty, had little reason to love either the Revolution or the new order, which had seen the death of her parents and the end of the life to which she had been born.

It had not hurt, either, that she was the sister of *Capitaine* Philippe Lambert, one of Napoleon's most decorated naval heroes. The soldiers who had come in pursuit of the escaped prisoners had not even searched the house.

Violet, lying in Dane's arms, had not found it difficult

to believe the beautiful Lynette had come quickly to love her fugitive captain. Dane, she knew from personal experience, was the sort of man women would find easy to love.

Still, Violet could not but think there was something Dane had not told her. The daring escape in a fishing boat, the rescue at sea by an East Indiaman, the wedding performed by the ship's captain had somehow left something out of the telling. Or perhaps, Violet told herself chidingly, she simply had no wish to accept that Lynette Lambert had fled her home, her country, and everything she had ever known out of an all-consuming passion for her British naval captain. The devil, it was a romantic tale to rival that of Genevieve Hayden and her beloved Edmond, Duke of Albermarle!

It was a romance, furthermore, Violet reminded herself, that had produced an offspring. Lord Fennington awaited her pronouncement of approval.

"I think," said Violet, placing the side of her index finger meditatively to her lips as she walked in a circle around the small figure of the boy, "that I have seldom seen a handsomer suit of clothes. They would appear to present a perfect fit. Would you not like to come and see for yourself, Philippe?" Violet asked, drawing the boy to the ormolu looking glass.

It was, perhaps, an infelicitous move on Violet's part. Upon viewing himself solemnly in the mirror for five or six seconds, Philippe's face crumpled, and he began to cry—loudly and vociferously.

"He . . . cut . . . off . . . my . . . *hair*," sobbed his six-year-old lordship between heartrending hiccoughs. "The big oaf. I will cut out his heart when he is sleeping. I will feed it to the dogs, and then he will be sorry."

"No less than should I, Philippe," said Violet, eyeing the child speculatively. "Or should your papa, for that matter. Mr. Murdoch is your father's very good friend. I believe you will find he is your friend, too, if you will only give him the chance."

"He is *not* my friend. I don't like him. I want Nanny Tidwell. I want to go home."

"Yes, of course you do," uttered Violet, reaching instinctively to pull the child to her. "But your home is with your papa and me now."

"I don't like it here," declared his lordship, twisting away from Violet's grasp. "I don't like you," he added, delivering her a well-placed kick to the shin. "You are not *ma mere.*"

Turning, he fled for the door—and collided with a pair of hard, muscular legs impeccably clad in skintight dove gray unmentionables tucked into the tops of brown Hessians shined to an uncanny sheen of perfection.

"Going somewhere?" queried a thrillingly soft masculine voice.

Tilting back his freshly shorn head, Lord Fennington peered doubtfully up into cold, hooded eyes the mesmeric blue of lapis lazuli.

"Yes, no doubt," murmured the gentleman, reaching down to grasp the young scapegrace by the scruff of his aristocratic neck before he could bolt again. "I beg your pardon, Lady Blackthorn. Does this belong to you?"

"Gideon!" exclaimed Violet, who, having dropped onto the sofa, was occupied with ruefully chafing her injured member. Coming to her feet, she limped across the room to plant a buss on her brother's smooth-shaven cheek. "Devil," she said fondly, stepping back to survey the Marquess of Vere's tall, handsome presence. "Where have you been keeping yourself? And however did you find me?"

"Having happened on the announcement of your nuptials in the *Gazette,* I was moved to try and discover how I came so suddenly to acquire a brother-in-law. A naval hero, Violet?" said the marquess, quizzing her with his eyes as he took her left hand in his. "I marvel he was ashore long enough for you to meet him, let alone persuade him to the altar." He saluted her knuckles, his glance lingering on the shiny band of gold as he lifted his head. "I believe I detect our grandsire's influence. But then, this is the approximate time one might expect to find our great uncle, the Right Reverend Long, at his yearly retreat at Albermarle, is it not?"

"You know very well it is," replied Violet, awarding him a grimace belied by the gleam of laughter in her eyes. "Or *was*, a little over three weeks ago. Directly after the wedding, we went to Blackthorn for a day or two before traveling to Kent to retrieve Philippe, along with his nanny. As it happens, you have already met Philippe, Viscount Fennington. Philippe, this is my brother, the Marquess of Vere."

"I believe Viscount Fennington is something less than pleased to make my acquaintance," observed Vere, his smile gently mocking the boy's stormy aspect. "No doubt he is contemplating making his apologies for his ungentlemanly conduct—are you not, your lordship?"

Violet held her breath as the boy and the man exchanged a long, assessing glance. She was hardly surprised when Philippe was the first to drop his eyes. Vere, in the proper mood, could freeze a grown man's blood with naught but a look.

"Beg your pardon," muttered the boy in an almost indistinguishable jumble of words. "Shouldn't've kicked you." Then, looking straight into Violet's eyes, "May I go now?"

Violet suppressed a sigh. "Yes, of course, Philippe. Nanny Tidwell is waiting for you in the nursery."

"Lord Fennington, one must presume," remarked Vere as the boy made a hasty escape through the door, "represents the *mixed* joys of parenthood. I suggest it would be wise never to turn your back on him, *enfant*."

"I fear in his present state you may be in the right of it," agreed Violet with a rueful grimace. "He took an instant dislike to me, and everything I have done since has seemed only to make matters worse."

A circumstance she did not hesitate to lay at Miss Hannah Tidwell's door, she added silently to herself.

The nanny was a consummate master at subtly undermining Violet's authority.

No matter what Violet tried, Miss Tidwell never ceased to remind the boy that his mama had done it differently. Worse, the woman must certainly be aware Violet dared not deprive Philippe of the one remaining link to his mama. Indeed, she must feel perfectly secure in her position.

"Still in the nursery, is he?" murmured Vere, leaning forward to examine, hanging over the mantelpiece, a Gainsborough landscape depicting a melancholy scene of the forest at twilight.

"Until recently and since the demise of his mama, he has been living in Kent with his nanny. He is very attached to Miss Tidwell, who, despite her advancing years, remains absolutely devoted to him."

"Yes, I shouldn't wonder if she is," agreed Vere, straightening. "On the other hand, perhaps the boy would benefit from a masculine influence. A tutor, for example, to broaden his education to include manly pursuits that Miss Tidwell, for all of her nurturing instincts, could not possibly provide him. Especially if the tutor should be a relatively young man, physically fit and of an even disposition suited to a high-spirited boy in need of a steadying hand."

Violet stared at her brother with a look of dawning comprehension. "Faith, Gideon. How did you know?"

"That Miss Tidwell was proving a disruptive influence in your new existence?" Vere shrugged an elegant shoulder. "Even if it had not been fairly obvious from the boy's behavior, it was, of course, a logical assumption. An aging nanny with a single chick in the nest must have very little to which to look forward, save for retirement on a pittance."

"Naturally, she would wish to hang on to her last charge for as long as possible before being put permanently out to pasture," declared Violet, seeing it suddenly as Vere must have seen it at once. Indeed, as

Miss Tidwell had visualized it when the boy's father had shown up with a new, young wife to remove nanny and child from the cozy cottage in Kent. "That is it, of course, and who could blame her? Miss Tidwell must naturally be assured of a comfortable pension. She has earned it, after all. Further, we shall engage a tutor to wean Philippe from the nursery so she may enjoy her retirement all the sooner. How very clever you are."

"Clever enough," Vere rejoined, giving her a gentle look, "to suspect all may not be quite as it should be."

Violet, who knew her brother far too well to suppose he was speaking idly, went pensively still, her hand on the bellpull preparatory to ringing for a tea tray.

"You have heard something, Gideon," she stated baldly, and gave the bellpull a tug.

"How not? I have never been one to carry tales, but I have eyes and ears." Waiting for her to arrange herself on the settee, Vere settled, one long leg stretched negligently out before him, in the armchair across from her. "The new Earl and Countess of Blackthorn have been in London barely a fortnight, and already the rumors run rife."

"No, do they?" Violet, studying the arrogant mask of her brother's face, felt a queasy sensation start in the pit of her stomach. Gideon at his most inscrutable must inevitably serve as a warning. For Vere to have bestirred himself to come to her was indicative of the gravity in which he viewed the matter that had brought him there. "Somehow I am not surprised. Still, I am curious. What are they saying about us?"

"Nothing to which I should lend any credence," Vere answered softly. His penetrating gaze beneath drooping eyelids held unnervingly calm on hers. "You have only to give me the word, *enfant*, and I shall naturally take steps to put an end to idle speculation."

Violet, far from being reassured by those remarks, felt a chill course down her spine. She had little doubt as to the sort of "steps" to which Vere was referring.

"You will do no such thing, Gideon," she said, thinking the last thing she could wish was to have her brother exiled from England for having cut someone's stick for him at twenty paces. And yet how like Gideon to think nothing of offering to fight a duel for her without even first bothering to ascertain if there was any truth to the rumors abounding. "Blackthorn and I are perfectly capable of dealing with the idle tongues of gossipmongers without resorting to the sacrifice of someone on the field of honor. Vere, pray do not be afraid to open the budget. Just tell me what is being said about us."

"Very well, if you insist, *enfant,*" shrugged the marquis. Then with brutal directness, "People are saying the new countess is as beautiful as ever, but it is a pity she apparently cannot hold her husband's attention in the bedroom. It has not been even a month since the wedding announcement and already Blackthorn seeks his pleasures elsewhere."

"The devil they do!" exclaimed Violet, bolting to her feet to pace forward and back in agitation. She had been expecting something of quite a different order. "What a parcel of nonsense. You may be sure that whatever he is about, it is not his pleasures he is seeking elsewhere. Blackthorn and I are doing perfectly fine in the bedroom," she stated unequivocally, little caring that she had made such a bald-faced claim to her brother, who received the news with the merest gleam of sardonic appreciation in his otherwise impenetrable eyes.

And why should she? Violet thought furiously. It was the one aspect of their marriage that had not given her pause for thought. There was not a night that her dearest captain had not come to her bed either to transport her to the blissful heights of passion or sometimes simply to hold her in the darkness, seemingly content merely to have her near.

When they were in bed together, the barriers melted away so that even in the absence of words there was yet a tender flow of communication between them. When she lay in her dearest captain's arms, she knew he was not indifferent to her—that, indeed, he needed her in a way perhaps he himself did not perfectly comprehend.

Perhaps in time he might even come to love her, she told herself even as it came to her with a pang to wonder if his need sprang only from grief. No matter how hard she tried, she could not dismiss the haunting thought that he would always wear the willow for his lost Lynette. Even that troubling possibility, however, did not change the certainty she felt in her heart that Blackthorn was not seeking pleasure in an illicit love.

"No," she declared, coming about in her restless pacing to view the marquess with unwavering eyes. "I do not believe it. It is a lie promulgated by Blackthorn's enemies. They will do anything to harm him."

Vere eyed her steadily, his handsome features impassive. "There is more. Shall I go on?"

Deliberately, Violet made herself return to her seat on the sofa.

"By all means," she said, folding her hands in her lap with at least an outward semblance of calm. "I want to hear all of it."

Retrieving an exquisite Sevres snuffbox from his coat pocket, Vere deftly flicked open the lid with his thumbnail. "It would seem," he said, retrieving a pinch of his favorite blend between thumb and forefinger, "that the earl has been so indiscreet as to take up with a Frenchwoman of questionable reputation." Inhaling the pinch, Vere returned the snuffbox to his pocket. "Her name is Madame Gabrielle Benneau. Perhaps you have heard of her."

"No," replied Violet, not in the least fooled by her brother's elaborate display of indifference. Vere might take perverse pleasure in generating gossip about himself, but he disliked intensely his present role of talebearer. She could not but be touched that he would do it solely for her benefit. "Who is she?"

"A French émigré who fancies herself a member of the literati," he said, brushing an imaginary speck from his coat sleeve. "She is the founder of a group whimsically named *le société des philosophes du jardin.*"

"Good heavens," exclaimed Violet in no little astonishment. "Do not tell me Blackthorn has taken a sudden interest in Epicureanism, for I shall not believe it. I have little doubt that were he to do anything so—so—delightfully out of the ordinary, he would not hesitate to ask me to join him."

"No doubt you are in the right of it," agreed Vere, who did not betray so much as a flicker of surprise at that revealing outburst from his outwardly demure younger sister. "I wonder if Albermarle is aware of the extent to which you have indulged yourself in his library. I cannot think he would consider *De Rerum Natura* proper for consumption by a female of gentle birth. It was from the poem by Lucretius that you learned of Epicurus and his 'philosophers of the garden' was it not, my surprising Violet?"

"Actually, it was Pierre Gassendi's life of Epicurus that caught my attention," confessed Violet, smiling with perfect understanding at her brother. "My French, thanks to *Maman,* is much better than my Latin. But that is neither here nor there. Tell me about Madame Benneau."

"There is not that much to tell." Vere shrugged, having no intention of revealing the full extent of the Frenchwoman's unsavory reputation to his enterprising sister. She, he did not doubt, would not be averse to seeking the woman out. "Madame Benneau was a member of the minor aristocracy who escaped the Terror by fleeing to England. She surrounds herself with émigrés who, like herself, espouse the philosophy that the pursuit of happiness is the only true goal of the enlightened. She enjoys a certain cachet among a select number of wealthy English gentlemen who frequent her salon. It is hardly to her credit, however, that she numbers among her followers Jean Morin, a gambler and soldier of fortune, and Paul Despagne, an exiled member of the French literati.''

"No, does she?" queried Violet in dulcet tones, her lovely eyes quizzing Vere. "A gambler and an adventurer, really?"

"Impertinent brat," pronounced Vere, with his gentle smile of self-mockery. "I believe I do not envy Blackthorn the acquisition of a wife who does not hesitate to cut a man to the quick with her tongue. I am well aware of my own reputation as a rake and a gambler, I assure you."

"A reputation you have cultivated with great care, my best loved Gideon," declared Violet, who knew well her brother's real worth. Despite his wild, rebellious streak that had led him to indulge in every sort of excess, he was a man to whom one could always look in a crisis. His reputation might be a deal less than exemplary, but his heart was true to the select few whom he held in his affections.

"I should never dispute the word of a lady," said Vere, clearly not disposed to discuss either his motives or his shortcomings with his younger sister. "It is not, however, my reputation that is relevant. It is that of Madame Benneau, who, deservedly or not, has fallen under a certain amount of suspicion as a possible Bonapartist sympathizer."

"A reputation that must inevitably rub off on anyone who associates with her?" queried Violet, who began to see at last where Vere had been leading all along.

"There is speculation one need look no farther than Blackthorn to discover the identity of the elusive *Le Corbeau*, who has become a thorn in the sides of the Admiralty. It remains to be seen how your brave captain managed to relay information to the French, but it would seem that is of little importance to those who would condemn him."

"No doubt he sent them coded messages in the cannon balls he used to sink them," Violet declared bitterly. "It is all too absurd, Gideon. I have no doubt these suspicions are based solely on the event of his daring escape from France in the company of Philippe Lambert's sister, whom he subsequently married. It is hardly his fault Lambert is a decorated French naval captain. I daresay they have never met before, save, perhaps, in the line of battle. And still he stands condemned for what was in fact an act of heroism. The devil! I should like to know more about this alleged French agent."

"No doubt I should oblige you an I could. Unfortunately, it seems very little is known about him," said Vere, who was equally curious—who, in fact, had exerted himself to make subtle inquiries about the French agent among certain of his Uncle Richard's intimates. "It would seem the Lords of the Admiralty have for some time entertained the suspicion that information concerning the strength of our blockade, orders to the fleet, and intelligence gathered by our ships at sea and relayed home were being somehow leaked to the enemy. It was not until a courier was intercepted and found to be carrying a message advising where an invasion of England by small craft would be most effective that he was given his peculiar sobriquet. Apparently, his signature consisted of the likeness of a raven impressed in ink on the bottom of the page."

"But then surely that must be proof enough Dane could not have been a part of it," declared Violet. "He could hardly have been sending messages out of England if he was on a ship at sea."

"That was my first thought," agreed Vere, his expression singularly impassive.

"Faith, do not tell me," groaned Violet, who knew that look too well to mistake its implication. "He was at home in England when it happened."

Vere's gaze remained unwavering on hers. "Two years ago, your Captain Dane, in command of His Majesty's Ship *Antiope*, was preparing to rejoin the blockade fleet.

He was in London at the time, my dearest Violet, saying good-bye to his French wife.''

It meant nothing, Violet told herself some time later, when Vere, claiming he had business elsewhere but could be reached at Albermarle House in the Campden Hill District, had taken his leave of her. It was only an unfortunate coincidence that Dane had been in England when the courier was intercepted. That his wife was French meant even less.

Violet's own mama, after all, had been the daughter of le Marquis d' Anguoille, who, along with his marquise, had fed the hunger of Madame Guillotine. And if the new Earl of Blackthorn had friends among the émigrés from France, it was hardly surprising. No doubt he knew them through the influence of his former wife, who naturally would seek acquaintances among people who at least spoke her own language. To remain always separate, isolated by her French origins, would have been a lonely existence indeed

These surely were not grounds for the vicious rumors that painted the new Earl of Blackthorn as a Bonapartist and French sympathizer. How fickle was the public, who only months before had lauded Dane as a hero! And how dared anyone to make aspersions on her ability to hold the interest of her own husband! She was suffering from the wholly unfamiliar urge to scratch somebody's eyes out. The question was, whose?

Really, it would seem to make little sense, fretted Violet, who could not but marvel there should be any talk at all about two people who had only just arrived in town. They had not even had time yet to make morning calls, let alone present an appearance in the usual haunts, such as Hyde Park at the fashionable hour of five or the opera or the theatre or Vauxhall Gardens or anyplace where the members of the *ton* were like to flock.

That, however, was about to change, she decided. Her head came up in unconscious, not to mention uncharacteristic, defiance. She, Violet Clarisse Rochelle, Lady Blackthorn, who never in her life before had stood up to anyone, had never deliberately courted attention or used her much vaunted beauty to her own personal advantage, and had never dared to do anything that might offend the sensibilities of anyone, was going to show the *ton* that Lady Blackthorn was a different proposition altogether.

Beginning this very day, the new Countess of Blackthorn would do the unthinkable. She would not only make an appearance at Hyde Park, followed by a night at the opera, but she would do so in a grand manner sure to attract the notice of everyone.

Giving the bellpull a decided yank, Violet faced the empty room with a martial light in her eyes. First, she would send an appeal to Aunt Roanna to come immediately to the town house on Grosvenor Square. Together, they would plan a campaign that would win over the *ton* and dispel all of the despicable rumors once and for all. Whoever had deliberately started them, and she did not doubt the perpetrators were the same villains who had deliberately set out to destroy her dearest captain, would learn they had barked up the wrong tree when they took on Lord and Lady Blackthorn.

At last she had found something for which she would fight to the last breath, if need be. She would fight for Blackthorn and for herself—and for Philippe, who would somehow in the end be brought to accept her.

Blackthorn stepped down from his carriage in the modest environs of Berners Street, which was noted for its resident artists, sculptors, and painters, and, instructing the coachman to walk 'em, strode briskly up to the door.

He was acutely aware of feeling distinctly uncomfortable in his new coat of blue superfine, never mind that it had been cut by Weston himself, and his pantaloons of yellow kersymere tucked into the tops of brown Hussars. His neck cloth, tied in something called the Italian by his newly engaged gentleman's gentleman, was like to give him a stiff neck, and the scent of Rowland's Macassar Oil emanating from his hair freshly cut in the Roman style annoyingly followed him everywhere.

At least he could comfort himself that William Pitt's guinea-a-year tax on hair powder had not only prompted the Duke of Beaufort and his intimates to swear off ever powdering their hair again, but had further relegated the style to oblivion, save for those willing to bear the sobriquet of "guinea pig" rather than give it up. He might have had that indignity added to all the rest—egad!

The door, opening to his rap on the knocker, was a welcome interruption to his disgruntled thoughts.

"Captain Dane, isn't it?" declared the maid, dimpling as she dipped him a curtsy. "Beggin' your pardon, but I'd hardly've known you. Be pleased to come in, sir," she added, taking his curly brimmed beaver, his greatcoat, and his gloves. "It's been that long since last you were here. The mistress is in the sitting room."

"Thank you, Maggie. I shall show myself in."

Suiting his action to his words, he stepped past the beaming maid and made his way up the staircase and along the cozy passage toward the sounds of muted laughter, which fell silent at his light rap on the door. The call to enter was uttered in a rich contralto charmingly inflected with a lilting French accent. Aware of a vague sense of reluctance, Blackthorn reached for the door handle.

He was greeted by the warm glow of candlelight augmented by the spill of afternoon sunlight through French windows; warm, rich colors of tapestry wallhangings and an Oriental carpet; and graceful furniture tastefully arranged about the room to create an atmosphere of congeniality.

"Dane, it *is* you," was followed swiftly by the rustle

of silk skirts and the figure of a woman crossing swiftly to fling her arms about his neck. "You did come. I was afraid you would change your mind."

"No, how should I?" said Blackthorn, drawing back to look at Gabrielle Benneau, who was smiling up at him with a question in her expressive brown eyes, exotically slanted upward.

A woman in her early thirties, she was small, her head only just reaching to his shoulder, and femininely plump in a manner pleasing to men. Her hair, questionably blond, was arranged in a tapering cone bound with bright green ribbons to match her dress, and loose ringlets fell to the nape of her neck.

"You have not changed, Gabrielle. You are as lovely as ever."

"And you are a charming liar, *mon cheri*," Gabrielle said, laughing and patting him playfully on the cheek. "You, on the other hand, have changed a great deal, I think. You are a lord, I hear. The Earl of Blackthorn, *n'est-ce pas?*"

"*Mais oui, ma petite*," smiled Blackthorn, allowing himself to be led toward the two gentlemen, who had risen with alacrity to their feet. "I have joined the ranks of the aristocrats."

"And we have fallen to the ranks of the peasants," observed Jean Morin, a slender, well-knit fellow with the rakish air of a ne'er-do-well and the laughing eyes of one who promised fair to be a devil with the women. "It is of the most droll, I think."

"It is better to descend to the ranks of the peasants than to be cut down to size by the loss of one's head," opined Paul Despagne, studying Dane through pince-nez eyeglasses clipped to the bridge of his long, pointed nose. "*Monsieur le Capitaine*, you have the look of a man who is made uncomfortable by unaccustomed prosperity. I, who have been made uncomfortable by too many years of poverty, would be glad to change places with you."

Dane laughed. He well knew Despagne's view of the privileged classes: they were a blight on the peace and prosperity of the rest of society. Despagne had fled the Terror because he entertained similar views of the Directory and Robespierre.

Immediately, Dane sobered. "You heard about Lynette? And Philippe, her brother?"

"It was a thing of the most *terrible*," said the petite Benneau with a shudder. "We were greatly saddened— Paul, Jean, all of us who knew and loved Lynette. Still, she will rest easier in heaven knowing Philippe escaped from Malta. *Peut-être* the Tyrant will not have his head cut off *maintenant.*"

"Escaped!" Blackthorn stared at Benneau, his ears ringing.

"You did not know," said Morin sympathetically. "It is plain to see. He is Philippe Lambert. You did not think he would be content to remain in the hands of the British? Hardly a week from the day of his surrender, he stole his own ship and took back his freedom."

"There has been nothing in the papers. I have heard not so much as a hint of it."

But then, it was hardly surprising he had not, thought Blackthorn grimly. Gabrielle and her friends had their own undisclosed sources of information, which he did not doubt came straight from France. The Admiralty, on the other hand, would hardly be anxious to release the information to the British public that the French hero had retaken his own ship and sailed out from under the noses of his British captors.

Little wonder the former Captain Dane found himself under a cloud of suspicion. He had gone to see Lambert in his prison cell in Malta, and hardly more than a day or two later Lambert had made his escape. It would have been marvelous only if Dane had *not* fallen under suspicion!

"You must not take it so to heart, *mon ami*," said Despagne, clapping a hand to Blackthorn's shoulder.

"Lambert is a magician with the luck of the devil. He and all of his crew were being transported to England aboard his very own *Liberté*. While his British captors were busy fighting a storm, the crew and the captain broke free and took over the ship. The devil looks after his own, *non?*"

"It would seem so," agreed Dane, seeing in his mind's eye how it must have been. The British prize crew would have been only of sufficient strength to sail the ship. If Lambert and his senior officers had refused to give their word not to attempt escape, they would of necessity have been confined in chains to the orlop deck, while their crew was shut below in the holds. In the midst of a sudden storm, the shorthanded British crew would have been hard-pressed to sail the ship. They would have stood hardly a chance against a full crew of escaped French sailors.

The devil's luck? Blackthorn did not doubt in the least help had come from somewhere. It would not, however, have been the devil's work that ordained Lambert and his crew would be transported together on Lambert's captured ship. That, he did not doubt, had come from some higher authority. Only the admiral who had been in charge of prisoner transport and harbor defenses could have signed the orders to make it possible.

"The devil," he said. "Landford."

"Vice Admiral Sir Oliver Landford?" lilted Gabrielle with a trill of laughter. "*Bah*, he is a buffoon, that one. *Mais* he has formed the *tendre* for Gabrielle. And he enjoys to buy her pretty things. You think he is the one who helped Philippe?"

"I'm afraid I really could not say, *ma petite*," Dane smiled grimly. "I confess, however, that I should like to know more about him."

Gabrielle returned his smile, her eyes never leaving his. "Tell me what you want to know, *mon cheri. Monsieur l' amiral* likes to drink the wine. It loosens his tongue.

When next he comes to see me, he will tell me everything."

"Yes, but will he tell you anything someone would wish to know?" said Despagne with a doubtful shrug. "He is full of talk, but he says nothing. He is either a fool or a fox."

"I think you should not be fooled by that one," warned Morin, his habitual air of insouciance markedly at abeyance in the look he gave Gabrielle. "I have seen his kind before. He is a man who would cheat at cards and condemn his own mother to Madame Guillotine. His loyalties lie with no one but himself."

"He is a vice admiral in His Britannic Majesty's Navy," Blackthorn said with a chilling lack of emotion. "Are you saying he would betray his king, his country, and his duty?"

"I know nothing of what you ask, *mon ami*," Morin answered steadily. "In my heart, I know only that this is a man to whom I would not wish to turn my back."

Blackthorn felt a tingling travel the length of his spine. Sternly, he told himself Morin's particular choice of words might mean anything or nothing. More than that, the Frenchman had said all he intended to say. It would be worse than bloody useless to try and force anything more out of him. The last thing Blackthorn could wish was to alienate Morin and the others. They were all the allies he had who did not require proof that he was not a traitor and a spy.

All, that was, save for Violet, he amended whimsically to himself, as some thirty minutes later he stepped up into his carriage and gave instructions to the coachman to return to the town house on Grosvenor Square. She, from the very first, had remained unshakable in her conviction that he was a man of honor. Settling back against the blue velvet squabs, he deliberately unclenched his misapprehension with thoughts of his dreamy-eyed enchantress, who had become indispensable to his future happiness.

With no little irony, he recalled the ease with which she had drawn him into talking about himself, about the ships upon which he had grown to manhood and learned to take up the lonely mantle of command, and about the men who looked to him to lead them. Catching himself describing in no little detail the scenes of everyday existence aboard a ship of war, he had marveled that his sweet Violet gave every appearance of one deeply enthralled. She had a rare capacity for listening without making him feel in the least self-aware, a trait that had the unsettling effect of unloosing his tongue. He told her things he had never told anyone, and she, unlike others he had known, never turned his words against him. She was like a soothing balm to his soul, which had known too much of isolation and too little of love and laughter.

The extent to which she had already worked her spell on him had become all too self-evident upon their arrival at the ancient pile in the north of Devon, an event to which he had been looking forward with mixed feelings of dread and something approaching a morbid curiosity.

Strangely, with Violet on his arm, the rambling Tudor house, which in his extreme youth had loomed as a dark and brooding place plagued with shadowy recesses and haunting noises of the sort that might have been especially designed to frighten children, had assumed a whole new dimension of bright possibilities. Through Violet's eyes, he was made to envision rooms stripped of their blood-red damask drapes, their heavy brocade and velvet upholstery, and their seeming profusion of ponderous objets d'art of questionable merit. In their place wafted cream-colored curtains of caffoy or lace, chairs and sofas done in satins and tapestry, and live plants in pots, along with freshly cut flowers in crystal vases.

In Violet's capable hands, he did not doubt Blackthorn Manor would be transformed from the oppressive elegance that had stifled and haunted his boyhood into a light and airy place in which Philippe and any aspiring young hopefuls that might come after him could blossom and grow in childish abandon.

Violet, too, had been the instrument of opening his eyes to a new and reluctant understanding of the uncle who had lived there in solitary wretchedness. She found the letters, carefully preserved and wrapped in tissue and bound in a pink velvet hair ribbon, which had belonged to Miss Meredith Michaels. The dark secret that had bred rancor between brothers was revealed in the script of a schoolgirl who had been loved by both.

That night, with Violet lying in his arms, it was perhaps inevitable that he had found himself suddenly seeing his uncle through her dreamy eyes.

"How very lonely he must have been in this great, empty house. All those years, Dane, and he never married, not even to get himself an heir. I wonder he ever let you go to sea, knowing that he never had any intention of setting up his nursery."

The devil, he thought. It was not something that had ever occurred to him—that his uncle's harshness toward a boy who was obdurate in his determination to pattern himself after the father who had perished at sea might have stemmed from Blackthorn's conviction he would never marry or sire a son to take the place of his nephew. Suddenly a great deal concerning his understanding of past events had been called into question. Looking back with new eyes, Dane had come to consider the possibility that Blackthorn had, in his own way, been trying to preserve the son that, had circumstances dictated otherwise, might have been his own. He had done all in his power to keep that boy from embracing the same fate that had befallen Morgan Dane, Blackthorn's brother.

It was not a thought to give him comfort. The devil! He had been visited with an uneasy feeling of guilt as unwonted as it was unfamiliar. But then Violet, who missed nothing, had assuaged even that, reminding him that a boy who had only recently lost both his mother and father could hardly have been expected to know and understand what actuated his uncle. Certainly he could not have known his uncle was suffering from unrequited love for the woman who had loved and married Morgan Dane.

The devil, thought Dane, sardonically aware of a mounting eagerness to see his countess. When he left the house that afternoon, ostensibly to visit the tailor Albermarle had recommended to him, Violet had promised him a surprise upon his return. He suffered a twinge of conscience at having deliberately failed to mention an additional call at the home of Madame Gabrielle Benneau. It was one thing to have invited speculation by marrying the duke's granddaughter. It was quite another to openly involve her in his efforts to discover the identity of the French agent, and he did not doubt that would be precisely what would happen were he to tell Violet about the woman who had been Lynette's closest intimate since childhood. The last thing he could wish was to wake up one morning to discover the Countess of Blackthorn was become the newest member of *la petite* Benneau's *société des philosphes du jardin!*

Blackthorn was aware of a quickening of his heartbeat as he stepped down from the carriage and, with a sardonic sense of the unreality of his newly elevated state, strode past the exceedingly superior Reginald Potter, his London butler, into the four-story brown brick, which had the distinction of also belonging to him.

"Be pleased to inform Lady Blackthorn I have arrived and desire her presence in the study," he said, allowing the wooden-faced Potter to relieve him of his curly brimmed beaver, greatcoat, and gloves.

"I beg your pardon, milord," intoned the butler, "but Lady Blackthorn is entertaining guests in the rose room. She requested you join her upon your arrival."

"I see," said Blackthorn, suffering a stab of disappointment. He had had in mind a more intimate homecoming than a ladies' tea party at which he would feel gauche in the extreme. "Very well. Thank you, Potter."

Mounting the stairs with a deal less enthusiasm than that with which he had entered the house, he turned his steps down the passage to the formal sitting room, which, decorated with wall hangings featuring a profusion of pink and white roses against a pale yellow background and furnished with téte-à-tétes and dainty chairs with spindly legs, he thoroughly detested.

Steeling himself for the ordeal before him, he opened the door—and was met with the sight of his countess holding court in the midst of a host of blue coats. At his first astonished glance, he picked out Admiral Sir Marcus Llewellyn, Admiral Sir William Stanhope, a commodore who, due to a marked family resemblance, he suspected to be Violet's Uncle Richard Rochelle, two captains, and a lieutenant!

Egad, he thought.

Chapter 9

It was to occur to Blackthorn often in the succeeding weeks that he would rather take on a fleet of enemy ships single-handedly than attend another soiree, dinner party, or gala. Indeed, he would rather face the wrath of the Admiralty for dereliction of duty than stand for one more fitting for a coat, waistcoat, or pair of unmentionables.

In his entire career as a naval officer, he had never possessed more than three uniforms at any given time, and he could well remember numerous occasions upon which he had no more than a single shirt to his name that could be considered remotely suitable to wear when summoned on board the ship of a superior. But then, a naval captain was a far cry from an earl, whose countess had become the town's reigning beauty.

Somehow he had never suspected that beneath the façade of the dreamy-eyed enchantress was a female who could ever entertain ambitions of setting herself up as the darling of the *ton.* Indeed, had anyone told him the woman who had sought refuge in her bedchamber to escape the adulation of an overabundance of admirers—

who, indeed, had fled her home in order to elude a siege of determined suitors—would seek to establish herself as London's leading hostess, he would have declared without hesitation that person was deluded.

And yet, in the six weeks following the eventful afternoon of what Blackthorn had come cynically to term the "Admirals' Tea Party," Violet, Lady Blackthorn, had launched herself on a veritable whirlwind of planned social events. They had included more dinner parties than he cared to count, at least half a dozen soirees with impromptu dancing and cards, an impromptu musicale in which Violet herself had performed, displaying a wholly enchanting mezzo soprano he had not known she possessed, and, finally and most significantly to Blackthorn, an alfresco children's party in honor of Viscount Fennington's momentous graduation from the nursery to the schoolroom.

And now, not satisfied at having achieved Princess Esterhazy's accolades, which proclaimed Lady Blackthorn's entertainments "the most delightful of the Season," Violet had determined on giving a masquerade ball three weeks hence for which she intended transforming the ballroom into a fantasy garden of forbidden delights. Blackthorn, who disliked the notion of having to play host to three hundred guests at a gala that was to feature any number of satyrs, wood sprites, and fantastical mythological creatures, had not pressed to learn what sort of forbidden delights Violet intended. It was enough that he had managed to impress upon his wife the fact that he had no intention of appearing in the guise of a trident-bearing Poseidon, not even to match her Venus.

The devil, he told himself, turning from contemplating the fire burning in his bedchamber fireplace. He should be pleased that Violet, far from occupying herself with trying to discover the identities of his enemies, who had turned from firing guns at him to sending poisoned barbs in the form of vicious rumors at his back, was busy with playing the hostess. Thus far it would seem her strategy of silencing the gabblemongers by charming them into submission was proving surprisingly effective.

According to Violet's Aunt Roanna, it was no longer being touted among the *ton* that the former Captain Trevor Dane had been, at the very least, hand-in-glove with a network of French spies and was, at the very worst, the infamous *Le Corbeau* himself. Now everyone, it would seem, was talking about the Earl of Blackthorn's good fortune in having won the hand of the enchanting Lady Blackthorn, who was as gracious as she was beautiful.

With that assessment he could not agree more, Blackthorn reflected wryly, as, stripped to the waist, he grasped Murdoch's huge-fisted hand in his own and braced himself to test the strength of his injured arm. The wound was well healed, offering little more than a twinge of pain as he flexed against the big coxswain's powerful grip. Still, he had learned from past experience the steps required for full recovery. Every day, even before the bandage had finally been discarded, he and Murdoch had played their game, working the muscles to keep them pliant.

"It's coming along fine, sir, and that's no lie," pronounced Murdoch with no little satisfaction. "We'll have you back where you belong in no time."

"Yes, no doubt," agreed Blackthorn, touched by his coxswain's unswerving faith.

Where he belonged, he thought. In Murdoch's mind there was little doubt that that was on the deck of a ship. That realization troubled Blackthorn more than he could previously have thought possible. For the first time in his life, he was no longer sure what he was doing or where he was going.

In his steady climb up the promotional chain of command, he had never faltered from his duty. It had been enough to meet the daily challenge of command without looking forward to where it might lead. He had known men to turn coward rather than take the risks that might jeopardize their hopes for promotion, and he had known men to lead their commands to disaster in a reckless bid for glory.

For Captain Trevor Dane, it had been the task at hand to seek out and engage the enemy. And the Earl of Blackthorn? Hellfire! He did not even know who he was.

"And you, Murdoch," he said, studying the man's strong, homely features, tanned to a nut brown from his years in the sun. Broad and powerful, the man gave the appearance of having been hewn out of sturdy old English oak. "How are you settling in?"

"I couldn't ask for anything more, Cap'n." Murdoch grinned, thinking of the plump widow belowstairs who was not averse to warming his bed at night. "I expect I never had it so good."

No, thought Blackthorn. For a man who had been impressed into the service at the age of eighteen and who for the most part had never known anything but the harsh discipline of the lower decks, his present duties must seem like the just rewards of heaven. Murdoch would never see forty again, from the looks of him. He was already old for a sailor who had done and experienced all that he had. And yet, if Blackthorn ever went back to sea, Murdoch would follow him without question, so long as he could serve the cap'n.

The devil, he thought, when the coxswain had gone, leaving Blackthorn prey once more to his brooding contemplation. Murdoch's sort of loyalty was as foreign to the world of wealth and privilege as was Blackthorn himself. Earl or not, he was ill-equipped to play the kind of games that used innuendo and lies as weapons, which could be more potentially deadly than cannon fire. At least in the line of battle, one could see the bloody enemy and fire back at him! This sort of insidious warfare, lacking in rules or honor, made him feel as if he were groping in the dark for answers while his courageous Violet led the vanguard of the attack. Hell and the devil confound it! All of his fighting instincts were crying out to him that he was walking into a trap and taking Violet with him.

It was not the rumors or the growing absence of them that troubled him. It was the circumstance that the rumors had had their inception before the events occurred that were supposed to have formed the basis for them.

His name had already been linked with Gabrielle Benneau days before he called on her for the first and only time since his return to the City. He had the indisputable evidence for that in the singular event of the Marquis of Vere's visit to his sister.

A smile, distinctly ironic, played about Blackthorn's stern lips at thought of his countess's reaction to the news he had reportedly taken up with a Frenchwoman who not only was alleged to be a Bonapartist sympathizer but advocated the Epicurean philosophy of the pursuit of pleasure as a way of life.

"You might say," replied Violet in answer to Blackthorn's demand to know how the devil she had managed in less than four hours to assemble the illustrious gathering that had attended the Admirals' Tea Party, "that it was the result of a most fortuitous chain of events. You must not think because you married a penniless orphan she is without influence. As it happens, my Aunt Roanna was to entertain the gentlemen and their ladies this afternoon. However, when she received my earnest request to come and help me plan how to launch my career as a hostess, she simply brought everyone with her."

"But of course she did," agreed Blackthorn, much struck at Aunt Roanna's practical outlook. "And your uncle, Commodore Rochelle, I must suppose, was perfectly amenable to the sudden change in plans?"

"My Uncle Richard understands my Aunt Roanna," Violet answered, smiling fondly. "She is the dearest, most generous soul, but she is also exceedingly indolent by nature. I daresay she could not have been more pleased to be relieved of the duties of hostess."

"And you, on the other hand, were exceedingly gratified to find yourself entertaining a dozen guests you had not anticipated," speculated Blackthorn, his gaze penetrating on her lovely face. "Why, Violet? You will no doubt pardon me if I find it curious."

"But it is obvious, is it not?" queried Violet, looking the picture of demureness.

"No doubt it should be, my dearest," admitted Blackthorn, who had learned that Violet at her most demure was a Violet who was evading something she had rather would simply go away. "Unfortunately, I'm afraid that it is beyond my immediate comprehension. You are up to something, Violet, and I feel I really must know what it is."

"Yes, I daresay you do," agreed Violet with perfect equanimity. "On the other hand, I feel that there are very likely some things that *you* have not told *me*. Naturally, I should never think of prying, Dane. You may be certain I shall never be the sort of wife to demand explanations for where you go or what you do when you are out."

"No doubt I am gratified to discover I am married to the most understanding of wives, my dear," said Blackthorn, who could not see precisely what his enchantress's assurances had to do with the Admirals' Tea Party, but who was somehow sure the two must be logically connected.

"For shame, my lord," continued Violet, awarding him a comical moue of displeasure, which had the effect of wrinkling her nose in a manner Blackthorn found utterly charming. "You are roasting me, when I am attempting to be perfectly serious."

"Then naturally I must beg your pardon," Blackthorn said, assuming an appropriate expression of gravity, which brought an answering gleam of rueful laughter to his enchantress's lovely eyes. "You were saying you would never question my comings and goings," he judiciously reminded her.

"Yes, I was," she agreed, immediately sobering. "And how not, Dane, when you know as well as I do that, for all practical purposes, I trapped you into a marriage that you did not want? No, pray do not deny it. You made your feelings plain enough, and that is why I am grateful circumstances led to today's hallmark event. It is but the first of many to demonstrate to the world that we are doing perfectly fine in our bedroom pursuits."

Blackthorn stared at her with startled eyes. Egad, he thought, contemplating the possible ramifications contained in that proclamation. "An end no doubt greatly to be desired," he observed.

"I knew you would understand," applauded Violet, positively beaming at him. "If I can do nothing else, I can at least put an end to the idle speculation of wagging tongues."

Blackthorn, who, strangely enough, was able to glean a deal of information from those otherwise seemingly disjointed utterances, understood one thing indisputably. His dreamy-eyed enchantress was once again launched on a course intended to protect him—from what?

Certainly, there had been little doubt Violet was referring to rumors of a malicious nature. Bloody hell, he did not give a tinker's damn about what people might think of him. Violet, however, was a different matter altogether. He felt the birth of a cold, burning rage at the thought that someone had deliberately set out to hurt Violet, his sweet enchantress, who made it a practice never to hurt anyone.

"About our bedroom pursuits," murmured Blackthorn. Drawing Violet deliberately into the circle of his arms, he pressed his lips to the top of her head. "Are you quite certain you have no room for complaints?"

"You know I do not," replied Violet, slipping her arms without hesitation around his waist. "Have you,

Dane? I realize I am new at the art of love. Very probably there is a great deal I have yet to learn. If there were something—well, different—that you wished to try, you would not be hesitant about trying it with me, would you?"

Blackthorn, who had been occupied with running his hand over the luxurious mass of Violet's hair, went suddenly still. "Something different, Violet?" he said, much struck at the possibilities inherent in that particular question. "What precisely did you have in mind?"

"Dear, how should I know?" countered Violet, obviously caught unprepared to have her question followed up with a demand for details. "I have already admitted I am a novice at such things. Something exotic, I should not doubt."

"Exotic," Blackthorn repeated in measured accents. Egad, every session in bed with his exquisitely responsive enchantress was a blissful experience in the exotic.

"Really, Dane," blurted Violet, "I daresay you would be better equipped than I to come up with a suitable suggestion. You, after all, have the advantage of numbering the founder of a society of garden philosophers among your acquaintances."

At last, thought Blackthorn, they had arrived at the heart of the matter.

"And if I do, Enchantress," he said, holding her away from him so he could look into her face, "it does not mean I am a practicing member either of her philosophy or her society. I came to know her through Lynette. She was, as it happens, Lynette's oldest, closest friend."

"But of course she was," exclaimed Violet, her face lighting up with understanding. "And naturally you would think nothing of calling on her, especially as you know no one else in London. I knew that it had to be something like that."

"Yes, no doubt," agreed Blackthorn, feeling a fist clench in the pit of his stomach. "Tell me, Violet. How did you come to know I went to see Gabrielle Benneau this afternoon?''

"Oh, but I didn't," Violet said. "Not that you went to her today. Indeed, I had no idea where you were."

"But you heard I was seeing her. How, Violet?"

"Vere told me. With great reluctance, I might add," Violet answered, her beautiful eyes searching Blackthorn's face. "He paid a call on me this morning for the sole purpose of offering to put an end to the rumors that you were seeking your pleasures in the arms of a Bonapartist sympathizer because I was unable to satisfy your needs at home. I told him we should be able to deal with the rumors without challenging anyone to a ridiculous duel." Blackthorn had suffered a wrench, as, placing the palm of her hand tenderly against the side of his face, she favored him with the full force of her magnificent eyes. "And we shall, Dane, I promise."

She had kept her promise—egad, how she had kept her promise! However, while the rumors had stopped, at least for the time being, there was still the intriguing question of who had fostered them. It had been immediately obvious to Blackthorn that it was someone who was familiar enough with him to know of his acquaintanceship with Gabrielle Benneau. There would seem no other plausible explanation for why the rumors should already have been in place before the event of his one and only visit to the house on Berners Street.

The difficulty was that there should have been *no one* who possessed that particular knowledge other than Gabrielle herself and her two friends, Morin and Despagne. Blackthorn knew Gabrielle too well to suppose she would let that information slip to anyone. Nor did he consider Morin or Despagne likely candidates for spreading tales about him. They were devoted to Gabrielle and, perhaps more importantly, to Lynette's memory. It would never occur to them to betray the trust of the man who had rescued Lynette from her hated existence in France. They, at least, were men of honor.

Then who, wondered Blackthorn, hardly noticing the entrance of his valet, who, after a single assessing glance at his employer's aspect of preoccupation, went wordlessly about the task of laying out the earl's evening apparel. It came perhaps inevitably to Blackthorn to speculate that the answer lay with Lynette, who had never been able to bring herself to confide in him.

Suddenly it occurred to him he had not the smallest notion how Lynette had lived her life, who she had seen, or how she had spent her time. And yet it was exceedingly ironic that the elusive woman who had been his wife would seem to hold all the answers to the questions that plagued him. The devil, he thought. Most ironic of all was that she had carried them to the grave with her!

Violet, riding in the carriage with her Aunt Roanna, who gave every appearance of having nodded off in the corner, could not but reflect that there was a great deal to be desired in leading the life of a social butterfly. It was not precisely that she had not enjoyed Mrs. Rutherford's dinner consisting of French haute cuisine or seeing Kean play Othello, for she had. Nor was it that she entirely disliked being whisked from Lady Wortham's soiree to Lady Wexler's rout, and now on once more to Lady Stanhope's gala. A very few moments in attendance at each of the gatherings had been enough to ascertain the absence of those she had a most particular interest in seeing. It was simply that gadding about from one social fling to the next left her little time to be with the one person with whom she would most like to be.

Really, she could not blame Blackthorn for his stubborn refusal to accompany her on her endless round of social events. It was sufficient that he agreed to make his appearance briefly at one or two in a se'nnight to dance at least one dance with his hostess and one with his countess. After all, it would have been thought exceedingly peculiar were he to be seen to live in Violet's pocket. It might be construed either that the Earl of Blackthorn was of a jealous, mistrusting disposition or, worse, that he was a henpecked husband. That would never do. Besides, she mused with a fondly amused smile, his rarely made appearances had served to give him an aura of mystery and allure that did him no harm in the eyes of a jaded *ton*.

Of course, Violet acknowledged ruefully to herself, it was customary for husbands and wives to live their own separate lives. Unfortunately, while Violet, despite her years of exile at Albermarle Castle, had a vast network of acquaintances upon whom to draw, Blackthorn, who had spent his entire life at sea, had practically no one.

It was true her Uncle Richard, who obviously respected Blackthorn for his record of command and who recognized in him a man of his own stamp, had sponsored the earl's membership in the private gaming club that he frequented occasionally on his rare visits home. Unfortunately—or fortunately, perhaps, depending on how one chose to look at it—Blackthorn entertained a distinct aversion to gambling, which aboard ship, whether in the officers' quarters or below decks among the common sailors, had proven the ruination of too many good men. Gambling was the curse of the sailor, who had few other diversions in the long months at sea. And while Blackthorn was not averse to a game of chess and enjoyed a hand at whist on occasion, he found little to amuse in entering his name in the betting book or whiling away his time at faro.

He was, further, the exception to the rule of his day in that, in the norm, he found little allure in drinking to the excess that would have clouded his mind and his judgment. There would seem, in short, little in the life of the town beau to appeal to a man who was accustomed to the rather more serious pursuit of commanding ships and men in times of war.

That realization endeared her to her best-loved captain, even as it gave birth to a hollow space somewhere in the vicinity of her breastbone.

She had married the Earl of Blackthorn, but Captain Trevor Dane had captured her heart, and Dane would be compelled in the end to leave her. His mistress, after all, was the true possessor of his soul, and his mistress was the sea.

Really, it was the shabbiest thing, she thought. Indeed, one might even have said it was the poorest sort of joke that she, who had been granted the dubious gift of attracting males the way sugared water attracted bees, should lose her heart to a man who could never be content merely to be with her. He was a sailor who had been born to command. He needed his ship and the sea to feel complete.

Rather than watch him grow in discontent with the passing weeks and months, Violet would settle for nothing less than to see him returned to the life for which he was singularly fitted, indeed, the only life he had ever known or wanted. She would see him once again in command of his own ship, she vowed. And to that end, she must first see him reinstated in the good graces of the Lords of the Admiralty if she had to sell her soul to the devil to do it.

Which was why, she told herself, as the carriage arrived before Admiral Sir William Stanhope's four-story brown brick, lit up from within by chandeliers and presenting every evidence of housing a crushing squeeze, she was most particularly looking forward to this particular ball.

"Aunt Roanna," she said, reaching across to give the older woman a gentle nudge. "Wake up, dearest. We are here."

"Here is where I should least like to be, if here is anywhere but Stratton Street. Pray tell me I have arrived home, Violet, or I promise I shall never forgive you."

"I daresay you will never forgive me anyway, dearest aunt, for having disturbed your tranquil existence." Violet smiled. "And so I shall not hesitate to tell you we are arrived at Lady Stanhope's ball. Come in with me at least until I am assured Blackthorn will make his obligatory appearance to escort me home. It is all I shall ask of you."

"It is all I have the energy to grant you, my troublesome niece," declared Aunt Roanna, rousing herself sufficiently to set her headdress of peacock feathers straight on her head. "Promise me you will find me a chair, Violet, before you are swept away by your ardent admirers. It is the very least you can do for one who has worn herself to the edge of a sharp decline for you. I am sure I shall fit in perfectly with the dowagers and wallflowers. I feel I must look quite old and fagged from burning the candle at both ends."

"Yes, dear. Now come along," urged Violet, who thought her aunt, a woman at the advanced age of three and thirty and possessed of pale blond hair and a flawless ivory complexion, had never looked more stunningly beautiful. "I shall find you a sofa, if that will make you happy."

"Nothing will make me happy ever again if Richard finds out what you are up to," predicted Roanna, obediently descending from the coach to the curb to proceed with languid grace through the door tended by a stone-faced butler, standing at rigid attention. "And as for Vere, I daresay he will have a great deal to say that is unpleasant when he hears you have been cultivating the attention of one he holds responsible for every ill that has befallen him."

"Not *every* ill, dearest aunt," demurred Violet, scanning the sea of faces as she gave up her ermine-lined mantle to a servant and proceeded onto the gallery overlooking the ballroom a full story below her. "Only the deaths of his parents and the loss of his inheritance. Ah, there he is now—Vice Admiral Sir Oliver Landford, in close conversation with Sir Henry Granville. I wonder what they could be talking about."

"Very likely some exceedingly boring nonsense about deployments and tactics," speculated Roanna, smothering a yawn behind her fan.

"Perhaps. Only, from the look on Landford's face, I should think it is something rather more unpleasant than that." The next moment, seeing herself about to be set upon by a bevy of eager admirers, Violet pulled her Aunt Roanna into the secluded environs of a love seat set in an alcove with potted ferns on either side. "Here, dearest aunt," she said. "You see, I am as good as my word. Wait for me. I shall return for you as soon as Blackthorn arrives."

She was gone, then, whisked away before Roanna could protest that she had a distinct aversion to potted ferns.

While she was trying to work her way around the dance floor to a vantage point from which she might observe Vice Admiral Sir Oliver Landford and be viewed by him, it was to occur to Violet that having anywhere from half a dozen to a score of gentlemen hanging on her every word and gesture at any given moment was a hindrance she would rather have done without.

Not that anyone observing her would have guessed that she would gladly have wished them all to the devil. Her beautiful eyes seemed to sparkle with laughter, even as her smile dazzled all who came within her sphere. To all appearances, she was enjoying herself immensely. And all the while, she was acutely aware that not ten feet away from her, Vice Admiral Sir Oliver Landford was holding a court of his own.

And, indeed, how could she not be aware of it, she marveled, observing Sir Oliver over the flutter of her fan even as she pretended an interest in the heated speculation as to whether Lord Shelby's matched team of grays could outrun Mr. Featherstone's bays on a race to Brighton, a debate being waged just then between Mr. Markham and Lord Winters, who sat on either side of her. Vice Admiral Sir Oliver Landford had, in the wake of his verbal exchange with Sir Henry, steadily progressed from sullen tippling to a state of rancorous obfuscation, evidenced not only in the heightened floridity of his normally pink and white complexion and the leering expression in his bleary pale blue eyes, but in his blurred speech, which carried over the roistering strains of the gavotte just then rollicking to a boisterous end.

She was not sure what she had hoped to gain by placing herself in proximity to Landford. She did not really entertain the notion that she would overhear him say something to implicate himself in a nefarious plot against Dane, his former subordinate. Nor did she imagine for one moment that he would behave in such a manner as to give himself away in front of a ballroom of people. She was the daughter of one whom he had openly held in aversion. Somehow, she simply had the feeling if she brought herself persistently to his notice, *something* would come of it.

Hardly had that thought crossed her mind than she became tinglingly aware of a pair of white breeches-clad legs directly in her line of vision. Glancing up, she discovered a gentleman in the crisp blue and white uniform of a naval lieutenant standing over her.

"I beg your pardon, Lady Blackthorn," said the officer, bowing a trifle self-consciously at the waist. "We m-met at Sir Henry Granville's house party some weeks ago. I am Lieutenant Alastair Cordell. I daresay you do not remember m-me."

"But of course I remember you, Lieutenant." Violet smiled, her pulse inexplicably leaping.

Indeed, Lieutenant Cordell would be difficult to forget. Possessed of blond hair and rather vulnerable brown eyes, he would have been strikingly handsome, rather in the manner of an aging Adonis. He would, that was, had he not the wilting aspect of a wallflower at a coming-out ball and the habit of casting his eyes downward in painful self-awareness. No doubt his obvi-

ous lack of confidence in himself could be blamed for
his failure to have ascended higher on the ladder of
promotion. In his middle thirties, he was old for his
rank.

"You are Vice Admiral Sir Oliver Landford's aide, are
you not?"

"I am, indeed, milady. M-may I say that I—I wish you
happy on your recent nuptials and further request the—
the honor of the next dance?"

"As to the first, you are very kind, sir. Thank you,"
replied Violet. Closing her fan, she rose to her feet.
"And as to the second, I regret I am not dancing this
evening. Perhaps you would care to take a stroll on the
balcony. I find it is rather close in here. I should not
be averse to some fresh air."

"N-nor should I, ma'am," said Cordell, finding the
courage, apparently, to offer her his arm. "I should in
fact be honored to stroll with you."

Violet, excusing herself to the gentlemen, who vociferously objected to her being stolen away from them,
placed her hand on Cordell's arm and allowed him to
lead her to French doors that opened onto a balcony
overlooking a small enclosed garden and the stables at
the back of the house.

"Ah, that is better," breathed Violet, turning her face
into the breeze. "And ever so much more peaceful, too.
I fear I have grown used to the quiet of the Devon
countryside and find on occasion that the constant bus-
tle of the City palls."

"No one would ever guess it, observing you with your
cortege of ad-admirers, milady," said Cordell, watching
her as she leaned her hands against the rail of the
balcony and gazed up at the stars peeking through the
drift of clouds. "You have taken the *ton* by storm."

"Everyone has been most kind to me," replied Violet,
coming about to face the admiral's aide. "And to Blackthorn, now that he is Blackthorn."

"You are right, of course," agreed Cordell, assuming

a grave expression. "I—I should be the f-first to declare Captain Dane was treated shabbily." A rueful smile flashed across his handsome face. "Not that it matters what a lieutenant th-thinks, milady. H-had it been up to me, Captain Dane would have received a new command along with a promotion for his defeat of the French seventy-four. Unfortunately, I am only a—a—"

"A lieutenant." Smiling, Violet finished for him. "A pity you are not an admiral. We might have avoided a great deal of foolishness and grief. Have you always been in the navy, Lieutenant?"

"I began my career rather l-late in life," submitted Cordell, suddenly inordinately fascinated with the toe of his left shoe, "thanks to an—an unfortunate incident w-with a lady who had been promised by her father to a g-gentleman of rather more consequence than I. There was the threat of a scandal, I—I'm afraid, and my uncle was k-kind enough to obtain a commission for me in the navy t-to get me out of the w-way."

"Your uncle?" queried Violet, her interest pricked. "Sir Oliver?"

"No, S-sir Oliver was only persuaded to take me on as his personal aide, a circumstance for which I—I should no doubt be grateful. I fear I should be ill suited to a career at sea—unlike your husband, who appears to have been born to it. Will you and the earl be making your home in London?"

"I should think not," said Violet, who could not have countenanced a life in the City, especially with Blackthorn away most of the time at sea. "I daresay Blackthorn Manor in the north of Devon will be better suited to rearing children, especially boys, who should have room to learn to ride and fish and do all the things upon which boys appear to thrive."

"Yes, of course. As a n-newlywed, it would be only natural for you to look forward to the future."

"Not so far into the future as that, Lieutenant," Violet said, thinking of Philippe, who appeared to be blossoming under the tutelage of young Mr. Timothy Greene. "My husband has a son from his first marriage."

"A son who has you for his stepmama. What b-boy could ask for more? He is indeed fortunate."

"He would be fortunate if he had not lost his own mama," rejoined Violet, unreasonably annoyed at what would seem Cordell's awkward attempt to flatter her at the expense of empathy for the child's probable feelings in the matter. Biting her tongue to keep from delivering a sharp retort, she turned away to conceal the angry sparkle in her eyes. "He is only a boy of seven," she added quietly. "He misses his *maman* exceedingly, and who can blame him?"

Her attention was drawn by the sudden hush from the ballroom.

"It would seem our dance is over, Lieutenant Cordell," said Violet, who was loath to return to the tiresome press of her importunate admirers, especially without having learned anything of a pertinent nature from Vice Admiral Sir Oliver's personal aide. Still, it would hardly have done to linger on the balcony with a man who was not her husband, even one as unobjectionable as the unassuming Lieutenant Cordell. To do so would be to start tongues wagging all over again.

Coming about again, she started to suggest that they go in. The utterance never left her lips.

She froze as the French doors were flung suddenly open to reveal the thick-bodied figure of a man reeling drunkenly on his wide-planted feet.

"That will be all, Lieutenant," announced Vice Admiral Sir Oliver Landford, staring through bleary eyes at Violet. "You may go now. Your services are no longer required."

Blackthorn, having submitted to being dressed by Morton, his newly acquired gentleman's gentleman, and having dutifully arrived at Lady Stanhope's ball, could not but reflect that Violet's cure for gossip was perhaps more distasteful than the bloody demmed affliction. It was bad enough that he was little more than passably adept at performing the barely remembered steps of the country dances that formed the greater part of the repertoire at the galas he had attended. Unfortunately, he was even less well equipped to engage in light badinage with anyone, let alone the numerous beauties of varying ages who surprisingly had demonstrated an inclination to make eyes at him. Finally, he entertained a strong distaste for requesting the dubious pleasure of a dance with females who were utter strangers to him.

He found it cynically amusing that in adopting a posture of polite aloofness, he had managed to make himself an object of a deal of feminine speculation, which manifested itself in everything from coy glances over the tops of fluttering fans to the surreptitious caress of a stockinged foot against his leg beneath dinner tables—egad! Indeed, it had become uncomfortably apparent that the more he maintained his distance, the greater grew his attraction.

The devil, he thought, stepping down from the carriage. He had sailed his sloop *Mercury* into the jaws of annihilation with less trepidation than he felt now at the prospect of stepping through that door into the confusion of laughter and music and unfamiliar faces. It came to him momentarily to wonder when it was that he had apparently lost the capacity for gaiety. Then, squaring his shoulders, he went inside.

Blackthorn, relieved of his greatcoat and other accoutrements, was quick to note that the receiving line had long since disbanded. He would be saved the discomfort at least of having to make small talk with his hosts. Further, the announcement of his name, practically indiscernible over the low roar of voices and the lilting strains of a country dance just then in progress, drew little or no notice.

Blackthorn paused near the head of the stairway to gaze down into the ballroom in search of his countess. His glance paused briefly on the unavoidable presence of Vice Admiral Sir Oliver Landford, one hand deftly plucking a glass of wine from the tray of a passing waiter, and then moved on.

He found her almost immediately. Indeed, it would have been difficult to miss the bevy of gentlemen clustered about the tall, slender figure stunningly gowned in rich mauve, more the color of deep purple. He was sardonically aware his blood had quickened at the mere sight of her. The devil, and why should it not? She was the most desirable woman in the room, and she was his wife.

He turned and started toward the stairs.

"Here you are," declared a deep feminine voice. "Lord Blackthorn, at last. I am so pleased you decided to join us. We had almost decided to give you up."

Blackthorn, coming about, was met with the sight of a still attractive middle-aged matron who appeared genuinely pleased at his presence. "Good evening, Lady Stanhope. It is a pleasure to see you again."

"And I am most particularly glad to see you." Taking his arm, she led him a little to one side. "I have been so wanting to talk to you. There was little opportunity the other day at your wife's delightful tea. I have wanted to thank you for looking out for my son. William wrote of you often; indeed, it seemed he could write of little else. He admires you greatly, my lord."

"He is young, ma'am," said Blackthorn, smiling gravely. "When I was his age, I, too, looked up to my captain. I believe it is a common enough failing among the junior officers."

"You are modest," said Lady Stanhope, studying his face with kindly interest. "William said you were. He also said there was no man under whom he would rather serve. I deeply regret he is not serving under you now. I should not worry so about him. Perhaps you can tell me something of his new commander—Captain James Travis, I believe. Are you acquainted with him?"

"Indeed, ma'am," answered Blackthorn, picturing the big, hardy Travis with his booming voice and bluff manner. "Captain Travis is a good officer and a fair man. Rest assured, young Parker-Stanhope is in good hands."

"You cannot know how relieved I am to hear it from you." Lady Stanhope smiled. "Admiral Stanhope would say nothing of it. You understand how it is. Young William is first lieutenant to Captain Travis. He must make his own way. 'Only God or the devil can help him now.' "

Blackthorn, watching her, was not fooled by her attempt at bravado. She was an admiral's wife. She had experienced it all—the loneliness, the waiting and wondering. And now she had it all to do over again, this time with her son. It had been just so with his own mother, who had tried to discourage her only son's eagerness to follow in the footsteps of his father. At least she had been spared that final torment of seeing her son go off to sea.

"I shall not tell you not to worry, ma'am," he said, knowing there were no words of comfort to offer her. "I can only say you can be proud of your son. It is clear he takes after you, ma'am, and the admiral."

He left her then, assuring her in answer to her request that he would be pleased in future to call on her. To the evening, however, there had been added a pall. William Parker-Stanhope was on a ship at sea, and as first lieutenant, he stood poised at the brink of having his own command one day, perhaps in the not too distant future. It was everything for which a young officer lived and breathed—if, that was, he was not killed before he could achieve it. And he, Captain Trevor Dane, was left to play Lord Blackthorn, the society fribble.

Blackthorn's mood was little improved to discover that, while he had been occupied with talking to Lady

Stanhope about her son, Violet had disappeared from view. The devil, he thought, aware of a fist closing like a vise on his vitals.

"Get out!" Landford's guttural command hung in the air like an unclean thing.

Cordell's face flushed an angry red, and for a moment it seemed he would find the courage to defy his superior.

"It is all right, Lieutenant," said Violet, who had no wish to be the inadvertent cause of the officer's ruin. "I shall join you directly."

Cordell hesitated a moment longer. Then, apparently convinced he would do greater harm by remaining, he stiffly inclined his head. "Very well, milady. I—I shall be just inside the door sh-should you require anything."

Stepping past the vice admiral, Cordell exited with obvious reluctance.

"Impertinent bastard," rasped Landford on a drunken wheeze. "Ought to have him cast out of the navy. Bloody demmed troublemaker, that's what he is. And you, Lady Blackthorn. What devilry are you up to is what I'd like to know. Always popping up wherever I go. Watching me with those angel eyes. Do you think I don't know you'd like nothing better than to see me burn in hell?"

"You are mistaken," replied Violet, gazing at him with limpid eyes. "I daresay I should not wish such a fate on anyone. Surely that is for a higher authority to decide. Have you reason, sir, to fear such an eventuality?"

"You're a clever one, I'll say that for you," wheezed Landford, eyeing her malevolently. "You and your bloody fine earl. But it will avail you nothing. D'you hear? You think you know things, the whole cursed lot of you, but you'll never prove anything."

Deliberately, Violet clasped her hands before her at her waist lest she betray the sudden leap of her heart at that declaration from Landford. "What should we possibly hope to prove, Sir Oliver?" she queried, wondering if she were about to find herself flung at any moment over the balcony rail. "I'm afraid I haven't the least notion of what you stand accused."

"Don't you?" Landford lurched toward her, his florid face contorted with dislike.

The smell of sweat mingled with the sour stench of wine on his breath sickened her. Indeed, only with the greatest effort did she hold her ground as he loomed over her.

"Then why the bloody hell are you following me around? If you choose to continue on your present course, you'll get nothing from me, girl, but grief, I promise you. More grief than you are able to imagine. You may tell that to your brother, the bloody marquis, the next time you see him. Or your grandfather, the duke, if you will."

"You may tell *me*, Landford, here and now," declared a soft voice, edged in steel, from behind him. "Indeed, I am waiting."

Landford went deathly still, his expression undergoing a rapid change from bestartlement to cunning.

"Blackthorn," he pronounced with undisguised loathing. Ponderously, he came about. "I suggest, sir, you watch your bloody damned tone when you address me."

Violet's breath caught at sight of the hard leap of Blackthorn's glittering eyes. What Landford in his drunken haze had failed to perceive was frighteningly clear to her. The vice admiral could not depend on his elevated rank to protect him—not this time, not from Dane.

Blackthorn's voice came with velvet-edged softness out of the silence.

"I shall thank you to cease to embarrass my wife with language better suited to the galleys. One more foul word out of your mouth, and I shall be forced to instruct you in gentlemanly conduct."

"Instruct *me?*" blustered Landford, his mouth working. "You fool. I shall have you hauled up before a court-martial for insubordination."

"You will do nothing of the kind." Blackthorn stepped out in the open. Balanced easily on the balls of his feet, his arms hanging loosely at his sides, he presented a poised and menacing presence. "You will instead apologize to my wife."

Landford swayed on his feet, his head jutting forward as if he could not see Blackthorn quite clearly. "You do not give orders to me, Captain. I shall bloody well—"

Blackthorn moved, his hand flashing out to deliver Landford an open-handed slap, forward and backward, across his cheeks.

"Why, *you . . . !*" Landford, his face turning a livid red, lunged at his tormentor.

Blackthorn was too swift for him. Slipping easily past the other man's guard, he closed powerful fingers about Landford's unprotected throat and rammed his back into the wall. Landford went still, his eyes bulging, as Blackthorn thrust his face close to his.

"I am not one of your captains. In case you have failed to understand, I resign my commission."

"Dane, *no!*" Violet gasped, one hand clutching at the balcony rail to keep her from falling. It was as if Blackthorn never heard her.

"Now you will beg the forgiveness of my lady wife, or you will face me on the field of honor."

Chapter 10

Feeling the sickness slowly recede to be replaced by a terrible hollow somewhere in the pit of her stomach, Violet struggled to assimilate the dreadful thing that had happened.

Blackthorn had severed his last hopes of ever reinstating himself in the good graces of the Admiralty. All in a single moment, he had cast aside what had once been one of the most promising careers in the navy. Somehow, Vice Admiral Sir Oliver Landford's choking apology seemed a pale victory in comparison, especially when taken in the context that Blackthorn had done it all for a woman who had trapped him in a marriage he could not want.

Really, she could not bear it, she thought, and yet somehow she must. Somehow she must find a way to make it all up to him. Better yet, she must think of something that would put it all right again.

"You are wrong, you know," Blackthorn said quietly. "You must stop blaming yourself for what was bound to happen sooner or later."

Violet went suddenly stiff in the cradle of his arms.

"I am not blaming myself," she retorted snappishly. "Indeed, why should I? You have flung away your career for me, when really it was not in the least necessary, and now you think you can read my mind. The truth is, I am quite sure I have never been more put out with you, Dane."

Blackthorn, smiling mirthlessly in the darkness of the carriage, felt the pressure ease ever so slightly in his chest. One moment she had been white-faced and trembling with reaction, and the next she had found the composure to return to the ballroom as if nothing had happened.

Roanna alone had seen past the thin edge of her control to the anguish just beneath the surface. After a single eloquent glance at Blackthorn, she had said nothing, but, clasping Violet's hand, had led her, unprotesting, through the milling press to the door. There they had waited for Blackthorn to retrieve their cloaks. Then at last they had gained the carriage, and all the time Violet had maintained a brittle silence.

Perhaps he should have acceded to Roanna's desire to accompany her niece home. Instead, he had seen Violet's aunt safely installed in her carriage. Then, climbing in beside Violet, sitting rigidly upright, her hands clasped tightly in her lap, he had said nothing, but had drawn her to him in the darkness.

Holding his apprehension rigidly in check, he had waited. All the while, he bitterly cursed the luck that had kept him from Violet's side. He had never known the sort of rage that sliced through him as he stepped through the French doors to find Landford standing over Violet. It was like a cold, burning thing deep in his belly that had spread outward, leaving his mind strangely clear. He had known what he would do before he did it, and, more strangely still, he did not regret it. He had known, too, he would kill Landford if ever he threatened Violet again.

"I collect I am mistaken," he said, knowing he was

not. She was Violet. Of course she was blaming herself. It had all been there to read in her face. "In which case, it is hardly necessary for me to point out that my naval career was finished long before tonight. I have not given up anything that was not already lost to me. Certainly I did not fling it away for you, my impetuous wife. No doubt I am sorry to disappoint you."

"Well, you *have* disappointed me," declared Violet, refusing to be mollified. Indeed, it seemed suddenly the floodgates had opened up, releasing all the emotions she had kept bottled up inside her, so everything came pouring out of her in a torrent. Really, she could not help herself. "Indeed, I shall not soon forgive you for ruining everything. All the endless nights of parties and making sure that Landford took notice of me in the hopes he would do precisely what he did tonight. Oh, it is too bad of you. And *just* when he was on the verge of revealing something of a significant nature, you came bursting in on us—and cast your career away as if it did not matter in the least. You had only to wait a little while longer, until we had time to discover the Raven's identity, which you know very well is bound up somehow with Landford. We shall only have to do it anyway, you know very well we shall. It is, after all, the only way we may be certain someone will not be trying to put another pistol ball in you the moment your back is turned. And that I will not have, Dane. I love you far too much to chance losing you. It was one thing to reconcile myself to having to give you up for months and years at a time at sea. It is quite another to lose you altogether, which is what is bound to happen if you fling away your career. If you do not now, you will in the end come to despise me for it, and I simply could not bear that, Dane. You know I could not."

"No more than could I, my sweet, impossible Violet," rumbled Blackthorn, who had *not* known it; who, indeed, had sustained a swift stab of elation at the realization his enchantress loved him to the extent that she would do anything to ensure his happiness. She would even have endured the solitary life of a captain's wife rather than see him grow bitter with discontent on shore.

Not since his extreme boyhood when he had lived with his mother and sisters had anyone cared what became of him. Nor had he missed what he had never known. It had been enough to pursue his duty, to command a king's ship, to seek out the enemy and pit his cunning and skills against him. He had never asked for or wanted anything more.

Now a beautiful woman with a caring soul and a generous heart had shown him what it might be to love and be loved, and suddenly he knew duty alone would no longer be enough.

Wanting her more than he had ever wanted anything else before in his life, Blackthorn pulled her to him, his lips seeking hers with a hunger born of all the lonely years, a hunger he had not even known he had growing inside him and which had centered on this one slender girl in his arms. With Violet, he glimpsed the lost meaning of joy. With Violet in his arms, he could face anything. The devil, there was not time to wait until they reached home to take her!

Covering her mouth with his, he reached for the hem of her gown.

Violet, who had been ignominiously on the verge of giving in to a wholly unaccustomed shed of tears, was instantaneously distracted by Blackthorn's fierce tenderness. Indeed, she was suddenly quite certain the last thing she could possibly wish at that moment was to indulge in a fit of the vapors.

Never in all the times Blackthorn had transported her to the blissful heights of passion had she felt anything quite like the savage need that drove him now. His lips, devouring the exquisitely tender flesh along the side of her neck and around to the racing pulse at the base of her throat, served to banish all thoughts of

Landford and the thing that she had sensed she had been very near to learning from him.

She knew only that Blackthorn was reaching out to her in a way he had never done before and that he aroused in her an answering need every bit as strong as his own. Breathing a tumultuous sigh, she gave herself to the emotions that were welling up inside her.

Not until she felt his hand working the hem of her dress up over her legs did it come to her in a delirious wave of sensations that they were in a closed carriage threading its way through hackneys and private conveyances on a thoroughfare that traversed the most fashionable part of London.

"*Dane?*" she gasped, prey to a blissful shudder of excitement as Blackthorn's fingers deftly found their way past the separation between the legs of her drawers to the pulsating warmth between her thighs. "I cannot think this is in the least proper."

"No, not in the least, my sweet enchantress," affirmed Blackthorn, delving a finger experimentally into the moist depths of her.

Violet, uttering a gasp, clutched at his shoulders.

Blackthorn smiled appreciatively. "You will agree, however, that it is *different*, will you not? Even exotic, perhaps," he uttered thickly, marveling to discover his delectable Violet was already flowing with the sweet nectar of arousal. He, moreover, was in an agony to possess her. Flinging his greatcoat open, he reached with hard, swift fingers to undo the fastenings at the front of his breeches.

Violet, given to see her dearest captain's magnificently erect manhood suddenly sprout from the front of his unmentionables, reached hastily to pull the shades down over the carriage windows. It was on her lips to ask how, precisely, he proposed to make love to her in the close confines of a moving carriage. Before she could utter it, however, Blackthorn's powerful hands closed about her waist.

"It is rather like mounting a horse, sweet Violet," he said, his voice sounding hoarse in the darkness. "I shall give you a boost and you—"

"Lift a leg up. I see," said Violet, giving vent to a delicious gurgle of laughter. Feeling delectably naughty, she hastily worked to gather her skirts up about her waist. "I am ready, Dane."

It was to come immediately to Violet, as she found herself suddenly sitting astraddle hard, muscular thighs, a knee on the seat on either side of her dearest captain and her dress gathered around her waist, that being poised to make love in the exotic environs of a moving carriage while fully dressed was a deal more exciting than she could previously have thought possible. If this was the sort of pleasurable pursuit advocated by the garden philosophers, no doubt it was perfectly understandable why Epicureanism had seen a revival in the modern century. Certainly her present position would seem to offer unique possibilities for exotic experimentation that must appeal to the creative spirit.

She was not to be given further time to contemplate the intriguing aspects of the philosophical pursuit of pleasure. Blackthorn, who was in the throes of an exquisite anguish, clasped her by the waist and guided her inexorably to the pinnacle of his manly desire.

"And now, Countess," he said, his voice taut with need, "I depend on you to carry us through." Pulling her savagely down on him, he buried his shaft in her.

Violet, finding herself suddenly filled with him, gave vent to a shuddering gasp of dawning enlightenment. It was the one thing that had not occurred to her—the freedom conferred in being the rider instead of the mount. Always before she had depended on Blackthorn's strength to guide them to the threshold of a glorious release and beyond. Now it was intriguingly up to her.

It was to occur to her no little time later that she must have a natural propensity for exotic pleasure. Indeed, how else could she explain her wholly abandoned response to the power Blackthorn had granted her to transport them both to the divine heights of rapture? She, who had ever abhorred the mere thought of conferring discomfort on anyone, discovered a delirious pleasure in teasing and tantalizing both him and herself. There was exquisite delight in slowly lifting herself off him only to fill herself with him again and again, until at last not even she could bear the suspense of waiting. Gloriously surrendering herself to the swell of passion building within her, she swiftly brought them both to the sweet ecstasy of release.

"Dane," she breathed several moments later, as, collapsed in sated abandonment against his chest, her arms clasped about his neck, she nuzzled her face into the strong column of his neck. "Promise me, my dearest, best loved captain, that we shall make love at least once every month or so in the exotic environs of a moving carriage."

"I promise we shall make love exotically with far greater frequency than once every month, my sweet, insatiable enchantress, though it may not be in a carriage," Blackthorn amended, running his hand over her back. "We shall be inordinately fortunate if we do not awaken in the morning to discover we are once again the talk of the town—if not for the incident on Lady Stanhope's balcony, then for our licentious behavior on the streets of London."

Violet went quite still as she digested that startling prediction. "You are roasting me, Dane—are you not?" she concluded a trifle uncertainly. "I daresay Landford will be as little desirous of spreading the story of his much deserved lesson in humility as are we. And as for the other, how could anyone possibly know we were being licentious within the privacy of our carriage?"

"A carriage, my girl, which has the distinction of bearing the Blackthorn coat of arms on the sides and which, in addition, is exceptionally well-sprung," offered Blackthorn, smiling reminiscently in the dark.

"Oh!" exclaimed Violet, after a very few moments. "Dear, I suppose it *was* perfectly obvious to anyone who came within view of the carriage that *something* was going on inside. Not that it matters. I daresay it will serve our purposes perfectly well to have people talking about the unbridled passions of the Earl and Countess of Blackthorn. I myself shall be tempted to gloat in their faces."

"You, my girl, will present an aspect of ladylike demureness," declared Blackthorn with a deep-throated chuckle, which had the effect of sending a thrill coursing through Violet. Faith, when before had she heard him laugh with such ease?

"And why is that, I wonder," she queried, though she knew perfectly well why.

"Because, my sweet, you are as aware as I am that that is the surest way to feed their curiosity, not to mention spark their imaginations. The gossipmongers will have a feeding frenzy of speculation, as will the servants if we arrive home in our present state of debauchery." Placing a kiss on the top of her head, he attempted to ease her arms from around his neck. "I suggest we should at least try and put ourselves to rights again."

Violet, who was utterly content where she was, clung stubbornly to him. "But this feels perfectly right, Dane. Can we not simply instruct Fisk to continue driving? I should like to remain like this forever."

"Naturally, I should never wish to deny you anything, Violet," said Blackthorn, who could not but marvel that he had once been fool enough to imagine he could ever return to an existence that did not include his sweet, passionate enchantress. "Unfortunately, even I have my limitations. I daresay if we remain in our present positions much longer, I am like to lose what little feeling I have left in my lower extremities."

"Devil," pronounced Violet with obvious emotion.

At last, heaving a sigh, she roused herself to relieve him of his burden. She suffered a pang of loss as, lifting herself, she felt him slip out of her. Indeed, she had the most peculiar urge to clasp him to her, as if by that she might prolong the moment of shared intimacy. Then his hands closed about her waist, and he was lifting, helping her to regain her seat next to him.

The moment could not have been more surely lost. Dane, working quickly to return himself to a semblance of a proper gentleman, settled back against the squabs. Violet smoothed her skirts and reached to lift the window shade. Swaying gently, the carriage turned into the square and stopped before Blackthorn House.

Violet, glancing out, was the first to experience a sense of misgiving.

Leaning forward, she clutched a hand on Blackthorn's arm. "Dane?"

"I see it." His hand covered hers on his arm. "Very likely it is nothing. A nightmare or a touch of the stomachache. Philippe is prone, I believe, to minor bouts of dyspepsia."

Moving past her as the door was opened, Blackthorn stepped down and reached back to help Violet dismount the carriage. Together, they strode briskly to the house.

"Potter, what is it?" Violet demanded quietly, tugging off her gloves. "The lamp is lit in the nursery. That is the doctor's horse and carriage in front, is it not? He was here to tend to Miss Tidwell only a few days ago. I am sure I recognize them. I never forget a horse."

"Mr. Greene thought it best to summon him, milady," the butler answered, relieving the earl of his greatcoat and other things. "Lord Fennington has a touch of the fever. The doctor is with him now."

Without waiting to hear more, Violet turned and crossed to the stairs.

"Violet." Blackthorn, striding after her, caught her arm. "I suggest until we know what the doctor has to say you would do better to wait below."

"I shall do no such thing, my lord," Violet quietly insisted. "I am not such a poor creature, I promise you. I have been in the sickroom before. The child needs his mother, and I'm afraid I am the closest we can come to that at the moment."

Cursing silently to himself, Blackthorn let her go. Wordlessly, they ascended the stairs to the nursery.

They entered to find the doctor just in the process of closing up his medical kit.

"It is the mumps, " he announced without preamble. "I'm afraid, my lord, I must ask you both to step outside at once."

"No, it is all right, Doctor," said Violet, her glance going to the child in the bed. "I have already had them—both sides, as fate would have it."

"Splendid. Then you will not mind staying with him while I summon a nurse. My lord, if you would be so kind?" the doctor added, ushering his lordship to the door. "At your age, the mumps are no laughing matter."

"Indeed, you must go, Blackthorn," said Violet, reading the refusal in his eyes. "We shall be fine, Philippe and I. Promise you will not worry."

He *would* worry, she thought, as, reluctantly, he allowed himself to be removed from the sickroom. Never mind that it would do no one any good, least of all himself. A pity he did not have some form of diversion aside from brooding about Landford and the troublesome business of the French agent, whom they were no closer to exposing. There had ought to be someone who could offer him some sort of distraction.

But then, there *was* someone, she realized, her lips curving irresistibly in a small, bemused smile. She would see to it first thing in the morning. In the meantime, however, there was Philippe. Pulling a chair up to the bed, she sat down and leaned over to put a hand to the child's forehead.

"There, now, Philippe," she said softly, smoothing the hair back from his hot brow. "You are feeling perfectly dreadful at the moment. But everything is going to be just fine. You will see. We shall have you back on your feet in no time."

It occurred to Blackthorn, sitting with his feet crossed at the ankles and propped on the great mahogany desk, that there was a great deal to be desired in the study of modern agricultural practices, which had seen little change since Lord Townshend, fondly known as "Turnip," had introduced the Norfolk System in 1730. The practice of yearly rotating crops from wheat to turnips to barley to clover and grass would seem to make sound economic as well as agronomic sense, which was undoubtedly why the previous Earl of Blackthorn had not deviated from the use of it. The three estates that he owned and maintained had, as a result, prospered greatly from it.

If nothing else, Blackthorn reflected, his uncle had been a fair and conscientious landlord to his numerous tenants and an excellent judge of men. The agents he employed for each of the three estates were, to all appearances, aboveboard and dedicated to the principles of stewardship that had been laid down by their previous employer.

Blackthorn snapped closed *The Scientific Study of the Effects of the Norfolk System on Agricultural Production,* which he had only just finished reading, and dropped his feet to the floor. There would seem little point in changing that which had already been demonstrated to be tried and true, he decided, setting the sizeable tome with a loud thump on the desk. Unlike the navy, he reflected ironically, which would have benefited by any number of changes, not the least of which was a policy designed to treat its common sailors with justice and humanity.

It was a subject to which he had given a great deal of consideration over the years. Naval tactics, thanks to Hood and Nelson, were undergoing swift and perma-

nent change. The navy, itself, however, which relied for
the most part on impressment gangs and the employment of convicts to man its ships, was slow to abandon
traditional practices that made the service of common
sailors on a ship of war little better than enslavement.

Blackthorn was wont to envision a permanent navy
of professional sailors treated with dignity and humanity, one in which floggings and the practice of keel-
hauling and hanging malefactors from the yardarms
were made things of the past. Decent wages, uniforms,
proper food, and medical treatment, the things that
gave dignity to men who sacrificed life and limb for
king and country, must eventually come if England, ever
dependent upon its fleets of ships, were to endure.
Certainly it was not enough to depend upon the discretion of individual captains, who ruled their ships as lord
and master.

The Spithead Mutiny would seem to give ample evidence of that, as did the punishment books of captains
who awarded more than a hundred floggings in a single
commission. Only a general policy would suffice, and
Parliament, occupied with a war of survival, was hardly
prepared to act for the betterment of the navy, which
at present was the only thing that stood between England and an invasion from France.

The devil, thought Blackthorn, rising abruptly from
the chair. There would seem little point in belaboring
something that apparently was no longer any of his
concern. He had resigned his commission. The navy
would go on without him. No doubt he was well out of
it, he told himself, absently flexing his recently healed
arm. His province now lay in the scintillating realm of
agronomy.

Hard upon that thought came a soft scratching at the
door.

"*Yes*, what is it!" burst angrily from him at the
untimely interruption.

The door opened to reveal Potter, who entered with

the unassailable dignity of an exceedingly superior servant in the presence of an employer who was obviously in an uncertain temper. "Begging your pardon, milord," intoned the butler. "The Marquis of Vere is here to see you."

Had Potter announced Admiral Lord Nelson himself had come to call, Blackthorn would hardly have been more surprised. Thus far his brother-in-law had demonstrated a marked lack of interest in his sister's newly acquired husband.

"Very good, then. You may show him in," said Blackthorn. "Oh, and, Potter."

"Yes, milord."

"I had no call to vent my ill humor on you just now."

"Yes, milord."

The butler stared at him with his peculiarly wooden expression, like that of a sailor afraid to draw the wrath of his captain down on his head, thought Blackthorn irritably.

"That is all, Potter. You may go."

"Yes, milord," said the butler, turning with staid dignity and exiting the room.

With the door shut behind him, Potter paused. The new master was a rare one, he thought, glancing briefly back at the wooden barrier. It was not uncommon for an employer to shout at a paid servant. He could not recall, however, that he had ever heard of one apologizing for it.

But then, he had seen at once his lordship was not of the common order. He was a gentleman in the truest sense of the word, Potter told himself with a faint, whimsical shake of his head. Then, schooling his features to their proper expression of superior impassivity, he proceeded to carry out his master's orders.

Blackthorn, who was unaware that he had won the unqualified approval of his butler, was instead pondering the purpose of his caller's visit. No doubt it was to inquire about his sister's well-being, a subject to which

Blackthorn could attest only from his infrequent brief snatches of conversation with her when she left the nursery to avail herself of an hour or two of rest from her self-imposed duties in the sickroom.

Hell and the devil confound it! He did not know whether to be relieved Violet had dismissed the nurse, who had proven both unclean in her personal habits and unappealing in her manner, or perturbed that his enchantress had taken too much upon herself. He was plagued with the thought that she was wearing herself to the nub, while he was prevented from doing anything to help her.

It had been three nights since Philippe had broken out with the mumps and Violet, with help from Miss Tidwell, had assumed full authority over the sickroom. Blackthorn chafed at his own inability to take some of the burden of caring for the child upon himself. It was the devil's own luck that he had never to his knowledge contracted the illness in childhood. Indeed, he could not recall that he had ever been sick a day in his life.

As for Philippe, Violet assured him the child was fast approaching the worst of the sickness and would soon begin to gain steadily in health. According to the doctor, who had only praise for Violet's comportment in the sickroom, it was to be expected the disease would have run its course in no less than two weeks.

Two bloody damned weeks, thought Blackthorn, slamming the side of his fist against the mantelpiece. It was to be hoped he was not driven to distraction before the quarantine was lifted.

"It would appear there is little improvement in Lord Fennington's condition," observed a dry masculine voice from the doorway. "I did knock, by the way. Apparently I failed to make myself heard. No doubt I beg your pardon, my lord, for intruding on your seemingly less than cheerful ruminations. Lady Blackthorn, I take it, has barricaded herself in the sickroom."

Blackthorn, coming about, was struck immediately

by the newcomer's unmistakable family resemblance to
Violet. It would appear, in fact, that jet-black hair in
sharp contrast to eyes the penetrating blue of steel or
ice could be traced directly back to the Marquess of
Vere's grandsire, the never-to-be-forgotten Duke of Albermarle. Rochelles, it would appear, bred true to their
type. He could only be grateful Violet demonstrated the
softening feminine influence of her French mother who
had, he did not doubt, bequeathed to her daughter her
ivory complexion and the dreamy, blue-violet cast of
her eyes.

"For three days and as many nights," said Blackthorn,
coolly assessing. Vere, he did not doubt, was as dangerous as he was cold-bloodedly arrogant. Curiously, he
wondered what else he was. Certainly, he would be
nobody's fool, Blackthorn surmised. "Would you care
to join me in a brandy, my lord marquess, while you
enlighten me as to why Violet has sent for you? I find
I am uncommonly curious to learn what new scheme
she has devised for my benefit."

"How well you would seem to know her," Vere
remarked, his eyes unreadable as they studied his host.
"Ah, but then I gave myself away, did I not? How else,
after all, should I have known about Lord Fennington's
unfortunate malady if I had not received a missive day
before yesterday from my sister?"

"How else, indeed?" said Blackthorn, filling two
glasses from a decanter set out on a silver grog tray on
the desk. Taking up the glasses, he handed one to his
visitor and with the other waved Vere to a seat. "Day
before yesterday, did you say?" Settling in the chair
behind the desk, Blackthorn absently swirled the liquid
in the glass. "She wasted little time. That would have
been the morning after Philippe first demonstrated the
symptoms of swelling."

"Yes, so she informed me in her letter," agreed Vere,
absently tapping the heel of his boot with the silver-
headed walking stick he affected when he was in town.

"I should have come sooner, of course, but I arrived back in town only this morning. How is young Lord Fennington, by the way?"

"Resting as comfortably as can be expected, I am told," replied Blackthorn, wondering when Vere would choose to come to the point of his visit.

Surely Violet had not seen fit to inform her brother of the incident with Landford. He could not doubt that the veteran of at least three duels that were of public knowledge would be little deterred in giving Sir Oliver instructions in gentlemanly conduct of a rather more permanent nature than those he had received from his former captain.

Taking a sip of the brandy, Blackthorn gazed speculatively at the marquess. "But then, I am convinced you did not come all this way to inquire about Philippe. What has my enterprising countess persuaded you to undertake for her, my lord?"

The marquess gazed back at Blackthorn, his smile cynically amused. "I, my lord," replied Vere, lifting his glass in a gesture of salute, "am your entertainment."

Violet, straightening from adjusting the clean flannel about Philippe's neck, could only be pleased that the child was sleeping peacefully at last. No doubt the hot fomentation of marigold steeped in cider vinegar had worked its magic. Philippe had dropped off before she had finished bathing his neck in it.

Quietly, she adjusted the screen to prevent the dim glow of lamplight from disturbing the sleeping child. Then, stretching her back, she walked to the window overlooking the square and parted the drapes just sufficiently to peek out at the morning, which was well advanced.

Below her, the square was a splash of color, with nannies out walking their charges in shaded prams and children playing catch-me-as-catch-can in the park. Inev-

itably her gaze was drawn across the way to the four-
story brown brick that belonged to her brother-in-law,
the Earl of Shields. A soft pang went through her at
sight of the door, its knocker removed as a sign that
the owners were not in residence.

She missed Elfrida, who, besides being her sister, was
her dearest friend and confidante. Unavoidably, it came
to her to wonder if Shields and Elfrida's retreat to Claverling had served its purpose. It had been Elfrida's
greatest disappointment that in the four years of her
marriage to Shields she had yet to conceive. Perhaps at
home in the quiet environs of Cheshire, Elfrida had
written in her last letter, she might at last be granted
the wish that remained closest to her heart. She had,
after all, seen it in a vision—Shields, dandling a boy
with raven curls on his knee. Clearly, it was meant to
be.

Feeling a ridiculous lump rise in her throat, Violet
shifted her gaze to the traffic on the streets. Instantly,
her momentary touch of gloom evaporated at sight of
a groom walking a magnificent pair of sweet-goers
hitched to an equally impressive curricle. Jet-black and
perfectly matched, the high-steppers had the small
heads, deep chests, and powerful quarters characteristic
of Irish thoroughbreds. Violet, who never forgot a horse
and who would, in any event, have had to be seriously
afflicted not to recognize these singular beauties
instantly, smiled bemusedly to herself.

Vere had come after all, just as she had known in her
heart he would. Now if only Blackthorn did not prove
ridiculously stubborn. Sternly, she quelled the urge to
summon Nanny Tidwell to relieve her in the sickroom
while she went to lend her persuasion to Vere's. Indeed,
she did not need to have done, she realized, as she saw
the curricle come to a halt in front of the house to
receive the two tall masculine figures that issued forth.

Watching the curricle depart, she could not but suffer
a fleeting quiver of uncertainty as it came to her to

wonder where the chain of events she had caused to be set in motion might lead her dearest Blackthorn. Vere, who was infamous for his jaded pursuits, perhaps inevitably inspired visions of smoke-filled drinking dens, gaming hells, and garish houses of disrepute peopled with painted, slink-hipped Paphians.

Instantly, she knew she was being ridiculous. Vere might be a dangerous rakehell and a gambler, but he was also her brother. He would never go so far as to betray her trust by deliberately seeking to corrupt Blackthorn simply for his own perverse amusement. Besides, it was not as if Blackthorn had not already seen it all for himself. He was a grown man of considerable experience in the world. Nothing untoward was going to happen to him.

Smiling at the absurdity of her thoughts, Violet turned away from the window. Everything was fine. She would be a perfect peagoose to wear herself out with worry. She, after all, had other matters to concern her, she reminded herself, as Philippe, moving fretfully in the bed, began to whimper for his *Maman Violette.*

Smiling whimsically, Violet sat in the chair at the bedside. "It is all right, Philippe," she said soothingly. "*Tout est bien, cheri. Je suis ici.*"

Violet might have been a deal less sanguine about her brother's intentions had she been given to see Vere some blocks later turn his curricle and pair over to his groom and, with Blackthorn, climb into a hackney cab. Indeed, she would undoubtedly have been plagued with doubt had she witnessed them some little time later enter the squalid environs of Wapping High Street and Penny Fields, which had the dubious distinction of housing the worst dens of iniquity in the east end of London.

"I give you Limehouse," cynically announced Vere, indicating the sordid maze of narrow, refuse-infested courts and alleys twisting through soot-blackened houses and teeming with a wretched array of humanity, most of whom had been unhappily transported from the Orient. "The Blue Dragon is only a short distance from here. I suggest you consider carefully whether you wish to continue. Once we leave the hackney, we shall find ourselves among the worst sort of thieves, cutthroats, and pickpockets."

"As it happens, I am not wholly unfamiliar with desperate people or difficult situations," said Blackthorn, who had little trouble assessing the liabilities of disembarking from the cab and setting out on foot.

"No, I do not suppose you are," agreed Vere, eyeing the earl with sardonic appreciation.

"I should be lying if I said I relished the prospect before us," continued Blackthorn, ironically aware Vere regarded him in the light of an oddity. "Especially as there is little guarantee the end result will have warranted the risk." Turning, he gave the marquess a level look. "I intend, however, to pursue the course before me. If what you have told me is true, I am already in your debt. I should understand if you wished to remain with the hackney coach. While *I* have a distinct interest in following through with this venture, you have little to gain beyond the distinct possibility of a bludgeoning to the head, or worse."

"You are mistaken surely, my lord," Vere countered, shrugging an elegant shoulder. "I have everything to gain in keeping you alive. In the unlikely event I should fail, I should, after all, have to face Violet."

Taking up his walking stick, Vere stepped lightly to the ground, followed in short order by Blackthorn.

"There will be twice this sum if you wait here for us," said Vere to the hackney driver as he reached up to hand him a bill. "We shall not be long."

"You won't be if you wants me to be here when you gets back, gov'nor," replied the driver. "I'll give you a quarter of an hour afore I takes me and old Bob there out of Limehouse. Beggin' your pardon, sir."

"He is right, of course," grinned Vere, setting off at a leisurely gait up the alley. "We shall be exceedingly fortunate if we do not have to make our way out on foot."

The prospect, Blackthorn noted with grim interest, rather than daunting, appeared to afford Vere no little source of entertainment. But then, it was obvious the marquess was no stranger either to risk-taking or the seedy environs of Penny Fields. He brought them with unerring directness to the unprepossessing façade of the Blue Dragon, which was remarkable only for the grimy impenetrability of its filth-encrusted windows and the weathered representation of a fire-breathing reptile of an indeterminate hue.

Blackthorn, steeling himself for what might lie within, entered the unsavory den.

The smoke-filled interior was to prove fully as unappealing as the exterior had given promise of its being. Gaunt figures, vacant-eyed with dreaming, sprawled in filthy abandon on rude couches consisting of little more than rough wooden frames draped with sacking and having the tattered remains of quilts for mattresses. Stacked three high to the ceiling, the cells of Morpheus lined the narrow confines of the dingy walls like the gaping tombs of a burial crypt. Blackthorn covered his nose and mouth with a handkerchief against the opium fumes mingled with the cloying scent of incense and the stench of unwashed bodies and began his grim search.

One never became totally inured to the horrors inflicted on men in the repeated broadsides of ships pitted in a fight to the finish. Smashed and headless bodies, ship's boys cut in two by cannon balls, men pierced by jagged splinters, the scuppers running red with blood—he had seen it all. There was little of glory in the hellish scenes on the orlop deck following a sea battle. There were the screams of men undergoing crude amputations at the hands of medical officers who, operating under primitive conditions, were rendered little better than butchers; and there were the loblolly boys carrying their gruesome bundles of severed limbs to cast overboard for the waiting sharks.

Not a man on shipboard did not live in dread of suffering disfiguration and loss of limb. But men fought and died, or they endured. The hell of the opium dens, however, was the silent hell of despair.

Blackthorn, moving from one living tomb to the next, found himself fiercely hoping Vere's information was in error. When he found him, lying like the others in slack-jawed unawareness, he felt a sickness claw at his throat. There was little to be seen of the young warrior in the pathetic creature who stared up at him with blurred, uncomprehending eyes. The blue coat with its single gold epaulet on the left shoulder was rumpled and covered with filth, but it was the coat of an officer who had stood fearlessly against the enemy.

Reaching down, Blackthorn shook him by the shoulder. "Steven. Steven, the devil, man. Come out of it!"

"He does not hear you," Vere said quietly. "Nor will he. He is now a captive to Morpheus."

Wordlessly, Blackthorn knelt to take the limp figure over his shoulder. Then, rising, he awarded Vere a hard, flat stare. "He is a British naval officer. He has faced far worse than this and lived to tell of it. He is coming with us."

"Naturally," agreed Vere with his gently mocking smile. "You may be sure I never doubted it."

It was instantly to prove, however, that there were others of a different persuasion. Hardly had Vere and Blackthorn, with his burden, taken a step toward the door than they found themselves confronted by one who was presumably the proprietor of the unwholesome establishment and three others who were obviously his henchmen.

"This is Mr. Wu," announced one of the henchmen, a slender individual who affected the skintight pantaloons and the narrow, high-waisted tailcoat with the stand-up collar and cuffless sleeves of an *Incroyable*. "He has been watching you."

"Has he, indeed," replied Vere, idly swinging his silver-headed walking stick between the thumb and index finger of one shapely hand.

"Mr. Wu says this man owes him money. Mr. Wu says this man stays. If you want to take him, you pay."

"Mr. Wu, it seems, is a talkative fellow," observed Blackthorn, slipping his hand into the pocket of his greatcoat. "You may tell Mr. Wu we have no intention of paying him anything."

"That would not be wise, mister. Mr. Wu is a man of business. He will not look kindly on the loss of his investment."

Blackthorn closed his fingers about the chequered grip of a pistol. "Mr. Wu is in danger of losing something a deal more valuable to him than his investment. Tell Mr. Wu he would be wise to step out of the way. My friends and I are leaving."

"You are too hasty," said the Oriental dandy, his eyes flicking from one to the other. "It will be better for all concerned if you choose instead to be reasonable. You, mister," he said to Vere. "You tell your friend it is better to pay."

There was something indescribably chilling about Vere's infinitely gentle smile, Blackthorn noted. Instinctively he tensed, ready to spring.

"I should no doubt be happy to oblige you," replied the marquess, observing with interest the sudden looming presence of a great, strapping hulk of a man in the shadows at Mr. Wu's back. The odds, it would seem, had just changed radically in Mr. Wu's favor. "Unfortunately," he added, the walking stick going suddenly still in his hand, "I could not agree with him more."

What happened next occurred with bewildering swiftness. The two large henchmen started menacingly forward. The Oriental dandy reached for the back of his neck. His arm flashing down let fly a deadly-looking knife at Vere, who neatly sidestepped the assault. Then, yanking his hands wide, Vere unsheathed the sword contained in his walking stick, even as Blackthorn's gun-filled hand emerged from the depths of his greatcoat pocket to hold with unnerving steadiness on Mr. Wu's bulging midriff.

"Hold, mateys," rumbled an intimidating voice from behind the stalking henchmen. Two massive hands reached out, the henchmen's heads came together with a sickening crunch, and the two dropped like oversized marionettes with their strings cut.

"Now," murmured Vere, the tip of his sword pressed against the dandy's throat, "you will inform Mr. Wu the account is paid."

"Mr. Murdoch," Blackthorn growled some moments later, as they emerged happily unscathed from the smoky entrails of the Blue Dragon, "you will kindly explain what the devil you are doing here."

"Beggin' your pardon, Cap'n," the coxswain said, shifting the weight of the unconscious officer onto his own broad shoulder, "but I was only doing what I always do. Watching your back, sir. You shouldn't've gone off the way you did, Cap'n. You and his lordship might not come out so lucky the next time."

"By all means, Blackthorn," agreed Vere in sardonic amusement, "if there is to be a next time, I suggest in future you do not leave this fellow behind. As fate would have it, he saved us a deal of unnecessary trouble."

"Do not encourage him, Vere, I beg you," Blackthorn retorted quellingly. "Murdoch is perfectly aware that was not the question I was asking. You will tell me, Murdoch. How did you manage to find us?"

"I've my own ways, Cap'n," replied the coxswain, lifting his burden into the hackney cab, which, the entire episode having consumed a maximum of twelve minutes, was still waiting at the head of the alley.

It was the only answer that Blackthorn, for all of his dire threats to consign the grinning Murdoch to perdition for his impertinence, was able to get from him. Nor was he soon to gain any pertinent information from the newly promoted Commander Steven Furneaux, who had until recently served as *Antiope's* first lieutenant under Captain Trevor Dane. He lay in a coma, his mind wandering among the dreams of Morpheus.

Chapter 11

"The ball will have to be postponed indefinitely. I'm afraid it cannot be helped," declared Violet to her Aunt Roanna, as they sat on the bench at the edge of the small park near the house on Stratton Street and watched Philippe and Violet's cousins playing with the newest addition to Violet's growing family—a puppy of indeterminate lineage, but with strong suggestions of the Welsh Corgi in its oversized ears and head, which Mr. Murdoch had discovered cowering in the stables.

"I really cannot see I have any other choice in the matter. I cannot possibly have everything ready in less than a week. Nor am I eager to compete with the Regent's Ball, which is to be held at the end of the three weeks I should require for all the preparations. After that, it is, for all practical purposes, the end of the Season. Not that it matters. In truth, I care not whether we have it at all. I am heartily weary of playing the role of the Incomparable. And how not, when I am even more besieged by admirers than I was before I was married?"

"Which is only to say that you are a *succes fou*,"

observed Roanna, who, despite the unseasonably warm weather, was wrapped in an ermine-lined mantle to ward off the merest possibility of contracting a chill while being exposed to an excess of fresh air. "I thought that was what you wanted. Why else, after all, should I have undertaken to play gooseberry to you, save that you implored me to help you launch your career in society?"

"It *was* what I wanted, dearest Aunt," Violet conceded, recalling with a whimsical smile the events that had led up to her momentous decision to become the darling of the *ton*. She could hardly have foreseen then that the strained state of affairs between Philippe and herself would undergo so swift and radical a transformation. Indeed, she found suddenly that she liked very well having her peace cut up by a six-year-old who, besides getting into every sort of mischief, would now refuse to go to bed unless his *Maman Violette* tucked him in and read him to sleep out of one of his storybooks. Had anyone told her only four weeks earlier she was to become so thoroughly attached to the boy that she would experience a growing ache in her heart at his father's marked display of indifference toward him, she undoubtedly would have thought that person deluded.

The truth was, however, that Philippe had inched his way into her heart, until now nothing could ever dislodge him. No doubt two weeks spent cooped up in a room with a sick child would tend to have that effect on one, she thought ruefully, as she bit off an exclamation of alarm at the sight of Philippe, running full tilt after the yapping puppy, trip and fall headlong in the grass.

She would have to control this unwonted urge of hers to mollycoddle him, she realized, watching him sit up, laughing, as the puppy excitedly gave his face a thorough washing with its wet, pink tongue. The boy's natural inclination to romp and play and do all the things that children did had been stifled enough not only by an aging nanny who could not have kept up with him, but by his mother, who, from all indications, had been protective of the child almost to the point of obsession.

It was, perhaps, the natural reaction of a woman who had suffered the violent loss of everything she knew and loved to develop an inordinate fear for the well-being of her only child. More difficult to explain was why a father who had been away at sea almost continuously for the first six years of the child's life should demonstrate an unnatural disinclination to become acquainted with his only son. Really, it would seem to make little sense, thought Violet, who knew Blackthorn was far from being an unfeeling man. But then, of late nothing about Blackthorn would seem to make any sense.

Indeed, she could not have anticipated that matters between her and Blackthorn could regress to the extent that a barrier of silence had settled between them or that, worse, it would seem he had embarked on a liaison with the probably beautiful and no doubt exotic practitioner of Epicurean philosophy, Madame Gabrielle Benneau.

It had never occurred to Violet to suspect there was anything amiss in Blackthorn's newly adopted practice of leaving the house every morning to remain away until the wee hours before dawn. She had naturally assumed Vere was doing just as she had asked him to do—introducing the new Earl of Blackthorn to the entertainments of a man about town. Occupied herself in the sickroom, she had been pleased Blackthorn was getting out. Though it had come to her on more than one occasion to wonder what sort of amusements Vere had chosen for his brother-in-law, she had trusted Blackthorn, at least, to keep a level head.

All that had changed when, at last judging Philippe to be sufficiently recovered neither to require her constant attendance nor to be contagious, she had relinquished his care to Nanny Tidwell and Mr. Greene and removed thankfully back to her own rooms.

The manner in which Blackthorn had greeted her

emergence from the sickroom had been something less than she might have wished. Having sent word after breakfast that he might visit the convalescent at his earliest possible convenience, she could not but be disappointed when he failed to avail himself immediately of her invitation.

She was subsequently to learn from Potter that the master was away from the house and, indeed, apparently had been since the break of dawn. Reasoning that it was not unusual for a gentleman to go for a gallop in Hyde Park in the early hours of the morning, Violet had swallowed her disappointment and gone about taking up the threads of her life where she had left them. She assumed, when he did not return for nuncheon or tea, that Vere very likely had taken him to Tattersall's to look over Lord Weston's breakdowns or to Gentleman Jackson's Gym to avail himself of a sparring match, perhaps even with Gentleman Jackson himself.

She had excused his absence from dinner by reminding herself that husbands and wives quite often dined separately and that he, after all, was not yet aware she had been liberated from her duties in the sickroom. Telling herself it would be the shabbiest thing if he returned to find her out, she had happily chosen to stay home and read the new anonymously published novel about which everyone was talking rather than attend any of the social functions for which she had received invitations. After the clock chimed three, she had gone to sleep, *Castle Rackrent* half-read and open across her lap in bed.

No doubt she should have been gratified that Blackthorn had been too solicitous of her rest to impose himself on her when he returned home some time later. She was not, however. She was acutely aware instead that she was hurt by his failure to come to her as had been his wont every night before Philippe had succumbed to the mumps. Still, she had promised she would never be the sort of demanding wife who questioned him about his comings and goings. When he finally presented himself to her, she was determined to receive him as if everything were just as it should be.

Violet suffered an unwitting pang at the memory of that momentous first meeting. There was no denying he had given every manifestation of a man who was exceedingly pleased to see his wife after more than a fortnight of being apart from her, the devil!

One moment, having only just risen from her bed, she was on the point of ringing for her abigail. The next she heard a light, thrilling step behind her and turned, her heart beating rapidly beneath her breast.

She was given no more than a fleeting impression of Blackthorn's tall, imposing presence before she was rendered singularly powerless by the fierce glow of warmth in his eyes. Faith, he had seemed to devour her with his gaze! The very next instant she was blissfully in his arms.

"The devil, Violet," he growled and covered her mouth with his.

He had kissed her with an aching tenderness, slowly, searchingly, his lips moving sensually over hers until she thought she must swoon from the emotions he drew seemingly from the depths of her. And when at last he released her to probe her face with his black, piercing eyes, she had felt strangely replete, as if all the hurt and doubt had been swept away in that single kiss. And then everything in a twinkling had changed. Really, it was too bad of him.

"I have missed you, Enchantress," he said, curling a wisp of hair behind her ear. "I am grateful you appear no worse for the wear. And Philippe. I must suppose that he is well recovered."

"Philippe is fine. He is waiting for you to come and see him, Dane. You will, will you not," she asked, "before you go out?"

To Violet's chagrin, she had felt him pull away, had seen his withdrawal like a mask drop in place. He had

regretted there was not time at present. He was already
late for an appointment that could not wait. He had
stopped in only for a moment to make sure all was well
with his enchantress. Then with a buss on the cheek for
Violet, he had made his departure. A plague take him!

Violet sighed heavily. These days there was always an
appointment that could not wait, and now Violet knew
with whom he met each day. Violet had done the
unthinkable. She had followed him to the house on
Berners Street. Not that time, of course, when he had
left her standing in her bedchamber. Still warm from
his kiss, she had not the wit then to realize just how far
he had distanced himself from her. Nor could she bring
herself later to blame him for it.

How could she, when she was to blame for everything?
she thought with a sharp, rending pain.

Faith, how easily she had allowed herself to be led
into believing he might come in time to care for her,
if only a little! The most odious part of all was that he
had never lied to her. He had told her from the very
beginning he had no wish to marry her. Good heavens,
he had told her repeatedly and often, and she, able to
see only that he was the only man she would ever love,
had refused to listen.

She, Violet Rochelle, who had never asserted her will
on anyone, had taken it upon herself to force a man
who did not love her into marriage. And now look what
had come of it. Her dearest captain was no longer a
captain. He was Lord Blackthorn, who had taken up
the pursuits of a town beau with all of its frivolities,
including a French mistress.

Really, it was too much, she thought, feeling her stomach turn with dismay at the terrible coil she had wrought
for herself—worse, wrought for Blackthorn, who had
lost everything that had ever mattered to him because
of it. *Because of her.* Indeed, she did not doubt that,
having found himself bereft of the career that meant

everything to him, he had plunged himself into the dissolute pleasures of the City in order to forget.

Still, perhaps it was not too late. If she could not free him from the marriage, she could at least do all in her power to return him to the life for which he yearned. She would not rest until she saw him captain of his own ship again. Indeed, she was quite determined on it. Then perhaps it would no longer matter that he was leg shackled to a wife he had never wanted and who, further, had caused him nothing but trouble.

"Violet? Violet, I do wish you would say something," declared Aunt Roanna, jarring Violet out of her exceedingly unrewarding thoughts. "I daresay you have not heard a word I have been saying."

"I beg your pardon, dearest aunt," said Violet, who was indeed guilty of having been preoccupied to the exclusion of all else, though she did recall her aunt having mentioned something about an Admirals' Ball to which she, Roanna, was promised to go, but from which Violet's name, understandably if regrettably, had been left off the list of invitations. "I fear I was woolgathering. Who did you say was hosting tomorrow night's gala?"

"Who else but that perfectly dreadful Vice Admiral Sir Oliver Landford?" replied Roanna, who had been observing her companion for some little time with a mounting sense of misapprehension. "Violet," she was moved to venture at last, "if something were troubling you, you would tell me, would you not? It is obvious something is disturbing your peace of mind—indeed, has been for some little time. I know you far too well to suppose this newfound propensity of yours for falling suddenly into distracted silences is not a manifestation of something amiss. Dear, only look at you. Your hands are clenched into fists, and only a moment ago your expression was positively daunting, which you will admit is nothing like you. Clearly, all is not as it should be, and pray do not bother to deny it, for I promise I shan't believe you."

"But nothing *is* wrong, Aunt Roanna," Violet denied, even as she made herself unclench her hands in her lap. "I'm afraid mention of Sir Oliver has the peculiar effect of making me wish to scratch somebody's eyes out. I pray you will think nothing of it."

"Think nothing of it? Really, Violet," said Roanna, taking the bull uncharacteristically by the horns, "I think it is time you told me what is truly bothering you. If it is Blackthorn, I feel compelled to point out it is hardly unusual for couples in their first months of marriage to experience some few little difficulties. I daresay Richard and I were saved from it only because hardly were we married than he was shipped off to sea for eleven months, having, I might add, left me in a delicate condition. And when he returned, I was far too happy to see him again to wish to indulge in histrionics. You must not take it to heart, my dear. These things have a way of working themselves out."

"Yes, of course they do, dearest aunt," agreed Violet, who could not envision the circumstance that would provide sufficient impetus to induce her Aunt Roanna out of her normal state of indolence to engage in anything so strenuous as a fit of histrionics must be. "However, Blackthorn is not responsible for this new turn of mine to abandon any ambition I might fleetingly have entertained to reign as London's leading hostess. It is all a parcel of nonsense, Roanna. I detest all the folderol. You know very well it was intended in the first place only as a means of putting an end to the ridiculous rumors circulating about Blackthorn. Now that it has achieved its purpose, I cannot think why I should continue to pursue it."

"Then by all means give it up," Aunt Roanna concluded with a shrug. "That is what I should do if I had my choice in the matter. You, at least, do not have your husband's naval career to consider." Realizing immediately what she had said, Roanna bolted upright in consternation at where her unruly tongue had led her. "Violet, I pray you will forgive me. I never meant—"

"No, of course you did not," Violet hastened to assure her flustered aunt before she could entangle herself in a hopeless string of apologies, which would only contribute further to her mortification. "Pray do not let it concern you. After all, I consider Blackthorn's having resigned his commission as only a minor setback in his career."

"A minor setback, Violet?" echoed Aunt Roanna, gazing in no little bewilderment at her niece by marriage. "But if he is no longer in the navy, I fail to see how his career is to be furthered."

"Never mind, dearest aunt," smiled Violet, who knew precisely how Blackthorn's career was to be benefited; indeed, who had never ceased through the two weeks of Philippe's recovery or the days afterward to contemplate what must be done to salvage it.

In truth, she had thought of little else when Philippe was sleeping and had not required her constant attention. She had gone over and over it in her head until she entertained not the slightest doubt that Vice Admiral Sir Oliver Landford had been on the verge of giving himself away to her when Blackthorn had disrupted his train of thought. And how not, when he had so vociferously protested nothing could be proven against him? As if the possibility there was some sort of evidence of his culpability lying around somewhere for someone to find had ever entered her head, mused Violet, who could only marvel that she had not previously considered it.

She had thought of it now, however. Indeed, Sir Oliver himself had planted the notion in her head until she was utterly convinced he had been prompted by his knowledge of the reality of just such proof to deny its existence to her.

The question was, what sort of evidence was it? Violet, who had spent a deal of her life devouring novels of a suspenseful nature and who had a vivid imagination, had little difficulty in conjuring up the notion of secret correspondences which Landford had kept to use for extortion or as some sort of leverage against his nefarious accomplices in crime. Or perhaps there were stolen papers, coded files, or lists of names of agents in an entire network of French spies.

The possibilities were practically endless. Indeed, the more she considered it, the more she was convinced Landford must have something in his possession, somewhere, which would at the very least implicate him in the conspiracy to ruin Captain Trevor Dane.

And where better to look than in the vice admiral's own house? she mused, a sudden gleam in her eye.

Blackthorn, sitting at the end of the table from Violet, could only reflect that nineteen years of living on ship's fare had hardly prepared him for the ordeal of dining in the fashion of an English earl. It was not only that thirty-eight feet of mahogany covered in white linen separated him from the only other person dining in the room, but he had the added discomfort, as well, of having been full to repletion well before the third cover was laid.

Clearly Violet was displeased with him, he thought, a wry smile twisting at his lips, as he ignored his plate of roast beef and Yorkshire pudding and reached for his glass of Medoc. There could hardly be another reason for her to have chosen the formal dining room for their first dinner alone since she had left Philippe's sickroom. No doubt that was the motive, too, for having caused a veritable profusion of spring flowers to be set in an oversized vase at the center of the table. She could not have devised a more effective means of rendering conversation singularly impossible.

How very unlike his normally forthright enchantress to employ obvious ruses to avoid the necessity of enjoying a tête-à-tête with him. If he did not know better, he might think she had some other reason than pique for holding him the length of the dining room from her.

But then, the truth was, he did *not* know better. If anything, he had been plagued all day with the demmed uneasy sensation that she was keeping something from him. Certainly her behavior at breakfast that morning, while outwardly as gay and charming as ever, had yet left something to be desired. The devil! Just as he had bent to kiss her lips, she had turned her head to present her cheek! The vixen.

When Violet chose to be, she could be as elusive as a fish avoiding the net, and that morning she had been at her slippery best. Nevertheless, despite her gay chatter about any number of things that could not have concerned him less, he had had the distinct impression she received the news of his intention to dine with her that night with something less than the enthusiasm that he might have expected from her. The word he might have chosen, in fact, to describe the fleeting expression in her eyes just before she had lowered her eyelashes was *consternation*.

The devil, he thought, what else should he have looked for from his sweet Violet? He was all too aware his own behavior the past few weeks had been less than exemplary for a husband who had been in the state of wedded bliss for little more than three months. Indeed, if he had been deliberately trying to alienate his countess's affections, he could have found no surer way than to absent himself on a daily basis without the smallest attempt at offering an explanation. Worse, he had not availed himself of his sweet Violet's delectable charms since the memorable night upon which he had taken her in the exotic environs of their carriage as it traversed one of the town's most fashionable thoroughfares.

Egad, she would never know how he had ached to possess her. In retrospect, he could not but think he would have done better to give in to temptation, even at the cost of disturbing her rest little more than an hour before the cock crowed. He had not done so in the past few weeks for the sole reason that it undoubtedly would have led to questions he was not then, nor was he now, prepared to answer.

Ironically, it would now seem that in his absence Violet had come up with her own secrets, which she was just as fully determined to keep to herself.

Blackthorn leaned far out to one side in order to obtain a glimpse of his troublesome countess. Catching her eye, he lifted his glass in a sardonic salute—and was awarded a wholly serene smile in return. The devil, he thought, as he settled back and took a good long swig from the glass. He had a distinct aversion to prying into the private affairs of his wife. Unfortunately, past experience with his dreamy-eyed enchantress had served to bring him to suffer a peculiar tingling sensation along the nape of his neck whenever she was up to something.

He felt it now with sufficient strength to find he was hard put not to bloody well squirm in his chair. Hellfire, it was time he took the tiller in his hands. His dearest Violet was about to discover once and for all he was not to be manipulated.

Taking up the glass, he stood up and with cool deliberation strolled the considerable distance to the other end of the table.

Violet, who had marked his steady progress with an odious quickening of her heartbeat, could not but think Blackthorn had never looked more formidable than he did then, garbed in black evening dress, his hair combed forward over his forehead in the Caesar, and his demon eyes, glittery and black, in the hard cast of his face. The devil, she thought, steeling herself for the inevitable confrontation. He would appear to be in a devil of a taking.

But then, she had hardly expected he would accept with sanguinity being subjected to sitting in august isolation the length of the formal dining table from her. Indeed, she had counted on his taking exception to it. If nothing else, she had meant to get his attention.

It was made immediately apparent that in that, at least, she had succeeded beyond her fondest expectations.

"No doubt you will pardon this intrusion, Countess," said Blackthorn in steely accents. Pulling out a chair at her elbow, he seated himself without preamble. "As it happens, I find little to recommend in dining alone. How do you find the roast? I trust it is to your taste."

"I daresay it is everything I might have wished," replied Violet, who found as little to recommend in the roast, which remained for the most part untouched, as in the asparagus soufflé, the pigeon pie, and the oxtail soup that had preceded it. "You, however, would appear to be singularly lacking in appetite, my lord. Surely you are not finished?"

"No doubt I should send my apologies to the cook, who has plainly outdone herself for my sake. Unfortunately, I fear I have never been much of a trencherman." He had been studying her face as he talked, and now he set his glass on the table with a deliberation that could hardly go unremarked by his companion, who demonstrated a sudden studious interest in cutting her meat with her knife and fork.

"Violet," said Blackthorn in the wake of breathing a heavy sigh. "It occurs to me we could do better than this."

"Does it, my lord?" queried Violet, betrayed into lifting her eyes to his, only immediately to lower them again. The devil, she must not let him work his spell on her. Really, it would not do at all—not *this* time and certainly not this night. She might never be presented with another opportunity like the one before her tonight. And it had been his idea, after all, to intrude on her privacy the one time she might least have wished him to do. "I am sure I do not know what you mean."

"No, of course you do not," agreed Blackthorn in

tones heavily laced with irony. "It is naturally the custom for a husband and wife, dining alone, to sit at the opposite ends of a dining table designed to seat forty guests."

"You must know very well it is not," Violet objected. Giving up all further attempts at pretending to eat, she carefully laid her utensils on the plate and folded her hands in her lap. "If you recall, I did tell you the fireplace in the family dining room had taken to smoking and until we have recourse to a chimney sweep to clean it out we must resign ourselves to the inconvenience of eating here. I am sorry, Blackthorn, if you have seen fit to read more into that than there is."

"If I am reading between the lines, Violet," said Blackthorn, sternly quelling the urge to shake her until she abandoned her demmed impenetrable façade of demure unassailability, "it is because I am regretfully aware I have been something less than an attentive husband of late."

Violet, he noted grimly, did not betray so much as a flicker of emotion at what amounted to a blatant concession of guilt on his part.

"If you have, Blackthorn," she replied as serenely as if he had just admitted to nothing more momentous than having spilt gravy on the tablecloth, "then I should not let it weigh heavily on you. I daresay you have had a great deal to occupy you, and I, I fear, have been far too busy to notice. I am not, you see, without my own pursuits."

One of which was demanding her immediate attention, thought Violet, put out of all countenance with her dearest Blackthorn. Indeed, she could not but be wishing him at Jericho at the moment. He would choose *now*, of all times, to salve what she did not doubt was a guilty conscience, when all he was really doing was battering at her meager defenses at a time when she might least have wished for him to do.

Blackthorn's eyebrows fairly snapped together over the bridge of his nose. Not noticed? Egad! Her answer was hardly what he might have wished, though, in light of the circumstances that must have prompted it, it was undoubtedly what he should have anticipated.

Hell and the devil confound it! The last thing he had ever intended was to hurt his sweet Violet, who had freely given so much of herself on his behalf and Philippe's. Telling himself it could not have been helped did little to assuage the sudden twist in his belly as it came to him insidiously to wonder if another man was occupying his enchantress's thoughts to the exclusion of himself.

His eyes narrowed to piercing points on the lovely profile of her face. The devil knew she had admirers enough to make up for the conspicuous absence of her husband.

"By that," he said in biting accents, "I must suppose you and the inimitable Aunt Roanna are happily launched once more into the gaiety of the Season."

"Oh, happily, indeed," Violet assured him airily, clenching her hands together in her lap to keep them from a wholly uncharacteristic propensity to flutter nervously. "We are gay every night practically to excess."

"You cannot know how glad I am to hear it," growled Blackthorn, fiercely waving away the footman who had had the unhappy misfortune to enter bearing a tray laden with hot lobster, roasted sweetbreads, and apricot tarts baked to a golden brown. "You are not further desirous, are you, of filling your plate?" he demanded harshly of Violet.

"No," replied Violet, who found the mere thought of food on a churning stomach revolting at best. "As it happens, I daresay I really haven't time to partake of anything more."

"Not with the press of all your planned social engagements," he prompted, heartily tempted to take her right then and there on the dining room table. It would be a feast, he did not doubt, to sate the most jaded of appetites, and he was bloody demmed starved from privation.

"Exactly so, my lord," replied Violet, as close as she had ever come to giving way to hysterics. "You know yourself how it is—always at least three or four balls from which to choose, not to mention soirees, romps, and musicales. It fair takes one's breath away."

At that glowing submission from Violet, Blackthorn drew up sharply. "A veritable merry-go-round of delights, as it were," he ventured silkily.

"Indeed, my lord," Violet said a trifle testily, feeling the beginnings of a headache coming on. "I believe I just said so."

Egad, thought Blackthorn, who had been made privy before to Violet's views on the whirl of the Season's social events, a view that had been rather different from the one which held she was rendered gay to excess by them. She was lying, he was sure of it—Violet, who never lied about anything!

"It is plain to see I needn't have worried you were wearying of your stay in London and had, perchance, grown homesick for Devon," he observed, leaning back in his chair. His eyes, demon black and unreadable, however, never left her face. "What plans have you and your aunt for tonight? I shall be pleased to make the effort to catch up with you to ask for the honor of a dance."

Inexplicably, he suffered a sudden wrench to his midsection as Violet at last lifted her eyes to his.

"Shall you, my lord?" she queried, little caring her whole heart must have shone in the look she gave him. "No doubt I should be pleased to dance with you. Unfortunately, Aunt Roanna has promised us to Vauxhall for the evening."

"No, has she?" queried Blackthorn, finding himself staring into blue-violet eyes which, far from being in the least dreamy, regarded him with a singular directness. "Aunt Roanna, then, is to accompany you herself?"

"We have been invited, as it happens, to share a booth with Lady and Sir Henry Granville," submitted Violet, ruefully amazed the lie should have come so easily to her tongue. Clearly, she was slipping into a veritable quagmire of depravity. "As I know your views regarding Sir Henry, I shall not hold you to your promise. Indeed," she added with pointed deliberation, "I daresay you already had plans of your own."

"Yes, of course," said Blackthorn, feeling peculiarly as if a cold vise had just clamped down on his vitals. Violet knew about *le petite* Benneau, he thought with bitter certainty. It was all there for him to see in her eyes, which dared him to deny it.

The devil! She knew nothing, and he was bound by honor not to tell her anything. A shadow of bitter self-mockery flickered briefly across his stern, handsome countenance, and then a shutter dropped over his face, and he was himself again. "You are right, of course. It would never do to inflict myself on Sir Henry and the rest of your party. We shall make it another time."

"I shall naturally look forward to it," Violet returned woodenly and hastily dropped her eyes to her untouched plate. Faith, it was truly over, she told herself, fighting against the feeling of nausea that threatened to rise to her throat. In spite of everything, she had hoped beyond reason that, once she had brought graphically to his attention the gulf that he had imposed between them, he might bring himself to trust her enough to tell her the truth. Surely she had earned that much from him, at least. He, however, had made it plain she meant less than nothing to him. Faith, what a fool she had been to think she knew his heart. In truth, she did not know him at all!

Wanting nothing more than to escape his disturbing presence, she summoned the wit to make her excuses. "Aunt Roanna is expecting me to call for her in the carriage in little more than an hour. I—I'm afraid I have still to dress."

"Then I shall not detain you further," said Black-thorn coldly.

He came smoothly to his feet and assisted Violet in rising from the table. Then, as she made as if to leave him, he caught her hand. "Violet," he said.

"Yes, my lord?"

The whimsical twist of his lips pulled at her heart. "You did not used to call me 'my lord.' I cannot but wonder when I became the earl to you."

If he had thought to win a smile from her, he was to be immediately disappointed.

Violet returned his look gravely. "I suppose," she said quietly, "it was when you began to behave like one. Was there anything else, my lord?"

A shadow of something like anger darkened his eyes, and it seemed for a moment he would say something more. But at last he only released her, his hand dropping to his side with a strange air of finality. "No, nothing. I wish you a good evening, Countess."

"As do I you, my lord," uttered Violet, marveling that her voice should sound calm and unruffled when inside her stomach was clenched in a hard knot.

Turning, she walked away without looking back. Consequently, she did not see Blackthorn stare after her, a curiously fixed expression in his dark, glittery eyes.

It was all Violet could do not to run from the dining room. Blackthorn must never know what it had cost her to spurn what she could only suppose had been meant as sops for his conscience. At least he had not offered to kiss her. That she could not have borne. Indeed, even knowing she meant nothing to him, she had no defenses against the power of his lips to melt her resistance. That had been amply demonstrated to her before.

She was grateful as she flung into her room at last that she had ordered the hackney coach to be waiting around the corner from the house by ten. There was not time to dwell on the unhappy scene in the dining room or her misery. She was forced to hurry out of her evening dress and into the gray serge gown which she had, with threats and persuasion, managed to borrow from her abigail.

Subduing the rebellious mass of her hair in a bun at the nape of her neck, she donned a plain white muslin cap. Moments later, her willowy figure draped in a long, black mantle, she made her way down the service stairs and out the back to the mews.

It was a still night with drifts of clouds scudding across the moon, and she was prey to the absurd fancy that a figure lurked in every shadow. Consequently, she could only be exceedingly grateful to discover the hackney coach was there before her.

Giving the coachman the direction, she settled back against the less than luxurious squabs and willed her heart to cease its ridiculous pounding. It was harder to stop the mist that persisted in blurring her vision.

Really, she could not think how she could have been so mistaken as to believe she and Blackthorn had had something together, something to which she might cling even knowing he did not love her. They had shared the blissful heights of passion. Surely it was inconceivable that it had meant nothing to him.

She, after all, had felt the tenderness in his touch—or had she been mistaken in that, too? she was brought suddenly to ask herself. It seemed in her distraction that she must question everything she had so blithely taken for granted. And if she could be so in error in her judgment concerning the things of the heart, could she not be wrong about Blackthorn himself?

Certainly Blackthorn would seem to be doing everything in his power to convince her of it, she bitterly reflected. He had not taken just any woman to be his mistress. He had chosen Madame Gabrielle Benneau, a Frenchwoman with unsavory friends and questionable loyalties. Really, it was too bad of him.

Things she had previously dismissed as being insignificant or merely coincidental now would appear to

loom as damning evidence against him. In his delirium
he had spoken in French. More than that, he had called
out to his French wife, who had the added distinction
of being the sister of Captain Philippe Lambert, one of
Napoleon's most decorated naval officers.

How could Violet now overlook the fact Dane had
been in London when the letter bearing the emblem
of the Raven was captured? Or, worse, that he had been
in Sir Henry's house when Granville was bludgeoned
from behind in an apparent attempt to steal secret government papers? It came to her with what would seem
a painful significance that he had never explained how
he came to receive the wound in his arm or why he had
been so certain Lieutenant Freeman and his men had
arrived at the inn with the intention of placing him
under arrest.

Faith, the one and only thing that she could say for
certain about the man she had married was that he was
consistent in never explaining anything to her! And
she, convinced he was her gallant captain, the hero of
countless naval battles, had been content to accept him
on faith alone.

The most dreadful thing of all, however, was that
no matter how damning the evidence might seem, she
simply could not bring herself to believe he was the
infamous French agent any more than she could cease
to love him.

He had betrayed her trust, but he could never betray
his king and country. In her heart, she knew it. In that,
she simply could not be wrong, she told herself as the
hackney coach came to a stop.

Handing the driver his fare with the instructions to
return for her in an hour, Violet dismounted into the
street at the head of a dark alley. At the very least,
she could not condemn him so long as there was the
remotest possibility that somewhere there was conclu-
sive proof of his innocence—or of the guilt of someone

other than Blackthorn. And that she was about to try and determine once and for all.

Waiting only long enough to see the hackney disappear around the corner, Violet gathered her mantle around her and entered the alley.

The four-story Georgian brick, which gave every evidence of a gala going forth, was bustling with activity belowstairs when Violet let herself in the service entrance with an air of quiet assurance. Even so, it was not long before a tall, spare woman wearing the harried authority of the housekeeper accosted her.

"You, miss, who are you? What are you doing there?"

"Miss Daisy Prill, ma'am," said Violet, dipping a brief curtsy. "Abigail to Mrs. Rochelle. The mistress broke a strap dancing." Violet shifted her arm to draw attention to what appeared to be a bundle carried under the loose folds of the mantle. "She sent for me to fetch her Egyptian sandals. Said she'd be waiting on me upstairs in the room next to the admiral's study."

"Then you had better be off, hadn't you?" determined the housekeeper, already turning away to see to the proper folding of the linens for the late supper. "The servants' stairs are through there," she added, briefly indicating a door at the far end of the pantry. "It's on the third floor, the fourth door to your right. You've only to follow your nose."

"Yes, ma'am." Violet, murmuring a thank-you, slipped quietly through the controlled chaos of the household staff catering to the needs of a house full of guests and let herself into the stairwell.

It was to occur whimsically to Violet as, thanks to the housekeeper's directions, she made her way unerringly to Vice Admiral Sir Oliver Landford's study, that she would seem to be blessed with unsuspected talents which lent themselves peculiarly well to criminal pursuits. Indeed, she might have been meant to be a burglar, she reflected, had it not been for an unfortunate accident of her birth into a family of wealth and position.

Lighting a lamp, she ran her glance over the glass-covered bookcases, leather-upholstered sofa and chairs, and oak desk, which constituted the study's furnishings. In search of something that might indicate a hidden vault or secret cabinet designed for concealing documents of an incriminating nature, she noted an oversized likeness of Sir Oliver, painted in the style of a David and ensconced on the wall between two book shelves. Aside from the fact that she had never felt an affinity for portraits of gentlemen depicted in the attire of a toga, riding boots, and a plumed hat, the painting would seem somehow singularly placed.

Drawn by curiosity, Violet ran her fingers along the back side of the frame. She sustained a small thrill of excitement as her fingertips brushed a small protuberance in the wall behind the frame. Then, pressing it, she stepped back, her heart leaping beneath her breast, as the painting shot upward to reveal a roomy priest hole behind it.

Congratulating herself on having so easily discovered Sir Oliver's secret cabinet, Violet failed to take note of the study door swinging open on silent hinges. Nor did she detect the tall figure garbed in black that, entering and closing the door behind it, moved silently toward her.

Violet stepped toward the gaping opening. The figure, looming over her, reached out a hand at her back. Violet, wondering where she should begin her search, halted uncertainly across the threshold—and the hand, clamping over her mouth, stifled her scream, even as an arm like a steel band imprisoned her against an unrelenting chest.

"Softly, *enfant*," a voice whispered in her ear. Carefully, the hand withdrew from her mouth.

Violet, nearly sagging with relief, turned, exclaiming, "Blackthorn! How the devil?"

Blackthorn silenced her with the side of his index finger placed to her lips. "I have been following you ever since you left the house. It was obvious you were up to something when you lied about your planned outing to Vauxhall Gardens. Your Aunt Roanna, after all, was promised to the Admirals' Ball. But this, Violet. What the devil did you hope to accomplish by dressing in the guise of an abigail and burglarizing Sir Oliver's house?"

"Evidence, my lord," declared Violet, hardly knowing whether, in the wake of his despicable behavior in the dining room, to be pleased or angry he had been concerned enough to come after her. "Proof Landford is behind the attempts to cut your stick for you as well as the attack on Sir Henry. He is involved, Dane, I am sure of it."

"I should not be at all surprised," agreed Blackthorn, suffering a pang of guilt for having suspected his enchantress was on an entirely different sort of assignation. The devil, he might have known Violet could never do anything that was not motivated by a selfless goal.

No doubt he should have been humbled by the realization she had succumbed to burglary for his sake. That he was not—indeed, that he was instead sorely tempted to throttle his meddling enchantress for having risked her pretty neck once again for him—could no doubt be attributed to a perversity in his character.

"Hell and the devil confound it, Violet," he said, taking a deliberate step toward her. "Have you the smallest notion what you are risking by simply being here, never mind the minor considerations of breaking and entering, not to mention intended burglary?"

"You may be sure I thought everything out very carefully beforehand, Dane," replied Violet, moving away from Blackthorn to examine a locked box set on what had obviously served as an altar when the priest hole was used for the secret practice of the then forbidden Catholic faith. "Have you, by any chance, a penknife?"

"And having thought it out, you decided it was prudent to burglarize Landford's house while the Admirals'

Ball was in full progress below?" demanded Blackthorn, kneeling before the box, the required article in his hand.

"It would seem the most opportune time with every-one occupied belowstairs," Violet submitted, watching as Blackthorn jiggled the point of the knife around in the keyhole. "Certainly, it was much simpler to gain admittance during all the confusion of a gala going forth than it would have been with the house quiet. Which brings me to wonder how you managed to enter without being detected."

"Through a ground story window, my enterprising enchantress," replied Blackthorn, smiling at the sudden click of the lock. "And *voila*." Lifting the lid, he reached in to remove the stack of documents contained within.

"Well?" demanded Violet, trying to peer over Black-thorn's shoulder. "What did we find?"

"I'm sorry, *enfant*," he said after a moment, "but there would seem to be nothing here to incriminate Landford in anything of a criminal nature. Aside from some deeds to apparent holdings, a few letters of credit, and various miscellaneous correspondences of no par-ticular interest to us, there are some articles of jewelry, and that is all."

Violet, however, was not listening. Feeling the blood drain from her face, she dropped slowly to her knees. Indeed, she could not control the trembling of the hand that reached down to retrieve a single item from the bottom of the box.

It was an exquisite thing of intricately wrought emer-alds interspersed with diamonds. Violet, holding it up to the lamplight, stared, entranced, at the glimmering heart of the stones, perfect in every detail.

Blackthorn, watching her, frowned. "Violet? What is it? You have seen this necklace before. Obviously, it means something to you."

Violet looked at him without really seeing him. "Yes,"

she said, "it means something to me. It was my mother's."

Then, carefully, she laid the necklace back in the box and, rising to her feet, stood with her back to Blackthorn, her arms clutched over her breasts.

"Return everything to the way it was, I pray you, Dane," she said in a muffled voice. "Then let us be away from this dreadful place. I wish to go home."

Chapter 12

"I was sixteen, and *Maman* thought it would be better if I stayed with Grandpapa in Devon," said Violet, staring at the spill of moonlight through her bedchamber window. "It was to be a yachting holiday, she said, just for the two of them. A fortnight of sailing along the coast with perhaps a stopover here and there if the fancy took them. I thought it was the most splendid thing I had ever heard of—Mama and Papa, at their age, stealing off to be alone. It never once entered my mind that I should never see them again. And afterward, when we learned they had gone to France to recover the fortune in gold her father had hidden away, I knew in my heart they had been betrayed. Like Gideon, I believed that Landford and his brother, the Earl of Blaidsdale, must somehow be behind it. But there was no proof, and I learned to accept that it was finished. *Maman* and Papa were dead, and nothing could ever bring them back again. But this." Turning her face into Blackthorn's shoulder, she clung to him, her pain reawakening. "Dane, how can I live with this, knowing the truth? And yet knowing, too, that it changes nothing? What am I to do?"

It was not a question that had any easy answers.

Wait and see. It was all Blackthorn, grimly holding Violet to him, could offer in the way of comfort. There was little that could be done. Even knowing the necklace had belonged to the marchioness was hardly sufficient evidence to convict Landford of piracy and murder. There would have to be proof Violet's mother had had the necklace with her on the yacht.

And therein lay the source of his enchantress's anguish. In a court of law, the necklace was all but meaningless. On the field of honor, it would be Landford's death warrant. Vere must never know what they had found in Landford's secret cabinet. And Violet must carry with her the knowledge of the necklace and all it signified.

There was, however, one other option Violet, in her anguish, had failed thus far to consider. She, after all, was not the only one who knew the truth.

Holding Violet in his arms, Blackthorn considered the proposition coldly. He was not averse to killing Landford in a duel. He would have done far more than invite exile upon himself if it would erase the pain from his sweet Violet's eyes.

Unfortunately, he knew Violet far too well to suppose she would not take the blame for his alienation and disgrace upon herself, and that burden he would not willingly place on her slender shoulders. Putting a period to Landford's existence would serve only as a last resort.

In the meantime, he reflected grimly, there would seem little he could do but continue on his present course. For now, his hopes rested in Gabrielle Benneau and the waiting game they played. Hellfire, he thought cynically. Thus far, that had yielded little enough beyond alienating him from his wife. His quarry had proven most damned elusive, a circumstance that could no doubt be attributed in part to his contretemps with Landford on the balcony at Lady Stanhope's ball.

In resigning his commission in the heat of anger, he surrendered the one advantage his enemies had believed they held over him—that he would remain reluctant to openly point the finger of accusation in their direction so long as he retained hopes of salvaging what was left of his career. Certainly they must now view him in the light of a loose cannon—wholly unpredictable and exceedingly dangerous. It was perhaps inevitable that they would proceed with a far greater caution than had been their previous wont.

It was one thing to frame and plot to murder a captain who was bound by the discipline of rank. It was quite another to arouse the enmity of an earl who had the advantages of wealth and position, not to mention powerful allies whose allegiance was based on family ties.

His lips curled in sardonic appreciation of the part Vere had played in bringing them to their present stalemate. The marquess presented a formidable ally who had proven to have access to sources of information beyond anything Blackthorn could have hoped to gain on his own. Indeed, he could only wonder at the sort of pursuits that had led Vere to discover the sinister plot unfolding in the seamy environs of the Blue Dragon.

Blackthorn's lips thinned to a hard line at the realization of how near they had come to arriving too late to rescue Furneaux from the clutches of Mr. Wu, who, Blackthorn did not doubt, had been in the employ of someone else. It was an unsavory conspiracy, indeed, if it involved the traffickers of opium and the soulless denizens of Limehouse in its machinations. They had done their work all too well on Steven Furneaux, whose recovery remained most damned uncertain. But then, Blackthorn did not doubt something else was working on Furneaux, something eating away at his will to live.

Blackthorn experienced the birth of a slow, burning rage at those who had sought to corrupt his former first lieutenant. Furneaux, a man of courage and honor who commanded the respect and loyalty of his men, had shown promise of becoming a more than able officer. Blackthorn could only wonder what had made Furneaux vulnerable to the manipulations of ruthless men who would do anything to achieve their nefarious ends.

And now Violet, too, had been touched by their evil, he thought, feeling her still awake in his arms. Even now he had only to close his eyes to see her, white-faced and stricken with the horror of her unlooked for discovery. The ride home in the carriage had been accomplished in silence with Violet lost in contemplation.

Blackthorn, drawing her to his side, had cursed the stupidity and greed of the man who could not bring himself to part with the necklace that incriminated him in murderous deeds. It was something Violet should never have been made to see.

Violet had not objected when Blackthorn, helping her from the carriage, had lifted her in his arms and carried her up the stairs to her bedchamber. Nor had she protested when he relieved her of the shapeless mantle and the ridiculous cap that hid her hair. Releasing the luxurious mass of curls from the pins that confined them, he had inhaled their sweet fragrance, rather than look into her eyes. Half afraid she would pull away, he had yet dared to minister to her as if she were a child in need of comforting, until at last, as he had slipped the gown off her slender frame, the haunted look had left her eyes to be replaced by a rueful grimace.

"This is not at all necessary, Dane," she said, half laughing, the color rising to her cheeks, as at last she met his dark, hooded gaze. "I am not like to go into a sharp decline over this."

"No, you will undoubtedly come about, just as you always do," he answered, his hands smoothing her hair back from her face.

The devil, he had never been able to hide anything from the enchantress who had cast her spell over him

from the very first. His uncertainty must have been plain
to read in his face.

Violet had grown suddenly still in his grasp, her gaze
searching his. A low, shuddering sigh breathed through
her lips, and she stepped into his arms. "Dane," she
breathed, laying her cheek against his chest. "Faith,
how I have missed you."

Egad, but she was magnificent, was his sweet, beautiful
Violet, he thought, remembering the feel of her in his
arms at that moment. She had come to him as naturally
as if the three weeks of his seeming disaffection had
never come close to touching her faith in him! The
devil, he had never dreamed there could be anyone in
the world like Violet.

Certainly he never could have imagined when he
broke into Sir Henry's country house that he would find
Violet waiting to tumble his defenses and forever change
the course of his existence. Violet, always and from the
very beginning, had come to his aid, giving of herself
with a selfless determination that had extended itself
even to the son who was not her own.

The realization that at last she had turned to him in
her sudden vulnerability had both humbled and moved
him. In that moment, he had wanted nothing more
than to be able to ease his sweet Violet's pain and make
her forget for a while the unwanted burden she carried.

Lifting her in his arms, he had carried her to her bed
and, ministering to her needs rather than his own, he
had made love to her. Egad, he had never had any
woman respond to his caresses the way Violet did. She
was all lithe, supple beauty reaching out to him. Accepting and giving, she drew emotions from him he
never knew he possessed, chief of which was an overpowering desire to cherish and render comfort.

A wry smile twisted at his lips at the thought. The devil,
he was becoming maudlin in his new role of husband,
something with which he had never come close to being
afflicted when he was married to Lynette. And yet he

could think of no other words to describe the unaccustomed well of emotions his sweet Violet had inspired in him.

More incredible yet, she had known and understood. He had seen it in her eyes, like moonlit pools, staring up at him, as he soothed and caressed her gently with his hands and lips.

A man had only to see Violet to be stricken with desire and plagued with lust-filled fantasies evoked by her lissome beauty. Egad, he knew well enough her power to inflame and incite him to a frenzied heat of passion.

This, however, had been something altogether of a different order. More than mere lust and yet fraught with passion, it had been a thing of feelings and emotion, of communication and trust. Hellfire, he had not the words to describe what it was. He was not even sure if he understood it.

As he had held himself over her, his eyes gazing deeply into hers, and made long, slow forays into her warm woman's flesh, he had experienced an unutterable sense of completion which had little to do with the swelling explosion of sexual release in which it had culminated. For those magnificent, seemingly timeless moments and afterward, he had felt closer to Violet than he had ever felt to anyone.

Violet, too, had been touched by it. Lying with him in the darkness, she had been brought at last to tell him about the tragic deaths of her mother and father, the suspicious circumstances surrounding their loss, and her now unshakable conviction that Blaidsdale and his brother had plotted to bring about the ruin of her house.

"Can you be so certain, Violet?" he asked quietly, trying to put it all together in his mind. "Blaidsdale, from all accounts, is a wealthy man. What would it serve him to attempt anything so risky as piracy? Even a fortune in gold would hardly seem sufficient motivation for one who was already more than plump in the pocket.

Is it at least possible there could be some other explanation for Landford's having possession of your mother's necklace?"

"I suppose anything is possible," sighed Violet, who had been able to think of little else on the interminable ride home from the vice admiral's town house. "Heaven knows I should be relieved to discover an alternative explanation that did not involve the murder of my parents. As for Blaidsdale, I cannot but think he is capable of anything. He never hid the fact he hated my father. Papa never talked about it, but I am reasonably certain it stemmed from something that happened between them when they were boys together at Eton. It was something *Maman* mentioned once about schoolboy grudges that come back to haunt one. She never explained what she meant, but somehow I know she was talking about Papa and Blaidsdale."

"And you believe Landford would do anything, even commit murder, out of loyalty to his brother?" said Blackthorn, Morin's judgment to the contrary yet fresh in his mind.

"It does seem rather farfetched when you put it that way," admitted Violet, who knew from her Uncle Richard, through her Aunt Roanna, how little Sir Oliver commanded the respect either of his subordinates or of his peers in the Admiralty. "A little over seven years ago, there was a scandalous episode which led to his court-martial for cowardice and dereliction of duty. I know that much. He was ultimately acquitted and the whole affair wrapped in clean linen. I am convinced, as well, he achieved his present rank not from merit but because of his brother's influence at court. I believe it is common knowledge he is given only the most mundane of assignments. But then, you were under his command, Dane. You should know even better than I what sort of man he is."

"I'm afraid the extent of my knowledge is based on only the two encounters I ever had with Sir Oliver," replied Blackthorn, who seven years before had been a prisoner in France. "One on the memorable occasion of Lady Stanhope's ball and the other in Malta, when he ordered me to transport Sir Henry Granville to Gibraltar."

"Sir Henry?" uttered Violet, lifting her head to peer into Blackthorn's shadowy features. "You had Sir Henry aboard the *Antiope* when you encountered the French seventy-four! You did, did you not, Dane? That is why you went to his house on another particularly memorable night. Pray do not bother to deny it, for I promise I shall not believe you."

"Then I won't deny it, my irrepressible Violet." Blackthorn smiled, well aware he had opened himself to a Spanish Inquisition, one Violet had been holding in reserve for no little time.

"*Well?*" demanded Violet, when Blackthorn odiously failed to expand on that intriguing admission.

"Well, what, Enchantress?" Blackthorn countered with the arch of a single arrogant eyebrow.

"You know very well what," declared Violet, mercilessly digging her fingers into his side between his ribs. "Why did you break into Sir Henry's house that night? And who assaulted him? You know who it was, I am certain of it. I daresay he was the reason you were forced to seek asylum in my bedchamber. He was, was he not? Oh, you will tell me!"

"Little *devil!*" gasped Blackthorn, subject to an exquisite torture at the hands of his enchantress. Lunging over onto his side, he clamped an iron fist about her wrist and pinned it to the pillow beside her head. "It would serve you right if, instead of satisfying your feminine curiosity, I turned you over my knee and beat you. Indeed, you may be sure I shall if ever you err again in trying my patience in a similar fashion."

"Blackthorn," crooned Violet, positively beaming up at him. "You are ticklish. Faith, I never should have thought the hero of countless naval battles would be possessed of a vulnerability on that particular order."

"As it happens, I am possessed of two older sisters who used to delight in holding me down and subjecting me to that sort of fiendish torture," growled Blackthorn, who had almost forgotten that episode in his life, but who had just had it vividly recalled to mind.

"No, are you?" queried Violet, immediately intrigued at what amounted to an exceedingly rare glimpse into her beloved captain's youth. "*Two* sisters, Dane? And you never told me anything about them. Who are they and where are they now?"

"Their names are Anne and Kathryn, and, as it happens, I have not the least idea where they might be. I have no doubt they are happily wed and occupied with the rearing of any number of aspiring hopefuls. I lost track of them longer ago than I care to think about. That, however, is neither here nor there," he added, reminded of her recent iniquity. "We were discussing the punishment you are about to receive for having inflicted yourself on me."

"Indeed, we were not," demurred Violet, who was not to be distracted from the original subject. "You were about to tell me why you broke into Sir Henry's. You did see him, Dane—the Raven. He *was* there."

"Naturally, I should not wish to dispute the word of a lady," said Blackthorn, reluctantly abandoning immediate implementation of the particular form of chastisement that had come to mind, one which had involved an exotic employment of leather bindings and peacock feathers. "*Monsieur Le Corbeau* had already bludgeoned Sir Henry on the back of the head and was busy rifling through the papers in Sir Henry's desk when I had the misfortune to burst in on them."

"I *knew* that must have been the way of it," interjected Violet, dazzling him with her smile of triumph. "It was obvious to me you could never have done anything so cowardly as to strike a man nearly twice your age from behind. Clearly, there had to be a second intruder."

"Oh, clearly, indeed," murmured Blackthorn, who could not but be gratified at his enchantress's acumen in the matter of character assessment. Egad, she had saved him from capture and subsequently had never once to all appearances altered in her unreasoning faith in him!

"You may choose to poke bogey at me if you wish, but I was right. You cannot deny it," scolded his perspicacious countess, awarding him a comical moue of disgust. "More to the point, however, what happened next?"

"What should have happened?" Blackthorn shrugged, thinking Violet had never looked more desirable than she did at that moment, with her hair tousled from their recent lovemaking and her lovely face animated with an insatiable curiosity. "The Raven and I exchanged a few pleasantries over Sir Henry, who was beginning to show distinct signs of returning to consciousness. He even went so far as to declare his positive delight that Captain Trevor Dane should have shown up in the nick of time to take the blame for having bludgeoned Sir Henry."

"The devil he did!" exclaimed Violet, who took immediate exception to the Raven's obvious intent to frame her dearest captain for his own dastardly deeds. "But, Dane," she added, as the full significance of what Blackthorn had just related struck her, "he *knew* you! Surely, then, he was no stranger to you either."

"I daresay you are in the right of it, Enchantress," submitted Blackthorn, who had frequently pondered that inescapable fact. "Unfortunately, he was masked. And I have since come to believe he must have deliberately altered his voice in some manner. I failed to recognize it or him."

"Still, you will admit his familiarity with you would

seem to narrow the field considerably," insisted Violet, who categorically refused to be discouraged by the small setback of Blackthorn's failure to recognize the assailant. "I am surprised he did not attempt to put a period to your existence in Sir Henry's study rather than run the risk of your eventually putting two and two together."

"As a matter of fact, he did take exception to the prospect of leaving me alive to identify him," Blackthorn admitted reminiscently. "He fired his pistol at me. He was generous enough, however, to miss. By the time I recovered my feet with the intent of returning the favor, he had vanished out the door—and completely out of sight, as I was immediately to discover when I pursued after him into the passage. A gathering at the foot of the stairs forced me to flee to the floor above."

"But of course," exclaimed Violet, who was already familiar with the events immediately subsequent to Blackthorn's flight up the stairs, "you were afraid you would be taken for Sir Henry's assailant. You really had no choice but to flee. Still, I fail to see how the Raven was able to so completely absent himself in the time it took you to appear in the passage. I promise he did not come upstairs. I had just gone up myself and was occupied with unlocking my door preparatory to entering. I most assuredly would have seen a masked gentleman fleeing through the passage. Unless—"

"He had discarded his disguise and fled to the floor below," Blackthorn, seeing her put it all together just as he himself had done, finished for her.

"Dane?" Violet said, gazing at him with disbelieving eyes.

"Yes, my sweet enchantress."

Wholly oblivious to the fact she was in her natural state, Violet sat perfectly upright in the bed. "He was one of Sir Henry's guests," she exclaimed. "Faith, he had to be."

"I believe it is of the very highest probability," agreed Blackthorn, who was *not* oblivious to her state and who, indeed, was fast losing interest in any further discussion of the elusive Raven and his undetermined identity. "Though I suppose it is conceivable he did just as I did and ducked into the nearest room. I daresay he would have done so, however, without the same intriguing results that attended my own fortuitous rescue."

"Then I daresay he must have had a devil of a time making his escape," postulated Violet, who could not but take note of the fact her dearest captain's attention had most certainly wandered. Already in a full state of arousal, he was, in fact, flying his colors. "There is not a ledge on the second story, and Sir Henry was exceedingly thorough in his search of the house and the grounds."

"The devil with Sir Henry," growled Blackthorn, pulling her down to him. "And with the cursed Raven," he added, molding the palm of his hand to one of her breasts. "They may both go to perdition for all I care at the moment."

"I daresay they shall, my dearest Blackthorn," submitted Violet, unable to suppress a shudder of pleasure, as he pressed his lips to the curve of her neck where it met her shoulder. "Whether you wish it or not. Only there is just one more thing. You have yet to tell me why you broke into Sir Henry's house in the first place."

"Because, my impossible Violet," Blackthorn replied thickly, well aware he would not be granted his infinitely desirable countess's full attention until he had first satisfied her curiosity, "I believed he had the answers to certain pertinent questions. Who shot me in the back, for example, from the decks of my own ship? And who made certain my career should be in a state of ruin when I recovered? I still believe he has the answers. Indeed, I fully intend to have them from him—after I have first dealt with the matter of *Le Corbeau* to my satisfaction."

Violet could not but feel a trifle chilled at the thought
Blackthorn had clearly suspected her godmother's husband of having attempted to cut his stick for him in the
despicable fashion of firing a bullet into his back. But
then, he would have to be one of the most obvious
suspects. Sir Henry, after all, was presumably the only
one onboard ship who was not a member of the ship's
company.

Still, Violet, who had known Sir Henry nearly the
entirety of her life, could not but find it exceedingly
difficult to believe the man who had dandled her on
his knee when she was five and who had presented
her with a Yorkshire terrier puppy when she was eight,
among a plethora of other kindnesses she could not
enumerate, was the sort of man who could commit cold-
blooded murder. Really, it would seem to her to be too
farfetched by half.

It was on her lips to suggest her dearest captain should
accompany her to Sir Henry's town house on the morrow and demand point-blank to be told the answers to
his questions. She did not doubt a great deal would be
immediately cleared up to his satisfaction. She was not
given the opportunity, however, to express that exceedingly practical opinion. Blackthorn, leaning over her,
chose just that moment to silence her with his lips on
hers, not to mention the thrust of his tongue between
her teeth.

It was, in fact, her last cogent thought as she was swept
away in a veritable whirlwind of emotions occasioned
by Blackthorn's hands moving over her, arousing her
as only he knew how.

This was not the slow-moving, achingly divine sharing
of emotions they had experienced earlier. Impatient to
possess her, Blackthorn teased and tormented her until
she writhed beneath him and begged him to end her
exquisite torture.

"Tell me . . . first . . . my sweet . . . tormentor," panted
Blackthorn, poised over her, his magnificently erect

manhood fitted against the swollen petals of her body. "Promise . . . you will trust me . . . to take care of Landford. Swear you will not . . . take matters . . . into your own hands . . . ever again."

Really, it was not in the least fair. Violet, who could never wish to hurt anyone, most especially her dearest captain, could not but be acutely aware she had been the source of no little concern to Blackthorn since the events at Landford's town house. Worse, she did not doubt she would continue to be a disturbing influence until he was reinstated in the good graces of the Admiralty.

"I promise, Dane," she said, cradling his face between the palms of her hands. "I promise always to trust you."

The devil, it was not what he had asked of her. And yet, she had promised to trust him—his sweet Violet, who would never break her word. It would have to be enough.

Plunging himself into her woman's flesh, he brought her swiftly to the pinnacle of desire, until at last she burst in a delirious explosion of release and, triumphantly, he spilled his seed inside her.

No doubt Blackthorn would have been rather less assured had he been given to see Violet depart the house the following morning and proceed directly to number twenty-two Portland Square. Violet, stepping past the butler, handed him her gloves and pelisse and requested Lady Granville be informed that her goddaughter, Lady Blackthorn, was there to see her.

"You cannot know how pleased I am you have come, Violet," declared Lady Granville some five minutes later as she pulled her young guest down beside her on the settee in her pink and lavender private sitting room. "We have missed you terribly these past weeks. How is Lord Fennington? I remember when Albert was taken by the mumps, followed in swift succession by Elizabeth,

Franklin, and Felicia. I was never so distraught. But that was all a long time ago now. Children have a disconcerting way of growing up seemingly overnight. Just look at you, dearest Violet. Here you are married and with a family of your own. I daresay your mother would have been so very happy for you. I know she would have liked your choice in husbands.''

Violet, who could only agree with her godmother, a woman in her middle fifties who was becomingly dressed in a Nile green morning dress that admirably set off her blond curls only just showing the first signs of frost. Violet did not doubt in the least that her mama would have liked Blackthorn exceedingly well; indeed, she knew they would have become the best of friends.

It was made clear to Violet after the first twenty minutes of hearing all the latest *on dits* that her godmother was not privy to anything concerning Sir Henry's private views on the former Captain Trevor Dane. She was, however, given the distinct impression something was troubling Lady Granville.

It was not like Lydia to refer constantly to fond memories of the past, especially reminiscences concerning her four children before they were grown. It seemed, however, that every subject upon which they touched over morning tea must inevitably remind the older woman of some little incident of domesticity. Having been given fond descriptions of Albert's childish propensity for inserting peas in his ears and Felicia's predilection for developing spots on her face at the least little thing, among other choice tidbits, Violet was moved at last to inquire if Lydia was feeling quite the thing.

"Faith," uttered Lady Granville, hastily averting her face. "Is it so obvious? I have tried to be sensible and brave. It is, after all, something that occurs all the time. Indeed, people think nothing of it. It is only that I never thought it could ever happen to me."

"Dear Lydia," exclaimed Violet softly, taking her godmother's fluttering hand in her own, "*what* has happened? Is it Albert or one of the others? Pray do not tell me one of them is—"

"No, oh, no, Violet," interrupted the other woman before Violet could finish. "The children are fine, I assure you. It is only that—"

Lady Granville broke off again, apparently unable to go on. Violet, watching in no little concern as the older woman struggled to regain her composure, could only wonder what could have overset her normally ebullient godmother. Faith, she could not recall ever having seen Lydia in dire straits before, save upon the tragic death of Violet's mother and father.

Involuntarily, Violet caught her breath as Lady Granville, clasping her hands firmly together in her lap, straightened her back.

"It is Sir Henry," she averred and immediately crumpled, one hand fumbling blindly for the lace handkerchief tucked in the neckline *en coulisse* of her gown. "If anyone had told me my own husband would fall to the lure of a—a *vampire* nearly half his age, I never should have believed it. Not in a hundred years, Violet, I assure you. And yet that is precisely what Lady Maheux was obliging enough to inform me not three days ago after she witnessed him emerging from a house on Berners Street where she had gone, if you must know, to commission Monsieur Pinchot to do a portrait of her son. I daresay you yourself will not believe it, Violet. Heaven knows I did not at first. Nevertheless, it is incontrovertible: Sir Henry has joined Madame Benneau's society of garden fanciers or some such thing, when you know he cannot tolerate the least suggestion of pollen without going off into a sneezing fit. Faith, when have you ever known him to wish to do anything that would require getting dirt under his fingernails? It is all a ridiculous fabrication, I tell you, meant to fling dust in my eyes. Madame Benneau has enticed him into her lair and, now that she has her clutches in him, you may be sure she will not be persuaded to let him go."

Whatever Violet had been expecting to hear from her godmother, it most certainly was not that Sir Henry had apparently taken up with Madame Gabrielle Benneau's *société des philosophes du jardin*. Good heavens, it would seem the revival of Epicurean philosophy was as contagious as the mumps!

And just as devastating to men old enough to know better, reflected Violet, as she exerted herself to reassure the wholly distraught Lady Granville that Sir Henry, far from taking up gardening, was undoubtedly pursuing an interest in the classical philosophy that advocated the doctrine of pleasure, or happiness, as the supreme good and principal goal in life.

"If you think to comfort me by telling me that Sir Henry has taken up with an entire society of persons dedicated to the pursuit of pleasure, Violet," declared Lydia, eyeing her goddaughter in no little horror, "then I fear I must question your sanity."

"You will understand, however," Violet hastened to amend, "when I explain that the real Epicurean believes true happiness or pleasure is achieved only through moderation and restraint as well as correct living."

"That is all very well for you to say, Violet," demurred Lady Granville, clearly doubtful. "But how are we to know that these are 'real' Epicureans with whom Sir Henry has involved himself? I have seen Madame Benneau at the opera surrounded by her cicisbeos, and you may be sure they did not appear to be practicing moderation, or a great deal of restraint, for that matter. I should have said they were gay to excess."

"No, were they?" queried Violet, who could not but experience a distinct prick of interest at that assertion from her godmother. Violet, after all, had never laid eyes on the woman. "And you have actually seen her? No doubt you will pardon my curiosity, dearest Lydia, but I have been wondering. What does she look like?"

"Precisely as you would imagine one of her calling would look," asserted Lady Granville, sniffing into her handkerchief. "*Voluptuous* would be the first word that comes to mind, followed by any number of others I should not dream of speaking out loud. She made her appearance in an Egyptian tunic open up the sides to an unseemly height that served to leave little to the imagination and no doubt at all that she was wearing next to nothing underneath it."

"Really? How very intriguing of her," commented Violet, forcefully reminding herself of her recently made promise to Blackthorn that she would always implicitly trust him.

"Disgraceful is more like," emended her godmother, draping herself over the arm of the sofa in an attitude of dejection. "And to think I have borne Sir Henry four children only to be cast off for a French *femme fatale* who paints her toenails and wears rings on her toes. Faith, it is too much."

Violet was rather more inclined to the opinion that Madame Benneau might very well be one of those free spirits who had embraced the precepts of such visionaries as Mrs. Wollstonecraft and Olympe de Gouges, who held that women were the equals of men in intellect and in essence and should not only enjoy equal opportunities in all ranges of life, but should be allowed, as well, to exercise the freedom to rule their own existences.

It was to come to her, as well, after an hour and a half of ministering to Lady Granville's fractured nerves, that there was a great deal more to Madame Gabrielle Benneau and *le société des philosophes du jardin* than she had previously been led to imagine. It was, after all, one thing for Blackthorn to be drawn to a woman who had been his former wife's closest intimate from childhood. It was quite another for a man like Sir Henry Granville, who had ever enjoyed a reputation for being staid in both his manners and his habits, to suddenly develop a taste for the gay existence of an Epicurean even of moderation. Really, it would seem too much to swallow.

Something was going on in the house on Berners Street, but somehow Violet did not think it was debauchery.

It was far more likely to have something to do with the pursuit of a certain French agent than with the quest for the true meaning of happiness or pleasure. Indeed, she could think of no other reason for a Whig of Sir Henry's remove, who in addition held the distinction of having been the victim of a cowardly assault by the villainous Raven, to insert himself into an environment of French intelligentsia. A whimsical smile played about her lips at the thought of Sir Henry happily discussing the philosophy of enlightenment, as espoused by Rousseau, Montesquieu, and Diderot, among other prominent French Encyclopedists. She did not doubt he would be subject in short order to a phlegmatic fit of the apoplexy if such were the case.

On the other hand, if *le société des philosophes du jardin* were what it would seem to claim to be, an intellectual gathering for the intelligent discussion of the true meaning of happiness and the human condition, then surely Blackthorn could find little in which to object if his wife chose to attend a session or two. She, as it happened, had developed an overweening curiosity to know what should have brought Blackthorn and Sir Henry Granville to a common meeting ground.

"He is a bloody hound on the trail," declared Blackthorn, stripping off his double-breasted coat of bottle green Superfine, followed in swift order by his yard-long white linen neck cloth, gray marcella waistcoat, and white silk shirt. "He appeared without warning three days ago at the house on Berners Street and has been nosing around ever since under the pretension of enjoying an interest in French Neoclassicism."

"I am hardly surprised," smiled Vere, who, likewise stripped to his lean, powerful waist, was occupied with shrugging into Jack Broughton padded gloves. "Sir

Henry is as shrewd as he is patient. I should not make the mistake of underestimating him if I were you. He is far from being the staid English gentleman he likes people to think he is."

"I have been convinced from the first he is every whit as deep as the game he is playing," Blackthorn said grimly, shaking his arms at his sides to loosen the muscles. "The question is, what is he after? I should give a deal to know what he was doing on my ship. I was informed he was some sort of government adviser who had been sent out with Landford to assess the fortifications at Malta."

"You, however, have reason to believe otherwise," concluded Vere, his hooded gaze coolly assessing his opponent, who displayed the lean, hard muscularity of a man who had known his share of fighting. With keen appreciation, Vere noted the scars of old wounds on the narrow torso. The fine art of pugilism, however, was a far cry from a free-for-all on the decks of a ship.

"You may be certain Nelson had already provided the Admiralty with everything they might require on the subject of the island's defenses," submitted Blackthorn in tones heavily laced with irony. Striking one gloved fist head-on against the other, he squared away in front of Vere, who waited, fists cocked before him, his left side turned a bit toward his opponent and his right shoulder held slightly down in readiness.

Oblivious to the drone of voices, the milling of gentlemen, the slap of leather-covered fists against flesh—all the activity, in short, that was normal to Gentleman Jackson's private gym on any given day of the week— the earl and the marquess warily began to circle one another

"If Granville was there in the capacity of an adviser, it had little to do with the conditions at Malta." Blackthorn, dodging an exploratory left from Vere, sidestepped and countered with a jab that glanced off the marquess's shoulder. "He was not on shore long enough to unpack before I was ordered to take him to Gibraltar.'' Gauging his opponent, Blackthorn drew a right cross from Vere, ducked, and came up under the other man's guard with a short jab to the jaw. ''I was given the distinct impression Landford was more than happy to see him go.''

Vere, pulling back with the speed of a cat, took the sting out of Blackthorn's punch and drove back with a blow straight from the shoulder. ''Which leads you to believe what?''

Blackthorn blocked and countered with an uppercut that missed as, grinning, Vere bobbed and retreated. Feinting with his left, Blackthorn let go with a hard right at Vere's midsection. ''That Granville was poking around in Landford's affairs.''

Vere, light and quick on his feet, only just danced away unscathed. The devil, he was beginning to enjoy himself. Blackthorn was proving to be far more amusing than Vere had dared to anticipate when he allowed himself to be lured, out of curiosity, into playing goose-berry to his sister's spouse. It had taken Vere only a very few moments in the same room with the earl to determine that what Blackthorn might be lacking in polish, he more than made up for in his quiet, yet unmistakable, command of presence. His new brother-in-law, he realized, was one of those curiosities—a man of integrity who was a man, not a prig. He had, in consequence, loomed as something of a novelty to Vere, who, having long since formed a cynical view of himself and his fashionable acquaintances, had made it a prac-tice to immerse himself in the rather more sordid walks of life. To a man familiar with all the worst sort of vices, Blackthorn's sober disposition should instantly have palled. Instead, he had turned out to be an unending source of surprise.

Who but Blackthorn, after all, would stroll into an opium den at the heart of Limehouse for the purpose of rescuing one of its lost souls and do it solely because the poor devil was a naval officer who had, before his fall from grace, faced the enemy bravely? It was obvious the stories of Blackthorn's exploits at sea were not exaggerated.

And yet, for one who must be termed a man of action, Blackthorn demonstrated a strength of intellect Vere could not but find singularly refreshing. It would seem the navy offered a unique source of education for its officers. Blackthorn was at least as well read in the classics, history, and mathematics as many of his contemporaries who had graduated from Eton, and more so than not a few of them. But then, no doubt, a captain would have a deal of leisure time on his hands in between fighting storms and the enemy, time that could be put to good use in reading.

Blackthorn's obvious skill in the art of pugilism, however, thought Vere, taking a glancing blow to the cheek, could only be explained by his having had a tutor of no little aptitude. Countering with a swift one-two combination to the head to draw Blackthorn's guard up, Vere lowered his shoulder and drove his right with all of his weight solidly behind it straight into the earl's exposed solar plexus. Blackthorn doubled, then came up, his face livid with the agony it cost him to drag in a shuddering gasp.

"Sorry, old man," said Vere, giving vent to a grin of pure enjoyment. "I'm afraid it was too good to pass up."

He was rewarded for his efforts with a sudden light, piercing glance filled with a fierce, savage joy—just before a gloved fist exploded against the side of his face.

"You may be certain Sir Henry is up to something," postulated Vere some little time later, as, fully dressed, he held a raw steak against the cheekbone beneath his left eye, which, considerably discolored, was already displaying a marked tendency to swell shut. "I confess, however, to no little difficulty in accepting he could do anything that might be remotely construed as treason. One is not made a Knight of the Grand Cross for plotting against one's king.''

Blackthorn, keenly aware of sore stomach muscles, lowered himself on to one of Madame Benneau's dimity-covered armchairs arranged next to the fireplace. The devil, he could not but agree that it would seem highly unlikely in view of the events at Sir Henry's country house to suspect Granville of anything more sinister than putting an end to the career of a naval captain. Still, he would like to know why Granville should have done it.

He would like to know, as well, why Sir Henry had taken a sudden interest in Gabrielle Benneau's little society of French literati. Somehow he did not think it was either the intellectual discussions or the undeniable charms of Madame Benneau that brought him to the house on Berners Street. *La petite* Gabrielle was no little amused that her newest cicisbeo tended to treat her in the manner of a fond but disapproving papa, who as little approved of her politics as he did of her philosophy of freethinking.

The only other explanation that occurred to Blackthorn for Sir Henry's eccentric behavior was that he was either convinced Gabrielle Benneau knew the secret of the Raven's identity or she knew the whereabouts of the missing captain of the schooner *Pegasus*—Commander Steven Furneaux. Either one would seem to imply he continued to hold Blackthorn in suspicion. Upon his first unheralded arrival at the house on Berners Street, he had not hesitated to use his acquaintanceship with the former Captain Trevor Dane as a reference.

If he had hoped in such a manner to gain Gabrielle's unwitting confidence, he had failed to take a proper measure of *la petite* Benneau. Before she made her perilous escape from France, Gabrielle had survived the Terror which had taken the life of her husband, Pierre, by masquerading as a peasant. Blackthorn doubted anyone could trick Gabrielle into saying or doing anything she had no wish to have done. She was as adept at charmingly evading questions as she was at juggling from one room to another the various gentlemen who called on her, he mused, with sardonic appreciation. Even now Sir Henry occupied the withdrawing room he and Vere had only recently evacuated for the more private environs of Gabrielle's boudoir and sitting room. Smiling mirthlessly to himself, he wondered where she would install Landford if the vice admiral should finally make his long delayed appearance. To say that the house on Berners Street was of only modest size would be a generous assessment.

Hardly had that thought crossed his mind than the silence was disturbed by a brisk rap of the knocker at the front door.

Blackthorn straightened in the chair, his head tilted, listening for the sounds of voices below.

"Can it possibly be our elusive vice admiral has decided to join us after all?" speculated Vere, a singular gleam in his unswollen eye.

"If he has, then it would seem we find ourselves in something of an awkward situation," said Blackthorn, a peculiarly fixed expression on his stern, handsome features. "Whoever it is, Gabrielle is bringing him upstairs to us."

"Indeed?" Vere murmured, likewise turning to look at the closed door. "I daresay this promises to be amusing."

When at last the sound of footsteps came to a halt on the other side of the oaken barrier, Blackthorn came instinctively out of his chair. The next moment the handle turned and the door swung open on its hinges.

"Blackthorn," pronounced the newcomer, gazing from the earl's tall figure to that of the marquess. "Good heavens, and Vere. What the devil are you doing here?"

"More to the point," declared Blackthorn in chilling accents, "is what the devil are *you* doing here, my dearest Lady Blackthorn?"

Chapter 13

"Vere, for heaven's sake," declared Violet, regarding her brother with no little astonishment, "what have you been up to? You look as if you had been in a Donnybrook fair. And you, Blackthorn," she added, turning her gaze speculatively on the earl, "I should be curious to know what you are doing in Madame Benneau's boudoir, save that I have given my promise to trust you."

"Precisely so, sweet Violet," said Blackthorn, ushering his wife into the room and firmly closing the door behind her. "I, on the other hand, shall not hesitate to ask you what *you* are doing here."

"Madame Benneau sent me up," replied Violet, who could not but think she had made a poor bargain with Blackthorn. "She said she was occupied for the moment in the withdrawing room and requested I wait for her in the upstairs sitting room. She *said* I should find some intriguing busts in the style of Nollekens within. She did not mention one of them would have a black eye."

"Gabrielle is possessed of a reprehensible sense of what is amusing," observed Blackthorn, advancing purposefully toward his enchantress. "Which is nothing to the point. You know very well that is not the question I was asking. I am in no mood for clever evasions, I warn you. Violet, why are you here?"

"I suppose if you really must know, I am here because I promised Lydia, my godmother, I should come," replied Violet, tugging off her lilac kid gloves one finger at a time. "It seems Epicureanism is not only undergoing a revival, but it is proving singularly irresistible to any number of English gentlemen, not the least of whom is her dearest husband. Indeed, if I am not mistaken, he is even now closeted in the withdrawing room with the founder of the society dedicated to its lofty principles. No doubt that is why you and Gideon are hiding upstairs in the lady's bedchamber."

"You are very astute, my dear," applauded Vere, moved to abandon the beefsteak for a glass of sherry. "I should point out, however, that we are in the lady's boudoir, not the bedchamber. That, as it happens, is occupied at present by someone else."

"Someone else?" lilted Violet, slipping past Blackthorn into the bedroom before he could put a hand out to stop her.

Violet came to a sudden standstill at the sight of the long, inert form lying covered to the chin in the bed. In the dim glow of a shaded lamp, she could just make out the exceedingly pallid features of a man little older than herself. With the greatest sense of dismay, she realized his eyes were open and staring at the ceiling with the chilling fixity of a corpse.

Indeed, she could only be grateful for Blackthorn's reassuring presence as he came to stand behind her, his hands resting lightly on her shoulders. Nor did she resist when he drew her back into the rather more comforting surrounds of the sitting room.

Turning into Blackthorn's arms, she lifted pity-filled eyes to his. "Who is he?" she asked, leaning the palms of her hands against his chest. "Why does he lie so still?"

"He is Commander Steven Furneaux. On *Antiope,* he served as my first lieutenant. It remains to be seen if he will ever serve again. It is my fear he may be lost to us."

"Lost? But why?" Violet, sensing some terrible mystery about to unfold, glanced from Blackthorn to Gideon, who merely shrugged and looked away. "What is the matter with him? How did he come to be like this?"

"The devil, Violet," uttered Blackthorn, cursing himself for not having foreseen this eventuality, "you should not have come. What would you have me tell you? That we found him in an opium den? That he had been there for far longer than was good for him? That he was like this when we carried him out of there and he has not altered for more than a bloody fortnight?" Angrily, he turned away and crossed to stare down into the embers of the fireplace. "You will no doubt pardon me if I failed to consider this a matter for feminine ears."

Violet, staring at Blackthorn's uncompromising back, could not but think that a great deal had been made suddenly exceedingly clear. No doubt Vere had been the one to come to Blackthorn with the dreadful news. She did not question how her brother had come by it. He was Vere. She had long since ceased to wonder at the things her brother did.

Together, he and Blackthorn had gone to the sort of sordid places she could not begin to imagine. Indeed, it must have been on the day she watched from the nursery window as they departed the house. They had found him, and they had brought him here to Madame Benneau, who could not possibly be the depraved creature Lady Granville believed her to be. In one corner of the room there had been a cot separated by a screen from the sickbed. She had sat with him night after night, no doubt murmuring words of comfort. And at dawn, Blackthorn had come to relieve her of her vigil.

Indeed, a great deal had been made clear. However, a great deal more made little sense at all! He was Blackthorn's former first lieutenant, a man who had faced and done battle with the enemy at Blackthorn's side. Blackthorn had called him Commander Furneaux. Obviously, he had received the promotion every young lieutenant dreamed of one day receiving.

More than that, he must certainly have been given command of his first ship, and no doubt he had earned it. This could not be the sort of man who would cast all away to embrace the sordid self-destruction of an opium den. If he had wished to kill himself, surely a warrior would have chosen a quicker and more certain exit.

"I am sorry, Blackthorn, if I have seemed to add to your burden," she said, suddenly sure of herself. "However, it appears to me you are allowing your feelings to cloud your judgment. And, indeed, who could blame you? It must naturally weigh heavily on you that one who was so promising has fallen, but you have seen men fall before in the fury of battle."

"Yes, in the fury of battle, but not like this." Blackthorn impaled her with black, searching eyes. "The devil, Violet! We dragged him out of an opium den."

"Yes, an opium den, but why?" persisted Violet.

"Do not think I have not asked myself that question a hundred times these past weeks," replied Blackthorn, who had thought of little else.

Those last weeks before Malta, it had been obvious something was troubling Furneaux. It had not been evident in the performance of his duties as first lieutenant. Those he had executed with his characteristic dedication and competence. It was rather that Blackthorn had sensed a sudden reserve in him, a restraint that had served to distance him from the other officers and men.

Hellfire! The signs had been there to read, and he, Blackthorn, had told himself it was not a captain's place to interfere in the private lives of his subordinates. He had confined himself to suggesting to his troubled lieutenant that if ever there were something about which he would like to talk, the captain's door was always open to him. Bloody hell! He had offered sops when he should have made at least an attempt to find out what was going on inside the man's head.

The truth was he had failed Furneaux, and now it would seem they had both paid the price. And now Violet, the one he would most wish to spare the sordid truth of his failure, had asked him a question. Hell and the devil confound it! He supposed she deserved an answer.

"I have come to the conclusion that, whoever or whatever drove Furneaux to the extreme of abandoning his duty and his career, his mind is now wandering in a darkness of his own making. Something is bloody well tearing him to pieces, and he has chosen to die rather than face it."

"What thing?" said Violet, her heart pierced by the hard bleakness in Blackthorn's grave features. Faith, he was blaming himself for what had happened to Furneaux. "Dane, what is it you are reluctant to say out loud?"

"I suggest you tell her, Blackthorn," said Vere, his hard eyes impenetrable, as he read the reluctance in his brother-in-law's grim aspect. It had been no different when he, Vere, had quizzed him about the scars of old battle wounds, one of them still livid on his back. No doubt it was a question of a warrior's honor, and honor, after all, was something Vere understood and respected.

Unfortunately, Vere knew his sister far too well to suppose she would be content to let it go without an answer. It were better to take the squirming earl off the hook. "Or shall I tell her my theory?" Vere said ever so gently. "I suspect, after all, Furneaux is guilty of trying to put a period to his captain—or at the very least he knew an attempt would be made and did nothing to prevent it, which, you will agree, amounts to the same thing. In any case, he would hardly seem to be worth the trouble he is costing you."

"Perhaps it would seem so to you," Blackthorn rejoined in even accents. "Nevertheless, he is my responsibility."

"Faith, is that it?" uttered Violet, feeling suddenly exceedingly sick to her stomach. "Dane? Is Furneaux the one who shot you in the battle against the French seventy-four?"

"In truth I do not know," answered Blackthorn, wondering how the devil Vere had known what he was thinking. The man had an uncanny knack for putting two and two together—in this instance his explanation for the scar on his back and his insistence on removing Furneaux from the Blue Dragon. Hellfire, he might have known Vere would figure it all out. "I haven't any proof he has done anything beyond abandon his duty and his ship. I know nothing for certain other than that we found him in an opium den in a state of oblivion."

"But that is just it," said Violet, clutching Blackthorn's sleeve in her eagerness to make him see what had come to her as most singularly peculiar about the lieutenant's fall from grace. "Does it not strike you as odd that he would choose such a manner in which to destroy himself? He had just been given his first command. If he were truly driven by guilt, would he not wish to redeem himself by doing the one thing that would make a difference—sail his ship against the enemy?"

"She would seem to have a point," observed Vere, giving Violet a long, steady look, which had the effect of sending a chill down her spine. "Perhaps it was never your first lieutenant's wish to lose himself in the dreams of Morpheus. Perhaps he knew something someone could not afford to have revealed. There are drugs known in the Orient that will steal a man's soul and leave his body with only a miserable facsimile of life."

Blackthorn's eyes gleamed, glittery hard, in the lamplight.

"Furneaux would be effectively silenced," he said with a chilling lack of emotion. "And there would not be the awkwardness of a corpse to be explained. It would seem to make a deal of sense."

"Commander Furneaux never stood a chance," uttered Violet, appalled at the sort of mentality that could have conceived anything so loathsome, let alone executed it. "Even if by some miracle he survived, he would still have been discredited, his word accounted for little or nothing. Faith, if only we knew what it is— something so dangerous that someone was willing to go to terrible lengths to keep it hidden."

"But I daresay that we do know what it is," said Blackthorn, recalling the two men in St. John's Cathedral and the package one man forced on the other. "Furneaux knows the identity of the Raven."

It was true. Violet knew it almost before Blackthorn voiced aloud what must have been evident to all of them. "But then somehow we must find a way to reach through to him," she exclaimed, looking from one to the other. "Vere, is there nothing that can be done for him?"

"It is difficult to say without knowing what drug was used, and I am no doctor. Perhaps if we could find someone versed in the Oriental art of healing?" Vere ended with a shrug, which would appear to indicate that for once he did not have an ace up his sleeve.

"But there *is* someone," declared Violet, glancing up at Blackthorn, who returned her look with a distinct glint in his eyes.

"Unfortunately, he is presently in Devon at Albermarle Castle," he said, leaving little doubt he knew precisely of whom Violet was thinking.

"Good God," exclaimed Vere, apparently much struck at the notion. "Do not say the duke has taken to studying Oriental medicine."

"As a matter of fact, he has, in a manner of speaking," submitted Violet, exchanging a smile with Blackthorn. "He has, after all, read Hufeland's learned treatise *Mac-*

robiotics, or the Art to Prolong One's Life. It is not the duke, however, of whom I am thinking. It is his cook."

"I had the pleasure of meeting Mr. Chan," said Blackthorn reminiscently, "when he applied a poultice to my wound. I believe he is a knowledgeable man. The question is, do you think His Grace will consent to do without his seaweed and rice for a few weeks?"

"One can never say from one moment to the next what the duke will do," replied Violet, who was already formulating the message to be sent to her grandpapa. "The first thing is simply to get his attention."

"Then naturally I must be the one to go to Albermarle," drawled the marquess, lifting the glass in a salute that was eminently self-mocking. "I daresay there is nothing more certain to jolt him to awareness than the sight of his doting grandson."

At that moment they were interrupted by a brisk rap on the door, which heralded the arrival of Madame Benneau in an undeniably striking tunic gown of powder blue gauze through which a distinct impression of her voluptuous feminine charms intriguingly showed.

"Ah, Madame *la comtesse,* I see you have found my collection of masterpieces well enough," she said, gaily entering and shutting the door behind her. "As you can see, one of them has the little damage, thanks to the 'handy pair of fives,' *n'est-ce pas?* I think, however, he will recover. Come," she added, slipping her arm through Violet's, "I wish for you to meet *mes amis, Monsieur* Despagne and *Monsieur* Morin, who are even now waiting with the profoundest curiosity to make your acquaintance." Sending a glance over her shoulder at Blackthorn, she ushered Violet through the door into the passage, where her maid stood, waiting. "You see, I have brought Maggie up to sit with our patient. You and *le marquis* must come, too, *oui?*"

Vere, who had risen at Gabrielle Benneau's entrance, paused before the dimpling maid. "Here, my girl," he said, proffering her the beefsteak between thumb and forefinger, "cook this for him. I myself have no further use for it."

"Yes, m'lord," giggled Maggie, dipping a curtsy. "Belike that'll bring 'im out'n 'is stupor, poor man that 'e is."

It was to prove, however, that nothing would serve to lure Commander Furneaux from the grips of whatever held him in its spell. Violet, who in the succeeding days had become a regular visitor to the house on Berners Street, was of the opinion he was still there, inside the seemingly lifeless body. She was nearly convinced upon occasion that she glimpsed glimmerings of intelligence behind the sightless eyes when, with Blackthorn supporting his head and shoulders, she spoon-fed Furneaux his broth.

In the hopes of keeping him from slipping farther into the dark place in which he wandered, she began to read to him—lively stories full of hope and good cheer and humorous passages designed to banish somber thoughts and lift the heart. Thinking to fling him a lifeline of sorts, she even read him the occasional reports in the *Gazette* concerning the naval blockade and England's ships at war.

Her time, however, was not all spent in the sickroom. Madame Benneau, she discovered, was as lively of intellect as she was engaging in her manner, and her friends Morin and Despagne, possessed of dry wit and droll humor, were a delightful change from Violet's fawning admirers. Had it not been for the sobering reminder of the patient upstairs that hung a cloud over the house, Violet could almost have been happy. Even so, the little house on Berners Street assumed a cozy atmosphere of warmth and conviviality Violet had not known since the death of her parents.

Indeed, for the first time since her sister Elfrida had married and left Albermarle Castle to take up her new life with Shields, Violet had found someone with whom she could talk about any number of things that had nothing to do with fashion or the latest *on dits*.

It was perhaps inevitable that the subjects of Lynette and Philippe should come up in the comfortable flow of feminine confidences. Indeed, it would seem to stem naturally from Gabrielle's suggestion one day as they sat in the withdrawing room that Violet might bring Philippe with her sometimes when she came. Gabrielle, after all, was the boy's godmother, and she had not seen him since before the unfortunate events on the road to Devon that had culminated in his mother's tragic demise.

"*Pauvre* Lynette. How I have missed her," sighed Gabrielle, sadly shaking her head. "*Peut-être* she is at peace *en fin*. I could never persuade her that happiness was a thing one made for oneself. *C'est dommage*—it is a pity—she could never see it for herself. But then, she could not stop being afraid. She had lost too much, I think. Perhaps if Dane had not had so much to be away." The Frenchwoman shrugged. "*Helas!* It could not be helped. Lynette knew that, and at least she had Philippe."

"Yes, Philippe," agreed Violet, who could not but wonder what Lynette had feared. No doubt it had been the waiting and wondering if Dane would find his way safely back to her, if only for the few brief days and weeks before he was sent to sea again.

Violet had seen how it was, after all, for her own Aunt Roanna. Indeed, it had often occurred to her that her dearest aunt's indolence was her own way of coping with the loneliness and uncertainty. "I daresay you will hardly recognize him. He has changed greatly even in the few weeks since I have come to know him."

"You, I think, are good for him," said Gabrielle, giving Violet one of her knowing looks. "Even as you are good for Dane. He, too, has changed, I think. More than he knows himself. You will listen to the advice of one who has lost her husband, *oui?* You will make sure he does not go back to sea."

It was hardly the sort of advice Violet was prepared to hear from the woman who had known Dane far longer than had she. Caught unawares, Violet rose abruptly to her feet and crossed to the window overlooking a walk peopled with artists busy at their easels.

"No, you are quite wrong," she said, pretending an interest in the scene below. "He must go back. Surely you, of all people, must see that."

"No, why should I?" returned Gabrielle with an eloquent wave of a white, shapely hand. "I am Madame Benneau of *le société des philosophes du jardin.* I see two people who are very much in love, I think. It is not given to everyone to know that kind of happiness, *cherie.* And happiness, after all, is the one good thing in this world. What a pity it would be to fling it all away."

Violet did know how to answer her. The truth was, she could not agree with Gabrielle more. Unfortunately, it was all an illusion that must vanish in the harsh light of reality. She loved Blackthorn, but he did not love her. His heart belonged to the sea and to the life of a naval captain who was very good at what he did.

She could not but think it ironic that in this house on Berners Street she had allowed herself to fall into a dream of what it might have been to be truly Blackthorn's wife. Here, in this house, of all places, she had let herself forget that she had trapped him into marrying her. Worse, she had begun to believe that in time she might have made the illusion a reality. She might have brought her gallant captain to love her.

And now, having gone so far as to fool herself into believing that one day he might love her, she had suddenly found herself visited with the terrible temptation to do what Gabrielle had suggested!

Faith, she could keep him from going back to sea. She need do nothing more than allow events to continue as they were. Thanks to her, he had already resigned his commission, and they were, after all, little closer than they had ever been to discovering the Raven's true identity. The devil, she had only to sit back and wait until Blackthorn himself realized the futility of pursuing their present course any further.

And then what? she asked herself, feeling on the verge of a ridiculous fit of the hysterics. Watch as Blackthorn tried to pretend an interest in farming, when in truth he was yearning with his whole heart and being to return to the life for which he had been born and to which he was singularly suited? How long would it be before he came to look upon her with disgust and perhaps to do so with every justification? It would, after all, be her fault.

Really, she could not bear it. Indeed, she had rather have him only for a few weeks in a year than to lose a little more of him with every passing day until there was nothing left of the illusion of happiness, but only the reality of his estrangement from her. And, after all, she, like Lynette before her, would have Philippe to give her comfort.

"You are perfectly in the right of it, Gabrielle," she said, turning at last to look at the other woman. "It would be a pity to fling happiness away. And that is why I shall continue to pray with my whole heart that somehow Blackthorn will one day have his beloved ship back again."

The same day Violet faced and conquered her greatest moment of temptation Vere returned with Mr. Chan, the duke's Oriental cook, who was well versed in the Chinese philosophy of yin and yang in the promotion of health and well-being.

Mr. Chan, a slight, well-knit gentleman with kind eyes and a mien of quiet perceptiveness, was pleased to inform Lady Blackthorn that her grandfather remained in excellent health and would continue so, thanks to Mr. Chan's understudy, whom he had left behind at the castle.

"I could not be more pleased to hear it, Mr. Chan," returned Violet, leading him into Madame Benneau's boudoir in which his patient resided in a state of unawareness. "You remember my husband, of course," she added, as Blackthorn set aside the book from which he been reading aloud and rose from his chair at the bedside.

"Very well," replied the Chinese gentleman, bowing. "I am gratified, my lord, to see you are recovered from your wound."

"A circumstance which may in no small measure be attributed to the poultice you applied, Mr. Chan," Blackthorn said. "It is to be hoped your cures will be of similar benefit to Commander Furneaux."

"We shall see what may be done," affirmed Mr. Chan, who, bending over the still form in the bed, was in the process of examining Furneaux's fingernails and hands. "I have brought with me the herbs I require. We are fortunate that we are in London. The foods I shall need may be obtained in Chinatown. I shall prepare a list for you. And now, if you would be so good as to leave me with him?"

"I believe your Commander Furneaux is in good hands," said Violet, as Blackthorn escorted her out into the passage and shut the door behind them. "What bothers me is the little Grandpapa told me about Oriental food cures leads me to believe it can be a lengthy process. It is, after all, based on the idea of bringing the energies of the body into balance. It could take weeks, perhaps even months, to return Furneaux to a semblance of his former self—if it can be done at all."

"I'm afraid we may not be able to wait that long," submitted Blackthorn, who for some time had been afflicted with a growing sense of unease concerning the passage of time. "It occurs to me the proprietor of the Blue Dragon must long since have reported Furneaux's removal to his employer. The Raven will be looking for him. How long do you think it will take for him to arrive at the notion of searching here for him?"

"I am sure I could not say, Dane," Violet replied, experiencing an inexplicable pang in the vicinity of her stomach. "I cannot think why it would occur to the Raven to look for him here at all. Surely the proprietor of the Blue Dragon could not have known you. In which case, why would he connect Gabrielle Benneau to the missing Furneaux?"

"Because, my dearest Violet," interjected Vere, stepping out of the withdrawing room where he had been occupied with apprising Madame Benneau in private of his return to London, "Mr. Wu was not unfamiliar with *me*. Naturally, it would take little imagination to connect me to Blackthorn, who not only has the distinction of being my sister's husband, but is Furneaux's former captain."

"The chain of connections must inevitably lead to Gabrielle," concluded Blackthorn, who was in any event fast wearing out of patience with waiting for the cursed Raven to make some sort of a move. "In which case, we are faced with the choice of moving our patient in the very near future for Gabrielle's protection as much as for his."

"Or what?" queried Violet, who could not think moving Furneaux would be in the least wise just when Mr. Chan was to begin his curative endeavors. "You did say we were faced with a choice, did you not? That would seem to imply you have some other option in mind."

"As a matter of fact, I have," admitted Blackthorn, a peculiar glint in his eye. "It has occurred to me that as long as we have Furneaux, it is not actually necessary to know the secret that he carries inside his head. It is merely enough that the Raven cannot be certain Furneaux has not recovered sufficiently to tell us what he knows."

"Really, Dane, I do not see how that is in the least helpful," objected Violet, allowing herself to be led into the withdrawing room, where Gabrielle waited expectantly for word of Mr. Chan's prognosis of Furneaux's condition. "If the Raven believes Furneaux has not talked, he will be more determined than ever to put a period to his existence. On the other hand, if he thinks Furneaux has told us what he knows, he will either do the sensible thing and flee the country posthaste, or he will be moved to silence everyone who has been in this house since Furneaux was brought here, which, you will admit, would make no practical sense at all."

"You have, as usual, managed to sum the situation up precisely, my perspicacious enchantress," applauded Blackthorn, awarding her one of his rare smiles, which had the effect of permeating her entire body with a warm, delectable glow.

"No doubt I am pleased that you think so," she retorted, wrinkling her nose at him as she obediently sank into the wing chair to which he led her. "On the other hand, you still have not answered my question. What other choice have we besides removing Furneaux from Gabrielle's house?"

"I, too, would like to know the answer, *mon ami*," spoke up Gabrielle, who could not be at all certain that *Le Corbeau* would choose to be practical and not kill them all as they lay in their beds. "You will tell us that you have some plan to stop this man *en fin*."

"I, too, am interested to know what you are contemplating," said Vere, settling easily on the sofa arm next to their hostess with a nonchalance not lost on Violet. Faith, she was hardly surprised to discover her brother had become rather better acquainted with the charming Madame Benneau than she had previously realized. He was Vere, after all, the devil.

One long leg stretched out to the side, Vere leaned his arm on the sofa back behind Gabrielle. "I believe I have a fair notion of how you intend to use the Raven's uncertainty to our advantage. Still, I confess I am all curiosity to hear it from you. Naturally, you have devised a scheme to draw the traitor out.''

"To draw him hopefully into a trap," amended Blackthorn, standing near the fireplace, an elbow propped on the mantelpiece. "Even without knowing who the Raven is, I believe it will be a relatively simple matter to convey to him the message that I have in my possession proof of his identity. Furthermore, I have every intention of turning that information over to the Admiralty in exchange for certain concessions to my benefit.''

"The devil you will," exclaimed Violet, who saw with horrifying clarity what her dearest Blackthorn intended. Bolting to her feet, she flew across the room to him. "You are going to set yourself up as the bait, Blackthorn, and I will not have it, do you hear?" she said, grasping the lapels of his coat in her agitation. "He has already come near to cutting your stick for you twice before, and I will not let you give him the opportunity to finish what he started. Why can you not simply let him go?''

"Because, my sweet, indomitable Violet," said Blackthorn, capturing her wrists in his hands and holding them captive at his chest, "exposing the identity of the Raven is the only way I shall ever clear myself of suspicion. And because even if it were not my duty to bring a traitor to justice, I should still owe it to Lynette to vindicate her murder.''

Violet, who had known beforehand all the arguments that he would bring to bear, yet sustained a rending stab of pain to her heart at that final justification for risking his life.

"And how will it serve Philippe if he is made to lose his father?" she demanded, little caring that she was behaving in a manner that must be wholly reprehensible to him—she, Violet, who had always retreated before submitting to being drawn into an argument.

It was immediately to prove just as she had always known it to be. One never changed another person's mind in an argument. One only created greater barriers between the two participants. It was evident in Blackthorn's face, which assumed a shuttered expression, just as it always did at the merest mention of Philippe.

"Philippe, I have no doubt, will grow up just fine whether I am there or not," said Blackthorn, putting Violet away from him. "He will, after all, have you to instruct him. And you at least have his affections. He can hardly miss a father he has never had or never known."

Violet bit her tongue to keep from giving voice to the retort that rose to her lips. It was, after all, hardly too late for Blackthorn to come to know his son—if, that was, he did not fling his life away in pursuit of the man who had nearly killed him twice before. He would do it for Lynette, who was beyond knowing or caring that he would die for her. It was bitter irony to Violet that he would not choose instead to live for those who were alive and held him dear to them. Really, it was too bad of him.

"I beg your pardon," she said instead, turning her face away. "You are right, of course. Naturally, you will do as you think fit. I shall undoubtedly remind myself in future that it was, after all, only the natural culmination of events. How, by the way, do you intend to bait the trap?"

Blackthorn, who could not fail to see the hurt in his sweet Violet's eyes before she turned away, cursed himself for a heartless brute. The last thing he could ever wish was to hurt Violet, who could never hurt anyone, who indeed had ever given of herself with a generosity that made him quite certain he could not bear to think of a life without her. Still, there would seem to be little help for it. He knew, if she did not, that none of them would ever be truly safe if he did not finish what had been set into motion with the cursed events in Malta. Hellfire! Even if he had not the constant threat of a bullet in the back to consider, there were questions to which he must have answers.

"I intend to send a message to each of the two men who would seem to be singularly involved in the events in which the Raven had a part," he said, his eyes on the averted profile of Violet's face.

"Landford, of course," remarked Vere, his handsome features peculiarly impassive. "And Granville."

"*Alors!*" exclaimed Gabrielle, her eyes expressive of understanding as she glanced from Blackthorn to Violet. "I cannot think either of them is *Le Corbeau*. One is too slow, and the other is too old."

"Yes, but then Blackthorn does not suspect Granville of being a spy," Vere pointed out, a queer sort of gleam in his hooded eyes. "And one does not have to be fast on one's feet to steal government secrets. It is enough to have access to them and be in addition utterly without scruples. I, for one, shall be looking forward to welcoming Vice Admiral Sir Oliver Landford to our little rendezvous."

Violet, who had reason enough to wish Landford to be the guilty party, could only agree with her brother. It would, after all, resolve two problems at once. On the other hand, there was, unfortunately, another possibility she had no wish even to contemplate. Nevertheless, she could not completely quash the small, nagging voice that insisted that Madame Gabrielle Benneau was also singularly well placed not only to gather secrets but to wield the reins of a network of agents as well. She was, after all, the founder of *le société des philosophes du jardin,* which not only espoused the notions of *liberté, egalité,* and *fraternité,* but also included any number of French *émigrés,* not to mention influential Englishmen drawn to her salons by her obvious feminine charms.

Even Granville had come to her, thought Violet, wondering what Sir Henry had been hoping to find. And Landford. The vice admiral had used to be a regular visitor to the house on Berners Street.

Insidiously, it came to Violet to wonder if Gabrielle Benneau had sat by Furneaux's bedside all those nights to care for him or to make sure he never talked. In her mind's eye she envisioned Gabrielle administering small doses of the debilitating drug—enough to keep him incapacitated, but not enough to kill him. After all, it was to her advantage to make sure Blackthorn continued to come on a regular basis to the house. An exceedingly clever, not to mention dangerous, French agent would wish to keep an eye on the man she had chosen to be her scapegoat.

And she had known Philippe Lambert and Lynette. What if Lynette had stumbled on to her bosom bow's nefarious activities and had threatened to tell Dane? Faith, what choice would Gabrielle have but to arrange to have both Lynette and Dane meet untimely demises? No doubt she had already seduced and corrupted Dane's unsuspecting first lieutenant. It had remained only for one of her agents to contact Furneaux in Malta, and, using either bribes or threats, persuade him to murder his captain.

As for the assault on Sir Henry on the particularly memorable occasion of Violet's first encounter with the gallant captain who was to win her heart and forever change the uneventful flow of her existence, there was every possibility the masked intruder had been Paul Despagne or Jean Morin—or someone else in league with Gabrielle. Dane, after all, suspected the villain had deliberately altered his voice to avoid recognition. And if it was true neither Frenchman had been a guest at Sir Henry's house party, it was not impossible Sir Henry's assailant had managed to escape without detection by any number of means, including slipping out the front door before anyone arrived at the foot of the stairs.

Faith, it would all seem to make perfect sense, thought Violet, glancing across the room at Gabrielle, who gave every manifestation of one wholly desirous of helping set the trap for the elusive Raven. Surely Violet could not have been so mistaken in the Frenchwoman. From the very first, she had felt an instant liking for Gabrielle, which had grown over the past several days to genuine fondness.

But then, one who practiced espionage for a living would have to be a consummate actress, Violet reminded herself with a distinctly queasy sensation in the pit of her stomach. Certainly Madame Benneau, who was at least five years his senior, would seem to have captivated Vere, who was never fooled by anyone, she thought. She felt her stomach positively beginning to churn with growing misapprehension as it came to her that Gideon might very well have seen through the Frenchwoman. After all, he could have found no better way to keep a close eye on her than to take her for his lover.

Violet was not to be given the opportunity to ponder the matter any further. Blackthorn, even as he had penned the two missives that would set the trap, had been acutely aware of his countess's distracted air. Rising from his seat at the secretary, he drew her quietly aside as soon as the messages had been dispatched.

"Violet," he said without preamble, "I want you to go home and stay with Philippe until this over. No, no arguments," he added, seeing the protest leap in her eyes. "There is not time. I want you well away from here before the Raven makes his appearance. If I am to be successful in this endeavor, I cannot afford the distraction of worrying about your safety."

"But I have every right to be here when you face Landford with the capture of the Raven," Violet insisted. "Surely you have not forgotten what we found in his secret cabinet. And, besides, I—"

It was on her lips to confide in him her doubts concerning Gabrielle Benneau, at the very least to give him a warning.

Blackthorn, however, was in no mood to humor her. "You, my girl, will leave this to me," he said, drawing her firmly into his arms. "You have not the smallest idea of the sort of men with whom we are dealing. *Le*

Corbeau will make his appearance. He has little choice in the matter if he is to have any hope of silencing me before Landford and Granville arrive. Go home, Violet. Wait for me. Trust me to see to everything."

"You should listen to him, *cherie,*" said Madame Benneau, coming up behind them. "Your Vice Admiral Landford is *tres stupide.* But he is a man who would stop at nothing, not even murder. Even so, he is only a pawn in the game of one who is far more dangerous. Go home. It will all be over soon."

Violet was given little other choice in the matter. Blackthorn, helping her into her pelisse, ushered her straight from the house to the carriage.

Only then did he turn to her. "Promise me you will go straight home and stay there," he said, clasping her firmly by the arms. "I warn you, I am not above sending Vere with you to make sure you do."

"Devil," she uttered, as close as she had ever been in her life to losing her temper with him. How dared he use her brother against her! He knew perfectly well he needed Vere with him to watch his back. "I promise. Only, give me your word you will be careful, Dane. I shall never forgive you if you are so careless as to forfeit your life over this."

"I give you my word." The devil, his enchantress had never looked more beautiful than she did at that moment with her eyes huge in her face and shadowed with fear for him. He was aware of a mounting impatience to be finished at last with the cursed Raven so he could turn his attentions to the far more important matter of learning everything there was to know about this woman in whom, he no longer doubted, resided the sum total of his future happiness.

Clasping her to him, he kissed her with a fierce, savage tenderness. And then he let her go. "Tell Murdoch I shall depend on him to keep you safe," he said, as he closed the carriage door and nodded to the coachman to send them on their way.

Murdoch, however, was not there when Violet arrived at the town house on Grosvenor Square.

"Begging your pardon, milady," intoned Potter, standing at rigid attention in the foyer, "but Mr. Murdoch did not say where he was going. There was a— er—gentleman who arrived inquiring after him early this morning. Mr. Murdoch appeared exceedingly pleased to see him. I might even say excited. They departed together immediately thereafter."

"What sort of a gentleman?" queried Violet, tugging at the fingers of her gloves.

"A seagoing gentleman, milady. He said something about the old *Antiope* and making things square for the captain, upon which they hastened out of the house. I'm afraid I know nothing more, milady."

"Very well, Potter," said Violet, crossing to the stairs. "I shall be in my room if I am needed."

Ascending the stair with a thoughtful frown, Violet proceeded first to the schoolroom, where she found Philippe mounted on his hobbyhorse and re-enacting the Battle of Agincourt.

"See, *Maman Violette,* I am D'Albret. My charger is caught in the mud. Mr. Greene is one of King Henry's archers. He is going to shoot me with his arrow."

"And take over nearly the entirety of France before he is finally done, I shouldn't doubt," smiled Violet, giving the tutor leave to let fly his imaginary dart.

Philippe, clutching his small chest, cast himself dramatically to the floor, where he lay most convincingly in a state of heroic expiration.

"Bravo, Philippe," applauded Violet, summoning the tutor to her with a silent gesture. "I shall return your archer to you in a moment, dearest. I should like a word with Mr. Greene.

"I should like you both to remain in the house the rest of the day, preferably in the schoolroom or nursery, if you will, Timothy. I do not like to alarm you, but the earl has received an anonymous threat, and I think it would be wise to keep a close eye on Philippe."

"I will, milady," replied the tutor, clearly bursting with questions he was too polite to ask. "You may be sure of it."

Torn between anxiety over Blackthorn's well-being and anger at his having exiled her to an agony of waiting, Violet sought in vain to distract herself with reading, only at length to fling the book aside and abandon herself to pacing restlessly about her room. Telling herself it was pointless to wear herself to the nub with worry was of precious little comfort. Indeed, it occurred to her to wonder what had happened to the serene Violet Rochelle who had believed so confidently that everything proceeded according to its natural course and must somehow turn out for the better. No doubt she was gone forever, to be replaced by this new creature who was naught but a bundle of nerves, she reflected, as she found herself glancing at the clock for the fifth time in less than five minutes.

She had long since sent down her supper tray all but untouched and was soundly berating herself for having given in to Blackthorn's insistence that she wait at home while he thoughtlessly set himself up to be the bait in a trap for a cold-blooded killer, when it came to her that she had utterly forgotten to tuck Philippe into bed and read him his customary story.

In spite of the fact it was past ten o'clock and he must surely have been asleep for hours, Violet, a burning taper in hand, let herself out of the bedchamber and made her way along the passage to the nursery. Even had she not detested the decor of blood-red damask interspersed with black and gold velvet and brocade furnishings, which she did not doubt had not been refurbished in the past fifty years, she would have been heartily weary of her suite of rooms. The nursery, at least, would offer a momentary diversion from the baroque.

Besides, she was suddenly aware she simply wished to see Philippe. There was a great deal of his father in him—the black, brilliant eyes, in addition to the firm little chin, even the texture of his hair, which she did not doubt would darken in time to be just as ebony-black as his father's.

Little wonder Lynette had derived no little comfort in little Philippe during Dane's long absences, she thought, as ever so quietly she turned the door handle and opened the nursery door.

As she lifted the candle and peered inside, the interior of the nursery appeared to leap out at her. For the barest instant it came to her that young Mr. Greene, in his eagerness to heed her warnings, was standing guard over Philippe's bed.

Violet drew breath to call the tutor's name. Then the figure straightened and turned.

Violet froze, the blood draining from her face.

"You!" she said with utter certainty. "Faith, I might have known."

Chapter 14

He was garbed in unrelieved black, his tall figure draped in a cloak that reached to his ankles, but even if he had not flung the hood down his back and discarded his mask, Violet would have known him. His eyes, a singularly liquid brown, must surely have given him away. At the moment, however, they were peculiarly lacking in the least hint of vulnerability, she could not but note with a shiver.

"Lieutenant Alastair Cordell," she pronounced with a chilly calm that was a far cry from the fear that gripped her heart. He was *Le Corbeau*, the Raven, and he had been bending over Philippe!

"Lady Blackthorn," said the lieutenant, executing an elegant bow at the waist. "Please do come in. And shut the door behind you."

"I shall do no such thing," said Violet, standing her ground. Surely at any moment someone would hear them. Nanny Tidwell was undoubtedly asleep in the next room, and Mr. Greene was only across the hall. "You, on the other hand, will come out. At once, Lieutenant. I will not have you disturbing my son."

"Your son, Lady Blackthorn?" His sudden bark of laughter had the peculiar effect of steeling her nerve.

It came to her with a terrible certainty he had not strayed into the nursery by accident. For whatever reason and for whatever sick purpose, he had come deliberately for the child, but he would not have him. She would die before she let him lay a hand on Philippe.

"Yes, *my* son, Lieutenant. Now, please come away from there. If you do not, I shall be forced to call for help to have you removed."

"You haven't enough help to remove me, Lady Blackthorn. Your husband's former coxswain is not here, and I fear your aging butler would have a difficult time even climbing the stairs. As for the boy's tutor, he, I am afraid, is indisposed."

With a sickening lurch of her stomach, Violet saw him then—Timothy Greene, lying sprawled on the floor at the foot of the bed. "You brute. What have you done to him? If you have—"

"He is not dead. At least not yet. Unfortunately, he took exception to my presence. I was forced to bludgeon him. I daresay he will have suffered no worse than a bump on the head and a headache when he awakens. You, however, will not be so fortunate. A pity, really. You have no idea how much I have admired you from afar. One thing I can say for the earl: He has the devil of the luck with women. Had there been time, I should have enjoyed teaching you the pleasures the lovely Lynette enjoyed in my bed. You may be sure I knew what she liked better than did her husband. I was with her so much more often. Even before she fled France to be with her beloved captain."

"You were the one who corrupted her innocence when she had no one to protect her," said Violet, realizing for the first time how truly wretched Lynette's life must have been. "She was fleeing you, not France. How dreadful for her that you should turn up in England just as she had begun to believe she would never have to set eyes on you again. What did you do? Threaten to kill Dane's son if she did not do as you told her?"

"Actually, I promised to kill Dane—after I had made certain his career was ruined and he had lost everything he had ever cared for. No doubt I should have killed his son, too—if he had ever had a son."

"Philippe *is* his son," declared Violet, sickened at the vile spitefulness of the man. "Anyone who looks at him can see he is Viscount Fennington, Blackthorn's true heir, and your filthy lies cannot change that."

"Can they not?" Cordell's smile should have warned Violet, but somehow it did not. "Ask your precious Blackthorn if Philippe is his son. Ask him what Lynette told him. Oh, but I forgot. You will not be seeing Blackthorn again, will you?" he said, taking a step toward her with obvious intent. "I'm afraid he will have to go on believing his precious heir is another man's by-blow."

Carefully, Violet backed before him, and Cordell followed, too obsessed with his malevolent enjoyment to notice she was leading him farther and farther away from the still sleeping child.

"You cannot know how greatly I shall enjoy that thought when I am back in Paris, living the life of gaiety and luxury."

Violet held her breath as she stepped backward through the doorway into the passage. One more step, and she would fling the candle in his face and run. "And to think I came here with the intent of killing the brat just to keep my promise to Lynette. I think killing you and leaving him with the brat will be much more satisfying, do not you?"

Cordell followed her through the door.

Violet thrust the candle in his face. Cordell screamed and, clawing at his eyes, lumbered backward into the wall. Violet turned and fled—straight into Blackthorn's waiting arms.

"Philippe!" demanded the earl, holding Violet away

from him so he could peer into her face. In the room behind them, Philippe awoke, wailing for his *maman*.

"He is unharmed, Dane. I promise. I interrupted Cordell before he could hurt him. Cordell is mad. He meant to kill Philippe."

Glancing up, Violet almost quailed before the terrible look in Blackthorn's eyes. Then he had put her from him. "Go to the boy," he said, striding toward the figure backing before him down the passage. "He is calling for you."

In horror Violet saw the flash of a knife in Cordell's hand. Then Blackthorn, moving purposefully, blocked her view of the Raven.

"We missed you at Madam Benneau's this evening, Cordell," he called out in a ringing voice, as Violet, held in the awful grip of fear, stood, powerless to move. "Fortunately, Sir Henry arrived to tell us whom we should have been expecting all along. Once I knew that, I had no doubt where you would be. It was not enough that you killed Lynette, was it, Cordell. Naturally, you would not be satisfied until you had sent Philippe to join her."

"She was deceived to think she could escape me by running away from France," Cordell flung back at him. His face, twisted with hatred and cunning, little resembled that of the uncertain, stammering lieutenant who had sought to elicit information about Philippe from Violet on Lady Stanhope's terrace. "She belonged to me. I swore I would kill her and the brat if she ever told you about me. Unfortunately, I could not be certain Lambert had not done that little service for her when you went to see him in Malta. Naturally, I could not allow you to continue to live."

"No, of course you could not," agreed Blackthorn, balanced easily on the balls of his feet, his hands hanging loosely at his sides. "Nor could you trust Lynette to keep her silence after you boasted that you had had me shot from the decks of my own ship. She knew you would come for her and Philippe."

"She hid the brat before I could keep my promise to her, the whore," said Cordell, peering at Blackthorn through the tops of his eyes. "But at least I shall send *you* to hell before me!"

Cordell lunged, the knife slashing at Blackthorn's chest. Blackthorn moved too quickly for Violet to see. One instant he was leaping to one side, his hand flashing out. The very next, his fingers clamped about Cordell's wrist, he forced the Raven back against the wall, the point of the knife at Cordell's stomach below the rib cage. Horror rose like bile to her throat, as she saw the terrible certainty transform Cordell's face into a mask of bitter hatred.

"What are you waiting for?" he gasped. "I killed Lynette, and I'd have killed your precious Lady Blackthorn—after I had sampled her pleasures for myself. I would have made her beg me to kill her before I was finished with her."

Cordell winced before the terrible leap of Blackthorn's eyes. Then, twisting the knife out of Cordell's fist, Blackthorn stepped back. "Killing you would be too easy," Blackthorn said contemptuously. "I'll see you hanged for your crimes, Cordell, and your body left to rot on the gallows."

Turning his back on Cordell, Blackthorn strode toward Violet, his eyes searching on her stricken face. Neither of them saw Cordell straighten, his hand delving into his coat pocket to come up with a pistol aimed at Blackthorn's retreating back.

A shot rang out, deafening in the narrow confines of the hallway.

Cordell went deathly still, his face frozen in startled realization. Then slowly he dropped to his knees to the floor. His eyes fixed and staring, he toppled forward on his face and lay still.

"I beg your pardon, Blackthorn," said Vere, standing

beyond Cordell's inert form. Deliberately, he lowered the pistol in his hand. "I'm afraid I really could not let him shoot you, old man. Not before we have had a rematch at Gentleman Jackson's, at any rate. You will not take me by surprise a second time, I promise you."

"Philippe!" cried Violet, freed at last from the immobilizing grip of dread. Slipping past Blackthorn, she hastened into the nursery to find Philippe, sitting up weeping in his bed while Miss Tredwell and Timothy Greene, looking pale, but otherwise little the worse for wear, did their best to console him.

"*Maman,*" sobbed the boy, reaching out for Violet. "It was Andre Renaud. I saw him. He was going to hurt you. I hate him. He is a bad man. He hurt *ma mere.*"

"It is all right, Philippe," soothed Violet, gathering the child up in her arms. "Mr. Renaud is gone. See? I am fine, Philippe. He did not hurt me."

Violet's heart leaped as a tall form loomed suddenly over them. Glancing up, she caught her breath at the look on her dearest Blackthorn's face. Even believing Philippe was another man's son, he had acknowledged him as his heir. She knew now that that was the terrible secret that had tormented him and kept him from relinquishing his heart to Philippe, the secret that he had kept from her, Violet. It would never stand between them again. All that was over and banished to the past where it belonged.

"Mr. Renaud will not hurt anyone ever again, Philippe," she said, meeting Blackthorn's eyes over the boy's head. "Your papa has sent him away for good."

"It is quite possible we will never know what happened to the real Alastair Cordell," said Sir Henry Granville, accepting a glass of brandy from Blackthorn. "I daresay this Renaud fellow dispatched him and took his place. There is little doubt, however, that Andre Renaud was *Le Corbeau.* With any luck Commander Furneaux will

recover to testify to that effect. And when he does, there
will be a ship waiting for him if he wants it. You must
know, Blackthorn, that he never wanted to spy on you.
I impressed upon him the fact that it was his duty to
clear you of the charges that Landford brought against
you, we know now at Cordell's instigation. It was Cordell,
of course, who forged the orders that placed Lambert's
crew on the ship that was transporting him to England.
I have no doubt he slipped Lambert the key to his irons
as the captain was being taken aboard. It was, unfortunately, a simple matter for Cordell to convince Landford
that you had performed that particular service when you
saw your brother-in-law in the prison at Malta."

"It is no doubt ironic," submitted Blackthorn, crossing to stand behind Violet seated on the withdrawing
room sofa beside Vere, "that Andre Renaud was the
one man Philippe Lambert hated most in this world.
He was the man who ruined his sister. Even at the risk
of forfeiting his own chances of escape, Lambert could
not overlook the opportunity to bring his personal
enemy to justice. It is obvious that Renaud had boasted
to Philippe that he was arranging to have his sister's
husband assassinated on his own ship. In sending me
to the meeting between Furneaux and Renaud, he was
doing what he could to warn me. Since I failed to recognize either man in the cathedral, it is fortunate Furneaux was working for you. Had he been the real
assassin, I should no doubt be dead."

"But you were very nearly killed," Violet could not
help but point out. "If it was not Steven Furneaux who
shot you, then who did?"

"As it happens, we may thank your man Murdoch
that we have the answer to that," interjected Sir Henry.
"He came to me this evening with what remained of a
seaman who had been impressed into service aboard
the *Antiope*. It seemed he was a malcontent who never
adjusted to the navy's discipline. You had him flogged
for stealing from his messmates."

"Tobias Endicott. Yes, of course, I remember," said Blackthorn, recalling the vituperative shrieks of pain and hatred. The punishment had had to be stopped before the full twenty lashes could be administered. Endicott had fainted. "The flogging, unfortunately, was necessary. He would undoubtedly have received worse had it been left to the discretion of the lower decks."

"I'm afraid Endicott did not see it that way," submitted Sir Henry, who knew well Blackthorn's views on flogging. He had, after all, availed himself of the captain's punishment book, which had been left lying on the chart table during a particularly memorable storm. A total of ten floggings in two years at sea was a remarkable record of a captain's restraint. "He was a more than willing instrument for Cordell's murderous plot. It was Murdoch who ferreted out Endicott in the Limehouse district and persuaded him to confess everything, not only to having shot you aboard the French man of war, but also of playing a part in the kidnapping of Commander Furneaux. I understand this Mr. Chan of yours believes he can bring Furneaux back."

"He appeared exceedingly hopeful," offered Vere, who had been listening with interest to the unfolding of the plot, which had ended that night with the death of *Le Corbeau*. "No doubt you will pardon my disbelief that you have found nothing that implicates Landford in any of these events. Cordell was his personal aide, and yet you would have me accept that Landford remained in ignorance of what was going on beneath his rather bulbous nose."

"I'm afraid so," admitted Granville, with sardonic appreciation of Vere's cynicism. "It would appear that Landford was guilty of nothing more than negligence and gross incompetence."

Violet, who had wished for something quite different for Landford, was made aware of the slight pressure from Blackthorn's hand where it rested on her shoulder. Blackthorn knew, as did she, that Landford had yet to meet the proper justice for his crimes. Vere, however, must never know. With Blackthorn's help, she would learn to bear that burden.

"More than that, however," Sir Henry had continued, "it has been conclusively proven that Captain Trevor Dane was guilty of nothing at all. I am pleased, my lord, to inform you that you have been completely exonerated of all charges. There will be no court-martial. I have, in fact, been commissioned to inform you that you have been promoted to the rank of commodore with a small squadron of your own to command. Naturally, you will be given the *Antiope* as your flagship with the captain of your choice to command her—if, that is, it is your wish to return to the service of your king and country."

Violet stilled, her heart seeming to stop beneath her breast. It had happened, just as she had known it would, and still she was not prepared for it. How could anyone ever expect her to be prepared to send her love into the arms of a mistress who had claimed him from his birth as her own? She very much feared that she had not the courage that Lynette had shown or, indeed, the courage of her dearest Aunt Roanna, who had learned to conceal her loneliness and fear behind a façade of indolence. Violet knew herself to be a coward. Indeed, she did not see how she could go back to the solitary existence she had known before Blackthorn had changed her life forever. And yet, somehow she must.

Violet summoned a smile and, reaching up, covered Blackthorn's hand with hers.

"Naturally, I should always wish to serve my king and my country, Sir Henry," said Blackthorn, gravely. "I have done so in the navy for nineteen years. And I had always thought to do so for as long as I was able. Now, however, I find myself unable to accept the honor either of a promotion or of command. I have come to believe that I may serve the navy and my country far more effectively in a different capacity. I have, in short, decided to take my seat in the House of Lords."

* * *

"Are you quite certain, my dearest Blackthorn?" queried Violet, when they were alone at last in her bedchamber. "I should understand perfectly if you wished to return to your beloved ships and the sea. It has been your whole life, and I, after all, trapped you into marriage. I am well aware that you may never feel for me as you did for Lynette. Nevertheless, *I* love *you*— far too much ever to wish to keep you here with me, when your heart must yearn for the freedom of the sea."

Blackthorn, who had for no little time been convinced that his happiness resided in the slender form of the woman clasped to his side, was quite sure that he would never feel for Violet what he had felt for Lynette. That poor, sad, lonely girl was at rest at last, and he need no longer bear the burden of guilt of knowing that he had married her without loving her. *She* had known it, and she had been content with the knowledge that he would have remained true to his oath to the rest of his days for her. No doubt she would not have condemned him now because a remarkable chain of circumstances, which had begun with her, should have led him to the woman who had irrevocably won his heart.

"Sweet, impossible Violet," he said, pulling her close to him. "Do you really think you could have forced me into marriage if it was not what I desired from the first moment that I burst into your bedchamber and stole a kiss from you? I have since come to love you far too much ever to contemplate leaving you for months, even years, at a time. The bloody sea will do well enough without me. I, however, cannot do without you. Or without Philippe, who, as you have so aptly pointed out, should not be required to grow up without his father."

He kissed her then with a slow, melting passion that quite took her breath away, and she knew at last that everything was just as it had been meant to be.

ABOUT THE AUTHOR

Sara Blayne lives with her family in New Mexico. She is the author of nine traditional Regency romances and five historical romances set in the Regency period. Sara is currently working on her next historical romance set in the Regency period—look for it in 2003. Sara loves to hear from readers and you may write to her c/o Zebra Books. Please include a self-addressed stamped envelope if you wish a reply.